MURDER AT THE OPERA

Great tales of Mystery and Suspense
at the Opera
edited and introduced
by Thomas Godfrey

MICHAEL O'MARA BOOKS LIMITED

Dedication
To the memory of
CALVIN SIMMONS
One of the best friends the Opera
ever had

05451907

First published in Great Britain in 1988 by
Michael O'Mara Books Ltd
20 Queen Anne Street
London W1N 9FB

Design: Mick Keates

British Library Cataloguing in Publication Data

Murder at the opera.
   1. Crime short stories in English, 1900- -
   Anthologies
   I. Godfrey, Thomas
   823′.0872 [FS]

ISBN 0-948397-13-6

Filmset by DP Photosetting, Aylesbury, Bucks
Printed and bound in Great Britain by
Mackays of Chatham PLC, Chatham, Kent

Contents:

Introduction

This collection draws its strengths from some unexpected sources. A contribution from Dame Agatha Christie is no surprise. She was one of the most prolific and successful mystery writers of all time. Before her years as a literary institution, she had embarked briefly on a vocal career, no doubt providing some of the background of 'Swan Song'. There is a second story with an operatic setting, 'The Face of Helen', that appears in *The Mysterious Mr Quin*.

If the heroine of Christie's tale is the prima donna of stereo-type, jealous, temperamental and tempestuous, Alberto Mion, the central figure in Rex Stout's 'The Gun With Wings', is her tenor counterpart, vain, golden-voiced, adulterous and none-too-bright – eminently well-suited to involvement in a juicy murder plot. Stout's celebrated detective, the corpulent Nero Wolfe, often called the American Sherlock Holmes for his powers of deductive reasoning, is on hand to solve the case.

New York of a slightly later period provides the setting of James Yaffe's 'Mom Sings an Aria'. Mom, Yaffe's series detective, is an elderly Jewish widow from the Bronx, who solves her detective-son's cases during traditional Friday night dinners. This tale evokes a special era at the Metropolitan Opera when Renata Tebaldi and Maria Callas rode the high C's on alternate nights, much to the delight of their passionate, and occasionally raucous fans.

That fans and their idols have not changed is demonstrated by the stories of Hector Berlioz (1804-1868) the famous French critic and composer (*Les Troyens*), and the American Storyteller O. Henry (William Sidney Porter, 1862-1910). Berlioz's 'Death by Enthusiasm' is excerpted from his *Evenings in the Orchestra*, in which fictional members of an opera orchestra exchange stories and discuss all matters musical during several weeks of performances. *La Vestale*, the opera that has captivated the hero of our story, was the biggest musical spectacle of its time. Not surprisingly, Berlioz's own extravaganza *Les Troyens* tops it. O. Henry's tale of an opera company on tour among the sagebrush and cactus is typical of his art. This great storyteller was as much at home in Delmonico's Restaurant in New York as he was in the

Long Branch Saloon in Wichita, Kansas. He was well-qualified to note that opera lovers' enthusiasms for their favourite had equal fervour, if differing manifestations, in either locale.

There is greater gentility to be found at Covent Garden's production of Wolf-Ferrari's *I Gioella della Madonna* in 1925, the setting for A.E.W. Mason's classic mystery story. Mason (1865-1948) was an accomplished playwright and novelist, best remembered for *The Four Feathers* (1902). However, his books featuring Inspector Hanaud, the hero of 'The Affair at the Semiramis Hotel', have earned classic status as well.

Less well known, but equally as classic, are the tales of Captain Duncan Maclain, the blind sleuth, created by Baynard Kendrick (1894-1970) the first president of the Mystery Writers of America. Kendrick's works were frequently serialized in magazines and newspapers in 1930s and '40s, and this tale of murder at the première of a new opera has a par-boiled, if not actually hard-boiled, style reminiscent of the popular 'pulp' literature of this era.

Vincent Starrett (1886-1974) the author of 'A Box at the Opera' was also a founding member of the American mystery writers' organization. A distinguished essayist and critic for several Chicago newspapers, he is perhaps best remembered for his work as a Sherlockian scholar, *The Private Life of Sherlock Holmes* (1933) and the pastiche 'The Unique Hamlet' (1920). Starrett's style harks back to an earlier period than his associate Kendrick's, and is well matched to this mannered tale of high society murder during an actual performance.

'Albert Herring', the author of the San Francisco contribution, hides a unique collaboration, that of a musician who knew the opera and the San Francisco house well, and a young mystery writer then at the start of his career. Their piece first appeared, on commission, for a special San Francisco issue of the American *Mystery Magazine* in 1981.

And finally to the most unusual story in this collection – a story ... with a story, *The Ptomaine Canary*, written by the American soprano Helen Traubel (1903-1972). In her years backstage at the Metropolitan Opera, she would pass the time devouring stacks of mystery novels. In 1949, she decided to try her hand at a story. She even sought out the advice of American mystery writer Harold Q. Masur on her effort. Later she went on to write a full-length book, *The Metropolitan Opera Murders* (considerably assisted by Masur).

Canary was privately printed and given to friends as a Christmas present. Later it was reportedly syndicated in several newspapers. And then it disappeared, occasionally talked about, but never seen.

A five-year search turned up a final draft among her papers in the Library of Congress weeks before this anthology's publication deadline. As a mystery, as a piece of great literature, it may be no lost masterpiece. But as a fantasy, as a memoir of perhaps America's greatest native Wagnerian talent and premier operatic mystery buff, it is delightful reading, revealing its author to be warm, witty, and full of fun, a woman not above getting a laugh at her own expense.

There have been many prolific authors in the mystery genre, but few have been so completely identified with the short story as Edward D. Hoch. In a time when writers were turning short story ideas into novels for greater financial gain Hoch has found equal success telling his stories in the form to which they are best suited.

Though he has written four novels, his reputation unquestionably rests on the hundreds of short stories that have come from his pen. He has created four series characters: Nick Velvet, the raffish, Rafflish thief; Simon Ark, the 2000 year-old detective; Captain Leopold; and 'Rand', the protagonist of 'The Spy Who Went to the Opera'.

And there you have it, something different for both the opera afficionado and the devotee of mystery-suspense stories.

Now. Come, put aside those bills and correspondence. Forget those cares of humdrum, everyday life. A theatre bright with lights, charged with anticipation, brimming with unusual patrons, awaits us. The call lights flicker. We ascend the grand staircase, find our doorway, hand our stubs to the attendant, and enter our private box. Glasses up. Lights down. The conductor makes his way through the orchestra to his place at the podium. A bow to the audience. A quick turn. The baton is poised. The curtain rises. And our entertainment begins ...

Thomas F. Godfrey, 1988

ADDIO, SAN FRANCISCO

by 'ALBERT HERRING'

Place: The San Francisco Opera
Time: 1981
Performance: *La Traviata*, by Giuseppe Verdi

Killing Louisa was like killing a part of myself.

The thought coursed through my brain as I watched her move.

How could it have happened? I watched her swirl onto the stage, while the orchestra announced the heady cadences of Act 1 *Traviata*.

How had it come to this? I tried to understand. Yet I could only watch in horror, as life drained away from her, and myself.

I tried to move the baton decisively, with authority. The musicians around me responded automatically, as though caught up by this force beyond my control.

There she was, before me, on stage, laughing amd moving with the music, her petulant lips mocking, her soft warm breasts strained against the tight lace bodice of her gown.

How had it happened?

The bright onyx eyes watched me, questioningly.

I could not look away, though I tried.

I could not cry out, though I willed it.

I could not breathe.

I could not understand.

How had it happened?

In these last moments, I had to know.

Alfredo was beginning his aria.

1

'Libiamo ne lieti calciti ...'

('Drink from the joyous glass ...')

Yes, Yes. If I could close my eyes, I could imagine the bottle of cognac I had carried to her dressing room earlier in the evening. I had been careful. Cunning. No one had seen me. There it was sitting innocently on the dressing table, a small thin-stemmed glass beside it, rimmed with the last drops of amber fluid. 'A gift from an admirer' the card read. And so it would appear later on, when they –

'Folie! Folie!'

Her voice was calling to me.

Was it madness?

The darkened hall echoed with accusation of my crime, threatening to drown out her performance. Her last performance.

How had it happened?

I had heard tales of Louisa before accepting this San Francisco engagement. But they were stories. Just stories. Part of the fragile fabric of fantasy that is The Opera.

There was a ridiculous account of Franconi walking out of a series of *Toscas* in New York after Louisa supposedly turned her amorous attentions to Norman Lewis, the Scarpia of the production. Silly stuff, really. Emiliano Franconi was incapable of loving anything, except one of his own press releases. It usually took him three or four performances just to notice there was anyone else on stage. And yet ...

What was the other one? About Baglioni, the intendant of one of Italy's smaller houses who'd supposedly climbed out on the ledge outside his office window and threatened to jump unless Louisa signed for *Adriana Lecouvreur* the next season. The Italian press was full of pictures. Just the sort of romantic twaddle Italians seem to love. Also, the stuff of which operatic legends are forged. Louisa the diva who drives men wild.

Someone, probably her press agent, once claimed that Callas gave the finest singing performances as Tosca, Tebaldi gave her incomparable vocal beauty and allure, Price gave her stature and force, but Louisa was Tosca, onstage and off.

I was immune to this sort of pre-packaged hyperbole. After all, a singer is nothing more than a set of vocal cords trained to make certain prescribed sounds at certain prescribed moments. It is the public, or publicists, who makes them into gods. Not professional musicians such as myself.

I had my little indulgences, my liaisons, but I knew when to cut them off. No one could make me look foolish. No one would make me look pathetic. Nothing must compromise my career in music, my reputation as an artist.

I'd learned, through discipline, to isolate my personal feelings and insulate them so they could never harm me. If one wants to succeed in the competitive world of serious music, one must be in control at all times. One miscalculation and you could be eaten alive. Look at ... Well, it doesn't matter.

I was prepared for some differences at our first rehearsal. Singers are by nature neurotic and difficult. It is as much a part of their make-up as sleeping and breathing. One's success as a conductor is often a measure of how one handles them. The routiniers kiss their feet and follow obediently behind like little dogs. The misguided often fight the good fight and lose. Only a Toscanini or a Karajan can expect to enforce their personalities over a production and emerge unscathed. I had learned when to be assertive, and when to accommodate and win.

But I was not prepared for Louisa. She arrived several days later than contracted and behaved abominably. She appeared very late the first morning behind dark glasses that failed to disguise a pair of puffy red-rimmed eyes encircled with ugly dark lines. She displayed a sharp tongue and proceeded to use it on everyone present. She was clearly unprepared herself but constantly interrupted others to offer unwanted suggestions on the faults of their performances. She picked on Spiccate the stage director, and reduced him to shrill hysteria in a matter of minutes, admittedly not a difficult thing to accomplish.

I could sense the other principals starting to chafe under her relentless interference. Finally I felt obliged to put her in her place. If this was a sampling of the Louisa legend, I was having no more. There followed the inevitable words. I lost my temper completely. She stormed backstage, vowing never to return.

After an endless wait, I went to her dressing room and found her seated by the table with a glass of cognac in her hand. She got up, as if to leave, but I blocked her exit.

For the good of the company, I told her, we were going to make amends. I met each of her protests with a firm, rational response. Finally her defenses fell away and she caved in completely.

She was weeping like a naughty child, clutching my hand pathetically, drawing me closer. She admitted I was right. She was overwhelmed by anxieties about her age and her voice. Her publicity had created a false image that she could not live up to. She was convinced the world was beginning to grow disillusioned. Her career was on the wane.

I was completely surprised. At first I thought this was some sort of act, some ludicrous play for sympathy, and protested.

Her voice, at least on the evidence of recent recordings, was silvery and accurate; if anything, more rich and skillful in its phrasing. As to her looks, well, a few good nights' sleep and less of this liquid reassurance and there would be no worry. I looked at the golden blonde hair as it fell around her softly sloped shoulders, the deep brown eyes, the perfectly shaped lips that pouted ever so slightly, the small snub nose that flared ever so slightly each time she smiled, the chin that curved so gently upwards accentuating the natural line of her eyes and lips.

I told her she was blowing this all out of proportion. It was discipline and assurance that preserved a legend and a long career. Liquor and foolish squabbling shortened it.

She admitted drinking lately to quiet her anxieties, though she insisted that other colleagues did the same. She mentioned one well-known conductor who always had someone standing by in the wings with a quick belt of whiskey which he downed in a gulp just prior to going on.

I took pains to make her understand that liquor in excess was poison to the voice. I tried to impress her with my firmness and fairness, my genuine concern. But I only seemed to upset her. And she was starting to upset me.

The rehearsal resumed, amid much grumbling, with only strained success. She was looking at me and I kept watching her.

We ended up the evening at L'Orangerie. It was Vanni's idea. The Alfredo. 'Just like Pavarotti,' one critic had observed of him, 'only with twice the girth and half the voice.' He had eaten his way through every emotional crisis since weaning, and was widely reputed to be the only tenor who could eat himself out of a costume in a two-week engagement. Still his was a reliable voice, pleasant company especially when there was food nearby.

At dinner, as Vanni overwhelmed several game birds, Arnold Praeger, the Germont, played the diplomat. He brought his gridiron physique and midwestern sense of fair play to bear with startling success. I don't remember what I ordered, but I distinctly recall that I had much too much to drink.

We left about midnight, laughing and chattering like old school friends. Louisa, too, seemed to unwind and join in the spirit. We sang the Brindisi from *Cavalleria Rusticana* several times with the cab driver joining in at one of the reprises. I have a passable bathroom tenor which gets sparing use, but I became another Domingo in crosstown traffic, rendering 'Mamma, Quel vino 'e generoso' with the utmost conviction. When we arrived at her hotel, I gallantly insisted on escorting Louisa to her room.

There was something unique about San Francisco that night, the same thing that is unique about it every night; only that night, we were lucky enough to catch it and experience it for ourselves. We watched from the window in her suite atop the Fairmount tower as the fog silently drifted in like cottony clouds blanketing the city below for the long night ahead.

Fortified with a bottle of Mumms from room service, we launched into an impromptu concert with Louisa giving renditions of *The Last Rose of Summer* in the styles of Sutherland, Sills, Price, Milanov and others upon request while I made vague accompaniment noises at the piano. Normally I can't stand *The Last Rose of Summer*, but I liked everything she did that night. We laughed and sang and made strange noises until we dissolved into torrents of laughter in each other's arms.

My next recollection was waking up on the rug beside her as the sun streamed through the drapes. The filtered pale light lent an air of unreality to what was happening. She awoke and we made love again.

How had it happened? If she sensed my inexperience, my clumsiness, she made no indication of it. If she cared I was younger and unsure of myself, it never showed. None of this mattered then. Not to her. Not to me.

The next few days passed like a dream. We were always together, caught up in the thrill of love and love returned. I remember once thinking I must be living someone else's life. None of this could be happening to me. Not this.

After rehearsals, after parties, after suppers with wealthy patrons, we were always together. We felt the special warmth, the special euphoria that people who live only for each other must feel. Whether it was reading Verlaine to each other in the basement of the City Lights Bookstore at 4:00 in the morning, or just watching the sun dip into the Pacific from the Top of the Mark, our lives seemed touched with a special magic that I prayed would never end.

I remember thinking in those days that the greatest experience one could feel was that fleeting moment when you can reach out and touch another's soul. It is a moment of supreme closeness and trusting, and the flow of it can carry through a lifetime. We became inseparable. When she was away, I suffered like a man with a fever. When we were together, I was everything to her: coach, friend, adviser, and lover. Nothing else mattered but Louisa.

I even grew so bold as to bring up the subject of drinking again one morning. I had no objections to a drink now and then. Good God, I'd had more to drink the past few days than in the whole rest of my life put together and more hangovers to show for it; but it was taking its toll on me and on her, too. There were Bloody Marys with lunch, cocktails and wine with dinner, champagne at all hours and always a bottle of cognac going in the dressing room. I was concerned what it would do to her.

She found this amusing now and made light of it. The more she tried to laugh it away, the more obsessed with it I became.

Perhaps I was just masking my fears that she would tire of me. I was terrified of losing her. I could not go back to my monastic existence. Not after this.

By then, the company was more than aware of my feelings for Louisa, but the spirit of our feelings for each other spilled over into the company and promoted accord from every quarter. If there were whisperings about us, I did not notice. All that mattered was Louisa and I.

We opened to good notices. One critic ungallantly pointed out that Louisa's voice had traces of roughness when pressed, but all had praise for her interpretation. I was conducting like 'a man transported' (the *Examiner*, I think), and even Vanni mustered his forces and performed with an ardour hitherto reserved only for lunch.

By the third performance, she was sounding a little tired. We had another discussion about her drinking, one that did not end well. I used the reviewer's remarks for corroboration, and she became touchy and defensive. My obsession meanwhile had grown to the point where I worried her drinking might destroy her looks, as well as her voice. I pushed it too hard and regretted it later alone in my hotel room.

After the fifth performance, we were making excuses not to see each other. I inevitably was bringing up the subject of drinking, even if it was only a display of not ordering one myself. She needed to rest, she protested. My agent was coming out from New York, I told her. After the sixth performance, she barely spoke to me, claiming she was tired and needed to turn in early, alone.

Two days later, in Herb Caen's column, I found an item saying that she'd been seen having dinner that night at Fourneau's Ovens with Arnold Praeger.

My nervous system short-circuited and exploded. I felt betrayed and humiliated. I couldn't face people. I wanted to withdraw from the engagement and let them get someone else for the final two performances.

The next night I conducted badly. If it had not been for the concertmaster, I would have missed a key entrance in Act 2. When we took our bows, Louisa reached out to clasp my hand and I made a point of withdrawing it. I went back to the hotel immediately and refused to answer the phone. I had never felt such pain in my life. I didn't know what to do about it. I tried reading, looking through the *Un Ballo* I'd brought with me, but it was impossible to concentrate. The pressures, the anger, the torment were driving me crazy.

How had this happened? I was exploding with anger. The thought of Louisa and Arnold Praeger together seethed in my mind. Praeger, the jock, the family man, the nice guy, everybody's trusted friend, Mr No-Ego, the man *Opera News* had almost raised to sainthood, was taking her away from me. Who knew the poison he was spreading about me. I wanted to kill him. I thought of a thousand ways to do it.

But it wasn't his fault. It was Louisa. She did this. She enticed men and made fools of them. Praeger was just another victim, the latest body to be tossed on the heap of Louisa's victims.

The next morning I awoke and knew what I must do. I had to kill her. It was the only way. She'd do this to others if she got the chance. She couldn't help herself. It would be best for her this way. Now she'd never have to worry about getting old anymore.

The plot presented itself fully laid out in my brain. I bought a bottle of the most expensive cognac I could find at the nearby liquor store off Union Square, then injected some arsenic through the cork with a syringe I had stolen out of the wastebasket of the diabetic Flora. It was simple enough. I just posted myself outside her hotel room until the maid came out to empty the wastebasket into her cart receptacle.

Finding the arsenic was more of a problem than I would have thought. However, I soon discovered you can get just about anything in San Francisco, including several things you never even knew existed.

I carried the bottle into the backstage area that night in an oversized case I used for scores. I arrived early and went immediately to her dressing room where I left it out on the dressing table in plain sight.

7

My plan was ingenious. Like Violetta in the opera, Louisa would sicken and die in the course of the evening. There was enough arsenic in the bottle that only a small amount would prove fatal. No one would really know what was happening until it was too late, and then there would be only the anonymous note to ponder, the scribblings of a crazed fan turned against his idol.

I found I was daydreaming through the prelude, turning the plan over and over in my mind in search of flaws. My conducting had a mechanical, robotized quality that might be mistaken for last-night boredom.

She was radiant at her entrance and in glorious voice throughout Act One, singing with a vivacity and femininity that swept all before it. Had she laughed with her eyes like this before? Had she danced like this before? I did not recall it, but I felt myself again being caught up by her charm.

By Act Two, I believed I saw traces of fatigue in her scene with Germont. The high spirits had eroded and now there was care and some anguish. Not enough to mar the performance. In fact, it gave the performance added meaning. I kept looking at her, feeling some pangs inside me. There was no mistaking it. I was falling in love with her all over again. My tempi were wild and impulsive. I could feel the players' eyes on me, but something was driving me on, fixing my attention on her.

In Act Three, she was noticeably pale and shaking. The poison was taking effect, and it was eating away at my insides. What was I doing? I was killing the thing I loved most in this world. Life would be agony without her. I could never live with the monstrosity of what I had done. I wanted to bolt up onto the stage and warn her. But how could I? It was I who had administered the poison and now it was too late.

Every note of her death scene broke the glass bubbles against my eardrums. I could not watch anymore. Tears were streaming down my cheeks. I wanted to blot out my senses and run from the auditorium.

I was perspiring heavily when I took my bows with the cast. My head was reeling. My stomach was tightly knotted. The hot lights had become oppressive. Louisa was obviously quite shaken and drawn and eager to get back to her dressing room. I knew something was wrong. I started backstage but the crowd gathering there made me turn away. I had to speak to her. I had to try to do something.

As I approached her dressing room, my worst fears were confirmed. One of Mr Adler's assistants was posted outside, blocking access.

'I'm sorry,' he addressed me, 'I cannot let you go inside. The doctor is with her.'

I felt my legs buckle under me as the room spun around.

'Here,' the man said, alarmed at my reaction. 'It isn't as bad as all that. Probably just the flu. There's been an early flu season this year.'

All I could see was Louisa gasping for air, fighting for life. I loved her so much and I had killed her.

'Quickly, Michael, get something for us,' he yelled at another assistant. 'Here, I think you'd better sit down.' He steered me to a nearby folding chair and forced me into the seat.

My head was throbbing and pounding. The light seemed to cut through my eyes. Everything was getting a strange yellowness to it.

'Maybe I should ask the doctor to look at you,' the assistant suggested over my shoulder.

'No,' I protested weakly, 'I'm all right.'

I was shaking my head 'no' with as much energy as I could muster. I felt like I was going out. Things were starting to slip away. I saw the other man approach and in a moment, the assistant was forcing something to my lips. It burned as it went down, but it brought me back.

As I struggled back to my feet, Louisa came into view.

'Darling, what's the matter? You look horrible,' she asked, regarding me with genuine concern.

I sank back into the chair speechless.

'You are all right?' I blurted out.

'I'm just fine, thanks to you,' she smiled. 'That's what the doctor says. I was having a few mild withdrawal symptoms, but I should be fine from here on in. As long as I stay away from the you-know-what.'

She bent down and kissed me with all the fondness in her heart.

'I was so foolish. Everyone could see it but me, and you were the only one who loved me enough to say anything. I finally forced Arnold to take me to dinner, and he told me the same thing.'

'Arnold Praeger?'

'Such a dear man. He could see this coming between us. He knew you were only trying to help me. And you have.'

She hugged me again and kept her arms around my neck.

'But the cognac.'

'Not for me. Not anymore. I have you, and you are all the intoxication I shall require. In fact, someone left me a very nice bottle in my dressing room and I gave it to one of the staff. So you see, I must be cured.'

She hugged me again with all the affection I could ever have wanted, and I hugged her back. It was magic there with her arms around me. But I knew it could not last.

Over her shoulder, I watched the man Michael walking away with an empty glass and the bottle of cognac in his hand.

SWAN SONG

by *AGATHA CHRISTIE*

Place: London, Covent Garden
Time: 1935
Performance: *Tosca*, by Giacomo Puccini

It was eleven o'clock on a May morning in London. Mr Cowan was looking out of the window; behind him was the somewhat ornate splendour of a sitting room in a suite at the Ritz Hotel. The suite in question had been reserved for Mme Paula Nazorkoff, the famous operatic star, who had just arrived in London. Mr Cowan, who was Madame's principal man of business, was awaiting an interview with the lady. He turned his head suddenly as the door opened, but it was only Miss Read, Mme Nazorkoff's secretary, a pale girl with an efficient manner.

'Oh, so it's you, my dear,' said Mr Cowan. 'Madame not up yet, eh?'

Miss Read shook her head.

'She told me to come round at ten o'clock,' Mr Cowan said. 'I have been waiting an hour.'

He displayed neither resentment nor surprise. Mr Cowan was indeed accustomed to the vagaries of the artistic temperament. He was a tall man, clean-shaven, with a frame rather too well covered, and clothes that were rather too faultless. His hair was very black and shining, and his teeth were aggressively white. When he spoke, he had a way of slurring his 's's' which was not quite a lisp, but came perilously near to it. At that minute a door at the other side of the room opened, and a trim French girl hurried through.

11

'Madame getting up?' inquired Cowan hopefully. 'Tell us the news, Elise.'

Elise immediately elevated both hands to heaven.

'Madame she is like seventeen devils this morning; nothing pleases her! The beautiful yellow roses which monsieur sent to her last night, she says they are all very well for New York, but that it is *imbécile* to send them to her in London. In London, she says, red roses are the only things possible, and straightaway she opens the door and precipitates the yellow roses into the passage, where they descend upon a monsieur, *très comme il faut*, a military gentleman, I think, and he is justly indignant, that one!'

Cowan raised his eyebrows, but displayed no other signs of emotion. Then he took from his pocket a small memorandum book and pencilled in it the words 'red roses'.

Elise hurried out through the other door, and Cowan turned once more to the window. Vera Read sat down at the desk and began opening letters and sorting them. Ten minutes passed in silence, and then the door of the bedroom burst open, and Paula Nazorkoff flamed into the room. Her immediate effect upon it was to make it seem smaller; Vera Read appeared more colourless, and Cowan retreated into a mere figure in the background.

'Ah, ha! My children,' said the prima donna. 'Am I not punctual?'

She was a tall woman, and for a singer not unduly fat. Her arms and legs were still slender, and her neck was a beautiful column. Her hair, which was coiled in a great roll halfway down her neck, was of a dark, glowing red. If it owed some at least of its colour to henna, the result was none the less effective. She was not a young woman, forty at least, but the lines of her face were still lovely, though the skin was loosened and wrinkled round the flashing dark eyes. She had the laugh of a child, the digestion of an ostrich, and the temper of a fiend, and she was acknowledged to be the greatest dramatic soprano of her day. She turned directly upon Cowan.

'Have you done as I asked you? Have you taken that abominable English piano away and thrown it into the Thames?'

'I have got another for you,' said Cowan, and gestured towards where it stood in the corner.

Nazorkoff rushed across to it and lifted the lid.

'An Erard,' she said; 'that is better. Now let us see.'

The beautiful soprano voice rang out in an arpeggio, then it ran lightly up and down the scale twice, then took a soft little run up to a high note, held it, its volume swelling louder and louder, then softened again till it died away in nothingness.

'Ah!' said Paula Nazorkoff in naïve satisfaction. 'What a beautiful voice I have! Even in London I have a beautiful voice.'

'That is so,' agreed Cowan in hearty congratulation. 'And you bet London is going to fall for you all right, just as New York did.'

'You think so?' queried the singer.

There was a slight smile on her lips, and it was evident that for her the question was a mere commonplace.

'Sure thing,' said Cowan.

Paula Nazorkoff closed the piano lid down and walked across to the table with that slow undulating walk that proved so effective on the stage.

'Well, well,' she said, 'let us get to business. You have all the arrangements there, my friend?'

Cowan took some papers out of the portfolio he had laid on a chair.

'Nothing has been altered much,' he remarked. 'You will sing five times at Covent Garden, three times in *Tosca*, and twice in *Aïda*.'

'*Aïda!* Pah,' said the prima donna, 'it will be unutterable boredom. *Tosca*, that is different.'

'Ah, yes,' said Cowan. '*Tosca* is *your* part.'

Paula Nazorkoff drew herself up.

'I am the greatest Tosca in the world,' she said simply.

'That is so,' agreed Cowan. 'No one can touch you.'

'Roscari will sing "Scarpia", I suppose?'

Cowan nodded.

'And Emile Lippi.'

'What?' shrieked Nazorkoff. 'Lippi – that hideous little barking frog, croak – croak – croak. I will not sing with him. I will bite him. I will scratch his face.'

'Now, now,' said Cowan soothingly.

'He does not sing, I tell you, he is a mongrel dog who barks.'

'Well, we'll see; we'll see,' said Cowan.

He was too wise ever to argue with temperamental singers.

'The Cavaradossi?' demanded Nazorkoff.

'The American tenor, Hensdale.

The other nodded.

'He is a nice little boy; he sings prettily.'

'And Barrère is to sing it once, I believe.'

13

'He is an artist,' said Madame generously. 'But to let that croaking frog Lippi be Scarpia! Bah – I'll not sing with him.'

'You leave it to me,' said Cowan soothingly.

He cleared his throat and took up a fresh set of papers.

'I am arranging for a special concert at the Albert Hall,'

Nazorkoff made a grimace.

'I know, I know,' said Cowan; 'but everybody does it.'

'I will be good,' said Nazorkoff, 'and it will be filled to the ceiling, and I shall have much money. *Ecco!*'

Again Cowan shuffled papers.

'Now here is quite a different proposition,' he said, 'from Lady Rustonbury. She wants you to go down and sing.'

'Rustonbury?'

The prima donna's brow contracted as if in the effort to recollect something.

'I have read that name lately, very lately. It is a town – or a village, isn't it?'

'That's right, pretty little place in Hertfordshire. As for Lord Rustonbury's place, Rustonbury Castle, it's a real dandy old feudal seat, ghosts and family pictures, and secret staircases, and a slap-up private theatre. Rolling in money they are, and always giving some private show. She suggests that we give a complete opera, preferably *Butterfly.*'

'*Butterfly?*'

Cowan nodded.

'And they are prepared to pay. We'll have to square Covent Garden, of course, but even after that it will be well worth your while financially. In all probability, royalty will be present. It will be a slap-up advertisement.'

Madame raised her still beautiful chin.

'Do I need advertisement?' she demanded proudly.

'You can't have too much of a good thing,' said Cowan, unabashed.

'Rustonbury,' murmured the singer; 'where did I see –'

She sprang up suddenly and, running to the centre table, began turning over the pages of an illustrated paper which lay there. There was a sudden pause as her hand stopped, hovering over one of the pages, then she let the periodical slip to the floor and returned slowly to her seat. With one of her swift changes of mood, she seemed now an entirely different personality. Her manner was very quiet, almost austere.

'Make all arrangements for Rustonbury. I would like to sing there, but there is one condition – the opera must be *Tosca*.'

Cowan looked doubtful.

'That will be rather difficult – for a private show, you know, scenery and all that.'

'*Tosca* or nothing.'

Cowan looked at her very closely. What he saw seemed to convince him; he gave a brief nod and rose to his feet.

'I will see what I can arrange,' he said quietly.

Nazorkoff rose too. She seemed more anxious than was usual, with her, to explain her decision.

'It is my greatest rôle, Cowan. I can sing that part as no other woman has ever sung it.'

'It is a fine part,' said Cowan. 'Jeritza made a great hit in it last year.'

'Jeritza?' cried the other, a flush mounting in her cheeks. She proceeded to give him at great length her opinion of Jeritza.

Cowan, who was used to listening to singers' opinions of other singers, abstracted his attention till the tirade was over; he then said obstinately:

'Anyway, she sings "Vissi D'Arte" lying on her stomach.'

'And why not?' demanded Nazorkoff. 'What is there to prevent her? I will sing it on my back with my legs waving in the air.'

Cowan shook his head with perfect seriousness.

'I don't believe that would go down any,' he informed her. 'All the same, that sort of thing takes on, you know,'

'No one can sing "Vissi D'Arte" as I can,' said Nazorkoff confidently. 'I sing it in the voice of the convent – as the good nuns taught me to sing years and years ago. In the voice of a choir boy or an angel, without feeling, without passion.'

'I know,' said Cowan heartily. 'I have heard you; you are wonderful.'

'That is art,' said the prima donna, 'to pay the price, to suffer, to endure, and in the end not only to have all knowledge, but also the power to go back, right back to the beginning and recapture the lost beauty of the heart of a child.'

Cowan looked at her curiously. She was staring past him with a strange, blank look in her eyes, and something about that look of hers gave him a creepy feeling. Her lips just parted, and she whispered a few words softly to herself. He only just caught them.

'At last,' she murmured. 'At last – after all these years.'

15

II

Lady Rustonbury was both an ambitious and artistic woman; she ran the two qualities in harness with complete success. She had the good fortune to have a husband who cared for neither ambition nor art and who therefore did not hamper her in any way. The Earl of Rustonbury was a large, square man, with an interest in horseflesh and nothing else. He admired his wife, and was proud of her, and was glad that his great wealth enabled her to indulge all her schemes. The private theatre had been built less than a hundred years ago by his grandfather. It was Lady Rustonbury's chief toy – she had already given an Ibsen drama in it, and a play of the ultra new school, all divorce and drugs, also a poetical fantasy with Cubist scenery. The forthcoming performance of *Tosca* had created widespread interest. Lady Rustonbury was entertaining a very distinguished house party for it, and all London that counted was motoring down to attend.

Mme Nazorkoff and her company had arrived just before luncheon. The new young American tenor, Hensdale, was to sing 'Cavaradossi', and Roscari, the famous Italian baritone, was to be Scarpia. The expense of the production had been enormous, but nobody cared about that. Paula Nazorkoff was in the best of humours; she was charming, gracious, her most delightful and cosmopolitan self. Cowan was agreeably surprised, and prayed that this state of things might continue.

After luncheon the company went out to the theatre and inspected the scenery and various appointments. The orchestra was under the direction of Mr Samuel Ridge, one of England's most famous conductors. Everything seemed to be going without a hitch, and strangely enough, that fact worried Mr Cowan. He was more at home in an atmosphere of trouble; this unusual peace disturbed him.

'Everything is going a darned sight too smoothly,' murmured Mr Cowan to himself. 'Madame is like a cat that has been fed on cream. It's too good to last; something is bound to happen.'

Perhaps as the result of his long contact with the operatic world, Mr Cowan had developed the sixth sense, certainly his prognostications were justified. It was just before seven o'clock that evening when the French maid, Elise, came running to him in great distress.

'Ah, Mr Cowan, come quickly; I beg of you, come quickly.'

'What's the matter?' demanded Cowan anxiously. 'Madame got her back up about anything – ructions, eh, is that it?'

'No, no, it is not Madame; it is Signor Roscari. He is ill; he is dying!'

'Dying? Oh, come now.'

Cowan hurried after her as she led the way to the stricken Italian's bedroom. The little man was lying on his bed, or rather jerking himself all over it in a series of contortions that would have been humorous had they been less grave. Paula Nazorkoff was bending over him; she greeted Cowan imperiously.

'Ah! There you are. Our poor Roscari, he suffers horrible. Doubtless he has eaten something.'

'I am dying,' groaned the little man. 'The pain – it is terrible. Ow!'

He contorted himself again, clasping both hands to his stomach, and rolling about on the bed.

'We must send for a doctor,' said Cowan.

Paula arrested him as he was about to move to the door.

'The doctor is already on his way; he will do all that can be done for the poor suffering one, that is arranged for, but never, never will Roscari be able to sing tonight.'

'I shall never sing again; I am dying,' groaned the Italian.

'No, no, you are not dying,' said Paula. 'It is but an indigestion, but all the same, impossible that you should sing.'

'I have been poisoned.'

'Yes, it is the ptomaine without doubt,' said Paula. 'Stay with him, Elise, till the doctor comes.'

The singer swept Cowan with her from the room.

'What are we to do?' she demanded.

Cowan shook his head hopelessly. The hour was so far advanced that it would not be possible to get anyone from London to take Roscari's place. Lady Rustonbury, who had just been informed of her guest's illness, came hurrying along the corridor to join them. Her principal concern, like Paula Nazorkoff's, was the success of *Tosca*.

'If there were only someone at hand,' groaned the prima donna.

'Ah!' Lady Rustonbury gave a sudden cry. 'Of course! Bréon.'

'Bréon?'

'Yes, Edouard Bréon, you know, the famous French baritone. He lives near here. There was a picture of his house in this week's *Country Homes*. He is the very man.'

'It is an answer from heaven,' cried Nazorkoff. 'Bréon as Scarpia, I remember him well, it was one of his greatest rôles. But he has retired, has he not?'

'I will get him,' said Lady Rustonbury. 'Leave it to me.'

And being a woman of decision, she straightway ordered out the Hispano Suiza. Ten minutes later, M. Edouard Bréon's country retreat was invaded by an agitated countess. Lady Runstonbury, once she had made her mind up, was a very determined woman, and doubtless M. Bréon realized that there was nothing for it but to submit. Also, it must be confessed, he had a weakness for countesses. Himself a man of very humble origin, he had climbed to the top of his profession, and had consorted on equal terms with dukes and princes, and the fact never failed to gratify him. Yet, since his retirement to this old-world English spot, he had known discontent. He missed the life of adulation and applause, and the English county had not been as prompt to recognize him as he thought they should have been. So he was greatly flattered and charmed by Lady Rustonbury's request.

'I will do my poor best,' he said, smiling. 'As you know, I have not sung in public for a long time now. I do not even take pupils, only one or two as a great favour. But there – since Signor Roscari is unfortunately indisposed –'

'It was a terrible blow,' said Lady Rustonbury.

'Not that he is really a singer,' said Bréon.

He told her at some length why this was so. There had been, it seemed, no baritone of distinction since Edouard Bréon retired.

'Mme Nazorkoff is singing "Tosca",' said Lady Rustonbury. 'You know her, I dare say?'

'I have never met her,' said Bréon. 'I heard her sing once in New York. A great artist – she has a sense of drama.'

Lady Rustonbury felt relieved – one never knew with these singers – they had such queer jealousies and antipathies.

She re-entered the hall at the castle some twenty minutes later waving a triumphant hand.

'I have got him,' she cried, laughing. 'Dear M. Bréon has really been too kind. I shall never forget it.'

Everyone crowded round the Frenchman, and their gratitude and appreciation were as incense to him. Edouard Bréon, though now close on sixty, was still a fine-looking man, big and dark, with a magnetic personality.

'Let me see,' said Lady Rustonbury. 'Where is Madame –? Oh! There she is.'

Paula Nazorkoff had taken no part in the general welcoming of the Frenchman. She had remained quietly sitting in a high oak chair in the shadow of the fireplace. There was, of course, no fire, for the evening was a warm one and the singer was slowly fanning herself with an immense palm-leaf fan. So aloof and detached was she, that Lady Rustonbury feared she had taken offence.

'M. Bréon.' She led him up to the singer. 'You have never yet met Madame Nazorkoff, you say.

With a last wave, almost a flourish, of the palm leaf, Paula Nazorkoff laid it down and stretched out her hand to the Frenchman. He took it and bowed low over it, and a faint sigh escaped from the prima donna's lips.

'Madame,' said Bréon, 'we have never sung together. That is the penalty of my age! But Fate has been kind to me, and come to my rescue.'

Paula laughed softly.

'You are too kind, M. Bréon. When I was still but a poor little unknown singer, I have sat at your feet. Your "Rigoletto" – what art, what perfection! No one could touch you.'

'Alas!' said Bréon, pretending to sigh. 'My day is over. Scarpia, Rigoletto, Radamès, Sharpless, how many times have I not sung them, and now – no more!'

'Yes – tonight.'

'True, madame – I forgot. Tonight.'

'You have sung with many "Toscas",' said Nazorkoff arrogantly, 'but never with *me!*''

The Frenchman bowed.

'It will be an honour,' he said softly. 'It is a great part, madame.'

'It needs not only a singer, but an actress," put in Lady Rustonbury.

"That is true,' Bréon agreed. 'I remember when I was a young man in Italy, going to a little out-of-the-way theatre in Milan. My seat cost me only a couple of lira, but I heard as good singing that night as I have heard in the Metropolitan Opera House in New York. Quite a young girl sang "Tosca"; she sang it like an angel. Never shall I forget her voice in "Vissi D'Arte", the clearness of it, the purity. But the dramatic force, that was lacking."

Nazorkoff nodded.

'That comes later,' she said quietly.

'True. This young girl – Bianca Capelli her name was – I interested myself in her career. Through me she had a chance of big engagements, but she was foolish – regrettably foolish.'

He shrugged his shoulders.

'How was she foolish?'

It was Lady Rustonbury's twenty-four-year-old daughter, Blanche Amery, who spoke – a slender girl with wide blue eyes.

The Frenchman turned to her at once politely.

'Alas! Mademoiselle, she had embroiled herself with some low fellow, a ruffian, a member of the Camorra. He got into trouble with the police, was condemned to death; she came to me begging me to do something to save her lover.'

Blanche Amery was staring at him.

'And did you?' she asked breathlessly.

'Me, mademoiselle, what could I do? A stranger in the country.'

'You might have had influence?' suggested Nazorkoff in her low, vibrant voice.

'If I had, I doubt whether I should have exerted it. The man was not worth it. I did what I could for the girl.'

He smiled a little, and his smile suddenly struck the English girl as having something peculiarly disagreeable about it. She felt that, at that moment, his words fell far short of representing his thoughts.

'You did what you could,' said Nazorkoff. 'That was kind of you, and she was grateful, eh?'

The Frenchman shrugged his shoulders.

'The man was executed,' he said, 'and the girl entered a convent. Eh, violà! The world has lost a singer.'

Nazorkoff gave a low laugh.

'We Russians are more fickle,' she said lightly.

Blanche Amery happened to be watching Cowan as the singer spoke, and she saw his quick look of astonishment, and his lips that half opened and then shut tight in obedience to some warning glance from Paula.

The butler appeared in the doorway.

'Dinner,' said Lady Rustonbury, rising. 'You poor things, I am so sorry for you. It must be dreadful always to have to starve yourself before singing. But there will be a very good supper afterwards.'

'We shall look forward to it,' said Paula Nazorkoff. She laughed softly. 'Afterwards!'

III

Inside the theatre, the first act of *Tosca* had just drawn to a close. The audience stirred, spoke to each other. The royalties, charming and gracious, sat in the three velvet chairs in the front row. Everyone was whispering and murmuring to each other; there was a general feeling that in the first act Nazorkoff had hardly lived up to her great reputation. Most of the audience did not realize that in this the singer showed her art; in the first act she was saving her voice and herself. She made of La Tosca a light, frivolous figure, toying with love, coquettishly jealous and exacting. Bréon, though the glory of his voice was past its prime, still struck a magnificent figure as the cynical Scarpia. There was no hint of the decrepit roué in his conception of the part. He made of Scarpia a handsome, almost benign figure, with just a hint of the subtle malevolence that underlay the outward seeming. In the last passage, with the organ and the procession, when Scarpia stands lost in thought, gloating over his plan to secure Tosca, Bréon had displayed a wonderful art. Now the curtain rose upon the second act, the scene in Scarpia's apartments.

This time, when Tosca entered, the art of Nazorkoff at once became apparent. Here was a woman in deadly terror playing her part with the assurance of a fine actress. Her easy greeting of Scarpia, her nonchalance, her smiling replies to him! In this scene, Paula Nazorkoff acted with her eyes; she carried herself with deadly quietness, with an impassive, smiling face. Only her eyes that kept darting glances at Scarpia betrayed her true feelings. And so the story went on, the torture scene, the breaking down of Tosca's composure, and her utter abandonment when she fell at Scarpia's feet imploring him vainly for mercy. Old Lord Leconmere, a connoisseur of music, moved appreciatively, and a foreign ambassador sitting next to him murmured:

'She surpasses herself, Nazorkoff, tonight. There is no other woman on the stage who can let herself go as she does.'

Leconmere nodded.

And now Scarpia has named his price, and Tosca, horrified, flies from him to the window. Then comes the beat of drums from afar, and Tosca flings herself wearily down on the sofa. Scarpia, standing over her, recites how his people are raising up the gallows – and then silence, and again the far-off beat of drums. Nazorkoff lay prone on the sofa, her head hanging downwards almost touching the floor, masked by her hair. Then, in exquisite contrast to the passion and stress of the last twenty minutes, her voice rang out, high and clear, the voice, as she had told Cowan, of a choir boy or an angel.

'Vissi d'arte, vissi d'amore, no feci mai male ad anima vival. Con man furtiva quante miserie conobbi, aiutai.'

21

It was the voice of a wondering, puzzled child. Then she is once more kneeling and imploring, till the instant when Spoletta enters. Tosca, exhausted, given in, and Scarpia utters his fateful words of double-edged meaning. Spoletta departs once more. Then comes the dramatic moment when Tosca, raising a glass of wine in her trembling hand, catches sight of the knife on the table and slips it behind her.

Bréon rose up handsome, saturnine, inflamed with passion. '*Tosca, finalmente mia!*' The lightning stab with the knife, and Tosca's hiss of vengeance:

'*Questo e il baccio di Tosca!* ('It is thus that Tosca kisses.')

Never had Nazorkoff shown such an appreciation of Tosca's act of vengeance. That last fierce whispered '*Muori dannato*,' and then in a strange, quiet voice that filled the theatre:

'*Or gli perdone!*' ('Now I forgive him!')

The soft death tune began as Tosca set about her ceremonial, placing the candles each side of his head, the crucifix on his breast, her last pause in the doorway looking back, the roll of distant drums, and the curtain fell.

This time real enthusiasm broke out in the audience, but it was short-lived. Someone hurried out from behind the wings and spoke to Lord Rustonbury. He rose, and after a minute or two's consultation, turned and beckoned to Sir Donald Calthorp, who was an eminent physician. Almost immediately the truth spread through the audience. Something had happened; an accident; someone was badly hurt. One of the singers appeared before the curtain and explained that M. Bréon had unfortunately met with an accident – the opera could not proceed. Again the rumour went round, Bréon had been stabbed, Nazorkoff had lost her head, she had lived in her part so completely that she had actually stabbed the man who was acting with her. Lord Leconmere, talking to his ambassador friend, felt a touch on his arm, and turned to look into Blanche Amery's eyes.

'It was not an accident,' the girl was saying. 'I am sure it was not an accident. Didn't you hear, just before dinner, that story he was telling about the girl in Italy? That girl was Paula Nazorkoff. Just after, she said something about being Russian, and I saw Mr Cowan look amazed. She may have taken a Russian name, but he knows well enough that she is Italian.'

'My dear Blanche,' said Lord Leconmere.

'I tell you I am sure of it. She had a picture paper in her bedroom opened at the page showing M. Bréon in his English country home.

She knew before she came down here. I believe she gave something to that poor little Italian man to make him ill.'

'But why? cried Lord Leconmere. 'Why?'

'Don't you see? It's the story of Tosca all over again. He wanted her in Italy, but she was faithful to her lover, and she went to him to try to get him to save her lover, and he pretended he would. Instead he let him die. And now at last her revenge has come. Didn't you hear the way she hissed '*I am Tosca*'? And I saw Bréon's face when she said it, he knew then – he recognized her!'

In her dressing room, Paula Nazorkoff sat motionless, a white ermine cloak held round her. There was a knock at the door.

'Come in,' said the prima donna.

Elise entered. She was sobbing.

'Madame, madame, he is dead! And–'

'Yes?'

'Madame, how can I tell you? There are two gentlemen of the police there; they want to speak to you.'

Paula Nazorkoff rose to her full height.

'I will go to them,' she said quietly.

She untwisted a collar of pearls from her neck and put them into the French girl's hands.

'Those are for you, Elise; you have been a good girl. I shall not need them now where I am going. You understand, Elise? I shall not sing "Tosca" again.'

She stood a moment by the door, her eyes sweeping over the dressing room, as though she looked back over the past thirty years of her career.

Then softly between her teeth, she murmured the last line of another opera:

'*La commedia e finita!*'

A MATTER OF MEAN ELEVATION

by O. HENRY

Place: Somewhere in Central America on Tour
Time: 1888
Performance: *Carmen*, by Georges Bizet

One winter the Alcazar Opera Company of New Orleans made a speculative trip along the Mexican, Central American, and South American coasts. The venture proved a most successful one. The music-loving, impressionable Spanish-Americans deluged the company with dollars and 'vivas.' The manager waxed plump and amiable. But for the prohibitive climate he would have put forth the distinctive flower of his prosperity – the overcoat of fur, braided, frogged, and opulent. Almost was he persuaded to raise the salaries of his company. But with a mighty effort he conquered the impulse toward such an unprofitable effervescence of joy.

At Macuto, on the coast of Venezuela, the company scored its greatest success. Imagine Coney Island translated into Spanish and you will comprehend Macuto. The fashionable season is from November to March. Down from La Guayra and Caracas and Valencia and other interior towns flock the people for their holiday season. There are bathing and fiestas and bull fights and scandal. And then the people have a passion for music that the bands in the plaza and on the sea beach stir but do not satisfy. The coming of the Alcazar Opera Company aroused the utmost ardor and zeal among the pleasure seekers.

The illustrious Guzman Blanco, President and Dictator of Venezuela, sojourned in Macuto with his court for the season. That potent ruler – who himself paid a subsidy of 40,000 pesos each year to grand opera in Caracas – ordered one of the government warehouses to be cleared for a temporary theatre. A stage was quickly constructed and rough wooden benches made for the audience. Private boxes were added for the use of the President and the notables of the army and Government.

The company remained in Macuto for two weeks. Each performance filled the house as closely as it could be packed. Then the music-mad people fought for room in the open doors and windows, and crowded about, hundreds deep on the outside. Those audiences formed a brilliantly diversified patch of color. The hue of their faces ranged from the clear olive of the pure-blood Spaniards down through the yellow and brown shades of the mestizos to the coal-black Carib and the Jamaica Negro. Scattered among them were little groups of Indians with faces like stone idols, wrapped in gaudy fibre-woven blankets – Indians down from the mountains states of Zamora and Los Andes and Miranda to trade their gold dust in the coast towns.

The spell cast upon these denizens of the interior fastnesses was remarkable. They sat in petrified ecstasy, conspicuous among the excitable Macutians, who wildly strove with tongue and hand to give evidence of their delight. Only once did the sombre rapture of these aboriginals find expression. During the rendition of 'Faust,' Guzman Blanco, extravagantly pleased by the 'Jewel Song,' cast upon the stage a purse of gold pieces. Other distinguished citizens followed his lead to the extent of whatever loose coin they had convenient, while some of the fair and fashionable señoras were moved, in imitation, to fling a jewel or a ring or two at the feet of the Marguerite – who was, according to the bills, Mlle Nina Giraud. Then from different parts of the house rose sundry of the stolid hillmen and cast upon the stage little brown and dun bags that fell with soft 'thumps' and did not rebound. It was, no doubt, pleasure at the tribute to her art that caused Mlle Giraud's eyes to shine so brightly when she opened these little deerskin bags in her dressing room and found them to contain pure gold dust. If so, the pleasure was rightly hers, for her voice in song, pure, strong, and thrilling with the feeling of the emotional artist, deserved the tribute that it earned.

But the triumph of the Alcazar Opera Company is not the theme: it but leans upon and colors it. There happened in Macuto a tragic thing, an unsolvable mystery, that sobered for a time the gaiety of the happy season.

One evening between the short twilight and the time when she should have whirled upon the stage in the red and black of the ardent Carmen, Mlle Nina Giraud disappeared from the sight and ken of 6,000 pairs of eyes and as many minds in Macuto. There was the usual turmoil and hurrying to seek her. Messengers flew to the little French-kept hotel where she stayed; others of the company hastened here or there where she might be lingering in some *tienda* or unduly prolonging her bath upon the beach. All search was fruitless. Mademoiselle had vanished.

Half an hour passed, and she did not appear. The dictator, unused to the caprices of prima donne, became impatient. He sent an aide from his box to say to the manager that if the curtain did not at once rise he would immediately hale the entire company to the calabosa, though it would desolate his heart, indeed, to be compelled to such an act. Birds in Macuto could be made to sing.

The manager abandoned hope, for the time, of Mlle Giraud. A member of the chorus, who had dreamed hopelessly for years of the blessed opportunity, quickly Carmenized herself and the opera went on.

Afterward, when the lost cantatrice appeared not, the aid of the authorities was invoked. The President at once set the army, the police, and all citizens to the search. Not one clue to Mlle Giraud's disappearance was found. The Alcazar left to fill engagements farther down the coast.

On the way back the steamer stopped at Macuto and the manager made anxious inquiry. Not a trace of the lady had been discovered. The Alcazar could do no more. The personal belongings of the missing lady were stored in the hotel against her possible later reappearance and the opera company continued upon its homeward voyage to New Orleans.

On the *camino real* along the beach the two saddle mules and the four pack mules of Señor Don Johnny Armstrong stood, patiently awaiting the crack of the whip of the *arriero*, Luis. That would be the signal for the start on another long journey into the mountains. The pack mules were loaded with a varied assortment of hardware and cutlery. These articles Don Johnny traded to the interior Indians for the gold dust that they washed from the Andean streams and stored in quills and bags against his coming. It was a profitable business, and Señor

Armstrong expected soon to be able to purchase the coffee plantation that he coveted.

Armstrong stood on the narrow sidewalk, exchanging garbled Spanish with old Peralto, the rich native merchant who had just charged him four prices for half a gross of pot-metal hatchets, and abridged English with Rucker, the little German who was Consul for the United States.

'Take with you, señor,' said Peralto, 'the blessings of the saints upon your journey.'

'Better try quinine,' growled Rucker through his pipe. 'Take two grains every night. And don't make your trip too long, Johnny, because we haf needs of you. It is ein villainous game dot Melville play of whist, and dere is no oder substitute. *Auf wiedersehen*, und keep your eyes dot mule's ear between when you on de edge of der brecipces ride.'

The bells of Luis's mule jingled and the pack train filed after the warning note. Armstrong waved a good-bye and took his place at the trail of the procession. Up the narrow street they turned, and passed the two-story wooden Hotel Inglés where Ives and Dawson and Richards and the rest of the chaps were dawdling on the broad piazza, reading week-old newspapers. They crowded to the railing and shouted many friendly and wise and foolish farewells after him. Across the plaza they trotted slowly past the bronze statue of Guzman Blanco, within its fence of bayoneted rifles captured from revolutionists, and out of the town between the rows of thatched huts swarming with the unclothed youth of Macuto. They plunged into the damp coolness of banana groves at length to emerge upon a bright stream, where brown women in scant raiment laundered clothes destructively upon the rocks. Then the pack train, fording the stream, attacked the sudden ascent, and bade adieu to such civilization as the coast afforded.

For weeks Armstrong, guided by Luis, followed his regular route among the mountains. After he had collected an arroba of the precious metal, winning a profit of nearly $5,000, the heads of the lightened mules were turned down-trail again. Where the head of the Guarico River springs from a great gash in the mountainside, Luis halted the train.

'Half a day's journey from here, Señor,' said he, 'is the village of Tacuzama, which we have never visited. I think many ounces of gold may be procured there. It is worth the trial.'

Armstrong concurred, and they turned again upward toward Tacuzama. The trail was abrupt and precipitous, mounting through a dense forest. As night fell, dark and gloomy, Luis once more halted. Before them was a black chasm, bisecting the path as far as they could see.

Luis dismounted. 'There should be a bridge,' he called, and ran along the cleft a distance. 'It is here,' he cried, and remounting, led the way. In a few moments Armstrong heard a sound as though a thunderous drum were beating somewhere in the dark. It was the falling of the mules' hoofs upon the bridge made of strong hides lashed to poles and stretched across the chasm. Half a mile further was Tacuzama. The village was a congregation of rock and mud huts set in that profundity of an obscure wood. As they rode in a sound inconsistent with that brooding solitude met their ears. From a long, low mud hut that they were nearing rose the glorious voice of a woman in song. The words were English, the air familiar to Armstrong's memory, but not to his musical knowledge.

He slipped from his mule and stole to a narrow window in one end of the house. Peering cautiously inside, he saw, within three feet of him, a woman of marvelous, imposing beauty, clothed in a splendid loose robe of leopard skins. The hut was packed close to the small space in which she stood with the squatting figures of Indians.

The woman finished her song and seated herself close to the little window, as if grateful for the unpolluted air that entered it. When she had ceased several of the audience rose and cast little softly falling bags at her feet. A harsh murmur - no doubt a barbarous kind of applause and comment - went through the grim assembly.

Armstrong was used to seizing opportunities promptly. Taking advantage of the noise he called to the woman in a low but distinct voice: 'Do not turn your head this way, but listen. I am an American. If you need assistance tell me how I can render it. Answer as briefly as you can.'

The woman was worthy of his boldness. Only by a sudden flush of her pale cheek did she acknowledge understanding of his words. Then she spoke, scarcely moving her lips.

'I am held a prisoner by these Indians. God knows I need help. In two hours come to the little hut twenty yards toward the mountainside. There will be a light and a red curtain in the window. There is always a guard at the door whom you will have to overcome. For the love of heaven, do not fail to come.'

The story seems to shrink from adventure and rescue and mystery. The theme is one too gentle for those brave and quickening tones. And

28

yet it reaches as far back as time itself. It has been named 'environment,' which is a weak a word as any to express the unnamable kinship
of man to nature, that queer fraternity that causes stones and trees and
salt water and clouds to play upon our emotions. Why are we made
serious and solemn and sublime by mountain heights, grave and
contemplative by an abundance of overhanging trees, reduced to
inconstancy and monkey capers by the ripples on a sandy beach? Did
the protoplasm – but enough. The chemists are looking into the matter,
and before long they will have all life in the table of the symbols.

Briefly, then, in order to confine the story within scientific bounds,
John Armstrong went to the hut, choked the Indian guard and carried
away Mlle Giraud. With her was also conveyed a number of pounds of
gold dust she had collected during her six months' forced engagement
in Tacuzama. The Carabobo Indians are easily the most enthusiastic
lovers of music between the equator and the French Opera House in
New Orleans. They are also strong believers that the advice of Emerson
was good when he said: 'The thing thou wantest, O discontented man
– take it, and pay the price.' A number of them had attended the
performance of the Alcazar Opera Company in Macuto, and found
Mlle Giraud's style and technique satisfactory. They wanted her, so
they took her one evening suddenly and without any fuss. They treated
her with much consideration, exacting only one song recital each day.
She was quite pleased at being rescued by Mr Armstrong. So much for
mystery and adventure. Now to resume the theory of the protoplasm.

John Armstrong and Mlle Giraud rode among the Andean peaks,
enveloped in their greatness and sublimity. The mightiest cousins,
furthest removed, in Nature's great family became conscious of the tie.
Among those huge piles of primordial upheaval, amid those gigantic
silences and elongated fields of distance the littlenesses of men are
precipitated as one chemical throws down a sediment from another.
They moved reverently, as in a temple. Their souls were uplifted in
unison with the stately heights. They traveled in a zone of majesty and
peace.

To Armstrong the woman seemed almost a holy thing. Yet bathed
in the white, still dignity of her martyrdom that purified her earthly
beauty and gave out, it seemed, an aura of transcendent loveliness, in
those first hours of companionship she drew from him an adoration
that was half human love, half the worship of a descended goddess.

Never yet since her rescue had she smiled. Over her dress she still
wore the robe of leopard skins, for the mountain air was cold. She

looked to be some splendid princess belonging to those wild and awesome altitudes. The spirit of the region chimed with hers. Her eyes were always turned upon the somber cliffs, the blue gorges, and the snow-clad turrets, looking a sublime melancholy equal to their own. At times on the journey she sang thrilling te deums and misereres that struck the true note of the hills, and made their route seem like a solemn march down a cathedral aisle. The rescued one spoke but seldom, her mood partaking of the hush of nature that surrounded them. Armstrong looked upon her as an angel. He could not bring himself to the sacrilege of attempting to woo her as other women may be wooed.

On the third day they had descended as far as the *tierra templada*, the zone of the table lands and foot hills. The mountains were receding in their rear, but still towered, exhibiting yet impressively their formidable heads. Here they met signs of man. They saw the white houses of coffee plantations gleam across the clearings. They struck into a road where they met travelers and pack-mules. Cattle were grazing on the slopes. They passed a little village where the round-eyed *niños* shrieked and called at sight of them.

Mlle Giraud laid aside her leopard-skin robe. It seemed to be a trifle incongruous now. In the mountains it had appeared fitting and natural. And if Armstrong was not mistaken she laid aside with it something of the high dignity of her demeanour. As the country became more populous and significant of comfortable life he saw, with a feeling of joy, that the exalted princess and priestess of the Andean peaks was changing to a woman – an earth woman, but no less enticing. A little color crept to the surface of her marble cheek. She arranged the conventional dress that the removal of the robe now disclosed with the solicitous touch of one who is conscious of the eyes of others. She smoothed the careless sweep of her hair. A mundane interest, long latent in the chilling atmosphere of the ascetic peaks, showed in her eyes.

This thaw in his divinity sent Armstrong's heart going faster. So might an Arctic explorer thrill at his first ken of green fields and liquescent waters. They were on a lower plane of earth and life and were succumbing to its peculiar, subtle influence. The austerity of the hills no longer thinned the air they breathed. About them was the breath of fruit and corn and builded homes, the comfortable smell of smoke and warm earth and the consolations man has placed between himself and the dust of his brother earth from which he sprung. While traversing those awful mountains, Mlle Giraud had seemed to be wrapped in their spirit of reverent reserve. Was this that same woman – now palpitating, warm, eager, throbbing with conscious life and charm, feminine to her fingertips? Pondering over this, Armstrong felt certain misgivings intrude upon his thoughts. He wished he could stop there with this changing creature, descending no farther. Here was the elevation and environment to which her nature seemed to respond with its best. He feared to go down upon the man-dominated levels. Would her spirit not yield still further in that artificial zone to which they were descending?

Now from a little plateau they saw the sea flash at the edge of the green lowlands. Mlle Giraud gave a little, catching sigh.

'Oh, look, Mr Armstrong, there is the sea! Isn't it lovely? I'm so tired of mountains.' She heaved a pretty shoulder in a gesture of repugnance. 'Those horrid Indians! Just think of what I suffered! Although I suppose I attained my ambition of becoming a stellar attraction, I wouldn't care to repeat the engagement. It was very nice of you to bring me away. Tell me, Mr Armstrong – honestly, now – do I look such an awful, awful fright? I haven't looked into a mirror, you know, for months.'

Armstrong made answer according to his changed moods. Also he laid his hand upon hers as it rested upon the horn of her saddle. Luis was at the head of the pack train and could not see. She allowed it to remain there, and her eyes smiled frankly into his.

Then at sundown they dropped upon the coast level under the palms and lemons among the vivid greens and scarlets and ochres of the *tierra caliente*. They rode into Macuto, and saw the line of volatile bathers frolicking in the surf. The mountains were very far away.

Mille Giraud's eyes were shining with a joy that could not have existed under the chaperonage of the mountain-tops. There were other spirits calling to her – nymphs of the orange groves, pixies from the chattering surfs, imps, born of the music, the perfumes, colours and the insinuating presence of humanity. She laughed aloud, musically, at the sudden thought.

'Won't there be a sensation?' she called to Armstrong. 'Don't I wish I had an engagement just now, though! What a picnic the press agent would have!' "Held a prisoner, by a band of savage Indians subdued by the spell of her wonderful voice" – wouldn't that make great stuff? But I guess I quit the game winner, anyhow – there ought to be a couple of thousand dollars in that sack of gold dust I collected as encores, don't you think?'

He left her at the door of the little Hotel de Buen Descansar, where she had stopped before. Two hours later he returned to the hotel. He glanced in at the open door of the little combined reception room and café.

Half a dozen of Macuto's representative social and official *caballeros* were distributed about the room. Señor Villablanca, the wealthy rubber concessionist, reposed his fat figure on two chairs, with an emollient smile beaming upon his chocolate-colored face. Guilbert, the French mining engineer, leered through his polished nose-glasses. Colonel Mendez, of the regular army, in gold-laced uniform and fatuous grin, was busily extracting corks from champagne bottles. Other patterns of Macutian gallantry and fashion pranced and posed. The air was hazy with cigarette smoke. Wine dripped upon the floor.

Perched upon a table in the centre of the room in an attitude of easy pre-eminence was Mlle Giraud. A chic costume of white lawn and cherry ribbons supplanted her traveling garb. There was a suggestion of lace, and a frill or two, with a discreet, small implication of hand-embroidered pink hosiery. Upon her lap rested a guitar. In her face was the light of resurrection, the peace of elysium attained through fire and suffering. She was singing to a lively accompaniment a little song:

> '*When you see de big round moon*
> *Comin' up like a balloon,*
> *Dis nigger skips fur to kiss de lips*
> *Of his stylish, black-faced coon.*'

The singer caught sight of Armstrong.

'Hi! there, Johnny,' she called; 'I've been expecting you for an hour. What kept you? Gee! but these smoked guys are the slowest you ever saw. They ain't on, at all. Come along in, and I'll make this coffee-colored old sport with the gold epaulettes open one for you right off the ice.'

'Thank you,' said Armstrong; 'not just now, I believe. I've several things to attend to.'

He walked out and down the street, and met Rucker coming up from the Consulate.

'Play you a game of billiards,' said Armstrong. 'I want something to take the taste of the sea level out of my mouth.'

MOM SINGS AN ARIA

by *JAMES YAFFE*

Place: New York, The Metropolitan Opera
Time: 1954
Performance: *Tosca*, by Giacomo Puccini

It was one of the greatest disappointments of my mother's life that I never turned out to be a musical genius. For a couple of years, when I was a kid, Mom made me take violin lessons. At the end of the first year I played a piece called 'Rustling Leaves'. At the end of the second year I was still playing 'Rustling Leaves'. Poor Mom had to admit I wasn't another Jascha Heifetz, and that was the end of my musical career.

Mom has always been crazy about music herself. She did a little singing when she was a girl, and might have done something with her voice – instead she got married, moved up to the Bronx, and devoted herself to raising a future Lieutenant in the New York City Homicide Squad. But she still listens regularly to the Saturday afternoon broadcasts of the Metropolitan Opera, and she can still hum along with all the familiar arias. That was why – when my wife Shirley and I went up to the Bronx the other night for our regular Friday dinner – I knew Mom would be interested in my latest case.

'You're a music lover, Mom,' I said. 'Maybe you can understand how a man could love music so much that he'd commit murder for it.'

'This is hard to understand?' Mom said, looking up from her roast chicken. 'Why else did I stop your violin lessons? Once, while you were playing one of your pieces, I happened to take a look at your teacher, Mrs Steinberg – and on her face was murder, if I ever saw it!'

33

'You don't mean that literally, do you, Mother?' Shirley said. 'A woman wouldn't *really* feel like murdering a little boy because he played the violin badly.'

'People can have plenty feelings that were never in your psychology books at college,' Mom said. 'Believe me, in my own family – my Aunt Goldie who thought the pigeon outside her window was actually her late husband Jake –'

Mom went into detail, and her story was fascinating. Then she passed the chicken a second time, and I was able to get back to my murder.

'Have you ever seen the standing-room line at the Metropolitan Opera House?' I said. 'Half an hour before every performance the box office sells standing-room tickets at two-fifty each, on a first-come first-served basis. The opera lovers start lining up outside the house hours ahead of time. They stand on their feet for three hours *before* the opera just so they can stand on their feet for three hours *during* the opera! Talk about crazy human motives!'

'People with no ears in their heads,' Mom said, 'shouldn't be so quick to call other people crazy.' And she gave me one of those glares which has been making me feel like a naughty little five-year-old ever since I *was* a naughty little five-year-old.

I turned my eyes away and pushed on. 'Well, there are certain people who show up on the opera standing-room line night after night, for practically every performance throughout the season. These "regulars" are almost always at the head of the line – they come earlier than anyone else, wait longer, and take the best centre places once they get inside the house. And since most of them have been doing this for years, they know each other by name, and they pass the time gossiping about the opera singers and discussing the performances. You could almost say they've got an exclusive little social club all their own – only their meeting place isn't a club-house, it's the sidewalk in front of the Met. Anyway, you couldn't imagine a more harmless collection of old fogeys – the last group on earth where you'd expect to find a murderer!'

'Even an opera lover has to have a private life,' Mom said. 'He enjoys himself with the beautiful music – but he's still got business troubles or love troubles or family troubles waiting for him at home.'

'That's just it, Mom. If one of these standing-room regulars had gone home and killed his wife or his mother-in-law or his business partner, this would just be a routine case. But what happened was, he killed one of the other people in the standing-room line.'

Mom was looking at me with her eyes narrowed – a sure sign that I had her interested. 'The two oldest regulars in the standing-room line,' I said, 'the charter members of the club, are Sam Cohen and Giuseppe D'Angelo. Cohen used to be a pharmacist, with his own drug store on West Eighty-third Street. He retired fifteen years ago, after his wife died, and turned the management of the store over to his nephew, though he went on living in the apartment above it. As soon as he retired, he started going to the opera almost every night of the season.

'D'Angelo was in the exterminating business out in Queens – insects, rodents, and so on – but *he* retired fifteen years ago too. His wife is alive but she doesn't care for music, so he's been in the habit of going to the opera by himself – almost every night of the season, just like Cohen.

'The two old men met on the standing-room line fifteen years ago, and have seen each other three of four nights a week ever since – but only at the opera, never anywhere else. As far as we know, they've never met for a drink or a lunch, they've never been to each other's homes, and they've never seen each other at all in the summer, when the opera is closed.

'Opera is the biggest thing in both their lives. Cohen's mother was a vocal coach back in Germany, and he cut his teeth on operatic arias – D'Angelo was born and brought up in the city of Parma, which they tell me is the most operatic city in Italy –'

'I've read about Parma,' Mom said. 'If a tenor hits a bad note there, they run him out of town.'

'How horrible!' Shirley said. 'It's positively uncivilized!'

Mom shrugged. 'A little less civilization here in New York, and maybe we wouldn't hear so many bad notes.'

I could see the cloud of indignation forming on Shirley's face – she never *has* caught on to Mom's peculiar sense of humor. I hurried on, 'Well, the two old men both loved opera, but their opinions about it have always been diametrically opposed. So for fifteen years they've been carrying on a running argument. If Cohen likes a certain soprano, D'Angels can't stand her. If D'Angelo mentions having heard Caruso sing *Aida* in 1920, Cohen says that Caruso never sang *Aida* after 1917.

'And the old men haven't conducted these arguments in nice soft gentlemanly voices either. They yell at each other, wave their arms, call each other all sorts of names. "Liar" and "moron" are about the tamest I can think of. In spite of their bitterness, of course, these fights have

35

never lasted long – before the night is over, or at least by the time of the next performance, the old men always make it up between them –'

'Until now?' Mom said.

'I'll get to that in a minute, Mom. Just a little more background first. According to the other regulars on the standing-room line, the fights between Cohen and D'Angelo have become even more bitter than usual in recent years. They've been aggravated by a controversy which has been raging among opera lovers all over the world. Who's the greatest soprano alive today – Maria Callas or Renata Tebaldi?'

Mom dropped her fork and clasped her hands to her chest, and on her face came that ecstatic almost girlish look which she reserves exclusively for musical matters. 'Callas! Tebaldi! Voices like angels, both of them! That Callas – such fire, such passion! That Tebaldi – such beauty, such sadness! To choose which one is the greatest – it's as foolish as trying to choose between noodle soup and borscht!'

'Cohen and D'Angelo made their choices, though,' I said. 'D'Angelo announced one day that Tebaldi was glorious and Callas had a voice like a rooster – so right away Cohen told him that Callas was divine and Tebaldi sang like a cracked phonograph record. And the argument has been getting more and more furious through the years.

'A week ago a climax was reached. Callas was singing *Traviata*, and the standing-room line started to form even earlier than usual. Cohen and D'Angelo, of course, were right there among the first. Cohen had a bad cold – he was sneezing all the time he stood in line – but he said he would't miss Callas' *Traviata* if he was down with double pneumonia. And D'Angelo said that personally he could live happily for the rest of his life without hearing Callas butcher *Traviata* – he was here tonight, he said, only because of the tenor, Richard Tucker.'

'That Richard Tucker!' Mom gave her biggest, most motherly smile. 'Such a wonderful boy – just as much at home in the *schul* as he is in the opera. What a proud mother he must have!' And Mom gave me a look which made it clear that she still hadn't quite forgiven me for 'Rustling Leaves.'

'With such a long wait on the standing-room line,' I said, 'Cohen and D'Angelo had time to whip up a first-class battle. According to Frau Hochschwender – she's a German lady who used to be a concert pianist and now gives piano lessons, and she's also one of the standing-room regulars – Cohen and D'Angelo had never insulted each other so violently in all the years she'd known them. If the box office had opened an hour later, she says they would have come to blows.

'As it turned out, the performance itself didn't even put an end to their fight. Ordinarily, once the opera began, both men became too wrapped up in the music to remember they were mad at each other – but this time, when the first act ended, Cohen grabbed D'Angelo by the arm and accused him of deliberately groaning after Callas' big aria. "You did it to ruin the evening for me!" Cohen said. He wouldn't pay attention to D'Angelo denials. "I'll get even with you," he said. 'Wait till the next time Tebaldi is singing!'

'And the next time Tebaldi was singing,' Mom said, 'was the night of the murder?'

Exactly. Three nights ago Tebaldi sang *Tosca* –'

'*Tosca!*'

Mom's face lighted up. 'Such a beautiful opera! Such a sad story! She's in love with this handsome young artist, and this villain makes advances and tries to force her to give in to him, so she stabs him with a knife. Come to think of it, the villain in that opera is a police officer.'

I looked hard, but I couldn't see any trace of sarcasm on Mom's face.

'Those opera plots are really ridiculous, aren't they?' Shirley said. 'So exaggerated and unrealistic.'

'Unrealistic!' Mom turned to her sharply. 'You should know some of the things that go on – right here in this building. Didn't Polichek the janitor have his eye on his wife's baby sitter?'

Another fascinating story came out of Mom, and then I went on. 'Anyway, for the whole week-end before *Tosca*, D'Angelo worried that Cohen would do something to spoil the performance for him. He worried so much that the night before, he called Cohen up and pleaded with him not to make trouble.'

'And Cohen answered?'

'His nephew was in the room with him when the call came. He was going over some account books and didn't really pay attention to what his uncle was saying – at one point he heard Cohen raise his voice angrily and shout out, "You can't talk me out of it! When Tebaldi hits her high C in the big aria, I'm going to start booing!"'

Mom shook her head. 'Terrible – a terrible threat for a civilized man to make! So does D'Angelo admit that Cohen made it?'

'Well, yes and no. In the early part of the phone conversation, D'Angelo says he and Cohen were yelling at each other so angrily that neither of them listened to what the other one was saying. But later on in the conversation – or so D'Angelo claims – Cohen calmed down and promised to let Tebaldi sing her aria in peace.'

37

'Cohen's nephew says he didn't?'

'Not exactly. He left the room while Cohen was still on the phone – he had to check some receipts in the cash register – so he never heard the end of the conversation. For all he knows Cohen *might* have calmed down and made that promise.'

'And what about D'Angelo's end of the phone conversation? Was anybody in the room with him?'

'His wife was. And she swears that he *did* get such a promise out of Cohen. But of course she's his wife, so she's anxious to protect him. And besides she's very deaf, and she won't wear a hearing aid – she's kind of a vain old lady. So what it boils down to, we've got nobody's word except D'Angelo's that Cohen didn't intend to carry out his threat.'

'Which brings us,' Mom said, 'to the night Tebaldi sang *Tosca?*'

'Cohen and D'Angelo both showed up early on the standing-room line that night. Frau Hochschwender says they greeted each other politely, but all the time they were waiting they hardly exchanged a word. No arguments, no differences of opinion – nothing. And her testimony is confirmed by another one of the regulars who was there – Miss Phoebe Van Voorhees. She's an old lady in her seventies, always dresses in black.

'Miss Van Voorhees came from a wealthy New York family, and when she was a young woman she used to have a regular box at the opera – but the money ran out ten or twelve years ago, and now she lives alone in a cheap hotel in the East Twenties, and she waits on the standing-room line two nights a week. She's so frail-looking you wouldn't think she could stay on her feet for five minutes, much less five hours – but she loves opera, so she does it.'

'For love,' Mom said, 'people can perform miracles.'

'Well, Miss Van Voorhees and Frau Hochschwender both say that Cohen and D'Angelo were unusually restrained with each other. Which seems to prove that they were still mad at each other and hadn't made up the quarrel over the phone, as D'Angelo claims –'

'Or maybe it proves the opposite,' Mom said. 'They *did* make up the quarrel, and they were so scared of starting another quarrel that they shut up and wouldn't express any opinions.'

'Whatever it proves, Mom, here's what happened. On cold nights it's the custom among the standing-room regulars for one of them to go to the cafeteria a block away and get hot coffee for the others –

38

meanwhile they hold his place in the line. The night of Tebaldi's *Tosca* was very cold, and it was D'Angelo's turn to bring the coffee.

'He went for it about forty-five minutes before the box office opened, and got back with it in fifteen or twenty minutes. He was carrying four cardboard containers. Three of them contained coffee with cream and sugar – for Frau Hochschwender, Miss Van Voorhees, and D'Angelo himself. In the fourth container was black coffee without sugar – the way Cohen always took it.

'Well, they all gulped down their coffee, shielding it from the wind with their bodies – and about half an hour later the doors opened. They bought their tickets, went into the opera house, and stood together in their usual place in the back, at the centre.

'At eight sharp the opera began. Tebaldi was in great voice, and the audience was enthusiastic. At the end of the first act all of the standing-room regulars praised her – except Cohen. He just grunted and said nothing. Frau Hochschwender and Miss Van Voorhees both say that he looked pale and a little ill.

' "Wait till she sings her big aria in the second act,' D'Angelo said. "I hope she sings it good," Cohen said – and Frau Hochschwender says there was a definite threat in his voice. But Miss Van Voorhees says she didn't notice anything significant in his voice – to her it just sounded like an offhand remark. Then the second act began, and it was almost time for Tebaldi's big aria –'

'Such a beautiful aria!' Mom said. '*Vissy Darty*. It's Italian. She's telling that police officer villain that all her life she's cared only for love and for art, and she never wanted to hurt a soul. She tells him this, and a little later she stabs him.' And in a low voice, a little quavery but really kind of pretty, Mom began to half sing and half hum – '*Vissy darty, vissy damory–*' Then she broke off, and did something I had seldom seen her do. She blushed.

There was a moment of silence, while Shirley and I carefully refrained from looking at each other. Then I said, 'So a few minutes before Tebaldi's big aria, Cohen suddenly gave a groan, then he grabbed hold of Frau Hochschwender's arm and said, "I'm sick –" And then he started making strangling noises, and dropped like a lead weight to the floor.

'Somebody went for a doctor, and D'Angelo got down on his knees by Cohen and said, "Cohen, Cohen, what's the matter?" And Cohen, with his eyes straight on D'Angelo's face, said, "You no-good! You deserve to die for what you did!" Those were his exact words, Mom – half a dozen people heard them.

'Then a doctor came, with a couple of ushers, and they took Cohen out to the lobby – and D'Angelo, Frau Hoshschwender, and Miss Van Voorhess followed. A little later an ambulance came, but Cohen was dead before he got to the hospital.

'At first the doctors thought it was a heart attack, but they did a routine autopsy – and found enough poison in his stomach to kill a man half his age and twice his strength. The dose he swallowed must've taken two to three hours to produce a reaction – which means he swallowed it while he was on the standing-room line. Well, nobody saw him swallow *anything* on the standing-room line except that container of hot black coffee.'

'And when the doctors looked at the contents of his stomach?'

'They found the traces of his lunch, which *couldn't* have contained the poison or he would've died long before he got to the opera house – and they found that coffee – and that was all they found. So the coffee had to be what killed him.'

'And since that old man D'Angelo was the one who gave him the coffee, you naturally think he's the murderer.'

'What else can we think, Mom? For five minutes or so – from the time he picked up the coffee at the cafeteria to the time he gave it to Cohen at the opera house – D'Angelo was alone with it. Nobody was watching him – he could easily have slipped something into it. And nobody else had such an opportunity. Cohen took the coffee from D'Angelo, turned away to shield the container from the cold wind, and drank it all down then and there. Only D'Angelo *could* have put the poison into it.'

'What about the man at the cafeteria who made the coffee?'

'That doesn't make sense, Mom. The man at the cafeteria would have no way of knowing who the coffee was meant for. He'd have to be a complete psycho who didn't care *who* he poisoned. Just the same, though, we checked him out. He poured the coffee into the container directly from a big urn – twenty other people had been drinking coffee from the same urn. Then in front of a dozen witnesses he handed the container to D'Angelo without putting a thing in it – not even sugar, because Cohen never took his coffee with sugar. So we're right back to D'Angelo – he *has* to be the murderer.'

'And where did he get it, this deadly poison? Correct me if I'm wrong, but such an item isn't something you can pick up at your local supermarket.'

'Sure, it's against the law to sell poison to the general public. But you'd be surprised how easy it is to get hold of the stuff anyway. The kind that killed Cohen is a common commercial compound – it's used to mix paints, for metallurgy, in certain medicines, in insecticides. Ordinary little pellets of rat poison are made of it sometimes, and you can buy them at you local hardware store – a couple of dozen kids swallow them by accident in this city every year. And don't forget, D'Angelo used to be in the exterminating business – he knows all the sources, it would be easier for him to get his hands on poison than for most people.'

'So you've arrested him for the murder?' Mom said.

I gave a sigh. 'No, we haven't.'

'How come? What's holding you up?'

'It's the motive, Mom. D'Angelo and Cohen had absolutely no connection with each other outside of the standing-room line. Cohen didn't leave D'Angelo any money, he wasn't having an affair with D'Angelo's wife, he didn't know a deep dark secret out of D'Angelo's past. There's only one reason why D'Angelo could have killed him – to stop him from booing at the end of Renata Tebaldi's big aria. That's why he committed the murder. I'm morally certain of it, and so is everyone else in the Department. And so is the D.A.'s office – but they won't let us make the arrest.'

'And why not?'

'Because nobody believes for one moment that we can get a jury to believe such a motive. Juries are made up of ordinary everyday people. They don't go to the opera. They think it's all a lot of nonsense – fat women screaming at fat men, in a foreign language. I can sympathize with them – I think so myself. Can you imagine the D.A. standing up in front of a jury and saying, "The defendant was so crazy about an opera singer's voice that he killed a man for disagreeing with him!" The jury would laugh in the D.A.'s face.'

I sighed harder than before. 'We've got an airtight case. The perfect opportunity. No other possible suspects. The dying man's accusation – "You no-good! You deserve to die for what you did!" But we don't dare bring the killer to trial.'

Mom didn't say anything for a few seconds. Her eyes were almost shut, the corners of her mouth were turned down. I know this expression well – her 'thinking' expression. Something always comes out of it.

Finally she looked up and gave a nod. 'Thank God for juries!'

'What do you mean, Mom?'

'I mean, if it wasn't for ordinary everyday people with common sense, God knows *who* you experts would be sending to jail!'

'Mom, are you saying that D'Angelo *didn't*–'

'I'm saying nothing. Not yet. First I'm asking. Four questions.'

No doubt about it, whenever Mom starts asking her questions, that means she's on the scent, she's getting ready to hand me a solution to another one of my cases.

My feelings, as always, were mixed. On the one hand, nobody admires Mom more than I do – her deep knowledge of human nature acquired among her friends and neighbors in the Bronx; her uncanny sharpness in applying that knowledge to the crimes I tell her about from time to time.

On the other hand – well, how ecstatic is a man supposed to get at the idea that his mother can do his own job better than *he* can? That's why I've never been able to talk about Mom's talent to anybody else in the Department – except, of course, to Inspector Milner, my immediate superior, and only because he's a widower, and Shirley and I are trying to get something going between Mom and him.

So I guess my voice wasn't as enthusiastic as it should have been, when I said to Mom, 'Okay, what are your four questions?'

'First I bring in the peach pie,' Mom said.

We waited while the dishes were cleared, and new dishes were brought. Then the heavenly aroma of Mom's peach pie filled the room. One taste of it, and my enthusiasm began to revive. 'What *are* your questions, Mom?'

She lifted her finger. 'Number One: you mentioned that Cohen had a cold a week ago, the night Maria Callas was singing *Traviata*. Did he still have the same cold three nights ago, when Tebaldi was singing *Tosca?*'

By this time I ought to be used to Mom's questions. I ought to take it on faith that they're probably not as irrelevant as they sound. But I still can't quite keep the bewilderment out of my voice.

'As a matter of fact,' I said, 'Cohen *did* have a cold the night of the murder. Frau Hochschwender and Miss Van Voorhees both mentioned it – he was sneezing while he waited in line, and even a few times during the performance, though he tried hard to control himself.'

Mom's face gave no indication whether this was or wasn't what she had wanted to hear. She lifted another finger. 'Number Two: after the opera every night, was it the custom for those standing-room regulars to separate right away – or did they maybe stay together for a little while before they finally said good night?'

'They usually went to the cafeteria a block away – the same place where D'Angelo bought the coffee that Cohen drank – and sat at a table for an hour or so and discussed the performance they'd just heard. Over coffee and doughnuts – or Danish pastry.'

Mom gave a nod, and lifted another finger. 'Number Three: at the hospital you naturally examined what was in Cohen's pockets? Did you find something like an envelope – a small envelope with absolutely nothing in it?'

This question really made me jump. 'We did find an envelope, Mom! Ordinary stationery size – it was unsealed, and there was no address or stamp on it. But how in the world did you –'

Mom's fourth finger was in the air. 'Number Four: how many more times this season is Renata Tebaldi supposed to sing *Tosca*?'

'It was Tebaldi's first, last, and only performance of *Tosca* this season,' I said. 'The posters in front of the opera house said so. But I don't see what that has to do with –'

'You don't see,' Mom said. 'Naturally. You're like all the younger generation these days. So scientific. Facts you see. D'Angelo was the only one who was ever alone with Cohen's coffee – so D'Angelo must have put the poison in. A fact, so you see it. But what about the *people* already? Who is D'Angelo – who was Cohen – what type human beings? This you wouldn't ask yourself. Probably you wouldn't even understand about my Uncle Julius and the World Series.'

'I'm sorry, Mom. I never knew you *had* an Uncle Julius –'

'I don't have him no more. That's the point of the story. All his life he was a fan from the New York Yankees. He rooted for them, he bet money on them, and when they played the World Series he was always there to watch them. Until a couple of years ago when he had his heart attack, and he was in the hospital at World Series time.

'"I'll watch the New York Yankees on television," he said. 'The excitement is too much for you," the doctor said. "It'll kill you." But Uncle Julius had his way, and he watched the World Series. Every day he watched, and every night the doctor said, "You'll be dead before morning." And Uncle Julius said, "I wouldn't die till I know how the

World Series comes out!" So finally the New York Yankees won the World Series – and an hour later Uncle Julius went to sleep and died.'

Mom stopped talking, and looked around at Shirley and me. Then she shook her head and said, 'You don't follow yet? A man with a love for something that's outside himself, that isn't even his family – with a love for the New York Yankees or for Renata Tebaldi – in such a man this feeling is stronger than his personal worries or his personal ambitions. He wouldn't let anything interrupt his World Series in the middle, not even dying. He wouldn't let anything interupt his opera in the middle – not even murdering.'

I began to see a glimmer of Mom's meaning. 'You're talking about D'Angelo, Mom?'

'Who else? Renata Tebaldi was singing her one and only *Tosca* for the year, and for D'Angelo, Renata Tebaldi is the greatest singer alive. Never – in a million years, never – would he do anything to spoil this performance for himself, to make him walk out of it before the end. Let's say he *did* want to murder Cohen. The last time in the world he'd pick for this murder would be in the middle of Tebaldi's *Tosca* – her one and only *Tosca!* Especially since he could wait just as easy till after the opera, when the standing-room regulars would be having cake and coffee at the cafeteria – he could just as easy poison Cohen then.'

'But Mom, isn't that kind of far-fetched, psychologically? If the average man was worked up enough to commit a murder, he wouldn't care about hearing the end of an opera first!'

'Excuse me, Davie – the average man's psychology we're not talking about. The opera lover's psychology we are talking about. This is why you and the Homicide Squad and the District Attorney couldn't make heads and tails from this case. Because you don't understand from opera lovers. In this world they don't live – they've got a world of their own. Inside their heads things are going on which other people's heads never even dreamed about. To solve this case you have to think like an opera lover.'

'To solve this case, Mom, you have to answer the basic question: if D'Angelo didn't poison that coffee who *could* have?'

'Who says the coffee was poisoned?'

'But I told you about the autopsy. The poison took two to three hours to work, and the contents of Cohen's stomach –'

'The contents of his stomach! You should show a little more interest in the contents of Cohen's pockets!'

'There was nothing unusual in his pockets –'

44

'Why should a man carry in his pocket an empty unsealed envelope, without any writing on it, without even a stamp on it? Only because it wasn't empty when he put it there. Something was in it – something which he expected to need later on in the evening – something which he finally took out of the envelope –'

'What are you talking about, Mom?'

'I'm talking about Cohen's cold. An ordinary man, he don't think twice about going to the opera with a cold. What's the difference if he sneezes a little? It's only music. But to an opera lover, sneezing during a performance, disturbing people, competing with the singers – this is worse than a major crime. A real opera lover like Cohen, he'd do everything he could to keep his cold under control.

'Which explains what he put in that envelope before he left his home to go to the opera house. A pill, what else? One of these new prescription cold pills that dries up your nose and keeps you from sneezing for five-six hours. And why was the evelope empty when you found it in his pocket? Because half an hour before the box office opened, he slipped out his pill and swallowed it down with his hot black coffee.

'Nobody saw him taking that pill, Mom.'

'Why should anybody see him? Like you explained yourself, to drink his coffee he had to turn his body away and shield the container from the wind.'

I was beginning to be shaken, no doubt about it. But Shirley spoke up now, in her sweet voice, the voice she alway uses when she thinks she's one up on Mom. 'The facts don't seem to bear you out, Mother. All the witnesses say that Mr Cohen went on sneezing after the opera had begun. Well, if he really did take a cold pill, as you believe, why didn't it have any effect on his symptoms?'

A gleam came to Mom's eyes, and I could see she was about to pounce. The fact is that Shirley never learns.

So to spare my wife's feelings I broke in quickly, before Mom could open her mouth. 'I'm afraid that confirms Mom's theory, honey. The reason why the cold pill didn't work was that it wasn't a cold pill. It looked like one on the outside maybe, but it actually contained poison.'

'I always knew I didn't produce a dope!' Mom said, with a big satisfied smile. 'So now the answer is simple, no? If Cohen was carrying around a poison pill in his pocket, where did he get it? Who gave it to him? Why should he think it was a cold pill? Because somebody told him it was. Somebody he thought he could trust – not

45

only personally but professionally. "Give me some of that new stuff, that new wonder drug, that'll keep me from sneezing during the opera—'"

'His nephew!' I interrupted. 'My God, Mom, I think you're right. Cohen's nephew *is* a pharmacist – he manages the drug store that Cohen owned. He has access to all kinds of poison and he could make up a pill that would look like a real cold pill. And what's more, he's the only relative Cohen has in the world. He inherits Cohen's store and Cohen's savings.'

Mom spread her hands. 'So there you are. You couldn't ask for a more ordinary, old-fashioned motive for murder. Any jury will be able to understand it. It isn't one bit operatic.'

'But Mom, you must've suspected Cohen's nephew from the start. Otherwise you wouldn't have asked your question about the empty envelope.'

'Naturally I suspected him. It was the lie he told.'

'What lie?'

'The night before the opera D'Angelo called up Cohen and tried to make up their quarrel. Now according to the nephew Cohen made a threat to D'Angelo over the phone. 'When Tebaldi hits her high C in the big aria, I'm going to start booing! A terrible threat – but Cohen never could have made it.'

'I don't see why not –'

'Because Cohen was an opera lover, that's why. A high C – in the *Vissy darty* from *Tosca* there isn't any such note. A high B flat is what the soprano is supposed to sing at the end of this aria. If Tebaldi ever made such a mistake – which in a million years she couldn't do – the conductor would have a conniption fit and Cohen would hide his head in shame. People who are ignoramuses about opera – people like Cohen's nephew – they never *heard* of anything except the high C. But an opera lover like Cohen – he positively couldn't get so mixed up. Now excuse me, I'll bring in the coffee.'

Mom got to her feet, and then Shirley called out, 'Wait a second, Mother. If his nephew committed the murder, why did Cohen accuse D'Angelo of doing it?'

'When did Cohen accuse D'Angelo?'

'His dying words. He looked into D'Angelo's face and said, 'You no-good! You deserve to die for what you did!''

'He looked into D'Angelo's face – but how do you know it was D'Angelo he was seeing? He was in delirium from the weakness and the pain, and before his eyes he wasn't seeing any D'Angelo, he wasn't seeing this world that the rest of us are living in. He was seeing the world he'd been looking at before he got sick, the world that meant the most to him – he was seeing the world of the opera, what else? And what was happening up there on that stage just before the poison hit him? The no-good villain was making advances to the beautiful heroine, and she was struggling to defend herself, and pretty soon she was going to kill him – and Cohen, seeing that villain in front of his eyes, shouted out at him, "You no-good! You deserve to die for what you did!"'

Mom was silent for a moment, and then she went on in a lower voice, 'An opera lover will go on being an opera lover – right up to the end.'

She went out to the kitchen for the coffee, and I went to the phone in the hall to call the Homicide Squad.

When I got back to the table, Mom was seated and the coffee was served. She took a few sips, and then gave a little sigh. 'Poor old Cohen – such a terrible way to go!'

'Death by poisoning *is* pretty painful,' I said.

'Poisoning?' Mom blinked up at me. 'Yes, that is terrible too. But the worst part of all – the poor man died fifteen minutes too soon. He never heard Tebaldi sing the *Vissy darty*.'

And Mom began to hum softly.

THE AFFAIR AT THE SEMIRAMIS HOTEL

by *A. E. W. MASON*

Place: London, Covent Garden
Time: 1925
Performance: *I Gioiella della Madonna,* by Ermanno Wolf-Ferrari

Mr Ricardo, when the excitements of the Villa Rose were done with, returned to Grosvenor Square and resumed the busy, unnecessary life of an amateur. But the studios had lost their savor, artists their attractiveness, and even the Russian opera seemed a trifle flat. Life was altogether a disappointment; Fate, like an actress at a restaurant, had taken the wooden pestle in her hand and stirred all the sparkle out of the champagne; Mr Ricardo languished – until one unforgettable morning.

He was sitting disconsolately at his breakfast-table when the door was burst open and a square, stout man, with the blue, shaven face of a French comedian, flung himself into the room. Ricardo sprang up in delight. 'My dear Hanaud!'

He seized his visitor by the arm, feeling it to make sure that here, in flesh and blood, stood the man who had introduced him to the acutest sensations of his life. He turned towards his butler, who was still beating expostulations in the doorway at Hanaud's unceremonious erruption.

'Another place, Burton, at once,' he cried, and as soon as he and Hanaud were alone: 'What good wind blows you to London?'

'Business, my friend. The disappearance of bullion somewhere on the line between Paris and London. But it is finished. Yes, I take a holiday.'

A light had suddenly flashed in Mr Ricardo's eyes, and was no less suddenly extinguished. Hanaud paid no attention whatever to his friend's disappointment. He pounced upon a piece of silver which adorned the tablecloth and took it over to the window.

'Everything is as it should be, my friend,' he exclaimed, with a grin. 'Grosvenor Square, the *Times* open at the money column, and a false antique upon the table. Thus I have dreamed of you. All Mr Ricardo is in that sentence.'

Ricardo laughed nervously. Recollection made him wary of Hanaud's sarcasms. He was shy even to protest the genuiness of his silver. But, indeed, he had not the time. For the door opened again and once more the butler appeared. On this occasion, however, he was alone.

'Mr Calladine would like to speak to you, sir,' he said.

'Calladine!' cried Ricardo in an extreme surprise. 'That is the most extraordinary thing.' He looked at the clock upon his mantelpiece. Its hands stood at barely half-past eight. 'At this hour, too?'

'Mr Calladine is still wearing evening dress,' the butler remarked.

Ricardo started in his chair. He began to dream of possibilities; and here was Hanaud miraculously at his side.

'Where is Mr Calladine?' he asked.

'I have shown him into the library.'

'Good,' said Mr Ricardo. 'I will come to him.'

But he was in no hurry. He sat and let his thoughts play with this incident of Calladine's early visit.

'It is very odd,' he said. 'I have not seen Calladine for months – no, nor has anyone. Yet, a little while ago, no one was more often seen.'

He fell apparently into a muse, but he was merely seeking to provoke Hanaud's curiosity. In this attempt, however, he failed. Hanaud continued placidly to eat his breakfast, so that Mr Ricardo was compelled to volunteer the story which he was burning to tell.

'Drink your coffee. Hanaud, and you shall hear about Calladine.'

Hanaud grunted with resignation, and Mr Ricardo flowed on:

'Calladine was one of England's young men. Everybody said so. He was going to do very wonderful things as soon as he had made up his mind exactly what sort of wonderful things he was going to do. Meanwhile, you met him in Scotland, at Newmarket, at Ascot, at Cowes, in the box of some great lady at the Opera, in any fine house where the candles that night happened to be lit. He went everywhere, and then a day came and he went nowhere. There was no scandal, no

49

trouble, not a whisper against his good name. He simply vanished. For a little while a few people asked: "What has become of Calladine?" But there never was any answer, and London has no time for unanswered questions. Other promising young men dined in his place. Calladine had joined the huge legion of the Come-to-nothings. No one even seemed to pass him in the street. Now unexpectedly, at half-past eight in the morning, and in evening dress, he calls upon me. "Why?" I ask myself.'

Mr Ricardo sank once more into a reverie. Hanaud watched him with a broadening smile of pure enjoyment.

'And in time, I suppose,' he remarked casually, 'you will perhaps ask him?'

Mr Ricardo sprang out of his pose to his feet.

'Before I discuss serious things with an acquaintance,' he said with a scathing dignity, 'I make it a rule to revive my impressions of his personality. The cigarettes are in the crystal box.'

'They would be,' said Hanaud, unabashed, as Ricardo stalked from the room. But in five minutes Mr Ricardo came running back, all his composure gone.

'It is the greatest good fortune that you, my friend, should have chosen this morning to visit me,' he cried, and Hanaud nodded with a little grimace of resignation.

'There goes my holiday. You shall command me now and always. I will make the acquaintance of your young friend.'

He rose and followed Ricardo into his study, where a young man was nervously pacing the floor.

'Mr Calladine,' said Ricardo. 'This is Mr Hanaud.'

The young man turned eagerly. He was tall, with a noticeable elegance and distinction, and the face which he showed to Hanaud was, in spite of its agitation, remarkably handsome.

'I am very glad,' he said. 'You are not an official of this country. You can advise – without yourself taking action.'

Hanaud frowned. He bent his eyes uncompromisingly upon Calladine.

'What does that mean?' he asked, with a note of sternness in his voice.

'I means that I must tell someone,' Calladine burst out in quivering tones, 'that I don't know what to do. I am in a difficulty too big for me.'

Hanaud looked at the young man keenly. It seemed to Ricardo that

50

he took in every excited gesture, every twitching feature, in one comprehensive glance. Then he said in a friendlier voice:

'Sit down and tell me' – and he himself drew up a chair to the table.

'I was at the Semiramis last night,' said Calladine, naming one of the great hotels upon the Embankment. 'There was a fancy-dress ball.'

All this happened, by the way, in those far-off days before the war when London, flinging aside its reticence, its shy self-consciousness, had become a city of carnivals and masquerades, rivaling its neighbors on the Continent in the spirit of its gaiety, and exceeding them by its stupendous luxury. 'I went by the merest chance. My rooms are in the Adelphi Terrace.'

'There!' cried Mr Ricardo in surprise, and Hanaud lifted a hand to check his interruptions.

Calladine drew up a chair opposite to Hanaud and, seating himself, told, with many nervous starts and in troubled tones, a story which, to Mr Ricardo's thinking, was as fabulous as any out of the 'Arabian Nights'.

'I had a ticket,' he began, 'but no domino. I was consequently stopped by an attendant in the lounge at the top of the staircase leading down to the ballroom.

' "You can hire a domino in the cloakroom, Mr Calladine," he said to me. I had already begun to regret the impulse which had brought me, and I welcomed the excuse with which the absence of a costume provided me. I was, indeed, turning back to the door, when a girl who had at that moment run down from the stairs of the hotel into the lounge, cried gaily: "That's not necessary"; and at the same moment she flung to me a long scarlet cloak which she had been wearing over her own dress. She was young, fair, rather tall, slim, and very pretty; her hair was drawn back from her face with a ribbon, and rippled down her shoulders in heavy curls; and she was dressed in a satin coat and knee-breeches of pale green and gold, with a white waistcoat and silk stockings and scarlet heels to her satin shoes. She was as straight-limbed as a boy, and exquisite like a figure in Dresden china. I caught the cloak and turned to thank her. But she did not wait. With a laugh she ran down the stairs, a supple and shining figure, and was lost in the throng at the doorway of the ballroom. I was stirred by the prospect of an adventure. I ran down after her. She was standing just inside the room alone, and she was gazing at the scene with parted lips and dancing eyes. She laughed again as she saw the cloak about my shoulders, and I said to her:

51

' "May I dance with you?"

' "Oh, do!" she cried, with a little jump, and clasping her hands. She was of a high and joyous spirit and not difficult in the matter of an introduction. "This gentleman will do very well to present us," she said, leading me in front of a bust of the God Pan which stood in a niche of the wall. "I am, as you see, straight out of an opera. My name is Celymène or anything with an eighteenth-century sound to it. You are – what you will. For this evening we are friends.'

' "And for tomorrow?" I asked.

' "I will tell you about that later on,' she replied, and she began to dance with a light step and a passion in her dancing which earned me many an envious glance from the other men. I was in luck, for Celymène knew no one, and though, of course, I saw the faces of a great many people whom I remembered, I kept them all at a distance. We had been dancing for about half an hour when the first queerish thing happened. She stopped suddenly in the midst of a sentence with a little gasp. I spoke to her, but she did not hear. She was gazing past me, her eyes wide open, and such a rapt look upon her face as I had never seen. She was lost in a miraculous vision. I followed the direction of her eyes and, to my astonishment, I saw nothing more than a stout, short, middle-aged woman, egregiously overdressed as Marie Antoinette.

' "So you do know someone here?" I said, and I had to repeat the words sharply before my friend withdrew her eyes. But even then she was not aware of me. It was as if a voice had spoken to her while she was asleep and had disturbed, but not wakened her. Then she came to – there's really no other word I can think of – she came to with a deep sigh.

' "No," she answered. "She is a Mrs Blumen from Chicago, a widow with ambitions and a great deal of money. But I don't know her."

' "Yet you know all about her," I remarked.

' "She crossed in the same boat with me," Celymène replied.

"Did I tell you that I landed at Liverpool this morning? She is staying at the Semiramis too. Oh, let us dance!"

'She twitched my sleeve impatiently, and danced with a kind of violence and wildness as if she wished to banish some sinister thought. And she did undoubtedly banish it. We supped together and grew confidential, as under such conditions people will. She told me her real name. It was Joan Carew.

' "I have come over to get an engagement if I can at Covent Garden. I am supposed to sing all right.'

' "You have some letters of introduction, I suppose?" I asked.

' "Oh, yes. One from my teacher in Milan. One from an American manager."

'In my turn I told her my name and where I lived, and I gave her my card. I thought, you see, that since I used to know a good many operatic people, I might be able to help her.

' "Thank you,' she said, and at that moment Mrs Blumen, followed by a party, came into the supper-room and took a table close to us. There was at once an end of all confidences – indeed, of all conversation. Joan Carew lost all the lightness of her spirit; she talked at random, and her eyes were drawn again and again to the grotesque slander on Marie Antoinette. Finally I became annoyed.

' "Shall we go?" I suggested impatiently, and to my surprise she whispered passionately:

' "Yes. Please! Let us go."

'Her voice was actually shaking, her small hands clenched. We went back to the ballroom, but Joan Carew did not recover her gaiety, and half way through a dance, when we were near the door, she stopped abruptly.

' "I shall go," she said. "I am tired."

'I protested, but she made a little grimace.

' "You'll hate me in half an hour. Let's be wise and stop now while we are friends," she said, and while I removed the domino from my shoulders she stooped very quickly. It seemed to me that she picked up something which had lain hidden beneath the sole of her slipper. She certainly moved her foot, and I certainly saw something small and bright flash in the palm of her glove as she raised herself again.

' "Yes, we'll go," she said, and we went up the stairs into the lobby.

' "But I shall meet you again?" I asked.

' "Yes. I have your address. I'll write and fix a time when you will be sure to find me in. Good night, and a thousand thanks."

'She was speaking lightly as she held out her hand, but her grip tightened a little and – clung.

' "I am half inclined to ask you to stay, however dull I am; and dance with me till daylight – the safe daylight," she said.

' "Let us go back then!" I urged. She gave me an impression suddenly of someone quite forlorn. But Joan Carew recovered her courage, "No, no," she answered quickly. She snatched her hand away and ran lightly up the staircase, turning at the corner to wave her hand and smile. It was then half-past one in the morning.'

'And when did you go home?' Hanaud asked of Calladine.

Calladine was not sure. His partner had left behind her the strangest medley of sensations in his breast. He was puzzled, haunted, and charmed. He had to think about her; sleep was impossible. He wandered for a while about the ballroom. Then he walked to his chambers along the echoing streets and sat at his window; and some time afterwards the hoot of a motorhorn broke the silence and a car stopped and whirred in the street below. A moment later his bell rang.

He ran down the stairs in a queer excitement, unlocked the street door, and opened it. Joan Carew, still in her masquerade dress with her scarlet cloak about her shoulders, slipped through the opening.

'Shut the door,' she whispered.

Calladine latched the door. Above, in the well of the stairs, the light spread out from the open door of his flat. Down here all was dark. He could just see the glimmer of her white face, the glitter of her dress, but she drew her breath like one who has run far. They mounted the stairs cautiously. He did not say a word until they were both safely in his parlor; and even then it was in a low voice.

'What has happened?'

'You remember a woman I stared at? You didn't know why I stared, but any girl would have understood. She was wearing the loveliest pearls I ever saw in my life.'

Joan was standing by the edge of the table. She was tracing with her finger a pattern on the cloth as she spoke. Calladine started with a horrible presentiment.

'Yes,' she said. 'I worship pearls. I always have done so. For one thing, they improve on me. I haven't got any, of course. I have no money. But friends of mine who do own pearls have sometimes given theirs to me to wear when they were going sick, and they have always got back their luster. I think that has had a little to do with my love of them. Oh, I have always longed for them.'

She was speaking in a dull, monotonous voice. But Calladine recalled the ecstasy which had shone in her face when her eyes first had fallen on the pearls, the passion with which she had danced to throw the obsession off.

'And I never noticed them at all,' he said.

'Yet they were wonderful. The color! The luster! All evening they tempted me. I was furious that a fat, coarse creature like that should have such exquisite things. Oh, I was mad.'

She covered her face suddenly with her hands and swayed. Calladine sprang towards her. But she held out her hand.

'No, I am all right.' And though he asked her to sit down she would not. 'You remember when I stopped dancing suddenly?'

'Yes. You had something hidden under your foot?'

The girl nodded.

'Her key!' And under his breath Calladine uttered a startled cry.

'A little Yale key,' the girl continued. 'I saw Mrs Blumen looking on the floor for something, and then I saw it shining on the very spot. Mrs Blumen's suite was on the same floor as mine, and her maid slept above. All the maids do. I knew that. Oh, it seemed to me as if I had sold my soul and was being paid.'

Now Calladine understood what she had meant by her strange phrase – 'the safe daylight'.

'I went up to my little suite,' Joan Carew continued. 'I sat there with the key burning through my glove until I had given her time enough to fall asleep. Then I crept out. The corridor was dimly lit. Far away below the music was throbbing. Up here it was as silent as the grave. I opened the door – her door. I found myself in a lobby. The suite, though bigger, was arranged like mine. I slipped in and closed the door behind me. I listened in the darkness. I couldn't hear a sound. I crept forward to the door in front of me. I stood with my fingers on the handle and my heart beating fast enough to choke me. I had still time to turn back. But I couldn't. There were those pearls in front of my eyes, lustrous and wonderful. I opened the door gently an inch or so – and then – it all happened in a second.'

Joan Carew faltered. The night was too near to her, its memory too poignant with terror. She shut her eyes tightly and cowered down in a chair.

'Go on,' Calladine said.

'I found myself inside the room with the door shut behind me. I had shut it myself in a spasm of terror. And I dared not turn round to open it. I was helpless.'

'What do you mean? She was awake?'

Joan Carew shook her head.

'There were others in the room before me, and on the same errand – men!'

Calladine drew back, his eyes searching the girl's face.

'Yes?' he said slowly.

'I didn't see them at first. I didn't hear them. The room was quite dark except for one jet of fierce white light which beat upon the door of a safe. And as I shut the door the jet moved swiftly and the light reached me and stopped. I was blinded. I stood in the full glare of it, drawn up against the panels of the door, shivering, sick with fear. Then I heard a quiet laugh, and someone moved softly towards me. Oh, it was terrible! I recovered the use of my limbs; in a panic I turned to the door, but I was too late. While I fumbled with the handle I was seized; a hand covered my mouth. I was lifted to the centre of the room. The jet went out, the electric lights were turned on. There were two men dressed as apaches in velvet trousers and red scarves, like a hundred others in the ballroom below, and both were masked. I struggled furiously; but, of course, I was like a child in their grasp. "Tie her legs," the man whispered who was holding me; "she's making too much noise." I kicked and fought, but the other man stooped and tied my ankles, and I fainted.

'When I came to, the lights were still burning, the door of the safe was open, the room empty; I had been flung onto a couch at the foot of the bed. I was lying there quite free.'

'Was the safe empty?' asked Calladine.

'I didn't look,' she answered. 'Oh!' – and she covered her face spasmodically with her hands. 'I looked at the bed. Someone was lying there – under a sheet and quite still. There was a clock ticking in the room; it was the only sound. I was terrified. If I didn't get out of the room at once I felt that I should scream and bring everyone to find me alone with – what was under the sheet in the bed. I ran to the door and looked out through a slit into the corridor. It was still quite empty, and below the music still throbbed in the ballroom. I crept down the stairs, meeting no one until I reached the hall. I looked into the ballroom as if I was searching for someone. I stayed long enough to show myself. Then I got a cab and came to you.'

Calladine sat watching the girl in silence.

Then he asked, and his voice was hard:

'Is that all you have to tell me?'

'Yes.'

Calladine rose to his feet and stood beside her.

'Then how do you come to be wearing this?' he asked, and he lifted a chain of platinum and diamonds which she was wearing about her shoulders. 'You weren't wearing it when you danced with me.'

Joan Carew stared at the chain.

'No. It's not mine. I have never seen it before.' Then a light came into her eyes. 'The two men – they must have thrown it over my head when I was on the couch – before they went.' She looked at it more closely. 'That's it. The chain's not very valuable. They could spare it, and – it would accuse me – of what they did.'

'Yes, that's very good reasoning,' said Calladine coldly.

Joan Carew looked quickly up into his face.

'Oh, you don't believe me,' she cried. 'You think – oh, it's impossible.'

'But you went to steal, you know,' he said gently.

'Yes, I did, but not this.' And she held up the necklace. 'Should I have stolen this, should I have come to you wearing it, if I had stolen the pearls, if I had' – and she stopped – 'if my story were not true?'

Calladine weighed her argument.

'No, I think you wouldn't,' he said frankly.

Calladine looked at the clock. It was nearly five o'clock in the morning, and though the music could still be heard from the ballroom in the Semiramis, the night had begun to wane upon the river.

'You must go back,' he said, 'I'll walk with you.'

They crept silently down the stairs and into the street. They met no one until they reached the Strand. There many, like Joan Carew in masquerade, were standing about, or walking hither and thither in search of carriages and cabs.

'You can slip in unnoticed,' said Calladine as he looked into the thronged courtyard. 'I'll telephone to you in the morning.'

'You will?' she cried eagerly.

'Yes, for certain,' he replied. 'Wait in until you hear from me. I'll think it over. I'll do what I can.'

'Thank you,' she said fervently.

He watched her scarlet cloak flitting here and there in the crowd until it vanished through the doorway. Then, for the second time, he walked back to his chambers, while the morning crept up the river from the sea.

This was the story which Calladine told in Mr Ricardo's library. Mr Ricardo heard it out with varying emotions. He began with a thrill of expectation, like a man on a dark threshold of great excitements. The setting of the story appealed to him too, by a sort of brilliant bizarrerie which he found in it. But, as it went on, he grew puzzled and a trifle disheartened. There were flaws and chinks; he began to bubble with unspoken criticisms, then swift and clever thrusts which he dared not deliver. He looked upon the young man with disfavor, as upon one who had half opened a door upon a theater of great promise and shown him a spectacle not up to the mark. Hanaud, on the other hand, listened imperturbably, without an expression upon his face, until the end. Then he pointed a finger at Calladine and asked him what to Ricardo's mind was a most irrelevant question.

'You got back to your rooms, then, before five, Mr Calladine, and it is now nine o'clock less a few minutes.'

'Yes.'

'Yet you have not changed your clothes. Explain to me that. What did you do between five and half-past eight?'

Calladine looked down at his rumpled shirt front.

'Upon my word, I never thought of it,' he cried. 'I was worried out of my mind. I couldn't decide what to do. Finally, I determined to talk to Mr Ricardo, and after I had come to that conclusion I just waited impatiently until I could come round with decency.'

Hanaud rose from his chair. His manner was grave, but conveyed no single hint of an opinion. He turned to Ricardo.

'Let us go round to your young friend's room in the Adelphi,' he said; and the three men drove there at once.

Calladine lodged in a corner house and upon the first floor. His rooms, large and square and lofty, with Adam mantelpieces and a delicate tracery upon their ceilings, breathed the grace of the eighteenth century. Broad high windows, embrasured in thick walls, overlooked the river and took in all the sunshine and the air which the river had to give. And they were furnished fittingly. When the three men entered the parlor, Mr Ricardo was astounded. He had expected the untidy litter of a man run to seed, the neglect and the dust of the recluse. But the room was as clean as the deck of a yacht; an Aubusson carpet made the floor luxurious underfoot; a few coloured prints of real value decorated the walls; and the mahogany furniture was polished so that a lady could have used it as a mirror. There was even a china bowl full of fresh red roses.

'So you live here, Mr Calladine?' said Hanaud.

'Yes.'

'With your servants, of course?'

'They come in during the day,' said Calladine, and Hanaud looked at him curiously.

'Do you mean that you sleep here alone?'

'Yes.'

'But your valet?'

'I don't keep a valet,' said Calladine; and again the curious look came into Hanaud's eyes.

'Yet,' he suggested gently, 'there are rooms enough in your set of chambers to house a family.'

Calladine colored.

'I prefer at night not to be disturbed,' he said, stumbling a little over the words.

Hanaud nodded his head with sympathy.

'Yes, yes. And it is a difficult thing to get – as difficult as my holiday,' he said ruefully, with a smile for Mr Ricardo. 'However' – he turned towards Calladine – 'no doubt, now that you are at home, you would like a bath and a change of clothes. And when you are dressed, perhaps you will telephone to the Semiramis and ask Miss Carew to come round here.'

Hanaud shut the door upon Calladine, then crossed the room to Mr Ricardo who, seated at the open window, was plunged deep in reflections.

'You have an idea, my friend,' cried Hanaud.

Mr Ricardo started out of an absorption which was altogether assumed.

'I was thinking,' he said, with a faraway smile, 'that you might disappear in the forests of Africa, and at once everyone would be very busy about your disappearance. You might leave your village in Leicestershire and live in the fogs of Glasgow, and within a week the whole village would know your postal address. But London – what a city! How different! How indifferent! Turn out of St James's into the Adelphi Terrace and not a soul will say to you: "Dr Livingstone, I presume?"'

'But why should they,' asked Hanaud, 'if your name isn't Dr Livingstone?'

Mr Ricardo smiled indulgently.

'Scoffer!' he said. 'You understand me very well,' and he sought to turn the tables on his companion. 'And you – does this room suggest nothing to you? Have you no ideas?' But he knew very well that Hanaud had. Ever since Hanaud had crossed the threshold he had been like a man stimulated by a drug.

'Yes,' he said, 'I have.'

He was standing now by Ricardo's side with his hands in his pockets, looking out at the trees on the Embankment and the barges swinging down the river. In a moment or two he began to walk about the room with that curiously light step which Ricardo was never able to reconcile with his cumbersome figure. With the heaviness of a bear he still padded. He went from corner to corner, opened a cupboard here, a drawer of the bureau there.

'You are looking for something,' Ricardo announced with sagacity.

'I am,' replied Hanaud; and it seemed that in a second or two he found it. Yet – yet – he found it with his hands in his pockets, if he had found it. Mr Ricardo saw him stop in that attitude in front of the mantelshelf, and heard him utter a long, low whistle. Upon the mantelshelf some photographs were arranged, a box of cigars stood at one end, a book or two lay between some delicate ornaments of china, and a small engraving in a thin gilt frame was propped at the back against the wall. Ricardo surveyed the shelf from his seat in the window, but he could not imagine which it was of these objects that so drew and held Hanaud's eyes.

Hanaud, however, stepped forward. He looked into a vase and turned it upside down. Then he removed the lid of a porcelain cup, and from the very look on his great shoulders Ricardo knew that he had discovered what he sought. He was holding something in his hands, turning it over, examining it. When he was satisfied he moved swiftly to the door and opened it cautiously. Both men could hear the splashing of water in a bath. Hanaud closed the door again with a nod of contentment and crossed once more to the window.

'Yes, it is all very strange and curious,' he said, 'and I do not regret that you dragged me into the affair. You were quite right, my friend, this morning. It is the personality of your young Mr Calladine which is the interesting thing. For instance, here we are in London in the early summer. The trees out, freshly green, lilac and flowers in the gardens, and I don't know what tingle of hope and expectation in the sunlight and the air.

'Can you understand a young man with money, with fastidious tastes, good-looking, hiding himself in a corner at such a time – except for some overpowering reason? No. Nor can I. There is another thing – I put a question or two to Calladine.

'He has no servants here at night. He is quite alone and – here is what I find interesting – he has no valet. That seems a small thing to you?' Hanaud asked at a movement from Ricardo. 'Well, it is no doubt a trifle, but it's a significant trifle in the case of a young rich man. It is generally a sign that there is something strange, perhaps even something sinister, in his life. Mr Calladine, some months ago, turned out of St James's into the Adelphi. Can you tell me why?'

'No,' replied Mr Ricardo.

Hanaud stretched out a hand. In his open palm lay a small round hairy bulb about the size of a big button and of a color between green and brown.

'Look!' he said. 'What is that?'

Mr Ricardo took the bulb wonderingly.

'It looks to me like the fruit of some kind of cactus.'

Hanaud nodded.

'It is. You will see some pots of it in the hothouses of any really good botanical gardens. They are labeled *Anhalonium Luinii*. But among the Indians of Yucatan the plant has a simpler name.'

'What name?' asked Ricardo.

'Mescal.'

Mr Ricardo repeated the name. It conveyed nothing to him.

'Mescal is a drug.'

Ricardo started.

'Yes, you are beginning to understand now,' Hanaud continued, 'why your young friend Calladine turned out of St James's into the Adelphi Terrace.'

Ricardo turned the little bulb over in his fingers.

'You make a decoction of it, I suppose?' he said.

'Or you can use it as the Indians do in Yucatan,' replied Hanaud. 'Mescal enters into their religious ceremonies. They sit at night in a circle about a fire built in the forest and chew it, while one of their number beats perpetually upon a drum.'

Hanaud looked round the room and took notes of its luxurious carpet, its delicate appointments. Outside the window there was a clamor of voices. Boats went swiftly down the river on the ebb. Beyond the mass of the Semiramis rose the great gray-white dome of St Paul's.

'It's a long way from the forests of Yucatan to the Adelphi Terrace of London,' said Hanaud. 'Yet here, I think, in these rooms, when the servants are all gone and the house is very quiet, there is a little corner of wild Mexico.'

A look of pity came into Mr Ricardo's face. He had seen more than one young man of great promise slacken his hold and let go, just for this reason.

'It's like bhang and kieff and the rest of the devilish things, I suppose,' he said, indignanantly tossing the button upon the table.

Hanaud picked it up.

'No,' he replied. 'It's not quite like any other drug. It has a quality of its own which just now is of particular importance to you and me. Yes, my friend, we must watch that we do not make the big fools of ourselves in this affair.'

'There,' Mr Ricardo agreed with an ineffable air of wisdom, 'I am entirely with you.'

'Now, why?' Hanaud asked. Mr Ricardo was at a loss for a reason, but Hanaud did not wait. 'I will tell you. Mescal intoxicates, yes – but it does more – it gives to the man who eats of it color-dreams.'

'Color-dreams?'

'Yes, strange heated charms, in which violent things happen vividly among bright colors. Color is the gift of this little prosaic brown button.' He spun the bulb in the air like a coin, and catching it again, took it over to the mantelpiece and dropped it into the porcelain cup.

'Are you sure of this?' Ricardo cried excitedly, and Hanaud raised his hand in warning. He went to the door, opened it for an inch or so, and closed it again.

'I am quite sure,' he returned. 'I have for a friend a very learned chemist in the Collège de France. He is one of those enthusiasts who must experiment upon themselves. He tried this drug.'

'Yes,' Ricardo said in a quieter voice. 'And what did he see then?'

'He had a vision of a wonderful garden bathed in sunlight, an old garden of gorgeous flowers and emerald lawns, ponds with golden lilies and thick yew hedges – a garden where peacocks stepped indolently and groups of gay people fantastically dressed quarreled and fought with swords. That is what he saw. And he saw it so vividly that, when the vapors of the drug passed from his brain and he waked, he seemed to be coming out of the real world into a world of shifting illusions.'

'Out of the real world,' Mr Ricardo quoted, 'I begin to see.'

'Yes, you begin to see, my friend, that we must be very careful not to make the big fools of ourselves. My friend of the Collège de France saw a garden. But had he been sitting alone in the window-seat where you are, listening through a summer night to the music of the masquerade at the Semiramis, might he not have seen the ballroom, the dancers, the scarlet cloak, and the rest of this story?'

'You mean,' cried Ricardo, now fairly startled, 'that Calladine came to us with the fumes of mescal still working in his brain, that the false world was the real one still for him.'

'I do not know,' said Hanaud. 'At present I only put questions. I ask them of you. I wish to hear how they sound. Let us reason this problem out. Calladine, let us say, takes a great deal more of the drug than my professor. It will have on him a more powerful effect while it lasts, and it will last longer. Fancy-dress balls are familiar things to Calladine. The music floating from the Semiramis will revive old memories. He sits here, the pageant takes shape before him, he sees himself taking his part in it. Oh, he is happier here sitting quietly in his window-seat than if he was actually at the Semiramis. For he *is* there more intensely, more vividly, more really, than if he had actually descended this staircase. He lives his story through, the story of a heated brain, the scene of it changes in the way dreams have, it becomes tragic and sinister, it oppresses him with horror, and in the morning, so obsessed with it that he does not think to change his clothes, he is knocking at your door.'

Mr Ricardo raised his eyebrows.

'Ah! You see a flaw in my argument,' said Hanaud. But Mr Ricardo was wary. Too often in other days he had been leaped upon and trounced for a careless remark.

'Let me hear the end of your argument,' he said. 'There was then to your thinking no temptation of jewels, no theft, no murder – in a word, no Celymène?'

'No!' cried Hanaud. 'Come with me, my friend. I am not so sure that there was no Celymène.'

With a smile upon his face, Hanaud led the way across the room. He had the dramatic instinct, and rejoiced in it. He was going to produce a surprise for his companion and, savouring the moment in advance, he managed his effects. He walked towards the mantelpiece and stopped a few paces away.

'Look!'

Mr Ricardo looked and saw a broad Adam mantelpiece. He turned a bewildered face to his friend.

'You see nothing?' Hanaud asked.

'Nothing!'

'Look again! I am not sure – but is not Celymène posing before you?'

Mr Ricardo looked again. There was nothing to fix his eyes. He saw a book or two, a cup, a vase or two, and nothing else except a very pretty and apparently valuable piece of – and suddenly Mr Ricardo understood. Straight in front of him, in the very centre of the mantelpiece, a figure in painted china was leaning against a china stile. It was the figure of a perfectly impossible courtier, feminine and exquisite, and appareled even to the scarlet heals, exactly as Calladine had described Joan Carew.

Hanaud chuckled with satisfaction when he saw the expression upon Mr Ricardo's face.

'Ah, you understand,' he said. 'Do you dream, my friend? At times – yes, like the rest of us. Then recollect your dreams? Things, people which you have seen perhaps that day, perhaps months ago, pop in and out of them without making themselves prayed for. Thus, our friend here sits in the window, intoxicated by his drug, the music plays in the Semiramis, the curtain goes up in the heated theater of his brain. He sees himself step upon the stage, and who else meets him but the china figure from his mantelpiece?'

Mr Ricardo for a moment was all enthusiasm. Then his doubt returned to him.

'What you say, my dear Hanaud, is very ingenious. The figure upon the mantelpiece is also extremely convincing. And I should be absolutely convinced but for one thing.'

'Yes?' said Hanaud.

'I am – I may say it, I think – a man of the world. And I ask myself whether a young man who has given up his social ties, who has become a hermit, and still more who has become the slave of a drug, would retain that scrupulous carefulness of his body which is indicated by dressing for dinner when alone?'

Hanaud struck the table with the palm of his hand.

'Yes. That is the weak point in my theory. You have hit it. I knew it was there – that weak point, and I wondered whether you would seize it. Yes the consumers of drugs are careless, untidy – even unclean as a rule. But not always. We must be careful. We must wait.'

'For what?' asked Ricardo.

'For the answer to a telephone message,' replied Hanaud.

Both men waited impatiently until Calladine came into the room. He wore now a suit of blue serge, he had a clearer eye, his skin a healthier look; he was altogether a more reputable person. But he was plainly very ill at ease. He offered his visitors cigarettes, he proposed refreshments, he avoided entirely and awkwardly the object of their visit. Hanaud smiled. His theory was working out. Sobered by his bath, Calladine had realized the foolishness of which he had been guilty.

64

'You telephoned to the Semiramis, of course?' said Hanaud cheerfully.

Calladine grew red.

'Yes,' he stammered.

'Yet I did not hear that volume of "Hallos" which precedes telephonic connection in your country of leisure,' Hanaud continued.

'I telephoned from my bedroom. You would not hear anything in this room.'

'Yes, yes; the walls of these old houses are solid.' Hanaud was playing with his victim. 'And when may we expect Miss Carew?'

'I can't say.' replied Calladine. 'It's very strange. She is not in the hotel.'

Mr Ricardo and Hanaud exchanged a look. They were both satisfied now. There was no word of truth in Calladine's story.

'Then there is no reason for us to wait,' said Hanaud. 'I shall have my holiday after all.' And while he was yet speaking the voice of a newsboy calling out the first edition of an evening paper became distantly audible. Hanaud broke off his farewell. For a moment he listened, with his head bent. Then the voice was heard again, confused, indistinct; Hanaud picked up his hat and cane and, without another word to Calladine, raced down the stairs. Mr Ricardo followed him, but when he reached the pavement, Hanaud was half down the little street. At the corner, however, he stopped, and Ricardo joined him, coughing and out of breath.

'What's the matter?' he gasped.

'Listen,' said Hanaud.

At the bottom of Duke Street, by Charing Cross Station, the newsboy was shouting his wares. Both men listened, and now the words came to them.

'*Mysterious crime at the Semiramis Hotel!*'

Ricardo stared at his companion.

'You were wrong, then!' he cried. 'Calladine's story was true.'

For once Hanaud was quite disconcerted.

But before he could move a taxicab turned into the Adelphi from the Strand, and wheeling in front of their faces, stopped at Calladine's door. From the cab a girl descended.

'Let us go back,' said Hanaud.

Mr Ricardo could no longer complain. It was half-past eight when Calladine had first disturbed the formalities of his house in Grosvenor

Square. It was barely ten now, and during that short time he had been flung from surprise to surprise.

'I am alive once more,' Mr Ricardo thought as he turned back with Hanaud, and in his excitement he cried his thought aloud.

'Are you?' said Hanaud. 'And what is life without a newspaper? If you will buy one from that remarkably raucous boy at the bottom of the street, I will keep an eye upon Calladine's house till you come back.'

Mr Ricardo sped down to Charing Cross and brought back a copy of the *Star*. He handed it to Hanaud, who stared at it doubtfully, folded as it was.

'Shall we see what it says?' Ricardo asked impatiently.

'By no means,' Hanaud answered, waking from his reverie and tucking the paper briskly away into the tail pocket of his coat. 'We will hear what Miss Joan Carew has to say, with our minds undisturbed by any discoveries.'

They went quickly to Calladine's rooms. As they entered Mr Ricardo saw a girl turn to them suddenly a white face of terror, and flinch as though already she felt the hand of a constable upon her shoulder. Calladine, on the other hand, uttered a cry of relief.

'These are my friends,' he exclaimed to the girl, 'the friends of whom I spoke to you;' and to Hanaud he said: 'This is Miss Carew.'

Hanaud bowed.

'You shall tell me your story, mademoiselle,' he said very gently, and a little color returned to the girl's cheeks.

'But you have heard it,' she answered.

'Not from you,' said Hanaud.

So for a second time in that room she told the history of that night. She was just a very young and very pretty girl, telling in a low and remorseful voice of the tragic dilemma to which she had brought herself. Of Celymène all that remained was something exquisite and fragile in her beauty, in the slimness of her figure, in her daintiness of hand and foot – something almost of the hothouse. But the story she told was the same which Calladine had already related.

'Thank you,' said Hanaud when she had done. 'Now I must ask you two questions.'

'I will answer them.'

'You will forgive me, Miss Carew. But have you ever stolen before?'

Joan Carew turned upon Hanaud with spirit. Then a change swept over her face.

'You have a right to ask,' she answered. 'Never.' She looked into his

66

eyes as she answered. Hanaud did not move. He sat with a hand upon each knee and led to his second question.

'Early this morning, when you left this room, you told Mr Calladine that you would wait at the Semiramis until he telephoned to you?'

'Yes.'

'Yet when he telephoned, you had gone out?'

'Yes.'

'Why?'

'I will tell you,' said Joan Carew. 'I could not bear to keep the little diamond chain in my room.

'I was terrified,' continued Joan Carew. 'I kept thinking: "They must have found out by now. They will search everywhere." I didn't reason. I lay in bed expecting to hear every moment a loud knocking on the door. Besides – the chain itself being there in my bedroom – her chain – the dead woman's chain – no, I couldn't endure it. I felt as if I had stolen it.'

Joan Carew explained how she had risen, dressed, wrapped the chain in a pad of cotton-wool and enclosed it in an envelope. The envelope had not the stamp of the hotel upon it. It was a rather large envelope, one of a packet which she had bought in a crowded shop in Oxford Street on her way from Euston to the Semiramis. She had bought the envelopes of that particular size in order that when she sent her letter of introduction to the Director of the Opera at Covent Garden she might enclose with it a photograph.

'And to whom did you send it?' asked Mr Ricardo.

'To Mrs Blumen at the Semiramis. I printed the address carefully. Then I went out and posted it.'

'Where?' Hanaud inquired.

'In the big letter-box of the Post Office at the corner of Trafalgar Square.'

Hanaud looked at the girl sharply.

'You had your wits about you, I see,' he said.

'What if the envelope gets lost?' said Ricardo.

Hanaud laughed grimly.

'If one envelope is delivered at its address in London today, it will be that one,' he said. 'The news of the crime is published, you see,' and he swung round to Joan. 'Did you know that, Miss Carew?'

'No,' she answered in an awestricken voice.

'Well, then, it is. Let us see what the special investigator has to say

67

about it.' And Hanaud, with a deliberation which Mr Ricardo found quite excruciating, spread out the newspaper on the table.

There was only one new fact in the couple of columns devoted to the mystery. Mrs Blumen had died from chloroform poisoning. She was of a stout habit, and the thieves were not skilled in the administration of the anesthetic.

'It's murder none the less,' said Hanaud, and he gazed straight at Joan, asking her by the direct summons of his eyes what she was going to do.

'I must tell my story to the police,' she replied, painfully and slowly.

Hanaud neither agreed nor differed. His face was blank, and when he spoke there was no cordiality in his voice. 'Well,' he asked, 'and what is it that you have to say to the police, miss? That you went into the room to steal, and that you were attacked by two strangers, dressed as Apaches, and masked? That is all?'

'Yes.'

'And how many men at the Semiramis ball were dressed as Apaches and wore masks? Come! Make a guess. A hundred at the least?'

'I should think so.'

'Then what will your confession do beyond – I quote your expressive English idiom – putting you in the coach?'

'Yet I think I must tell the police,' she repeated, looking up and dropping her eyes again. Mr Ricardo noticed that her eyelashes were very long. For the first time Hanaud's face relaxed.

'And I think you are quite right,' he cried heartily, to Mr Ricardo's surprise. 'Tell them the truth before they suspect it, and they will help you out of the affair if they can. Not a doubt of it. Come, I will go with you myself to Scotland Yard.'

'Thank you,' said Joan, and the pair drove away in a cab together.

Hanaud returned to Grosvenor Square alone and lunched with Ricardo.

'It was all right,' he said. 'The police were very kind. Miss Joan Carew told her story to them as she had told it to us. Fortunately, the envelope with the platinum chain had already been delivered, and was in their hands. They were much mystified about it, but Miss Joan's story gave them a reasonable explanation. I think they are inclined to believe her; and if she is speaking the truth, they will keep her out of the witness-box if they can.'

'She is to stay here in London, then?' asked Ricardo.

'Oh, yes; she is not to go. She will present her letters at the Opera House and secure an engagement, if she can. The criminals might be lulled thereby into a belief that the girl had kept the whole strange incident to herself, and that there was nowhere even a knowledge of the disguise which they had used.' Hanaud spoke as carelessly as if the matter was not very important; and Ricardo, with an unusual flash of shrewdness, said:

'It is clear, my friend, that you do not think those two men will ever be caught at all.'

Hanaud shrugged his shoulders.

'But,' exclaimed Ricardo, 'those pearls were of great value, and pearls of great value are known; so, when they come upon the market –'

'That is true,' Hanaud interrupted imperturbably. 'But how are they known?'

'By their weight,' said Mr Ricardo.

'Exactly,' replied Hanaud. 'But did you not know that pearls can be peeled like an onion? No? It is true. Remove a skin, two skins, the weight is altered, the pearl is a trifle smaller. It has lost a little of its value, yes – but you can no longer identify it as the so-and-so pearl which belonged to this or that sultan, was stolen by the vizier, bought my Messrs Lustre and Steinopolis, of Hatton Garden, and subsequently sold to the wealthy Mrs Blumen. No, your pearl has vanished altogether. There is a new pearl which can be traded.' He looked at Ricardo. 'Who shall say that those pearls are not already in one of the queer little back streets of Amsterdam, undergoing their transformation?'

The days flew by. It was London's play-time. The green and gold of early summer deepened and darkened. Hanaud made acquaintance with the wooded reaches of the Thames; Joan Carew sang *Louise* at Covent Garden with notable success; and the affair of the Semiramis Hotel, in the minds of the few who remembered it, was already added to the long list of unfathomed mysteries.

But towards the end of May there occurred a startling development. Joan Carew wrote to Mr Ricardo that she would call upon him in the afternoon, and she begged him to secure the presence of Hanaud. She came as the clock struck; she was pale and agitated; and in the room where Calladine had first told the story of her visit she told another story which, to Mr Ricardo's thinking, was yet more strange.

'It has been going on for some time,' she began. 'I thought of coming to you at once. Then I wondered whether, if I waited – oh, you'll never believe me!'

'Let us hear,' said Hanaud.

'I began to dream of that room, the two men disguised and masked, the still figure in the bed. Night after night! I was terrified to go to sleep. I felt the hand upon my mouth. I used to catch myself falling asleep, and walk about the room with all the lights up to keep myself awake. Oh, my nights were horrible until' – she paused and looked at her companions doubtfully – 'until one night the mask slipped.'

'What–?' cried Hanaud.

'It is true, the mask slipped on the face of one of the men – the man who held me. Only a little way; it just left his forehead visible.'

'Well?' asked Hanaud.

'I waked up,' the girl continued, 'in the darkness, and for a moment the whole scene remained vividly with me – for just long enough for me to fix clearly in my mind the figure of the Apache with the white forehead showing above the mask.'

'When was that?' asked Ricardo.

'A fortnight ago.'

'Why didn't you come with your story then?'

'I waited,' said Joan. 'What I had to tell wasn't yet helpful. I thought that another night the mask might slip lower still. Besides, I – it is difficult to describe just what I felt. I felt it important just to keep that photograph in my mind, not to think about it, not to talk about it, not even to look at it too often lest I should begin to imagine the rest of the face and find something familiar in the man's carriage and shape when there was nothing really familiar to me at all. Do you understand that?'

'Yes,' replied Hanaud.

'I thought there was a chance now – the strangest chance – that the truth might be reached. I did not wish to spoil it,' and she turned eagerly to Ricardo, as if, having persuaded Hanaud, she would now turn her batteries on his companion. 'My whole point of view was changed. I was no longer afraid of falling asleep lest I should dream. I wished to dream, but –'

'But you could not,' suggested Hanaud.

'No, that is the truth,' replied Joan Carew. 'Whereas before I was anxious to keep awake and yet must sleep from sheer fatigue, now that I tried consciously to put myself to sleep I remained awake all through

70

the night, and only towards morning, when the light was coming through the blinds, dropped off into a heavy, dreamless slumber.

'Then came my rehearsals,' Joan Carew continued, 'and that wonderful opera drove everything else out of my head. I had such a chance, if only I could make use of it! When I went to bed now, I went with that haunting music in my ears – the call of Paris – oh, you must remember it. But can you realize what it must mean to a girl who is going to sing it for the first time in Covent Garden?'

Mr Ricardo saw his opportunity. He, the connoisseur, could answer that question.

'It is true, my friend,' he informed Hanaud with quiet authority. 'The great march of events leave the artist cold. He lives aloof. While the tumbrils thunder in the streets he adds a delicate tint to the picture he is engaged upon or recalls his triumph in his last great art.'

'Thank you,' said Hanaud gravely. 'And now Miss Carew may perhaps resume her story.'

'It was the very night of my début,' she continued. 'I had supper with some friends. A great artist, Carmen Valeri, honored me with her presence. I went home excited, and that night I dreamed again.'

'Yes?'

'This time the chin, the lips, the eyes were visible. There was only a black strip across the middle of the face. And I thought – nay, I was sure – that if that strip vanished I should know the man.'

'And it did vanish?'

'Three nights afterwards.'

'And you did know the man?'

The girl's face became troubled.

'I knew the face, that was all,' she answered. 'I was disappointed. I had never spoken to the man. I am sure of that still. But somewhere I have seen him.'

'You don't even remember when?' asked Hanaud.

'No.' Joan Carew reflected for a moment with her eyes upon the carpet, and then flung up her head with a gesture of despair. 'No. I try all the time to remember. But it is no good.'

'How did you pass the evening of that night when you first dreamed complete the face of your assailant?'

Joan Carew reflected. Then her face cleared.

'I know,' she exclaimed. 'I was at the opera.'

'And what was being given?'

'*The Jewels of the Madonna.*'

71

Hanaud nodded his head. To Ricardo it seemed that he had expected precisely that answer.

'Now,' he continued, 'you are sure that you have seen this man?'

'Yes.'

'Very well,' said Hanaud. 'There is a game you play at children's parties – is there not? – animal, vegetable, or mineral, and always you get the answer. Let us play that game for a few minutes, you and I.'

Joan Carew drew up her chair to the table and sat with her chin propped upon her hands and her eyes fixed on Hanaud's face. As he put each question she pondered on it and answered.

'You crossed on the *Lucania* from New York?'

'Yes.'

'Picture to yourself the dining-room, the tables. You have the picture quite clear?'

'Yes.'

'Was it at breakfast that you saw him?'

'No.'

At luncheon?'

'No.'

'At dinner?'

'No.'

'In the library, when you were writing letters, did you not one day lift your head and see him?'

'No.'

'On the promenade deck? Did he pass you when you sat in your deck-chair?

'No.'

Step by step Hanaud took her back to New York to her hotel, to journeys in the train. Then he carried her to Milan where she had studied. It was extraordinary to Ricardo to realize how much Hanaud knew of the curriculum of a student aspiring to grand opera. From Milan he brought her again to New York, and at the last, with a start of joy, she cried: 'Yes, it was there.'

Hanaud took his handkerchief from his pocket and wiped his forehead.

'Ouf!' he grunted. 'To concentrate the mind on a day like this, it makes one hot, I can tell you. Now, Miss Carew, let us hear.'

It was at a concert at the house of a Mrs Starlingshield on Fifth Avenue and in the afternoon. Joan Carew sang. She was a stranger to New York and very nervous. She saw nothing but a mist of faces while she sang, but when she had finished, the mist cleared, and as she left the improvised stage she saw the man. He was standing against the wall in a line of men. There was no particular reason why her eyes should single him out, except that he was paying no attention to her singing, and, indeed, she forgot him altogether afterwards.

'I just happened to see him clearly and distinctly,' she said. 'He was tall, clean-shaven, rather dark, not particularly young – thirty-five or so, I should say – a man with a heavy face and beginning to grow stout. He moved away while I was bowing to the audience, and I noticed him afterwards talking to people.'

'Do you remember to whom?'

'No.'

'Did he notice you, do you think?'

'I am sure he didn't,' the girl replied emphatically.

She gave, so far as she could remember, the names of such guests and singers as she knew at that party. 'And that is all,' she said.

'Thank you,' said Hanaud. 'It is perhaps a good deal.'

'You will let me hear from you?' she cried, as she rose to her feet.

'Miss Carew, I am at your service,' he returned. She gave him her hand timidly and he took it cordially. For Mr Ricardo she had merely a bow, a bow which recognized that he distrusted her and that she had no right to be offended. Then she went, and Hanaud smiled across the table at Ricardo.

'Yes,' he said, 'all that you are thinking is true enough. A man who slips out of society to indulge a passion for a drug in greater peace, a girl who, on her own confession, tried to steal, and, to crown all, this fantastic story. It is natural to disbelieve every word of it. But we disbelieved before, when we left Calladine's lodging in the Adelphi, and we were wrong.'

'You have an idea?' exclaimed Ricardo.

'Perhaps!' said Hanaud. And he looked down the theatre column of the *Times*. 'Let us distract ourselves by going to the theatre.'

'You are the most irritating man!' Mr Ricardo broke out impulsively. 'If I had to paint your portrait, I should paint you with your finger against the side of your nose, saying mysteriously: 'I know,' when you know nothing at all.'

Hanaud made a schoolboy's grimace. 'We will go and sit in your box at the opera tonight,' he said.

They reached Covent Garden before the curtain rose. Mr Ricardo's box was on the lowest tier and next to the omnibus box.

'We are near the stage,' said Hanaud, as he took his seat in the corner and so arranged the curtain that he could see and yet was hidden from view. 'I like that.'

The theatre was full; stalls and boxes shimmered with jewels and satin, and all that was famous that season for beauty and distinction had made its tryst there that night.

'Yes, this is wonderful,' said Hanaud. 'What opera do they play?' He glanced at his program and cried, with a little start of surprise: 'We are in luck. It is *The Jewels of the Madonna*.'

'Do you believe in omens?' Mr Ricardo asked coldly. He had not yet recovered from his rebuff of the afternoon.

'No, but I believe that Carmen Valeri is at her best in this part,' said Hanaud.

Mr Ricardo belonged to that body of critics which must needs spoil your enjoyment by comparisons and recollections of other great artists. He was at a disadvantage certainly tonight, for the opera was new. But he did his best. He imagined others in the part, and when the great scene came at the end of the second act, and Carmen Valeri, on obtaining from her lover the jewels stolen from the sacred image, gave such a display of passion as fairly enthralled that audience, Mr Ricardo sighed quietly and patiently.

'How Calvé would have brought out the psychological value of that scene!' he murmured; and he was quite vexed with Hanaud, who sat with his opera glasses held to his eyes, and every sense apparently concentrated on the stage. The curtains rose and rose again when the act was concluded, and still Hanaud sat motionless as the Sphinx, staring through his glasses.

'That is all,' said Ricardo when the curtains fell for the fifth time.

'They will come out,' said Hanaud. 'Wait!' And from between the curtains Carmen Valeri was led out into the full glare of the footlights. Then at last Hanaud put down his glasses and turned to Ricardo with a look of exultation and genuine delight.

'What a night!' said Hanaud. 'What a wonderful night!' And he applauded until he split his gloves. At the end of the opera he cried: 'We will go and take supper at the Semiramis. Yes, my friend, we will finish our evening like gallant gentlemen. Come!'

In spite of his boast, however, Hanaud hardly touched his supper, and he played with, rather than drank, his brandy and soda. He sat with his back to the wall watching the groups which poured in. Suddenly his face lighted up.

'Here is Carmen Valeri!' he cried. 'Once more we are in luck. It is not that she is beautiful?'

Mr Ricardo turned languidly about in his chair and put up his eyeglass.

'So-so,' he said.

'Ah!' returned Hanaud. 'Then her companion will interest you still more. For he is the man who murdered Mrs Blumen.'

Mr Ricardo jumped so that his eyeglass fell and tinkled on its cord against the buttons of his waistcoat.

'What!' he exclaimed. 'It's impossible!' He looked again. 'Certainly that man fits Joan Carew's description. But –' He turned back to Hanaud utterly astounded. And as he looked at the Frenchman all his earlier recollections of him, of his swift deductions, of the subtle imagination which his heavy body so well concealed, crowded in upon Ricardo and convinced him.

'How long have you known?' he asked in a whisper of awe.

'Since ten o'clock tonight.'

'But you will have to find the necklace before you can prove it.'

'The necklace!' said Hanaud carelessly. 'That is already found.'

Mr Ricardo had been longing for a thrill. He had it now.

'It's found?' he said in a startled whisper.

'Yes.'

Ricardo turned again, with as much indifference as he could assume, towards the couple who were settling down at their table, the man with a surly indifference, Carmen Valeri with the radiance of a woman who has just achieved a triumph and is now free to enjoy the fruits of it. Confusedly, recollections returned to Ricardo of questions put that afternoon by Hanaud to Joan Carew – subtle questions into which the name of Carmen Valeri was continually entering. She was a woman of thirty, certainly beautiful, with a clear, place face and eyes like the night.

'Then she is implicated too!' he said. What a change for her, he thought, from the stage of Covent Garden to the felon's cell.

'She!' exclaimed Hanaud; and in his passion for the contrasts of drama Ricardo was almost disappointed. 'She has nothing whatever to do with it. She knows nothing. André Favart there – yes. But Carmen Valeri! She's as stupid as an owl, and loves him beyond words. Do you

75

want to know how stupid she is? You shall know. I asked Mr Clements, the director of the opera house, to take supper with us, and here he is.'

Hanaud stood up and shook hands with the director. He was of the world of business rather than of art, and long experience of the ways of tenors and primadonnas had given him a good-humored cynicism.

'They are spoilt children, all tantrums and vanity,' he said, 'and they would ruin you to keep a rival out of the theatre.'

He told them anecdote upon anecdote.

'And Carmen Valeri,' Hanaud asked in a pause. 'Is she troublesome this season?'

'Has been,' replied Clements dryly. 'At present she is playing at being good. But she gave me a turn some weeks ago.' He turned to Ricardo. 'Superstition's her trouble, and André Favart knows it. She left him behind in America this spring.'

'America!' suddenly cried Ricardo; so suddenly that Clements looked at him in surprise.

'She was singing in New York, of course, during the winter,' he returned. 'Well, she left him behind, and I was shaking hands with myself when he began to deal the cards over there. She came to me in a panic. She had just had a cable. She couldn't sing on Friday night. There was a black knave next to the nine of diamonds. She wouldn't sing for worlds. And it was the first night of *The Jewels of the Madonna!* Imagine the fix I was in!'

'What did you do?' asked Ricardo.

'The only thing there was to do,' replied Clements with a shrug of the shoulders. 'I cabled Favart some money and he dealt the cards again. She came to me beaming. Oh, she had been so distressed to put me in the cart! But what could she do? Now there was a red queen next to the ace of hearts, so she could sing without a scruple so long, of course, as she didn't pass a funeral on the way down to the opera house. Luckily she didn't. But my money brought Favart over here, and now I'm living on a volcano. For he's the greatest scoundrel unhung. He never has a farthing, however much she gives him; he's a blackmailer, a swindler, has no manners and no graces, looks like a butcher and treats her as if she were dirt, never goes near the opera except when she is singing this part, and she worships the ground he walks on. Well, I suppose it's time to go.'

The lights had been turned off, the great room was emptying. Mr Ricardo and his friends rose to go, but at the door Hanaud detained Mr

Clements, and they talked together alone for some little while, greatly to Mr Ricardo's annoyance.

Hanaud's good humor, however, when he rejoined his friend, was enough for two.

'I apologize, my friend, with my hand on my heart. But it was for your sake that I stayed behind. You have a meretricious taste for melodrama which I deeply deplore, but which I mean to gratify. I ought to leave for Paris tomorrow, but I shall not. I shall stay until Thursday.'

Mr Ricardo bubbled with questions, but he knew his man. He would get no answer to any of them tonight. So he worked out the problem for himself as he lay awake in his bed, and he came down to breakfast next morning fatigued but triumphant. Hanaud was already chipping off the top of his egg at the table.

'So I see you have found it all out, my friend,' he said.

'Not all,' replied Ricardo modestly, 'and you will not mind, I am sure, if I follow the usual custom and wish you a good morning.'

'Not at all,' said Hanaud. 'I am all for good manners myself. But I am longing to hear the line of your reasoning.'

Mr Ricardo did not need much pressing.

'Joan Carew saw André Favart at Mrs Starlingshield's party, and saw him with Carmen Valeri. For Carmen Valeri was there. I remember that you asked Joan for the names of the artists who sang, and Carmen Valeri was among them.'

Hanaud nodded his head.

'No doubt Joan Carew noticed Carmen Valeri particularly, and so took unconsciously into her mind an impression of the man who was with her, André Favart – of his build, of his walk, of his type.'

Again Hanaud agreed.

'She forgets the man altogether, and the picture remains latent in her mind – an undeveloped film.

'Then came the tragic night at the Semiramis. She does not consciously recognize her assailant, but she dreams the scene again and again, and by a process of unconscious cerebration the figure of the man becomes familiar. Finally she makes her début, is entertained at supper afterwards, and meets once more Carmen Valeri.'

'Yes, for the first time since Mrs Starlingshield's party,' interjected Hanaud.

'She dreams again, she remembers asleep more than she remembers when awake. The presence of Carmen Valeri at her supper-party has its

77

effect. By a process of association she recalls Favart, and the mask slips on the face of her assailant. Some days later she goes to the opera. She hears Carmen Valeri sing in *The Jewels of the Madonna*. No doubt the passion of her acting, which I am more prepared to acknowledge this morning than I was last night, affects Joan Carew powerfully, emotionally. She goes to bed with her head full of Carmen Valeri, and she dreams not of Carmen Valeri in her thoughts. The mask vanishes altogether. She sees her assailant now, has his portrait limned in her mind.'

'Yes,' said Hanaud. 'It is curious, the brain working while the body sleeps, the dream revealing what thought cannot recall.'

Mr Ricardo was delighted. He was taken seriously.

'But of course,' he said, 'I could not have worked the problem out but for you. You knew of André Favart and the kind of man he was.'

Hanaud laughed.

'Yes. That is always my one little advantage. I know all the cosmopolitan blackguards of Europe.' His laughter ceased suddenly, and he brought his clenched fist heavily down upon the table. 'Here is one of them who will be very well out of the world, my friend,' he said very quietly.

For a few moments there was silence. Then Ricardo asked: 'But have you evidence enough?'

'Yes.'

'Your two chief witnesses, Calladine and Joan Carew – you said it yourself – there are facts to discredit them. Will they be believed?'

'But they won't appear in the case at all,' Hanaud said. 'Wait, wait!' and once more he smiled. 'By the way, what is the number of Calladine's house?'

Ricardo gave it, and Hanaud thereupon wrote a letter. 'It is all for your sake, my friend,' he chuckled.

'Nonsense,' said Ricardo. 'You have the spirit of the theater in your bones.'

'Well, I shall not deny it,' said Hanaud, and he sent out the letter to the nearest pillar-box.

Mr Ricardo waited in a fever of impatience until Thursday came. At breakfast Hanaud would talk of nothing but the news of the day. At luncheon he was no better. The affair of the Semiramis Hotel seemed a thousand miles from his thoughts. But at five o'clock he said as he drank his tea:

'You know, of course, that we go to the opera tonight?'

'Yes. Do we?'

'Yes. Your young friend Calladine, by the way, will join us in your box.'

'That is very kind of him, I am sure,' said Mr Ricardo.

The two men arrived before the rising of the curtain, and in the crowded lobby a stranger spoke a few words to Hanaud, but what he said Ricardo could not hear. They took their seats in the box, and Hanaud looked at his program.

'Ah! It is *Il Ballo de Maschera* tonight. We always seem to hit upon something appropriate, don't we?'

Then he raised his eyebrows.

'Oh-o! Do you see that our pretty young friend, Joan Carew, is singing in the role of the page? It is a showy part. There is a particular melody with a long-sustained trill in it. By the way, I should let Calladine find it all out for himself.'

Mr Ricardo nodded sagely.

'Yes. That is wise. I had thought of it myself.' But he had done nothing of the kind. He was only aware that the elaborate stage-management in which Hanaud delighted was working out to the desired climax, whatever that climax might be. Calladine entered the box a few minutes later and shook hands with them awkwardly.

'It was kind of you to invite me,' he said, and very ill at ease, he took a seat between them.

'There's the overture,' said Hanaud. The curtains divided and were festooned on either side of the stage. The singers came on in their turn; the page appeared to a burst of delicate applause (Joan Carew had made a small name for herself that season), and with a stifled cry Calladine shot back in the box as if he had been struck. Even then Mr Ricardo did not understand. He only realized that Joan Carew was looking extraordinarily trim and smart in her boy's dress. He had to look from his program to the stage and back again several times before the reason of Calladine's exclamation dawned on him. When it did, he was horrified. Hanaud, in his craving for dramatic effects, must have lost his head altogether. Joan Carew was wearing, from the ribbon in her hair to the scarlet heels of her buckled satin shoes, the same dress as she had worn on the tragic night at the Semiramis Hotel. He leaned forward in his agitation to Hanaud.

'You must be mad. Suppose Favart is in the theatre and sees her. He'll be over on the Continent by one in the morning.'

'No, he won't,' replied Hanaud. 'For one thing, he never comes to

Covent Garden unless one opera, with Carmen Valeri in the chief part, is being played, as you heard the other night at supper. For a second thing, he isn't in the house. I know where he is. He is gambling in Dean Street, Soho. For a third thing, my friend, he couldn't leave by the nine o'clock train for the Continent if he wanted to. Arrangements have been made. For a fourth thing, he wouldn't wish to. He has really remarkable reasons for desiring to stay in London. But he will come to the theater later. Clements will send him an urgent message, with the result that he will go straight to Clements's office. Meanwhile, we can enjoy ourselves, eh?'

Never was the difference between the amateur dilettante and the genuine professional more clearly exhibited than by the behaviour of the two men during the rest of the performance. Mr Ricardo might have been sitting on a coal fire from his jumps and twistings; Hanaud stolidly enjoyed the music, and when Joan Carew sang her famous solo his hands clamoured for an encore. Certainly, whether excitement was keeping her up or no, Joan Carew had never sung better in her life. Her voice was clear and fresh as a bird's – a bird with a soul inspiring its song. Even Calladine drew his chair forward again and sat with his eyes fixed upon the stage and quite carried out of himself. He drew a deep breath at the end.'

'She is wonderful,' he said.

'We will go round to the back of the stage,' said Hanaud.

They passed through the iron door and across the stage to a long corridor with a row of doors on one side. There were two or three men standing about in evening dress, as if waiting for friends in the dressing-rooms. At the third door Hanaud stopped and knocked. The door was opened by Joan Carew, still dressed in her green and gold. Her face was troubled, her eyes afraid.

'Courage, little one,' said Hanaud, and he slipped past her into the room. 'It is as well that my ugly, familiar face should not be seen too soon.'

The door closed and one of the strangers loitered along the corridor and spoke to a call-boy. The call-boy ran off. For five minutes more Mr Ricardo waited with a beating heart. He had the joy of a man in the center of things. All those people driving homewards in their motor-cars along the Strand – how he pitied them! Then, at the end of the corridor, he saw Clements and André Favart. They approached, discussing the possibility of Carmen Valeri's appearance in London opera during the next season.

'We have to look ahead, my dear friend,' said Clements, 'and though I should be extremely sorry –'

At that moment they were exactly opposite Joan Carew's door. It opened, she came out; with a nervous movement she shut the door behind her. At the sound André Favart turned, and he saw up against the panels of the door, with a look of terror in her face, the same gay figure which had interrupted him in Mrs Blumen's bedroom.

Favart stared and uttered an oath. His face turned white; he staggered back, as if he had seen a ghost. Then he made a wild dash along the corridor, and was seized and held by two of the men in evening dress. Favart recovered his wits. He ceased to struggle.

'What does this outrage mean?' he asked, and one of the men drew a warrant and notebook from his pocket.

'You are arrested for the murder of Mrs Blumen in the Semiramis Hotel,' he said, 'and I have to warn you that anything you may say will be taken down and may be used in evidence against you.'

'Preposterous!' exclaimed Favart. 'There's a mistake. We will go along to the police and put it right. Where's your evidence against me?'

Hanaud stepped out of the doorway of the dressing-room.

'In the property-room of the theater,' he said.

At the sight of him Favart uttered a violent cry of rage. 'You are here, too, are you?' and he sprang at Hanaud's throat. Hanaud stepped lightly aside. Favart was borne down to the ground, and when he stood up again the handcuffs were on him. Favart was led away, and Hanaud turned to Ricardo and Clements.

'Let us go to the property-room,' he said. They passed along the corridor, and Ricardo noticed that Calladine was no longer with them. He turned and saw him standing outside Joan Carew's dressing-room. In the property-room there was already a detective in plainclothes.

'What is it you really want, sir?' the property-master asked of the director.

'Only the jewels of the Madonna,' Hanaud answered.

The property-master unlocked a cupboard and took from it the sparkling cuirass. Hanaud pointed to it, and there, lost among the huge glittering stones of paste and false pearls, Mrs Blumen's necklace was entwined.

'Then that is why Favart came always to Covent Garden when *The Jewels of the Madonna* was being performed!' exclaimed Ricardo.

Hanaud nodded.

'He came to watch over his treasure.'

Ricardo was piecing together the sections of the puzzle.

'No doubt he knew of the necklace in America. No doubt he followed it to England.'

'But to hide them here!' cried Mr Clements. 'He must have been mad.'

'Why?' asked Hanaud. 'Can you imagine a safer hiding place? Who is going to burgle the property-room of Covent Garden? Who is going to look for a priceless string of pearls among the stage jewels of an opera house?'

'You did,' said Mr Ricardo.

'I?' replied Hanaud, shrugging his shoulders. 'Joan Carew's dreams led me to André Favart. The first time we came here and saw the pearls of the Madonna, I was on the lookout, naturally I noticed those pearls through my opera glasses.'

'At the end of the second act?' cried Ricardo suddenly. 'I remember now.'

'Yes,' replied Hanaud. 'But for that second act the pearls would have stayed comfortably here all through the season. Carmen Valeri – a fool as I told you – would have tossed them about in her dressing-room without a notion of their value, and at the end of July, when the murder at the Semiramis Hotel had been forgotten, Favart would have taken them to Amsterdam and made his bargain.'

They left the theater together and walked down to the grill-room of the Semiramis. But as Hanaud looked through the glass door he turned and drew back.

'We will not go in, I think, eh?'

'Why?' asked Ricardo.

Hanaud pointed to a table. Calladine and Joan Carew were seated at it taking their supper.

'Perhaps,' said Hanaud with a smile, 'perhaps, my friend – what? Who shall say that the rooms in the Adelphi will not be given up?'

They turned away from the hotel. But Hanaud was right, and before the season was over Mr Ricardo had to put his hand in his pocket for a wedding present.

DEATH BY ENTHUSIASM

by *HECTOR BERLIOZ*

(translated by Jacques Barzun)

Place: The Paris Opera
Time: 1808
Performance: *La Vestale*, by Gaspare Spontini

I shall call my story *Death by Enthusiasm*. In 1808 a young musician had for three years been serving, with obvious distaste, as first violin in a theater in southern France. The boredom he carried with him every evening to the orchestra, where he had to play *The Barrel-Maker, The King and the Farmer, The Betrothed*[1] or some such score of the kind, meant that he was looked upon by his colleagues as a stuck-up prig. 'He thinks,' said they, 'that he alone in all the world has learning and taste; he scorns the opinion of the public, whose applause makes him shrug his shoulders, and also the opinion of other musicians, whom he affects to consider mere babes.' His contemptuous laugh and impatient gestures every time that he had to play some platitude had repeatedly brought down on him severe reprimands from the conductor, and he would long ago have sent in his resignation if poverty, which always seems to choose for its victims temperaments of this sort, had not hopelesly nailed him to his post in front of a greasy and grimy old music-stand.

Adolphe D. obviously was one of those artists predestined to suffering; men who carry within themselves an ideal of the beautiful,

[1] Operas by, respectively: Isouard, who used the name Nicolo (1799); Monsigny (1762); and Lemoyne (1780).

83

pursue it unremittingly, and feel intense hatred for everything alien to it. Gluck, whose scores he knew by heart (for he had copied them in order to be better acquainted with them), was his idol.[2] He read him, played him, and sang him night and day. A misguided amateur to whom he was giving lessons in solfeggio was once incautious enough to tell him that Gluck's operas were merely shouting and plainsong. D. flushed with indignation, yanked open the drawer of his desk, took from it the ten vouchers for the fees due him by this particular pupil, and flung them in his face, roaring: 'Get out of here! I don't want you or your money, and if you ever step inside this door again, I will throw you out the window!'

It is easy to see that with so much tolerance for his pupils' tasts, D. hardly made a fortune giving lessons. Spontini was just then in all his glory. The dazzling success of *La Vestale*, proclaimed by the thousand tongues of the press, made all the provincial dilettanti anxious to hear a score so touted by the Parisians. Accordingly the unfortunate theater managers strained themselves to circumvent, if not to overcome, the difficulties of staging and performing the new work.

Not wanting to lag behind, D.'s manager, like the rest, shortly announced that *La Vestale* was in preparation. D., as is true of all fiery spirits whom a sound education has not taught to reason out their judgments, was an exclusivist in taste. He was at the outset full of prejudice against Spontini's opera, of which he knew not a single note: 'They say it is in a new style, more melodic than Gluck's. So much the worse for the new style! Gluck's melody is good enough for me; the better is the enemy of the good. I bet it is detestable.'

It was in this frame of mind that he took his seat in the orchestra on the day of the first stage rehearsal. As concertmaster he had not had to attend the earlier partial rehearsals. The other players, though they admired Lemoyne,[3] found merit just the same in Spontini's score, and on seeing D. said among themselves: 'Let's see what the great Adolphe's verdict about it is!' The latter went through the rehearsal without a word or a sign of either praise or blame. His ideas were undergoing a curious transformation. He realized fully from the very first scene that this was a noble and powerful work and that Spontini was a genius whose greatness he could not ignore. But not conceiving

[2] This sentence applies in every detail to the young Berlioz.
[3] See above, note 1, for his popular opera *The Betrothed*. The composer's real name was Jean Baptiste Moyne (1751-96).

clearly what the composer's methods were, for they were new to him and the poor provincial performance made them still more difficult to grasp, D. borrowed the score, began by reading the words attentively, studied the spirit and character of the persons in the drama, then gave his whole mind to the analysis of the music, thus following a path that could not but lead him to a real and complete understanding of the opera as a perfect whole.

From that time forward it was noticed that he was becoming more and more sulky and taciturn; he evaded any questions put to him, or laughed sardonically when he heard his colleagues vent their admiration of Spontini. 'Fools,' he seemed to be saying, 'how can you understand his work when you admire *The Betrothed*?'

Noticing the ironic expression on D.'s features, the players were sure that he judged Spontini as severely as he had Lemoyne, and that he bracketed both composers in one and the same reprobation. But one day when the performance was a trifle less execrable than usual, it was seen that the finale of the second act had moved him to tears, and they no longer knew what to think. 'He is mad,' said some; 'he is play-acting,' said others. And all together: 'He is a second-rate musician.'

Motionless in his chair, sunk in deep abstraction, and furtively wiping his eyes, D. said not a word to all this impertinence, but was hoarding a treasure of contempt and fury in his heart. The inadequacy of the orchestra, the even greater incompetence of the chorus, the lack of intelligence and feeling in the actors, the vocal ornaments added by the prima donna, the mutilation of every phrase and rhythm, the arrogant cuts – in short, the relentless beating and torturing he saw inflicted on the score which had become the object of his deepest worship and of which he knew every detail, caused him torments with which I am well acquainted, but which I am unable to described.

One night after the second act, the whole house having risen to its feet with cries of enthusiasm, D. felt fury overwhelm him; and as an enraptured hatitué asked him the commonplace question: 'Well, M. Adolphe, what do you say?'

'I say,' shouted D., pale with anger, 'that you and all the others who are carrying on like lunatics in this theater are fools, asses, louts fit only to hear Lemoyne's music. If you weren't, you would break in the skulls of the manager, the singers, and the musicians, instead of condoning by your applause the most shameful profanation that genius can endure.'

This time the insult was too great, and despite the fiery artist's performing talent, which made him invaluable; despite, also, the dreadful poverty which dismissal would entail, the manager could not avoid placating the public for the insult by relieving him of his duties.

Unlike the generality of men of his caliber, D. was not given to expensive tastes. He had some savings from his salary and from the lessons he had been giving, and was secure for three months at least. This cushioned the blow of his dismissal and even made him look upon it as likely to be useful for his artistic career by restoring his freedom. But the chief appeal of his unexpected liberation lay in the possibility of a journey which D. had been vaguely planning ever since the genius of Spontini had been revealed to him. To hear *La Vestale* in Paris had become the fixed goal of his ambition.

The hour of reaching this goal was at hand, when an incident that our enthusiast could not foresee threw a hurdle in his path. Though born with a fiery character and unconquerable passions, Adolphe was nevertheless shy in the presence of women, and apart from some less than poetic affairs with the princesses of his theater, love, all-devouring love, frantic love, the only love that could seem genuine to him, had not yet dug a crater in his heart. On returning home one evening, he found the following note:

Sir,

If you should find it possible to devote a few hours to the musical education of a pupil who is already sufficiently advanced not to put too great a strain on your patience, I should be glad if you would place them at my disposal. Your talents are better known and better appreciated than perhaps you yourself suspect, so you must not be surprised if immediately on her arrival in your city, a Parisian woman hastens to charge you with the direction of her studies in the great art which you honour and so thoroughly understand.

Hortense N

This blend of flattery and self-conceit, the tone at once detached and engaging, aroused D.'s curiosity so that instead of answering the letter, he decided to call on the Parisian lady herself, thank her for her expression of confidence, assure her that she in now way 'surprised' him, and inform her that, being on the point of leaving for Paris, he could not undertake the unquestionably agreeable task that she proposed.

This little speech, rehearsed beforehand with the appropriate irony, expired on his lips the moment he entered the stranger's sitting-room. The unusual and challenging grace of Hortense, her deftly fashionable mode of dress, the something indefinable that is so fascinating in the gait and carriage and all the movements of a beauty from the Chaussée d'Antin, made their impact on Adolphe. Instead of irony, he began to utter regrets at his approaching departure. The tone of his voice, the dismay visible in his features gave proof of his sincerity, but Mme N., like a clever woman, interrupted him:

'You are leaving? Then I was well advised to lose no time. You are going to Paris, but let us begin our lessons during the few days that remain. As soon as the cure season in your city is over, I am going back to the capital, where I shall be charmed to see you again and to take further advantage of your instruction.'

Adolphe, secretly happy to see his arguments for refusing so easily disposed of, promised to begin the next day and left the house in a dream. That day he did not give one thought to *La Vestale*.

Mme N. was one of those adorable women (as they say at the Café de Paris, Tortoni's, and three or four of the other resorts of dandyism) who find their slightest whims 'delightfully novel,' and feel that it would be tantamount to murder not to gratify them. They profess a species of respect for their own fancies, however absurd they are.

'My dear Fr–' said one of these charming creatures to a celebrated dilettante a few years ago, 'you know Rossini: tell him from me that his *William Tell* is a deadly thing, it is enough to bore one to extinction; he must *not* take it into his head to write a second opera in that vein – otherwise Mme M. and I, who have always given him our support, will abandon him to his fate.' And on another occasion: 'Who on earth is this new Polish pianist whom all you artists are so crazy about and whose music is so *queer*? I want to see him; bring him around tomorrow.'

'Madam, I will do my best, but I must confess that I am but slightly acquainted with him and that he is not mine to command.'

'No, no, of course not; you can't issue an order, but he will obey mine, so I count on his coming.'

This strange invitation not having been accepted, the queen told her subjects that M Chopin was 'an odd little body,' who played the piano 'passably well,' but that his music was simply 'one long riddle, a ridiculous acrostic.'

A fancy of this sort was the main motive behind the rather impertinent note that Adolphe had received from Mme N. as he was preparing to leave for Paris. The beautiful Hortense was a most accomplished pianist and gifted with a magnificent voice which she used as well as it is possible to do when the soul is not in it. She therefore stood in no need of the lessons of the Provençal musician. But his shouting defiance to the public in the theatre had had reverberations throughout the town, and our Parisian lady, hearing them talked about on all sides, obtained particulars about the hero of an adventure which to her seemed full of piquancy.

She too 'wanted to have him brought around,' fully intending, after she had ascertained at leisure what sort of 'odd little body' he was, and after she had played with him and upon him as on a new instrument, to send him about his business for good.

But matters turned out quite differently, much to the annoyance of the pretty *Simia parisiensis*.[4] Adolphe was very handsome. Great black eyes full of flame, regular features, which a habitual pallor invested with a slight tinge of melancholy, but into which the warmest color came from time to time as enthusiasm or indignation quickened his pulse; a distinguished bearing, and manners rather different from what might have been expected from someone who had seen almost nothing of the world except through the curtainhole of his theater; a character at once passionate and reserved, with the most singular mixture of stiffness and grace, brusqueness and forbearance, suddenly gaiety and deep abstraction – such traits made him, by their the unexpectedness, the man most capable of catching a coquette in her own net.

And that is just what happened, though without premeditation on Adolphe's part, for he was smitten before she was. From the very first lesson Mme N.'s musical mastery shone forth in all its splendour. Far from needing advice, she was in a position to give some to her new teacher. The sonatas of Steibelt – the Hummel of the day – the arias of Paisiello and Cimarosa, which she smothered with ornaments that were often original and daring, gave her an opportunity to make each facet of her talent sparkle in turn. Adolphe, to whom such a woman and so fine an execution were something new, soon fell completely under her spell. After Steibelt's grand fantasia, 'The Storm,' in which Hortense seemed to him to display all the powers of musical art,[5] he said to her,

[4] Parisian she-ape.
[5] This reference to Steibelt's 'Storm' confirms the likely supposition that Hortense is a portrait of Camile Moke (Mme Pleyel) at a time when Berlioz himself bore a great resemblance to Adolphe D. But differences of more than detail should not be overlooked.

88

trembling with emotion: 'Madam, you were making fun of me when you asked me to give you lessons. But how could I take it amiss when your hoax has opened to my unsuspecting eyes the portals of the world of poetry, the artistic paradise of my dreams, turning these dreams into a dazzling reality? Please prolong the hoax, madam, I implore you – tomorrow, next day, every day. I shall be indebted to you for the most intoxicating joys it has ever been given me to know.'

The tone in which these words were spoken, the tears which welled up in his eyes, the nervous spasm which shook his frame, astonished Hortense even more than her talent had surprised the young artist. If, on the one hand, the arpeggios, the turns, the showy harmonies, the finely chopped melodies, that rippled from the hands of the graceful fairy caused, so to speak, a paralysis of amazement in Adolphe; on the other, his impressionable nature, his lively sensibility, the picturesque expressions he used, their very exaggeration, affected Hortense no less powerfully.

His impassioned praise, springing from true artistic bliss, was such a far cry from the lukewarm and studied approval of the dandies of Paris that self-esteem alone would have sufficed to make her look indulgently upon a man less outwardly favored than our hero. Art and enthusiasm were face to face for the first time; the result of the encounter was easy to foresee: Adolphe, drunk with love, seeking neither to conceal nor to moderate the impetus of his altogether southern passion, disconcerted Hortense completely, and thus unwittingly upset the plan of defense prepared by the coquette. It was all so new to her! Though not actually feeling anything like the devouring ardor of her lover, she nevertheless understood that here was a whole world of sensations (not to say emotions) that the insipidity of her earlier affairs had never disclosed.

They were thus both happy, each in his own way, for a few weeks. The departure for Paris, as may be imagined, was postponed indefinitely. Music was to Adolphe an echo of his profound happiness, the mirror in which were reflected the rays of his frenzied passion, whence they returned more scorching to his heart. To Hortense, on the contrary, music was but a relaxation about which she had long been blasé. It procured her some agreeable diversions, and the pleasure of shining in the eyes of her lover was often the only motive that could bring her to the piano.

Wholly given over to his rage for loving, Adolphe had during the first few days partly forgotten the fanaticism that had filled his life until then. Though far from sharing Mme N.'s sometimes strange opinions about the merits of the various works in her repertory, he none the less made extraordinary concessions to her, avoiding in their conversations, without quite knowing why, the broaching of musical doctrine. A vague instinct warned him that the divergence between them would have been too great. Nothing less than some frightful blasphemy, such as the one that had made him show the door to one of his pupils, could have upset the balance in Adolphe's heart between his violent love and his despotically impassioned artistic convictions. And this blasphemy, one day, did escape Hortense's pretty lips.

It was on a fine morning in the autumn. Adolphe, lying at his mistress's feet, was reveling in the melancholy happiness, the delightful dejection, that follows the great climaxes of voluptuous bliss. The atheist himself, in such moments, hears within himself a hymn of gratitude rising toward the unknown cause that gave him life. And at the same moment, death – a death 'dreamy and calm as night,' in Moore's beautiful words – is the goal earnestly desired, the only fitting one that our eyes, dimmed with celestial tears, can glimpse as the gift to crown that superhuman intoxication. The common life, life devoid of poetry and love, *prose* life, in which one walks instead of flying, speaks instead of singing, in which so many bright-colored flowers lack perfume and grace, in which genius is worshipped for a day or done glacial homage to, in which art is too often the partner of a misalliance, *this* life, in short, shows itself under so gloomy an aspect, feels so empty, that death, even stripped of the real charm it holds for a man drowned in happiness, would still seem desirable to him, by offering him an assured refuge from the insipid existence he above all things dreads.

Lost in thoughts of this kind, Adolphe was holding one of the delicate hands of his lady-love, imprinting on every finger slight nibbles which he effaced with endless kisses, while Hortense with her free hand, humming the while, ruffled the black locks of her lover. Hearing that voice, so pure, so full of seduction, he felt an irrestible impulse to ask: 'Oh, do sing me the elegy in *La Vestale*, my love; you know the one I mean:

> *Thou whom I leave on earth,*
> *Mortal I dare not name.*

Sung by you, that inspired melody will be incredibly sublime. I can't imagine why I haven't asked you before. Sing, sing Spontini to me; let me enjoy every kind of happiness all at once.'

'Really? Is that what you would like?' replied Mme N., with a slight pout she thought charming. 'You *enjoy* that long, monotonous dirge? It's the most boring thing – like monks chanting! Still, if you insist–'

The cold blade of a dagger plunging into Adolphe's heart would not have lacerated it more cruelly than her words. Starting up like a man who discovers an unclean animal in the grass he has been sitting on, he first riveted on Hortense a dark glance full of threatening fire. Then, striding restlessly about the room, fists clenched, teeth convulsively set, he seemed to be taking counsel with himself about the way in which he should speak to signify their breaking off. To forgive such a remark was impossible. Love and admiration had fled, the angel had become an ordinary woman; the superior artist had fallen to the level of the ignorant and superficial amateurs who want art to 'amuse them', never suspecting that it has a nobler mission. Hortense was now but a graceful form without mind or soul; the musician had nimble fingers and a warbler's throat, nothing more.

In spite of the torments Adolphe felt at his discovery, in spite of the horror of so abrupt a disenchantment, he would not have been likely to fail in consideration and tact when breaking off with a woman whose sole crime, after all, was to have perceptions inferior to his own and to love the pretty without understanding the beautiful. But as Hortense was not able to credit the violence of the storm she had just raised, the sudden contraction of Adolphe's features, his excited striding about the sitting-room, his barely controlled indignation – all this seemed to her so comical that she could not restrain a burst of mad merriment and she let out a peal of strident laughter.

Have you ever noticed how hateful a high cackling laugh can be in certain women? To me it seems the sure sign of a withered heart, selfishness, and coquetry. Just as the expression of great joy is in some women marked by charm and modesty, so in others it takes on a tone of indecent sarcasm. Their voice becomes harsh, impudent, and shameless, which is all the more odious the younger and prettier the woman is. At such times I can understand the pleasure of murdering, and I absent-mindedly reach for Othello's pillow. Adolphe no doubt had the same feelings in the matter. A moment before, he was already out of love with Mme N., but he had pity for her and her limited faculties; he would have left her coldly, but without insulting her. The stupid noise of her laughter, at the very instant when the wretched man

91

felt his heart torn, exasperated him. A flash of hatred and unutterable contempt suddenly darted from his eyes. Wiping the cold perspiration from his brow with an angry gesture, he said in a voice she had never heard him use: 'Madam, you are a fool.'

That same evening he was on his way to Paris.

No one knows what the modern Ariadne thought on finding herself thus forsaken. At all events Bacchus, who was to console her and heal the cruel wound inflicted on her self-esteem, was probably not slow in making his apearance. Hortense was not the woman to stay moping. 'Her mind and heart required sustenance.' Such is the usual phrase with which such women poetize and try to justify their most prosaic lapses from grace.

Be that as it may, from the second day of his journey, Adolphe had completely broken the spell and was all wrapped up in the joy of seeing his darling hope, his obsessive dream, on the verge of realization. At last he was to see Paris, to be in the center of the musical world. He was about to hear the magnificent orchestra of the Paris Opéra, with its large and powerful chorus, he would see Mme Branchu in *La Vestale*. A review by Geoffroy,[6] which he read on reaching Lyon, further increased his impatience. Contrary to custom, the famous critic had uttered nothing but praise.

'Never,' he wrote, 'had Spontini's beautiful score been given with such fine ensemble by orchestra and chorus, nor with such passionate inspiration by the principal actors. Mme Branchu, among others, soared to the highest pitch of tragedy; a finished singer, gifted with an incomparable voice, a consummate actress, she is perhaps the most valuable member that the Opéra has been able to boast of since the day of its foundation – be it said with due deference to the admirers of Mme Saint-Huberty. Mme Branchu is, unfortunately, small in stature; but the naturalness of her attitudes, the energetic truth of her gestures, and the fire in her eyes make this lack of stature pass unnoticed. In her exchanges with the priests of Jupiter her acting is so expressive that she seems to tower a full head above Dérivis, who is a colossus.

'Last night a very long intermission preceded the third act. The reason for this unusual pause in the performance was the violent state of excitement into which the part of Julia and Spontini's music had thrown the singer. In the prayer ('O ye unfortunates') her tremulous

---

[6] Louis Geoffroy (1743-1814) was a critic of drama and opera, whose opinions carried weight throughout the Continent during the Napoleonic period.

voice already betrayed an emotion she could scarcely control, but in the finale ('Of this temple priestess lost in sin'), her part being all pantomime and not requiring her to restrain so completely the transports that agitated her, tears flooded her cheeks, her gestures became disordered, incoherent, wild; and when the pontiff threw over her head the huge black veil which covers her like a shroud, instead of fleeing distracted, as she had always done before, Mme Branchu dropped fainting at the feet of the Grand Vestal. The public, mistaking this for a new invention by the actress, covered with applause the peroration of this magnificent finale. Chorus, orchestra, Dérivis, the gong – all was drowned out by the shouts of the audience. The house was in a state of frenzy.'

'My kingdom for a horse!' exclaimed Richard III. Adolphe would have given the whole world to have been able to gallop from Lyon to Paris then and there. He could hardly breathe as he read Geoffroy's words. The blood throbbed in his head and made him deaf, he was in a fever. Perforce he had to wait till the starting-time of the lumbering coach, so inappropriately called a diligence, in which he had reserved a seat for the next day.

During his few hours in Lyon, Adolphe took good care not to enter a theater. On any other occasion he would have been eager to do so; but feeling sure as he now did that he would soon hear Spontini's masterpiece worthily performed, he wished to remain until then virginally pure of all contact with the provincial Muses.

At last they were off. Ensconced in a corner of the carriage, buried in thought, D. maintained an unsociable silence and took no part in the cackling of three ladies who were taking pains to keep up a steady conversation with a couple of soldiers. The talk, as usual, ran on every conceivable subject, and when the turn of music came, the thousand and one absurdities retailed barely drew from Adolphe the laconic aside: 'Old hens!' But the next day he was forced to answer the questions that the eldest of the women was determined to ask him. All three of them had lost patience with his persistent silence and the sardonic smile that played from time to time on his features. They made up their minds that he should speak and tell them the object of his journey.

'You are no doubt going to Paris?'

'Yes, madam.'

'To study law?'

'No, madam.'

'Ah, then, you are a medical student?'

'Not at all, madam.'

The questioning had come to an end for the time being. It was resumed the next day with an importunity fit to make the most forbearing man lose patience.

'Can it be that our young friend is about to enter the Polytechnic School?'

'No, madam.'

'Some business firm, then?'

'Heavens, no, madam.'

'As a matter of fact, nothing is nicer than to travel for pleasure, as you appear to be doing.'

'That may have been my object in setting out, madam, but I am doomed to miss it altogether, if the future is anything like the present.'

This rejoinder, dryly uttered, had the effect of silencing the impertinent questioner at last, and Adolphe was able to take up the thread of his thoughts. How was he going to manage in Paris? His whole fortune consisted of his violin and a purse containing two hundred francs. By what means could he put the former to use and save the contents of the latter? Would he find a way to make something of his talent? But what matter all these worries about trifles and fears about the future? Was he not going to hear *La Vestale*? Was he not on the point of enjoying to its fullest the happiness so long dreamed of? Even if he should die the moment after, he would have no complaint. It was in truth perfectly fair that life should come to an end when the sum of the possible joys that fill a human existence is spent at one stroke.

In this state of exaltation our Provençal reached Paris. Hardly out of the carriage, he rushed to look at the playbills. But what does he see on the Opéra's: *The Betrothed*! 'A barefaced fraud!' he exclaims; 'what was the use of getting myself expelled from my theater and flying from Lemoyne's music as from plague and leprosy, only to find it again at the Paris Opéra?'

The fact is that this mongrel work, this archetype of the powdered, embroidered, gold-laced rococo style, which seems to have been composed expressly for the Viscount Jodelet and the Marquis de Mascarille,[7] was then in high favour. Lemoyne shared the programs in alternation with Gluck and Spontini. In Adolphe's eyes the putting of

---

[7] The lackeys masquerading as noblemen in Molière's *Précieuses Ridicules*.

these names cheek by jowl was a desecration. It seemed to him that a stage adorned by the finest geniuses of Europe should not be open to such pallid mediocrities; that the noble orchestra, still vibrating with the virile tones of *Iphigenia in Tauris* or *Alcestis*, should not be debased by having to accompany the twitterings of Mondor and la Dandinière. As for the comparison between *La Vestale* and those ghastly and stale potpourris, he tried to drive the thought from his mind. Such an abomination curdled his blood, and to this day there still exist a few ardent or *extravagant* minds (you may call them either way) who take exactly the same view of the matter.

Swallowing his disappointment, Adolphe was glumly going home when chance made him meet a fellow countryman to whom he had formerly given lessons. The latter, a wealthy amateur and well known in musical circles, readily told his former teacher all he knew about what was going on, and reported that the performances of *La Vestale*, which had been suspended because of Mme Branchu's indisposition, would in all probability not be resumed for some weeks to come. As for Gluck's works, which ordinarily formed the core of the Opéra's repertory, they were not scheduled during the first days of Adolphe's stay in Paris. This circumstance made it easier for him to fulfill the vow he had made of preserving his musical virginity for Spontini. He did not set foot in any theater and abstained from every kind of music.

Meanwhile he sought a position that would give him his daily bread without condemning him anew to the humiliating role he had so long occupied in the provinces. He played to Persuis, at that time conductor at the Opéra.[8] Persuis saw that he had talent, invited him to come and see him again, and promised him the first opening among the violins of the Opéra. Thus reassured, and banking for his livelihood on a couple of pupils whom his patron had found for him, the worshipper at Spontini's shrine felt increasing impatience to hear the magic score. Every day he ran out to scan the playbills, only to have his hopes dashed to the ground.

On the morning of the 22nd of March, reaching the corner of the rue Richelieu just as the billposter was climbing up his ladder, and seeing the placard of, successively, the Vaudeville, the Opéra-Comique, the Italian Theater, and the Porte-Saint-Martin, finally saw the slow

---

[8] Luc Loiseau de Persuis (1769-1839) was a violinist and composer who rose to the musical direction of the Opéra in 1817 and made his management notable. He also wrote some two dozen operas, ballets, and oratorios.

unfolding of the large brown sheet bearing as headline the words 'Académie impériale de Musique'. He nearly collapsed in the street on reading at last the title so greatly desired: La Vestale.

Hardly had Adolphe seen this promise of La Vestale for the next day when he was seized by a sort of delirium. He rushed madly through the streets, bumping into the jutting angles of houses, elbowing passers-by, laughing at their insults, talking, singing, gesticulating like an escaped lunatic.

Dead with fatigue, spattered with mud, he finally entered a café, ordered dinner, wolfed down without noticing what the waiter set before him, and lapsed into a strange fit of melancholy. Suddenly a prey to anxiety without quite discerning what could be causing it, and overawed by the nearness of the stupendous event which was to come into his life, he listened awhile to the violent thumping of his heart, he wept, and letting his poor, emaciated head drop to the table, he fell into a deep sleep.

The following day he was calmer. A call on Persuis shortened his wait. The manager, on receiving Adolphe, handed him a letter bearing the official stamp of the Opéra: it was his appointment as second violin. Adolphe thanked him, though with much alacrity. This favor, which at any other time would have overwhelmed him with joy, had become to him hardly more than a secondary matter of little interest. A few minutes later he had forgotten it. He avoided speaking to Persuis of the performance that was to take place that evening; the subject would have shaken him to the core. He dreaded it. Persuis, not knowing what to think of the young man's strange looks and incoherent speech, was about to ask the cause of the trouble, when Adolphe noticed this, rose and left.

He strolled awhile in front of the Opéra, looked again at the bill to make sure there was no change in the program or in the cast. All this helped him to wait till the close of that interminable day. At last the clock struck six. Twenty minutes later Adolphe was in his box, for in order to be undisturbed in his ecstatic admiration, and to enhance the solemnity of his happiness, he had taken, regardless of the extravagant expenditure, and entire box for himself alone.

We shall now let our enthusiast give his own account of that memorable evening. A few lines that he wrote on reaching home, as a sequel to the sort of diary from which I have culled the foregoing particulars, show but too well the state of his mind and the inconceivable frenzy which formed the groundwork of his temperament. I give them here without alteration.

'March 23rd, midnight

'This, then, is life! I gaze upon it from the pinnacle of my happiness ... it is impossible to go further. ... I have reached the summit. ... Come down again? Go back? ... Certainly not! I prefer making my exit before nauseating tastes poison that of the delicious fruit I have just plucked. What would my life be if it were to go on? – that of the thousands of insects I hear buzzing about me. Chained once more to a music-stand, forced to play in alternation masterpieces and filthy platitudes, I should end like the rest and become hardened. The exquisite sensibility that enables me to enjoy so many sensations and gives me access to so many emotions unknown to the common herd would gradually become blunted, and my enthusiasm would cool, even supposing it did not die out altogether under the ashes of habit. I might perhaps come to speak of geniuses as if they were ordinary beings; I might utter the names of Gluck and Spontini without raising my hat. I am fairly sure that I should always hate with all my soul anything I now hate; but is it not a cruel necessity to husband one's energy only for the purposes of hatred?

'Music occupies too large a place in my life. My passion for it has killed and absorbed all the rest. My last experience of love has disillusioned me only too harshly. Could I ever find a woman whose being would be tuned to the same high pitch as mine? No, I'm afraid they are all more or less like Hortense. I had forgotten her name – Hortense – odd how a single word from her mouth broke the spell! Oh, the humiliation of having loved with the most ardent and poetic love, with all the strength of my heart and soul, a woman possessed of neither, and radically incapable of understanding the meaning of the words 'love' and 'poetry'. Fool, thrice-silly fool, of whom I still cannot think without a blush.

'Yesterday I thought of writing to Spontini and begging him to let me pay a call. But even if my request had been granted, the great man would never have believed me capable of understanding his work as I do understand it. I should probably appear to him merely as an excited young man, childishly infatuated with a work miles above his grasp. He would think of me what he must necessarily think of the public. He might even attribute my transports of admiration to shameful self-interest, thus confusing the most sincere enthusiasm with the meanest flattery. Horrible! No, no, better make an end of it. I am alone in the world, an orphan from childhood; my death will grieve no one. A few will say: "He was crazy." That will be my epitaph.

'I shall die day after tomorrow. *La Vestale* is to be performed again, I want to hear it a second time. What a work! How love is pictured in it! as well as fanaticism! All those mastiff-priests barking at their wretched victim! And what harmonies in that gigantic finale! What melody even in the recitatives! What an orchestra! It moves so majestically; the basses swell and sink like the waves of the ocean. The instruments are actors whose language is as expresive as that spoken on the stage. Dérivis was superb in his recitative of the second act: he was *Jupiter Tonans*. In the aria "Unrelenting gods," Mme Branchu tore my heart out; I nearly fainted. That woman is lyric tragedy incarnate; she would reconcile me to her sex. Yes! I shall see her again ... once ... this *Vestale* ... a superhuman work, which could have come to birth only in an age of miracles like Napoleon's. I shall focus into three hours the life force of twenty years' existence. Afterwards, I shall go ... and ponder over my happiness in eternity.'

Two days later, at ten o'clock at night, a report was heard at the corner of the rue Rameau, opposite the entrance to the Opéra. Some footmen in gorgeous liveries rushed to the spot on hearing the noise, and raised the body of a man bathed in blood who showed no signs of life. At that instant a lady who was leaving the theater came to find her carriage and recognizing the blood-bespattered face of Adolphe, said: 'Oh, mercy! It's that unhappy young man who's been following me all the way from Marseille!'

Hortense (for it was she) had then and there seen the way to make her vanity benefit from the death of the man who had vexed her by his humiliating departure. The next day the talk in the club in the rue de Choiseul was: 'That Mme N. is really a captivating woman! When she went south some time ago, a Provençal fell so madly in love with her that he followed her all the way to Paris and blew his brains out at her feet last night, just outside the Opéra. That's success, as you might say; it will make her absolutely irresistible.'

Poor Adolphe! ...

THE GUN WITH WINGS

by REX STOUT

Place: New York

Time: 1948

Performance: *La Forza del Destino*, by Giuseppe Verdi

The young woman took a pink piece of paper from her handbag, got up from the red leather chair, put the paper on Nero Wolfe's desk, and sat down again. Feeling it my duty to keep myself informed and also to save Wolfe the exertion of leaning forward and reaching so far, I arose and crossed to hand the paper to him after a glance at it. It was a check for five thousand dollars, dated that day, August fourteenth, made out to him, and signed Margaret Mion. He gave a look and dropped it back on the desk.

'I thought,' she said, 'perhaps that would be the best way to start the conversation.'

In my chair at my desk, taking her in, I was readjusting my attitude. When early that Sunday afternoon, she had phoned for an appointment, I had dug up a vague recollection of a picture of her in the paper some months back, and had decided it would be no treat to meet her, but now I was hedging. Her appeal wasn't what she had, which was only so-so, but what she did with it. I don't mean tricks. Her mouth wasn't attractive even when she smiled, but the smile was. Her eyes were just a pair of brown eyes, nothing at all sensational, but it was a pleasure to watch them move around, from Wolfe to me to the man who had come with her, seated off to her left. I guessed she had maybe three years to go to reach thirty.

'Don't you think,' the man asked her, 'we should get some questions answered first?'

His tone was strained and a little harsh, and his face matched it. He was worried and didn't care who knew it. With his deep-set gray eyes and well-fitted jaw he might on a happier day have passed for a leader of men, but not as he now sat. Something was eating him. When Mrs Mion had introduced him as Mr Frederick Weppler I had recognized the name of the music critic of the *Gazette*, but I couldn't remember whether he had been mentioned in the newspaper accounts of the event that had caused the publication of Mrs Mion's picture.

She shook her head at him, not arbitrarily. 'It wouldn't help, Fred, really. We'll just have to tell it and see what he says.' She smiled at Wolfe – or maybe it wasn't actually a smile, but just her way of handling her lips. 'Mr Weppler wasn't quite sure we should come to see you, and I had to persuade him. Men are more cautious than women, aren't they?'

'Yes,' Wolfe agreed, and added, 'Thank heaven.'

She nodded. 'I suppose so.' She gestured. 'I brought that check with me to show that we really mean it. We're in trouble and we want you to get us out. We want to get married and we can't. That is – if I should just speak for myself – I want to marry him.' She looked at Weppler, and this time it was unquestionably a smile. 'Do you want to marry me, Fred?'

'Yes,' he muttered. Then he suddenly jerked his chin up and looked defiantly at Wolfe. 'You understand this is embarrassing, don't you? It's none of your business, but we've come to get your help. I'm thirty-four years old, and this is the first time I've ever been –' He stopped. In a moment he said stiffly, 'I am in love with Mrs Mion and I want to marry her more than I have ever wanted anything in my life.' His eyes went to his love and he murmured a plea. 'Peggy!'

Wolfe grunted. 'I accept that as proven. You both want to get married. Why don't you?'

'Because we can't,' Peggy said. 'We simply can't. It's on account – you may remember reading about my husband's death in April, four months ago? Alberto Mion, the opera singer?'

'Vaguely. You'd better refresh my memory.'

'Well, he died – he killed himself.' There was no sign of a smile now. 'Fred – Mr Weppler and I found him. It was seven o'clock, a Tuesday evening in April, at our apartment on East End Avenue. Just that afternoon Fred and I had found out that we loved each other, and –'

'Peggy!' Weppler called sharply.

Her eyes darted to him and back to Wolfe. 'Perhaps I should ask you, Mr Wolfe. He thinks we should tell you just enough so you understand the problem, and I think you can't understand it unless we tell you everything. What do you think?'

'I can't say until I hear it. Go ahead. If I have questions, we'll see.'

She nodded. 'I imagine you'll have plenty of questions. Have you ever been in love but would have died rather than let anyone see it?'

'Never,' Wolfe said emphatically. I kept my face straight.

'Well, I was, and I admit it. But no one knew it, not even him. Did you, Fred?'

'I did not.' Weppler was emphatic too.

'Until that afternoon,' Peggy told Wolfe. 'He was at the apartment for lunch, and it happened right after lunch. The others had left, and all of a sudden we were looking at each other, and then he spoke or I did, I don't know which.' She looked at Weppler imploringly. 'I know you think this is embarrassing, Fred, but if he doesn't know what it was like he won't understand why you went upstairs to see Alberto.'

'Does he have to?' Weppler demanded.

'Of course he does.' She returned to Wolfe. 'I suppose I can't make you see what it was like. We were completely – well, we were in love, that's all, and I guess we had been for quite a while without saying it, and that made it all the more – more overwhelming. Fred wanted to see my husband right away, to tell him about it and decide what we could do, and I said all right, so he went upstairs –'

'Upstairs?'

'Yes, it's a duplex, and upstairs was my husband's soundproofed studio, where he practiced. So he went –'

'Please, Peggy,' Weppler interrupted her. His eyes went to Wolfe. 'You should have it firsthand. I went up to tell Mion that I loved his wife, and she loved me and not him, and to ask him to be civilized about it. Getting a divorce has come to be regarded as fairly civilized, but he didn't see it that way. He was anything but civilized. He wasn't violent, but he was damned mean. After some of that I got afraid I might do to him what Gif James had done, and I left. I didn't want to go back to Mrs Mion while I was in that state of mind, so I left the studio by the door to the upper hall and took the elevator there.'

He stopped.

'And?' Wolfe prodded him.

'I walked it off. I walked across to the park, and after a while I had calmed down and I phoned Mrs Mion, and she met me in the park. I told her what Mion's attitude was, and I asked her to leave him and come with me. She wouldn't do that.' Weppler paused, and then went on, 'There are two complications you ought to have if you're to have everything.'

'If they're relevant, yes.'

'They're relevant all right. First, Mrs Mion had and has money of her own. That was an added attraction for Mion. It wasn't for me. I'm just telling you.'

'Thank you. And the second?'

'The second was Mrs Mion's reason for not leaving Mion immediately. I suppose you know he had been the top tenor at the Met for five or six years, and his voice was gone – temporarily. Gifford James, the baritone, had hit him on the neck with his fist and hurt his larynx – that was early in March – and Mion couldn't finish the season. It had been operated, but his voice hadn't come back, and naturally he was glum, and Mrs Mion wouldn't leave him under those circumstances. I tried to persuade her to, but she wouldn't. I wasn't anything like normal that day, on account of what had happened to me for the first time in my life, and on account of what Mion had said to me, so I wasn't reasonable and I left her in the park and went downtown to a bar and started drinking. A lot of time went by and I had quite a few, but I wasn't pickled. Along toward seven o'clock I decided I had to see her again and carry her off so she wouldn't spend another night there. That mood took me back to East End Avenue and up to the twelfth floor, and then I stood there in the hall a while, perhaps ten minutes, before my finger went to the pushbutton. Finally I rang, and the maid let me in and went for Mrs Mion, but I had lost my nerve or something. All I did was suggest that we should have a talk with Mion together. She agreed, and we went upstairs and –'

'Using the elevator?'

'No, the stairs inside the apartment. We entered the studio. Mion was on the floor. We went over to him. There was a big hole through the top of his head. He was dead. I led Mrs Mion out, made her come, and on the stairs – they're too narrow to go two abreast – she fell and rolled halfway down. I carried her to her room and put her on her bed, and I started for the living room, for the phone there when I thought of something to do first. I went out and took the elevator to the ground floor, got the doorman and elevator man together, and asked them who had been taken up to the Mion apartment, either the twelfth floor or the

102

thirteenth, that afternoon. I said they must be damn sure not to skip anybody. They gave me the names and I wrote them down. Then I went back up to the apartment and phoned the police. After I did that it struck me that a layman isn't supposed to decide if a man is dead, so I phoned Dr Lloyd, who has an apartment in the building. He came at once, and I took him up to the studio. We hadn't been there more than three or four minutes when the first policeman came, and of course –'

'If you please,' Wolfe put in crossly. 'Everything is sometimes too much. You haven't even hinted at the trouble you're in.'

'I'll get to it –'

'But faster, I hope, if I help. My memory has been jogged. The doctor and the police pronounced him dead. The muzzle of the revolver had been thrust into his mouth, and the emerging bullet had torn out a piece of his skull. The revolver, found lying on the floor beside him, belonged to him and was kept there in the studio. There was no sign of any struggle and no mark of any other injury on him. The loss of his voice was an excellent motive for suicide. Therefore, after a routine investigation, giving due weight to the difficulty of sticking the barrel of a loaded revolver into a man's mouth without arousing him to protest, it was recorded as suicide. Isn't that correct?'

They both said yes.

'Have the police reopened it? Or is gossip at work?'

They both said no.

'Then let's get on. Where's the trouble?'

'It's us,' Peggy said.

'Why? What's wrong with you?'

'Everything.' She gestured. 'No. I don't mean that – not everything, just one thing. After my husband's death and the – the routine investigation, I went away for a while. When I came back – for the past two months Fred and I have been together some, but it wasn't right – I mean we didn't feel right. Day before yesterday, Friday, I went to friends in Connecticut for the weekend, and he was there. Neither of us knew the other was coming. We talked it out yesterday and last night and this morning, and we decided to come and ask you to help us – anyway, I did, and he wouldn't let me come alone.'

Peggy leaned forward and was in deadly earnest. 'You *must* help us, Mr Wolfe. I love him so much – so much! – and he says he loves me, and I know he does! Yesterday afternoon we decided we would get married in October, and then last night we got started talking – but it isn't what we say, it's what is in our eyes when we look at each other.

We just can't get married with that back of our eyes and trying to hide it –'

A little shiver went over her. 'For years – forever? We can't! We know we can't – it would be horrible! What it is, it's a question: who killed Alberto? Did he? Did I? I don't really think he did, and he doesn't really think I did – I hope he doesn't – but it's there back of our eyes, and we know it is!'

She extended both hands. 'We want you to find out!'

Wolfe snorted. 'Nonsence. You need a spanking or a psychiatrist. The police may have shortcomings, but they're not nincompoops. If they're satisfied –'

'But that's it! They wouldn't be satisifed if we had told the truth!'

'Oh.' Wolfe's brows went up. 'You lied to them?'

'Yes. Or if we didn't lie, anyhow we didn't tell them the truth. We didn't tell them that when we first went in together and saw him, there was no gun lying there. There was no gun in sight.'

'Indeed. How sure are you?'

'Absolutely positive. I never saw anything clearer than I saw that – that sight – all of it. There was no gun.'

Wolfe snapped at Weppler, 'You agree, sir?'

'Yes. She's right.'

Wolfe sighed. 'Well,' he conceded, 'I can see that you're really in trouble. Spanking wouldn't help.'

I shifted in my chair on account of a tingle at the lower part of my spine. Nero Wolfe's old brownstone house on West Thirty-fifth Street was an interesting place to live and work – for Fritz Brenner, the chef and housekeeper, for Theodore Horstmann, who fed and nursed the ten thousand orchids in the plant rooms up on the roof, and for me, Archie Goodwin, whose main field of operations was the big office on the ground floor. Naturally I thought my job the most interesting, since a confidential assistant to a famous private detective is constantly getting an earful of all kinds of troubles and problems – everything from a missing necklace to a new blackmail gimmick. Very few clients actually bored me. But only one kind of case gave me that tingle in the spine: murder. And if this pair of lovebirds were talking straight, this was it.

II

I had filled two notebooks when they left, more than two hours later.

If they had thought it through before they phoned for an appointment with Wolfe, they wouldn't have phoned. All they wanted, as Wolfe pointed out, was the moon. They wanted him, first, to investigate a four-month-old murder without letting on there had been one; second, to prove that neither of them had killed Alberto Mion, which could be done only by finding out who had; and third, in case he concluded that one of them had done it, to file it away and forget it. Not that they put it that way, since their story was that they were both absolutely innocent, but that was what it amounted to.

Wolfe made it good and plain. 'If I take the job,' he told them, 'and find evidence to convict someone of murder, no matter who, the use I make of it will be solely in my discretion. I am neither an Astraea nor a sadist, but I like my door open. But if you want to drop it now, here's your check, and Mr Goodwin's notebooks will be destroyed. We can forget you have been here, and shall.'

That was one of the moments when they were within an ace of getting up and going, especially Fred Weppler, but they didn't. They looked at each other, and it was all in their eyes. By that time I had about decided I liked them both pretty well and was even beginning to admire them, they were so damn determined to get loose from the trap they were in. When they looked at each other like that their eyes said, 'Let's go and be together, my darling love, and forget this – come on, come on.' Then they said, 'It will be so wonderful!' Then they said, 'Yes, oh yes, but – But we don't want it wonderful for a day or a week; it must be always wonderful – and we know ...'

It took strong muscles to hold onto it like that, not to mention horse sense, and several times I caught myself feeling sentimental about it. Then of course there was the check for five grand on Wolfe's desk.

The notebooks were full of assorted matters. There were a thousand details which might or might not turn out to be pertinent, such as the mutual dislike between Peggy Mion and Rupert Grove, her husband's manager, or the occasion of Gifford James socking Alberto Mion in front of witnesses, or the attitudes of various persons toward Mion's demand for damages; but you couldn't use it all, and Wolfe himself never needed more than a fraction of it, so I'll pick and choose. Of course the gun was Exhibit A. It was a new one, having been bought by Mion the day after Gifford James had plugged him and hurt his larynx

– not, he had announced, for vengeance on James but for future protection. He had carried it in a pocket whenever he went out, and at home had kept it in the studio, lying on the base of a bust of Caruso. So far as known, it had never fired but one bullet, the one that killed Mion.

When Dr Lloyd had arrived and Weppler had taken him to the studio the gun was lying on the floor not far from Mion's knee. Dr Lloyd's hand had started for it but had been withdrawn without touching it, so it had been there when the law came. Peggy was positive it had not been there when she and Fred had entered, and he agreed. The cops had made no announcement about fingerprints, which wasn't surprising since none are hardly ever found on a gun that are any good. Throughout the two hours and a half, Wolfe kept darting back to the gun, but it simply didn't have wings.

The picture of the day and the day's people was all filled in. The morning seemed irrelevant, so it started at lunch time with five of them there: Mion, Peggy, Fred, one Adele Bosley, and Dr Lloyd. It was more professional than social. Fred had been invited because Mion wanted to sell him the idea of writing a piece for the *Gazette* saying that the rumours that Mion would never be able to sing again were malicious hooey. Adele Bosley, who was in charge of public relations for the Metropolitan Opera, had come to help work on Fred. Dr Lloyd had been asked so he could assure Weppler that the operation he had performed on Mion's larynx had been successful and it was a good bet that by the time the opera season opened in November the great tenor would be as good as ever. Nothing special had happened except that Fred had agreed to do the piece. Adele Bosley and Lloyd had left, and Mion had gone up to the soundproofed studio, and Fred and Peggy had looked at each other and suddenly discovered the most important fact of life since the Garden of Eden.

An hour or so later there had been another gathering this time up in the studio, around half-past three, but neither Fred nor Peggy had been present. By then Fred had walked himself calm and phoned Peggy, and she had gone to meet him in the park, so their information on the meeting in the studio was hearsay. Besides Mion and Dr Lloyd there had been four people: Adele Bosley for operatic public relations; Mr Rupert Grove, Mion's manager; Mr Gifford James, the baritone who had socked Mion in the neck six weeks previously; and Judge Henry Arnold, James' lawyer. This affair had been even less social than the lunch, having been arranged to discuss a formal request that Mion had made of Gifford James for the payment of a quarter of a million bucks for the damage to Mion's larynx.

Fred's and Peggy's hearsay had it that the conference had been fairly hot at points, with the temperature boosted right at the beginning by Mion's getting the gun from Caruso's bust and placing it on a table at his elbow. On the details of its course they were pretty sketchy, since they hadn't been there, but anyhow the gun hadn't been fired. Also there was plenty of evidence that Mion was alive and well – except for his larynx – when the party broke up. He had made two phone calls after the conference had ended, one to his barber and one to a wealthy female opera patron; his manager, Rupert Grove, had phoned him a little later; and around five-thirty he had phoned downstairs to the maid to bring him a bottle of vermouth and some ice, which she had done. She had taken the tray into the studio, and he had been upright and intact.

I was careful to get all the names spelled right in my notebook, since it seemed likely the job would be to get one of them tagged for murder, and I was especially careful with the last one that got in: Clara James, Gifford's daughter. There were three spotlights on her. First, the reason for James' assault on Mion had been his knowledge or suspicion – Fred and Peggy weren't sure which – that Mion had stepped over the line with James' daughter. Second, her name had ended the list, got by Fred from the doorman and elevator man, of people who had called that afternoon. They said she had come about a quarter past six and had got off at the floor the studio was on, the thirteenth, and had summoned the elevator to the twelfth floor a little later, maybe ten minutes, and had left. The third spotlight was directed by Peggy, who had stayed in the park a while after Fred had marched off, and had then returned home, arriving around five o'clock. She had not gone up to the studio and had not seen her husband. Sometime after six, she thought around half-past, she had answered the doorbell herself because the maid had been in the kitchen with the cook. It was Clara James. She was pale and tense, but she was always pale and tense. She had asked for Alberto, and Peggy had said she thought he was up in the studio, and Clara had said no, he wasn't there, and never mind. When Clara went for the elevator button, Peggy had shut the door, not wanting company anyway, and particularly not Clara James.

Some half an hour later Fred showed up, and they ascended to the studio together and found that Alberto was there all right, but no longer upright or intact.

That picture left room for a whole night of questions, but Wolfe concentrated on what he regarded as the essentials. Even so, we went into the third hour and the third notebook. He completely ignored some spots that I thought needed filling in; for instance, had Alberto had a habit of stepping over the line with other men's daughters and/ or wives, and if so, names please. From things they said I gathered that Alberto had been broad-minded about other men's women, but apparently Wolfe wasn't interested. Along toward the end he was back on the gun again, and when they had nothing new to offer he scowled and got caustic. When they stayed glued he finally snapped at them, 'Which one of you is lying?'

They looked hurt. 'That won't get you anywhere,' Fred Weppler said bitterly, 'or us either.'

'It would be silly,' Peggy Mion protested, 'to come here and give you that check and then lie to you. Wouldn't it?'

'Then you're silly,' Wolfe said coldly. He pointed a finger at her. 'Look here. All of this might be worked out, none of it is preposterous, except one thing. Who put the gun on the floor beside the body? When you two entered the studio it wasn't there; you both swear to that, and I accept it. You left and started downstairs; you fell, and he carried you to your room. You weren't unconscious. Were you?'

'No.' Peggy was meeting his gaze. 'I could have walked, but he – he wanted to carry me.'

'No doubt. He did so. You stayed in your room. He went to the ground floor to compile a list of those who had made themselves available as murder suspects – showing admirable foresight, by the way – came back up and phoned the police and then the doctor, who arrived without delay since he lived in the building. Not more than fifteen minutes intervened between the moment you and Mr Weppler left the studio and the moment he and the doctor entered. The door from the studio to the public hall on the thirteenth floor has a lock that is automatic with the closing of the door, and the door was closed and locked. No one could possibly have entered during the fifteen minutes. You say that you had left your bed and gone to the living room, and that no one could have used that route without being seen by you. The maid and cook were in the kitchen, unaware of what was going on. So no one entered the studio and placed the gun on the floor.'

'Someone did,' Fred said doggedly.

Peggy insisted, 'We don't know who had a key.'

'You said that before.' Wolfe was at them now. 'Even if everyone had keys, I don't believe it and neither would anyone else.' His eyes came to me. 'Archie. Would you?'

'I'd have to see a movie of it,' I admitted.

'You see?' he demanded of them. 'Mr Goodwin isn't prejudiced against you – on the contrary. He's ready to fight fire for you; see how he gets behind on his notes for the pleasure of watching you look at each other. But he agrees with me that you're lying. Since no one else could have put the gun on the floor, one of you did. I have to know about it. The circumstances may have made it imperative for you, or you thought they did.'

He looked at Fred. 'Suppose you opened a drawer of Mrs Mion's dresser to get smelling salts, and the gun was there, with an odour showing it had been recently fired – put there, you would instantly conjecture, by someone to direct suspicion at her. What would you naturally do? Exactly what you did do: take it upstairs and put it beside the body, without letting her know about it. or –'

'Rot,' Fred said harshly. 'Absolute rot.'

Wolfe looked at Peggy. 'Or suppose it was you who found it there in your bedroom, after he had gone downstairs. Naturally you would have –'

'This is absurd,' Peggy said with spirit. 'How could it have been in my bedroom unless I put it there? My husband was alive at five-thirty, and I got home before that, and was right there, in the living room and my room, until Fred came at seven o'clock. So unless you assume –'

'Very well,' Wolfe conceded. 'Not the bedroom. But somewhere. I can't proceed until I get this from one of you. Confound it, the gun didn't fly. I expect plenty of lies from the others, at least one of them, but I want the truth from you.'

'You've got it,' Fred declared.

'No. I haven't.'

'Then it's a stalemate.' Fred stood up. 'Well, Peggy?'

They looked at each other, and their eyes went through the performance again. When they got to the place in the script where it said, 'It must be wonderful always,' Fred sat down.

But Wolfe, having no part in the script, horned in. 'A stalemate,' he said dryly, 'ends the game, I believe.'

Plainly it was up to me. If Wolfe openly committed himself to no dice nothing would budge him. I arose, got the pretty pink check from his desk, put it on mine, placed a paperweight on it, sat down, and grinned at him.

'Granted that you're dead right,' I observed, 'which is not what you call apodictical, someday we ought to make up a list of the clients that have sat here and lied to us. There was Mike Walsh, and Calida Frost, and that cafeteria guy, Pratt – oh, dozens. But their money was good, and I didn't get so far behind with my notes that I couldn't catch up. All that for nothing?'

'About those notes,' Fred Weppler said firmly. 'I want to make something clear.'

Wolfe looked at him.

He looked back. 'We came here,' he said, 'to tell you in confidence about a problem and get you to investigate. Your accusing us of lying makes me wonder if we ought to go on, but if Mrs Mion wants to I'm willing. But I want to make it plain that if you divulge what we've told you, if you tell the police or anyone else that we said there was no gun there when we went in, we'll deny it in spite of your damn notes. We'll deny it and stick to it!' He looked at his girl. 'We've got to, Peggy! All right?'

'He wouldn't tell the police,' Peggy declared, with fair conviction.

'Maybe not. But if he does, you'll stick with me on the denial. Won't you?'

'Certainly I will,' she promised, as if he had asked her to help kill a rattlesnake.

Wolfe was taking them in, with his lips tightened. Obviously, with the check on my desk on its way to the bank, he had decided to add them to the list of clients who told lies and go on from there. He forced his eyes wide open to rest them, let them half close again, and spoke.

'We'll settle that along with other things before we're through,' he asserted. 'You realize, of course, that I'm assuming your innocence, but I've made a thousand wrong assumptions before now so they're not worth much. Has either of you a notion of who killed Mr Mion?'

They both said no.

He grunted. 'I have.'

They opened their eyes at him.

He nodded. 'It's only another assumption, but I like it. It will take work to validate it. To begin with, I must see the people you have mentioned – all six of them – and I would prefer not to string it out. Since you don't want them told that I'm investigating a murder, we must devise a stratagem. Did your husband leave a will, Mrs Mion?'

She nodded and said yes.

'Are you the heir?'

'Yes, I –' She gestured. 'I don't need it and don't want it.'

'But it's yours. That will do nicely. An asset of the estate is the expectation of damages to be paid by Mr James for his assault on Mr Mion. You may properly claim that asset. The six people I want to see were all concerned in that affair, one way or another. I'll write them immediately, mailing the letter tonight special delivery, telling them that I represent you in the matter and would like them to call at my office tomorrow evening.'

'That's impossible!' Peggy cried, shocked. 'I couldn't! I wouldn't dream of asking Gif to pay damages –'

Wolfe banged a fist on his desk. 'Confound it!' he roared. 'Get out of here! Go! Do you think murders are solved by cutting out paper dolls! First you lie to me, and now you refuse to annoy people, including the murderer! Archie, put them out!'

'Good for you,' I muttered at him. I was getting fed up too. I glared at the would-be clients. 'Try the Salvation Army,' I suggested. 'They're old hands at helping people in trouble. You can have the notebooks to take along – at cost, six bits. No charge for the contents.'

They were looking at each other.

'I guess he has to see them somehow,' Fred conceded. 'He has to have a reason, and I must admit that's a good one. You don't owe them anything – not one of them.'

Peggy gave in.

After a few details had been attended to, the most important of which was getting addresses, they left. The manner of their going, and of our speeding them, was so far from cordial that it might have been thought that instead of being the clients they were the prey. But the check was on my desk. When, after letting them out, I returned to the office, Wolfe was leaning back with his eyes shut, frowning in distaste.

I stretched and yawned. 'This ought to be fun,' I said encouragingly. 'Making it just a grab for damages. If the murderer is among the guests, see how long you can keep it from him. I bet he catches on before the jury comes in with the verdict.'

'Shut up,' he growled. 'Blockheads.'

'Oh, have a heart,' I protested. 'People in love aren't supposed to think, that's why they have to hire trained thinkers. You should be happy and proud they picked you. What's a good big lie or two when you're in love? When I saw –'

'Shut up,' he repeated. His eyes came open. 'Your notebook. Those letters must go at once.'

III

Monday evening's party lasted a full three hours, and murder wasn't mentioned once. Even so, it wasn't exactly jolly. The letters had put it straight that Wolfe, acting for Mrs Mion, wanted to find out whether an appropriate sum could be collected from Gifford James without resort to lawyers and a court, and what sum would be thought appropriate. So each of them was naturally in a state of mind: Gifford James himself; his daughter Clara; his lawyer, Judge Henry Arnold; Adele Bosley for Public Relations; Dr Nicholas Lloyd as the technical expert; and Rupert Grove, who had been Mion's manager. That made six, which was just comfortable for our big office. Fred and Peggy had not been invited.

The James trio arrived together and were so punctual, right on the dot at nine o'clock, that Wolfe and I hadn't yet finished our after-dinner coffee in the office. I was so curious to have a look that I went to answer the door instead of leaving it to Fritz, the chef and house overseer who helps to make Wolfe's days and years a joy forever almost as much as I do. The first thing that impressed me was that the baritone took the lead crossing the threshold, letting his daughter and his lawyer tag along behind. Since I have occasionally let Lily Rowan share her pair of opera seats with me, James' six feet and broad shoulders and cocky strut were nothing new, but I was surprised that he looked so young, since he must have been close to fifty. He handed me his hat as if taking care of his hat on Monday evening, August 15, was the one and only thing I had been born for. Unfortunately I let it drop.

Clara made up for it by looking at me. That alone showed she was unusually observant, since one never looks at the flunkey who lets one in, but she saw me drop her father's hat and gave me a glance, and then prolonged the glance until it practically said, 'What are you, in disguise? See you later.' That made me feel friendly, but with reserve. Not only was she pale and tense, as Peggy Mion had said, but her blue eyes glistened, and a girl her age shouldn't glisten like that. Nevertheless, I gave her a grin to show that I appreciated the prolonged glance.

Meanwhile the lawyer, Judge Henry Arnold, had hung up his own hat. During the day I had of course made inquiries on all of them, and had learned that he rated the 'Judge' only because he had once been a city magistrate. Even so, that's what they called him, so the sight of him was a let-down. He was a little sawed-off squirt with a bald head so flat on top you could have kept an ashtray on it, and his nose was pushed in. He must have been better arranged inside than out, since he had quite a list of clients among the higher levels on Broadway.

Taking them to the office and introducing them to Wolfe, I undertook to assign them to some of the yellow chairs, but the baritone spied the red leather one and copped it. I was helping Fritz fill their orders for drinks when the buzzer sounded and I went back to the front.

It was Dr Nicholas Lloyd. He had no hat, so that point wasn't raised, and I decided that the searching look he aimed at me was merely professional and automatic, to see if I was anemic or diabetic or what. With his lined handsome face and worried dark eyes he looked every inch a doctor and even surgeon, fully up to the classy reputation my inquiries had disclosed. When I ushered him to the office his eyes lighted up at the sight of the refreshment table, and he was the best customer – bourbon and water with mint – all evening.

The last two came together – at least they were on the stoop together when I opened the door. I would probably have given Adele Bosley the red leather chair if James hadn't already copped it. She shook hands and said she had been wanting to meet Archie Goodwin for years, but that was just public relations and went out the other ear. The point is that from my desk I get most of a party profile or three-quarters, but the one in the red leather chair fullface, and I like a view. Not that Adele Bosley was a pin-up, and she must have been in the fifth or sixth grade when Clara James was born, but her smooth tanned skin and pretty mouth without too much lipstick and nice brown eyes were good scenery.

Rupert Grove didn't shake hands, which didn't upset me. He may have been a good manager for Alberto Mion's affairs, but not for his own physique. A man can be fat and still have integrity, as for instance Falstaff or Nero Wolfe, but that bird had lost all sense of proportion. His legs were short, and it was all in the middle third of him. If you wanted to be polite and look at his face you had to concentrate. I did so, since I needed to size them all up, and saw nothing worthy of recording but a pair of shrewd shifty black eyes.

When these two were seated and provided with liquid, Wolfe fired the starting gun. He said he was sorry it had been necessary to ask them to exert themselves on a hot evening, but that the question at issue could be answered fairly and equitably only if all concerned had a voice in it. The responding murmurs went all the way from acquiescence to extreme irritation. Judge Arnold said belligerently that there was no question at legal issue because Alberto Mion was dead.

'Nonsense,' Wolfe said curtly. 'If that were true, you, a lawyer, wouldn't have bothered to come. Anyway, the purpose of this meeting is to keep it from becoming a legal issue. Four of you telephoned Mrs Mion today to ask if I am acting for her, and were told that I am. On her behalf I want to collect the facts. I may as well tell you, without prejudice to her, that she will accept my recommendation. Should I decide that a large sum is due her you may of course contest; but if I form the opinion that she has no claim she will bow to it. Under that responsibility I need all the facts. Therefore –'

'You're not a court,' Arnold snapped.

'No, sir, I'm not. If you prefer it in a court you'll get it.' Wolfe's eyes moved. 'Miss Bosley, would your employers welcome that kind of publicity? Dr Lloyd, would you rather appear as an expert on the witness-stand or talk it over here? Mr Grove, how would your client feel about it if he were alive? Mr James, what do you think? You wouldn't relish the publicity either, would you? Particularly since your daughter's name would appear?'

'Why would her name appear?' James demanded in his trained baritone.

Wolfe turned up a palm. 'It would be evidence. It would be established that just before you struck Mr Mion you said to him, "You let my daughter alone, you bastard."'

I put my hand in my pocket. I have a rule, justified by experience, that whenever a killer is among those present, or may be, a gun must be handy. Not regarding the back of the third drawer of my desk, where they are kept, as handy enough, the routine is to transfer one to my pocket before guests gather. That was the pocket I put my hand in, knowing how cocky James was. But he didn't leave his chair. He merely blurted, 'That's a lie!'

Wolfe grunted. 'Ten people heard you say it. That would indeed be publicity, if you denied it under oath and all ten of them, subpoenaed to testify, contradicted you. I honestly think it would be better to discuss it with me.'

'What do you want to know?' Judge Arnold demanded.

'The facts. First, the one already moot. When I lie I like to know it. Mr Grove, you were present when that famous blow was struck. Have I quoted Mr James correctly?'

'Yes.' Grove's voice was a high tenor, which pleased me.

'You heard him say that?'

'Yes.'

'Miss Bosley. Did you?'

She looked uncomfortable. 'Wouldn't it be better to –'

'Please. You're not under oath, but I'm merely collecting facts, and I was told I lied. Did you hear him say that?'

'Yes, I did.' Adele's eyes went to James. 'I'm sorry, Gif.'

'But it's not true!' Clara James cried.

Wolfe rasped at her, 'We're all lying?'

I could have warned her, when she gave me that glance in the hall, to look out for him. Not only was she a sophisticated young woman, and not only did she glisten, but her slimness was the kind that comes from not eating enough, and Wolfe absolutely cannot stand people who don't eat enough. I knew he would be down on her from the go.

But she came back at him. 'I don't mean that,' she said scornfully. 'Don't be so touchy! I mean I had lied to my father. What he thought about Alberto and me wasn't true. I was just bragging to him because – it doesn't matter why. Anyway, what I told him wasn't true, and I told him so that night!'

'Which night?'

'When we got home – from the stage party after *Rigoletto*. That was where my father knocked Alberto down, you know, right there on the stage. When we got home I told him that what I had said about Alberto and me wasn't true.'

'When were you lying, the first time or the second?'

'Don't answer that, my dear,' Judge Arnold broke in, lawyering. He looked sternly at Wolfe. 'This is all irrelevant. You're welcome to facts, but relevant facts. What Miss James told her father is immaterial.'

Wolfe shook his head. 'Oh no.' His eyes went from right to left and back again. 'Apparently I haven't made it plain. Mrs Mion wants me to decide for her whether she has a just claim, not so much legally as morally. If it appears that Mr James' assault on Mr Mion was morally justified that will be a factor in my decision.' He focused on Clara. 'Whether my question was relevant or not, Miss James, I admit it was embarrassing and therefore invited mendacity. I withdraw it. Try this instead. Had you, prior to that stage party, given your father to understand that Mr Mion had seduced you?'

'Well –' Clara laughed. It was a tinkly soprano laugh, rather attractive. 'What a nice old-fashioned way to say it! Yes, I had. But it wasn't true!'

'But you believed it, Mr James?'

Gifford James was having trouble holding himself in, and I concede that such leading questions about his daughter's honour from a stranger must have been hard to take. But after all it wasn't new to the rest of the audience, and anyway it sure was relevant. He forced himself to speak with quiet dignity. 'I believed what my daughter told me, yes.'

Wolfe nodded. 'So much for that,' he said in a relieved tone. 'I'm glad that part is over with.' His eyes moved. 'Now, Mr Grove, tell me about the conference in Mr Mion's studio, a few hours before he died.'

Rupert the Fat had his head tilted to one side, with his shrewd black eyes meeting Wolfe's. 'It was for the purpose,' he said in his high tenor, 'of discussing the demand Mion had made for payment of damages.'

'You were there?'

'I was, naturally. I was Mion's adviser and manager. Also Miss Bosley, Dr Lloyd, Mr James, and Judge Arnold.'

'Who arranged the conference, you?'

'In a way, yes. Arnold suggested it, and I told Mion and phoned Dr Lloyd and Miss Bosley.'

'What was decided?'

'Nothing. That is, nothing definite. There was the question of the extent of the damage – how soon Mion would be able to sing again.'

'What was your position?'

Grove's eyes tightened. 'Didn't I say I was Mion's manager?'

'Certainly. I mean, what position did you take regarding the payment of damages?'

'I thought a preliminary payment of fifty thousand dollars should be made at once. Even if Mion's voice was soon all right he had already lost that and more. His South American tour had been cancelled, and he had been unable to make a lot of records on contract, and then radio offers –'

'Nothing like fifty thousand dollars,' Judge Arnold asserted aggressively. There was nothing wrong with his larynx, small as he was. 'I showed figures –'

'To hell with your figures! Anybody can –'

'Please!' Wolfe rapped on his desk with a knuckle. 'What was Mr Mion's position?'

'The same as mine, of course.' Grove was scowling at Arnold as he spoke to Wolfe. 'We had discussed it.'

'Naturally.' Wolfe's eyes went left. 'How did you feel about it, Mr James?'

116

'I think,' Arnold broke in, 'that I should speak for my client. You agree, Gif?'

'Go ahead,' the baritone muttered.

Arnold did, and took most of one of the three hours. I was surprised that Wolfe didn't stop him, and finally decided that he let him ramble on just to get additional support for his long-standing opinion of lawyers. If so, he got it. Arnold covered everything. He had a lot to say about tort-feasors, going back a couple of centuries, with emphasis on the mental state of a tort-feasor. Another item he covered at length was proximate cause. He got really worked up about proximate cause, but it was so involved that I lost track and passed.

Here and there, though, he made sense. At once point he said, 'The idea of a preliminary payment, as thĕy called it, was clearly inadmissible. It is not reasonable to expect a man, even if he stipulates an obligation, to make a payment thereon until either the total amount of the obligation, or an exact method of computing it, has been agreed upon.'

At another point he said, 'The demand for so large a sum can in fact be properly characterized as blackmail. They knew that if the action went to trial, and if we showed that my client's deed sprang from his knowledge that his daughter had been wronged, a jury would not be likely to award damages. But they also knew that we would be averse to making that defense.'

'Not his knowledge,' Wolfe objected. 'Merely his belief. His daughter says she had misinformed him.'

'We could have showed knowledge,' Arnold insisted.

I looked at Clara with my brows up. She was being contradicted flatly on the chronology of her lie and her truth, but either she and her father didn't get the implication of it or they didn't want to get started on that again.

At another point Arnold said, 'Even if my client's deed was tortious and damages would be collectable, the amount could not be agreed upon until the extent of the injury was known. We offered, without prejudice, twenty thousand dollars in full settlement, for a general release. They refused. They wanted a payment forthwith on account. We refused that on principle. In the end there was agreement on only one thing: that an effort should be made to arrive at the total amount of damage. Of course that was what Dr Lloyd was there for. He was asked for a prognosis, and he stated that – but you don't need to take hearsay. He's here, and you can get it direct.'

Wolfe nodded. 'If you please, Doctor?'

I thought, My God, here we go again with another expert.

But Lloyd had mercy on us. He kept it down to our level and didn't take anything like an hour. Before he spoke he took another swallow from his third helping of bourbon and water with mint, which had smoothed out some of the lines on his handsome face and taken some of the worry from his eyes.

'I'll try to remember,' he said slowly, 'exactly what I told them. First I described the damage the blow had done. The thyroid and arytenoid cartilages on the left side had been severely injured, and to a lesser extent the criciod.' He smiled – a superior smile, but not supercilious. 'I waited two weeks, using indicated treatment, thinking an operation might not be required, but it was. When I got inside I confess I was relieved; it wasn't as bad as I had feared. It was a simple operation, and he healed admirably. I wouldn't have been risking much that day if I had given assurance that his voice would be as good as ever in two months, three at the most, but the larynx is an extremely delicate instrument, and a tenor like Mion's is a remarkable phenomenon, so I was cautious enough merely to say that I would be surprised and disappointed if he wasn't ready, fully ready, for the opening of the next opera season, seven months from then. I added that my hope and expectation were actually more optimistic than that.'

Lloyd pursed his lips. 'That was it, I think. Nevertheless, I welcomed the suggestion that my prognosis should be reinforced by Rentner's. Apparently it would be a major factor in the decision about the amount to be paid in damages, and I didn't want the sole responsibility.'

'Rentner? Who was he?' Wolfe asked.

'Dr Abraham Rentner of Mount Sinai,' Lloyd replied, in the tone I would use if someone asked me who Jackie Robinson was. 'I phoned him and made an appointment for the following morning.'

'I insisted on it,' Rupert the Fat said importantly. 'Mion had a right to collect not sometime in the distant future, but then and there. They wouldn't pay unless a total was agreed on, and if we had to name a total I wanted to be damn sure it was enough. Don't forget that that day Mion couldn't sing a note.'

'He wouldn't have been able even to let out a pianissimo for at least two months,' Lloyd bore him out. 'I gave that as the minimum.'

'There seems,' Judge Arnold interposed, 'to be an implication that we opposed the suggestion that a second professional opinion be secured. I must protest –'

'You did!' Grove squeaked.

'We did not!' Gifford James barked. 'We merely –'

The three of them went at it, snapping and snarling. It seemed to me that they might have saved their energy for the big issue, was anything coming to Mrs Mion and if so how much, but not those babies. Their main concern was to avoid the slightest risk of agreeing on anything at all. Wolfe patiently let them get where they were headed for – nowhere – and then invited a new voice in. He turned to Adele and spoke.

'Miss Bosley, we haven't heard from you. Which side were you on?'

IV

Adele Bosley had been sitting taking it in, sipping occasionally at her rum collins – now her second one – and looking, I thought, pretty damn intelligent. Though it was the middle of August, she was the only one of the six who had a really good tan. Her public relations with the sun were excellent.

She shook her head. 'I wasn't on either side, Mr Wolfe. My only interest was that of my employer, the Metropolitan Opera Association. Naturally we wanted it settled privately, without any scandal. I had no opinion whatever on whether – on the point at issue.'

'And expressed none?'

'No. I merely urged them to get it settled if possible.'

'Fair enough!' Clara James blurted. It was a sneer. 'You might have helped my father a little, since he got your job for you. Or had you –'

'Be quiet, Clara!' James told her with authority.

But she ignored him and finished it. 'Or had you already paid in full for that?'

I was shocked. Judge Arnold looked pained. Rupert the Fat giggled. Doc Lloyd took a gulp of bourbon and water.

In view of the mildly friendly attitude I was developing toward Adele I sort of hoped she would throw something at the slim and glistening Miss James, but all she did was appeal to the father. 'Can't you handle the brat, Gif?'

Then, without waiting for an answer, she turned to Wolfe. 'Miss James likes to use her imagination. What she implied is not on the record. Not anybody's record.'

Wolfe nodded. 'It wouldn't belong on this one anyhow.' He made a face. 'To go back to relevancies, what time did that conference break up?'

'Why – Mr James and Judge Arnold left first, around four-thirty. Then Dr Lloyd, soon after. I stayed a few minutes with Mion and Mr Grove, and then went.'

'Where did you go?'

'To my office, on Broadway.'

'How long did you stay at your office?'

She looked surprised. 'I don't know – yes, I do too, of course. Until a little after seven. I had things to do, and I typed a confidential report of the conference at Mion's.'

'Did you see Mion again before he died? Or phone him?'

'See him?' She was more surprised. 'How could I? Don't you know he was found dead at seven o'clock? That was before I left the office.'

'Did you phone him? Between four-thirty and seven?'

'No.' Adele was puzzled and slightly exasperated. It struck me that Wolfe was recklessly getting onto thin ice, mighty close to the forbidden subject of murder. Adele added, 'I don't know what you're getting at.'

'Neither do I,' Judge Arnold put in with emphasis. He smiled sarcastically. 'Unless it's force of habit with you, asking people where they were at the time a death by violence occurred. Why don't you go after all of us?'

'That's what I intend to do,' Wolfe said imperturbably. 'I would like to know why Mion decided to kill himself, because that has a bearing on the opinion I shall give his widow. I understand that two or three of you have said that he was wrought up when that conference ended, but not despondent or splenetic. I know he committed suicide; the police can't be flummoxed on a thing like that; but why?'

'I doubt,' Adele Bosley offered, 'if you know how a singer – especially a great artist like Mion – how he feels when he can't let a sound out, when he can't even talk except in an undertone or a whisper. It's horrible.'

'Anyway, you never knew with him,' Rupert Grove contributed. 'In rehearsal I've heard him do an aria like an angel and then rush out weeping because he thought he had slurred a release. One minute he was up in the sky and the next he was under a rug.'

Wolfe grunted. 'Nevertheless, anything said to him by anyone during the two hours preceding his suicide is pertinent to this inquiry, to establish Mrs Mion's moral position. I want to know where you people were that day, after the conference up to seven o'clock, and what you did.'

'My God!' Judge Arnold threw up his hands. The hands came down again. 'All right, it's getting late. As Miss Bosley told you, my client and I left Mion's studio together. We went to the Churchill bar and drank and talked. A little later Miss James joined us, stayed long enough for a drink, I suppose half an hour, and left. Mr James and I remained together until after seven. During that time neither of us communicated with Mion, nor arranged for anyone else to. I believe that covers it?'

'Thank you,' Wolfe said politely. 'You corroborate, of course, Mr James?'

'I do,' the baritone said gruffly. 'This is a lot of goddam nonsense.'

'It does begin to sound like it,' Wolfe conceded. 'Dr Lloyd? If you don't mind?'

He hadn't better, since he had been mellowed by four ample helpings of our best bourbon, and he didn't. 'Not at all,' he said cooperatively. 'I made calls on five patients, two on upper Fifth Avenue, one in the East Sixties, and two at the hospital. I got home a little after six and had just finished dressing after taking a bath when Fred Weppler phoned me about Mion. Of course I went at once.'

'You hadn't seen Mion or phoned him?'

'Not since I left after the conference. Perhaps I should have, but I had no idea – I'm not a psychiatrist, but I was his doctor.'

'He was mercurial, was he?'

'Yes, he was.' Lloyd pursed his lips. 'Of course, that's not a medical term.'

'Far from it,' Wolfe agreed. He shifted his gaze. 'Mr Grove, I don't have to ask you if you phoned Mion, since it is on record that you did. Around five o'clock?'

Rupert the Fat had his head tilted again. Apparently that was his favourite pose for conversing. He corrected Wolfe. 'It was after five. More like a quarter past.'

'Where did you phone from?'

'The Harvard Club.'

I thought, I'll be damned, it takes all kinds to make a Harvard Club. 'What was said?'

'Not much.' Grove's lips twisted. 'It's none of your damn business, you know, but the others have obliged, and I'll string along. I had forgotten to ask him if he would endorse a certain product for a

121

thousand dollars, and the agency wanted an answer. We talked less than five minutes. First he said he wouldn't and then he said he would. That was all.'

'Did he sound like a man getting ready to kill himself.'

'Not the slightest. He was glum, but naturally, since he couldn't sing and couldn't expect to for at least two months.'

'After you phoned Mion what did you do?'

'I stayed at the club. I ate dinner there and hadn't quite finished when the news came that Mion had killed himself. So I'm still behind that ice cream and coffee.'

'That's too bad. When you phoned Mion, did you again try to persuade him not to press his claim against Mr James?'

Grove's head straightened up. 'Did I what?' he demanded.

'You heard me,' Wolfe said rudely. 'What's surprising about it? Naturally Mrs Mion has informed me, since I'm working for her. You were opposed to Mion's asking for payment in the first place and tried to talk him out of it. You said the publicity would be so harmful that it wasn't worth it. He demanded that you support the claim and threatened to cancel your contract if you refused. Isn't that correct?'

'It is not.' Grove's black eyes were blazing. 'It wasn't like that at all! I merely gave him my opinion. When it was decided to make the claim I went along.' His voice went up a notch higher, though I wouldn't have thought it possible. 'I certainly did!'

'I see.' Wolfe wasn't arguing. 'What is your opinion now, about Mrs Mion's claim?'

'I don't think she has one. I don't believe she can collect. If I were in James' place I certainly wouldn't pay her a cent.'

Wolfe nodded. 'You don't like her, do you?'

'Frankly, I don't. No. I never have. Do I have to like her?'

'No, indeed. Especially since she doesn't like you either.' Wolfe shifted in his chair and leaned back. I could tell from the line of his lips, straightened out, that the next item on the agenda was one he didn't care for, and I understood why when I saw his eyes level at Clara James. I'll bet that if he had known that he would have to be dealing with that type he wouldn't have taken the job. He spoke to her testily. 'Miss James, you've heard what has been said?'

'I was wondering,' she complained, as if she had been holding in a grievance, 'if you were going to go on ignoring me. I was around too, you know.'

'I know. I haven't forgotten you.' His tone implied that he only wished he could. 'When you had a drink in the Churchill bar with your father and Judge Arnold, why did they send you up to Mion's studio to see him? What for?'

Arnold and James protested at once, loudly and simultaneously. Wolfe, paying no attention to them, waited to hear Clara, her voice having been drowned by theirs.

'... nothing to do with it,' she was finishing. 'I sent myself.'

'It was your own idea?'

'Entirely. I have one once in a while, all alone.'

'What did you go for?'

'You don't need to answer, my dear,' Arnold told her.

She ignored him. 'They told me what had happened at the conference, and I was mad. I thought it was a holdup – but I wasn't going to tell Alberto that. I thought I could talk him out of it.'

'You went to appeal to him for old times' sake?'

She looked pleased. 'You have the nicest way of putting things! Imagine a girl my age having old times!'

'I'm glad you like my diction, Miss James.' Wolfe was furious. 'Anyhow, you went. Arriving at a quarter past six?'

'Just about, yes.'

'Did you see Mion?'

'No.'

'Why not?'

'He wasn't there. At least –' She stopped. Her eyes weren't glistening quite so much. She went on, 'That's what I thought then. I went to the thirteenth floor and rang the bell at the door to the studio. It's a loud bell – he had it loud to be heard above his voice and the piano when he was practicing – but I couldn't hear it from the hall because the door is soundproofed too, and after I had pushed the button a few times I wasn't sure the bell was ringing so I knocked on the door. I like to finish anything I start, and I thought he must be there, so I rang the bell some more and took off my shoe and pounded on the door with the heel. Then I went down to the twelfth floor by the public stairs and rang the bell at the apartment door. That was really stupid, because I know how Mrs Mion hates me, but anyway I did. She came to the door and said she thought Alberto was up in the studio, and I said he wasn't, and she shut the door in my face. I went home and mixed myself a drink – which reminds me, I must admit this is good scotch, though I never heard of it before.'

She lifted her glass and jiggled it to swirl the ice. 'Any questions?'

'No,' Wolfe growled. He glanced at the clock on the wall and then along the line of faces. 'I shall certainly report to Mrs Mion,' he told them, 'that you were not grudging with the facts.'

'And what else?' Arnold inquired.

'I don't know. We'll see.'

That they didn't like. I wouldn't have supposed anyone could name a subject on which those six characters would have been in unanimous accord, but Wolfe turned the trick in five words. They wanted a verdict; failing that, an opinion; failing that, at least a hint. Adele Bosley was stubborn, Rupert the Fat was so indignant he squeaked, and Judge Arnold was next door to nasty. Wolfe was patient up to a point, but finally stood up and told them good night as if he meant it. The note it ended on was such that before going not one of them shelled out a word of appreciation for all the refreshment, not even Adele, the expert on public relations, or Doc Lloyd, who had practically emptied the bourbon bottle.

With the front door locked and bolted for the night, I returned to the office. To my astonishment Wolfe, was still on his feet, standing over by the bookshelves, glaring at the backbones.

'Restless?' I asked courteously.

He turned and said aggressively, 'I want another bottle of beer.'

'Nuts. You've had five since dinner.' I didn't bother to put much feeling into it, as the routine was familiar. He had himself set the quota of five bottles between dinner and bedtime, and usually stuck to it, but when anything sent his humour far enough down he liked to shift the responsibility so he could be sore at me too.

It was just part of my job. 'Nothing doing,' I said firmly. 'I counted 'em. Five. What's the trouble, a whole evening gone and still no murderer?'

'Bah.' He compressed his lips. 'That's not it. If that were all we could close it up before going to bed. It's that confounded gun with wings.' He gazed at me with his eyes narrowed, as if suspecting that I had wings too. 'I could, of course, just ignore it – No. No, in view of the state our clients are in, it would be foolhardy. We'll have to clear it up. There's no alternative.'

'That's a nuisance. Can I help any?'

'Yes. Phone Mr Cramer first thing in the morning. Ask him to be here at eleven o'clock.'

My brows went up. 'But he's interested only in homicides. Do I tell him we've got one to show him?'

'No. Tell him I guarantee that it's worth the trouble.'

Wolfe took a step toward me. 'Archie.'

'Yes, sir.'

'I've had a bad evening and I'll have another bottle,'

'You will not. Not a chance.' Fritz had come in and we were starting to clear up. 'It's after midnight and you're in the way. Go to bed.'

'One wouldn't hurt him,' Fritz muttered.

'You're a help,' I said bitterly. 'I warn both of you, I've got a gun in my pocket. What a household!'

V

For nine months of the year Inspector Cramer of Homicide, big and broad and turning gray, looked the part well enough, but in the summertime the heat kept his face so red that he was a little gaudy. He knew it and didn't like it, and as a result he was some harder to deal with in August than in January. If an occasion arises for me to commit a murder in Manhattan I hope it will be winter.

Tuesday at noon he sat in the red leather chair and looked at Wolfe with no geniality. Detained by another appointment, he hadn't been able to make it at eleven, the hour when Wolfe adjourns the morning session with his orchids up in the plant rooms. Wolfe wasn't exactly beaming either, and I was looking forward to some vaudeville. Also I was curious to see how Wolfe would go about getting dope on a murder from Cramer without spilling it that there had been one, as Cramer was by no means a nitwit.

'I'm on my way uptown,' Cramer grumbled, 'and haven't got much time.'

That was probably a barefaced lie. He merely didn't want to admit that an inspector of the NYPD would call on a private detective on request, even though it was Nero Wofle and I had told him we had something hot.

'What is it,' he grumbled on, 'the Dickinson thing? Who brought you in?'

Wolfe shook his head. 'No one, thank heaven. It's about the murder of Alberto Mion.'

I goggled at him. This was away beyond me. Right off he had let the dog loose, when I had thought the whole point was that there was no dog on the place.

'Mion?' Cramer wasn't interested. 'Not one of mine.'

125

'It soon will be. Alberto Mion, the famous opera singer. Four months ago, on April nineteenth. In his studio on East End Avenue. Shot –'

'Oh.' Cramer nodded. 'Yeah, I remember. But you're stretching it a little. It was suicide.'

'No. It was first-degree murder.'

Cramer regarded him for three breaths. Then, in no hurry, he got a cigar from his pocket, inspected it, and stuck it in his mouth. In a moment he took it out again.

'I have never known it to fail,' he remarked, 'that you can be counted on for a headache. Who says it was murder?'

'I have reached that conclusion.'

'Then that's settled.' Cramer's sarcasm was usually a little heavy. 'Have you bothered any about evidence?'

'I have none.'

'Good. Evidence just clutters a murder up.' Cramer stuck the cigar back in his mouth and exploded, 'When did you start keeping your sentences so goddam short? Go ahead and talk!'

'Well –' Wolfe considered. 'It's a little difficult. You're probably not familiar with the details, since it was so long ago and was recorded as suicide.'

'I remember it fairly well. As you say, he was famous. Go right ahead.'

Wolfe leaned back and closed his eyes. 'Interrupt me if you need to. I had six people here for a talk last evening.' He pronounced the names and identified them. 'Five of them were present at a conference in Mion's studio which ended two hours before he was found dead. The sixth, Miss James, banged on the studio door at a quarter past six and got no reply, presumably because he was dead then. My conclusion that Mion was murdered is based on things I have heard said. I'm not going to repeat them to you – because it would take too long, because it's a question of emphasis and interpretation, and because you have already heard them.'

'I wasn't here last evening,' Cramer said dryly.

'So you weren't. Instead of "you", I should have said the Police Department. It must all be in the files. They were questioned at the time it happened, and told their stories as they have now told them to me. You can get it there. Have you ever known me to have to eat my words?'

126

'I've seen times when I would have liked to shove them down your throat.'

'But you never have. Here are three more I shall not eat: Mion was murdered. I won't tell you, now, how I reached that conclusion; study your files.'

Cramer was keeping himself under restraint. 'I don't have to study them,' he declared, 'for one detail – how he was killed. Are you saying he fired the gun himself but was driven to it?'

'No. The murderer fired the gun.'

'It must have been quite a murderer. It's quite a trick to pry a guy's mouth open and stick a gun in it without getting bit. Would you mind naming him?'

Wolfe shook his head. 'I haven't got that far yet. But it isn't the objection you raise that's bothering me; that can be overcome; it's something else.' He leaned forward and was earnest. 'Look here, Mr Cramer. It would not have been impossible for me to see this through alone, deliver the murderer and the evidence to you, and flap my wings and crow. But first, I have no ambition to expose you as a zany, since you're not; and second, I need your help. I am not now prepared to prove to you that Mion was murdered; I can only assure you that he was and repeat that I won't have to eat it – and neither will you. Isn't that enough, at least to arouse your interest?'

Cramer stopped chewing the cigar. He never lit one. 'Sure,' he said grimly. 'Hell, I'm interested. Another first-class headache. I'm flattered you want me to help. How?'

'I want you to arrest two people as material witnesses, question them, and let them out on bail.'

'Which two? Why not all six?' I warned you his sarcasm was hefty.

'But' – Wolfe ignored it – 'under clearly defined conditions. They must not know that I am responsible; they must not even know that I have spoken with you. The arrests should be made late this afternoon or early evening, so they'll be kept in custody all night and until they arrange for bail in the morning. The bail need not be high; that's not important. The questioning should be fairly prolonged and severe, not merely a gesture, and if they get little or no sleep so much the better. Of course this sort of thing is routine for you.'

'Yes, we do it constantly.' Cramer's tone was unchanged. 'But when we ask for a warrant we like to have a fairly good excuse. We wouldn't like to put down that it's to do Nero Wolfe a favour. I don't want to be contrary.'

'There's ample excuse for these two. They *are* material witnesses. They are indeed.'

'You haven't named them. Who are they?'

'The man and woman who found the body. Mr Frederick Weppler, the music critic, and Mrs Mion, the widow.'

This time I didn't goggle, but I had to catch myself quick. It was a first if there ever was one. Time and again I have seen Wolfe go far, on a few occasions much too far, to keep a client from being pinched. He regards it as an unbearable personal insult. And here he was, practically begging the law to haul Fred and Peggy in, when I had deposited her check for five grand only the day before!

'Oh,' Cramer said. 'Them?'

'Yes, sir,' Wolfe assured him cooperatively. 'As you know or can learn from the files, there is plenty to ask them about it. Mr Weppler was there for lunch that day, with others, and when the others left her remained with Mrs Mion. What was discussed? What did they do that afternoon; where were they? Why did Mr Weppler return to the Mion apartment at seven o'clock? Why did he and Mrs Mion ascend together to the studio? After finding the body, why did Mr Weppler go downstairs before notifying the police, to get a list of names from the doorman and elevator man? An extraordinary performance. Was it Mion's habit to take an afternoon nap? Did he sleep with his mouth open?'

'Much obliged,' Cramer said not gratefully. 'You're a wonder at thinking of questions to ask. But even if Mion did take naps with his mouth open, I doubt if he did it standing up. And after the bullet left his head it went up to the ceiling, as I remember it. Now.' Cramer put his palms on the arms of the chair, with the cigar in his mouth tilted up at about the angle the gun in Mion's mouth had probably been. 'Who's your client?'

'No,' Wolfe said regretfully. 'I'm not ready to disclose that.'

'I thought not. In fact, there isn't one single damn thing you have disclosed. You've got no evidence, or if you have any you're keeping it under your belt. You've got a conclusion you like, that will help a client you won't name, and you want me to test it for you by arresting two reputable citizens and giving them the works. I've seen samples of your nerve before, but this is tops. For God's sake!'

'I've told you I won't eat it, and neither will you. If –'

'You'd eat one of your own orchids if you had to earn a fee!'

That started the fireworks. I have sat many times and listened to that pair in a slugging match and enjoyed every minute of it, but this one got so hot that I wasn't exactly sure I was enjoying it. At 12:40 Cramer was on his feet, starting to leave. At 12:45 he was back in the red leather chair, shaking his fist and snarling. At 12:48 Wolfe was leaning back with his eyes shut, pretending he was deaf. At 12:52 he was pounding his desk and bellowing.

At ten past one it was all over. Cramer had taken it and was gone. He had made a condition, that there would first be a check of the record and a staff talk, but that didn't matter, since the arrests were to be postponed until after judges had gone home. He accepted the proviso that the victims were not to know that Wolfe had a hand in it, so it could have been said that he was knuckling under, but actually he was merely using horse sense. No matter how much he discounted Wolfe's three words that were not to be eaten – and he knew from experience how risky it was to discount Wolfe just for the hell of it – they made it fairly probable that it wouldn't hurt to give Mion's death another look; and in that case a session with the couple who had found the body was as good a way to start as any. As a matter of fact, the only detail that Cramer choked on was Wolfe's refusal to tell who his client was.

As I followed Wolfe into the dining room for lunch I remarked to his outspread back, 'There are already eight hundred and nine people in the metropolitan area who would like to poison you. This will make it eight hundred and eleven. Don't think they won't find out sooner or later.'

'Of course they will,' he conceded, pulling his chair back. 'But too late.'

The rest of that day and evening nothing happened at all, as far as we knew.

VI

I was at my desk in the office at 10:40 the next morning when the phone rang. I got it and told the transmitter, 'Nero Wolfe's office, Archie Goodwin speaking.'

'I want to talk to Mr Wolfe.'

'He won't be available until eleven o'clock. Can I help?'

'This is urgent. This is Weppler, Frederick Weppler. I'm in a booth in a drugstore on Ninth Avenue near Twentieth Street. Mrs Mion is with me. We've been arrested.'

'Good God!' I was horrified. 'What for?'

'To ask us about Mion's death. They had material-witness warrants. They kept us all night, and we just got out on bail. I had a lawyer arrange for the bail, but I don't want him to know about – that we consulted Wolfe, and he's not with us. We want to see Wolfe.'

'You sure do,' I agreed emphatically. 'It's a damn outrage. Come on up here. He'll be down from the plant rooms by the time you arrive. Grab a taxi.'

'We can't. That's why I'm phoning. We're being followed by two detectives and we don't want them to know we're seeing Wolfe. How can we shake them?'

It would have saved time and energy to tell him to come ahead, that a couple of official tails needn't worry him, but I thought I'd better play along.

'For God's sake,' I said, disgusted. 'Cops give me a pain in the neck. Listen. Are you listening?'

'Yes.'

'Go to the Feder Paper Company, Five-thirty-five West Seventeenth Street. In the office ask for Mr Sol Feder. Tell him your name is Montgomery. He'll conduct you along a passage that exits on Eighteenth Street. Right there, either at the curb or double-parked, will be a taxi with a handkerchief on the door handle. I'll be in it. Don't lose any time climbing in. Have you got it?'

'I think so. You'd better repeat the address.'

I did so, and told him to wait ten minutes before starting, to give me time to get there. Then, after hanging up, I phoned Sol Feder to instruct him, got Wolfe on the house phone to inform him, and beat it.

I should have told him to wait fifteen or twenty minutes instead of ten, because I got to my post on Eighteenth Street barely in time. My taxi had just stopped, and I was reaching out to tie my handkerchief on the door handle, when here they came across the sidewalk like a bat out of hell. I swung the door wide, and Fred practically threw Peggy in and dived in after her.

'Okay driver,' I said sternly, 'you know where,' and we rolled.

As we swung into Tenth avenue I asked if they had had breakfast and they said yes, not with any enthusiasm. The fact is, they looked as if they were entirely out of enthusiasm. Peggy's lightweight green jacket, which she had on over a tan cotton dress, was rumpled and not very clean, and her face looked neglected. Fred's hair might not have been combed for a month, and his brown tropical worsted was anything but natty. They sat holding hands, and about once a minute Fred twisted around to look through the rear window.

'We're loose all right,' I assured him. 'I've been saving Sol Feder just for an emergency like this.'

It was only a five-minute ride. When I ushered them into the office Wolfe was there in his custom-made chair behind his desk. He arose to greet them, invited them to sit, asked if they had breakfasted properly, and said that the news of their arrest had been an unpleasant shock.

'One thing,' Fred blurted, still standing. 'We came to see you and consult you in confidence, and forty-eight hours later we were arrested. Was that pure coincidence?'

Wolfe finished getting himself re-established in his chair. 'That won't help us any, Mr Weppler,' he said without resentment. 'If that's your frame of mind you'd better go somewhere and cool off. You and Mrs Mion are my clients. An insinuation that I am capable of acting against the interest of a client is too childish for discussion. What did the police ask you about?'

But Fred wasn't satisfied. 'You're not a double-crosser,' he conceded. 'I know that. But what about Goodwin here? He may not be a double-crosser either, but he might have got careless in conversation with someone.'

Wolfe's eyes moved. 'Archie. Did you?'

'No, sir. But he can postpone asking my pardon. They've had a hard night.' I looked at Fred. 'Sit down and relax. If I had a careless tongue I wouldn't last at this job a week.'

'It's damn funny,' Fred persisted. He sat. 'Mrs Mion agrees with me. Don't you, Peggy?'

Peggy, in the red leather chair, gave him a glance and then looked back at Wolfe. 'I did, I guess,' she confessed. 'Yes, I did. But now that I'm here, seeing you –' She made a gesture. 'Oh, forget it! There's no one else to go to. We know lawyers, of course, but we don't want to tell a lawyer what we know – about the gun. We've already told you. But now the police suspect something, and we're out on bail, and you've got to do something!'

'What did you find out Monday evening?' Fred demanded. 'You stalled when I phoned yesterday. What did they say?'

'They recited facts,' Wolfe replied. 'As I told you on the phone, I made some progress. I have nothing to add to that – now. But I want to know, I *must* know, what line the police took with you. Did they know what you told me about the gun?'

131

They both said no.

Wolfe grunted. 'Then I might reasonably ask that you withdraw your insinuation that I or Mr Goodwin betrayed you. What did they ask about?'

The answers to that took a good half an hour. The cops hadn't missed a thing that was included in the picture as they knew it, and, with instructions from Cramer to make it thorough, they hadn't left a scrap. Far from limiting it to the day of Mion's death, they had been particularly curious about Peggy's and Fred's feelings and actions during the months both prior and subsequent thereto. Several times I had to take the tip of my tongue between my teeth to keep from asking the clients why they hadn't told the cops to go soak their heads, but I really knew why: they had been scared. A scared man is only half a man. By the time they finished reporting on their ordeal I was feeling sympathetic, and even guilty on behalf of Wolfe, when suddenly he snapped me out of it.

He sat a while tapping the arm of his chair with a fingertip, and then looked at me and said abruptly, 'Archie. Draw a check to the order of Mrs Mion for five thousand dollars.'

They gawked at him. I got up and headed for the safe. They demanded to know what the idea was. I stood at the safe door to listen.

'I'm quitting,' Wolfe said curtly. 'I can't stand you. I told you Sunday that one or both of you were lying, and you stubbornly denied it. I undertook to work around your lie, and I did my best. But now that the police have got curious about Mion's death, and specifically about you, I refuse any longer to risk it. I am willing to be a Quixote, but not a chump. In breaking with you, I should tell you that I shall immediately inform Inspector Cramer of all that you have told me. If, when the police start the next round with you, you are fools enough to contradict me, heaven knows what will happen. Your best course will be to acknowledge the truth and let them pursue the investigation you hired me for; but I would also warn you that they are not simpletons and they too will know that you are lying – at least one of you. Archie, what are you standing there gaping for? Get the checkbook.'

I opened the safe door.

Neither of them had uttered a peep. I suppose they were too tired to react normally. As I returned to my desk they just sat, looking at each other. As I started making the entry on the stub, Fred's voice came.

'You can't do this. This isn't ethical.'

'Pfui.' Wolfe snorted. 'You hire me to get you out of a fix, and lie to me about it, and talk of ethics! Incidentally, I did make progress Monday evening. I cleared everything up but two details, but the devil of it is that one of them depends on you. I have got to know who put that gun on the floor beside the body. I am convinced that it was one of you, but you won't admit it. So I'm helpless and that's a pity, because I am also convinced that neither of you was involved in Mion's death. If there were –'

'What's that?' Fred demanded. There was nothing wrong with his reaction now. 'You're convinced that neither of us was involved?'

'I am.'

Fred was out of his chair. He went to Wolfe's desk, put his palms on it leaned forward, and said harshly. 'Do you mean that? Look at me. Open your eyes and look at me! Do you mean that?'

'Yes,' Wolfe told him. 'Certainly I mean it.'

Fred gazed at him another moment and then straightened up. 'All right,' he said, the harshness gone. 'I put the gun on the floor.'

A wail came from Peggy. She sailed out of her chair and to him and seized his arm with both hands. 'Fred! No! Fred!' she pleaded. I wouldn't have though her capable of wailing, but of course she was tired to begin with. He put a hand on top of hers and then decided that was inadequate and took her in his arms. For a minute he concentrated on her. Finally he turned his face to Wolfe and spoke.

'I may regret this, but if I do you will too. By God, you will.' He was quite positive of it. 'All right, I lied. I put the gun on the floor. Now it's up to you.' He held the other client closer. 'I did, Peggy. Don't say I should have told you – maybe I should – but I couldn't. It'll be all right, dearest, really it will –'

'Sit down,' Wolfe said crossly. After a moment he made it an order. 'Confound it, sit down!'

Peggy freed herself, Fred letting her go, and returned to her chair and dropped into it. Fred perched on its arm, with a hand on her far shoulder, and she put her hand up to his. Their eyes, suspicious, afraid, defiant, and hopeful all at once, were on Wolfe.

He stayed cross. 'I assume,' he said, 'that you see how it is. You haven't impressed me. I already knew one of you had put the gun there. How could anyone else have entered the studio during those few minutes? The truth you have told me will be worse than useless, it will be extremely dangerous, unless you follow it with more truth. Try another lie and there's no telling what will happen; I might not be able to save you. Where did you find it?'

'Don't worry,' Fred said quietly. 'You've screwed it out of me and you'll get it straight. When we went in and found the body I saw the gun where Mion always kept it, on the base of Caruso's bust. Mrs Mion didn't see it; she didn't look that way. When I left her in her bedroom I went back up. I picked the gun up by the trigger guard and smelled it; it had been fired. I put it on the floor by the body, returned to the apartment, went out, and took the elevator to the ground floor. The rest was just as I told you Sunday.'

Wolfe grunted. 'You may have been in love, but you didn't think much of her intelligence. You assumed that after killing him she hadn't had the wit to leave the gun where he might have dropped –'

'I did not, damn you!'

'Nonsense. Of course you did. Who else would you have wanted to shield? And afterward it got you in a pickle. When you had to agree with her that the gun hadn't been there when you and she entered, you were hobbled. You didn't dare tell her what you had done because of the implication that you suspected her, especially when she seemed to be suspecting you. You couldn't be sure whether she really did suspect you, or whether she was only –'

'I never did suspect him,' Peggy said firmly. It was a job to make her voice firm, but she managed it. 'And he never suspected me, not really. We just weren't sure – sure all the way down – and when you're in love and want it to last you've got to be sure.'

'That was it,' Fred agreed. They were looking at each other. 'That was it exactly.'

'All right, I'll take this,' Wolfe said curtly. 'I think you've told the truth, Mr Weppler.'

'I know damn well I have.'

Wolfe nodded. 'You should like it. I have a good ear for the truth. Now take Mrs Mion home. I've got to work, but first I must think it over. As I said, there were two details, and you've disposed of only one. You can't help with the other. Go home and eat something.'

'Who wants to eat?' Fred demanded fiercely. 'We want to know what you're going to do!'

'I've got to brush my teeth,' Peggy stated. I shot her a glance of admiration and affection. Women saying things like that at times like that is one of the reasons I enjoy their company. No man alive, under those circumstances, would have felt that he had to brush his teeth and said so.

Besides, it made it easier to get rid of them without being rude. Fred tried to insist that they had a right to know what the program was, and to help consider the prospects, but was finally compelled to accept Wolfe's mandate that when a man hired an expert the only authority he kept was the right to fire. That, combined with Peggy's longing for a toothbrush and Wolfe's assurance that he would keep them informed, got them on their way without a ruckus.

When, after letting them out, I returned to the office, Wolfe was drumming on his desk blotter with a paperknife, scowling at it, though I had told him a hundred times that it ruined the blotter. I went and got the checkbook and replaced it in the safe, having put nothing on the stub but the date, so no harm was done.

'Twenty minutes till lunch,' I announced, swivelling my chair and sitting. 'Will that be enough to hogtie the second detail?'

No reply.

I refused to be sensitive. 'If you don't mind,' I inquired pleasantly, 'what is the second detail?'

Again no reply, but after a moment he dropped the paperknife, leaned back, and sighed clear down.

'That confounded gun,' he growled. 'How did it get from the floor to the bust? Who moved it?'

I stared at him. 'My God,' I complained, 'you're hard to satisfy. You've just had two clients arrested and worked like a dog, getting the gun from the bust to the floor. Now you want to get from the floor to the bust again? What the hell!'

'Not again. Prior to.'

'Prior to what?'

'To the discovery of the body.' His eyes slanted at me. 'What do you think of this? A man – or a woman, no matter which – entered the studio and killed Mion in a manner that would convey a strong presumption of suicide. He deliberately planned it that way: it's not as difficult as the traditional police theory assumes. Then he placed the gun on the base of the bust, twenty feet away from the body, and departed. What do you think of it?'

'I don't think; I know. It didn't happen that way, unless he suddenly went batty after he pulled the trigger, which seems far-fetched.'

'Precisely. Having planned it to look like suicide, he placed the gun on the floor near the body. That is not discussible. But Mr Weppler found it on the bust. Who took it from the floor and put it there, and when and why?'

'Yeah.' I scratched my nose. 'That's annoying. I'll admit the question is relevant and material, but why the hell do you let it in? Why don't you let it lay? Get him or her pinched, indicted, and tried. The cops will testify that the gun was there on the floor, and that will suit the jury fine, since it was framed for suicide. Verdict, provided you've sewed up things like motive and opportunity, guilty.' I waved a hand. 'Simple. Why bring it up at all about the gun being so fidgety?'

Wolfe grunted. 'The clients. I have to earn my fee. They want their minds cleared, and they know the gun wasn't on the floor when they discovered the body. For the jury, I can't leave it that the gun was on the bust, and for the clients I can't leave it that it stayed on the floor where the murderer put it. Having, through Mr Weppler, got it from the bust to the floor, I must now go back and get it from the floor to the bust. You see that?'

'Only too plain.' I whistled for help. 'I'll be damned. How're you coming on?'

'I've just started.' He sat up straight. 'But I must clear my own mind, for lunch. Please hand me Mr Shanks's orchid catalogue.'

That was all for the moment, and during meals Wolfe excludes business not only from the conversation but also from the air. After lunch he returned to the office and got comfortable in his chair. For a while he just sat, and then began pushing his lips out and in, and I knew he was doing hard labour. Having no idea how he proposed to move the gun from the floor to the bust, I was wondering how long it might take, and whether he would have to get Cramer to arrest someone else, and if so who. I have seen him sit there like that, working for hours on end, but this time twenty minutes did it. It wasn't three o'clock yet when he pronounced my name gruffly and opened his eyes.

'Archie.'

'Yes, sir.'

'I can't do this. You'll have to.'

'You mean dope it? I'm sorry, I'm busy.'

'I mean execute it.' He made a face. 'I will not undertake to handle that young woman. It would be an ordeal, and I might botch it. It's just the thing for you. Your notebook. I'll dictate a document and then we'll discuss it.'

'Yes, sir. I wouldn't call Miss Bosley really young.'

'Not Miss Bosley. Miss James.'

'Oh.' I got the notebook.

VII

At a quarter past four, Wolfe having gone up to the plant rooms for his afternoon session with the orchids, I sat at my desk, glowering at the phone, feeling the way I imagine Jackie Robinson feels when he strikes out with the bases full. I had phoned Clara James to ask her to come for a ride with me in the convertible, and she had pushed my nose in.

If that sounds as if I like myself beyond reason, not so. I am quite aware that I bat close to a thousand on invitations to damsels only because I don't issue one unless the circumstances strongly indicate that it will be accepted. But that has got me accustomed to hearing yes, and therefore it was a rude shock to listen to her unqualified no. Besides, I had taken the trouble to go upstairs and change to a Pillater shirt and a tropical worsted made by Corley, and there I was, all dressed up.

I concocted three schemes and rejected them, concocted a fourth and bought it, reached for the phone, and dialed the number again. Clara's voice answered, as it had before. As soon as she learned who it was she got impatient.

'I told you I had a cocktail date! Please don't –'

'Hold it,' I told her bluntly. 'I made a mistake. I was being kind. I wanted to get you out into the nice open air before I told you the bad news. I –'

'What bad news?'

'A woman just told Mr Wolfe and me that there are five people besides her, and maybe more, who know that you had a key to Alberto Mion's studio door.'

Silence. Sometimes silences irritate me, but I didn't mind this one. Finally her voice came, totally different. 'It's a silly lie. Who told you?'

'I forget. And I'm not discussing it on the phone. Two things and two only. First, if this gets around, what about your banging on the door for ten minutes, trying to get in, while he was in there dead? When you had a key? It would make even a cop skeptical. Second, meet me at the Churchil bar at five sharp and we'll talk it over. Yes or no.'

'But this is so – you're so –'

'Hold it. No good. Yes or no.'

Another silence, shorter, and then, 'Yes,' and she hung up.

I never keep a woman waiting and saw no reason to make an exception of this one, so I got to the Churchill bar eight minutes ahead of time. It was spacious, air-conditioned, well-fitted in all respects, and even in the middle of August well-fitted also in the matter of customers, male and female. I strolled through, glancing around but not expecting her yet, and was surprised when I heard my name and saw her in a booth. Of course she hadn't had far to come, but even so she had wasted no time. She already had a drink and it was nearly gone. I joined her and immediately a waiter was there.

'You're having?' I asked her.

'Scotch on the rocks.'

I told the waiter to bring two and he went.

She leaned forward at me and began in a breath, 'Listen, this is absolutely silly, you just tell me who told you that, why, it's absolutely crazy –'

'Wait a minute.' I stopped her more with my eyes than my words. Hers were glistening at me. 'That's not the way to start, because it won't get us anywhere.' I got a paper from my pocket and unfolded it. It was a neatly typed copy of the document Wolfe had dictated. 'The quickest and easiest way will be for you to read this first, then you'll know what it's about.'

I handed her the paper. You might as well read it while she does. It was dated that day:

I, Clara James, hereby declare that on Tuesday, April 19, I entered the apartment house at 620 East End Avenue, New York City, at or about 6:15 P.M., and took the elevator to the 13th floor. I rang the bell at the door of the studio of Alberto Mion. No one came to the door and there was no sound from within. The door was not quite closed. It was not open enough to show a crack, but was not latched or locked. After ringing again and getting no response, I opened the door and entered.

Alberto Mion's body was lying on the floor over near the piano. He was dead. There was a hole in the top of his head. There was no question whether he was dead. I got dizzy and had to sit down on the floor and put my head down to keep from fainting. I didn't touch the body. There was a revolver there on the floor, not far from the body, and I picked it up. I think I sat on the floor about five minutes, but it might have been a little more or less. When I got back on my feet and started for the door I became aware that the revolver was still in my hand. I placed it on the base of the bust of Caruso. Later I realized I shouldn't have done that, but at the time I was too shocked and dazed to know what I was doing.

I left the studio, pulling the door shut behind me, went down the *public stairs to the twelfth floor, and rang the bell at the door of the Mion apartment. I intended to tell Mrs Mion about it, but when she appeared there in the doorway it was impossible to get it out. I couldn't tell her that her husband was up in the studio, dead. Later I regretted this, but I now see no reason to regret it or apologize for it, and I simply could not get the words out. I said I had wanted to see her husband, and had rung the bell at the studio and no one had answered. Then I rang for the elevator and went down to the street and went home.*

Having been unable to tell Mrs Mion, I told no one. I would have told my father, but he wasn't at home. I decided to wait until he returned and tell him, but before he came a friend telephoned me the news that Mion had killed himself, so I decided not to tell anyone, not even my father, that I had been in the studio, but to say that I had rung the bell and knocked on the door and got no reply. I thought that would make no difference, but it has now been explained to me that it does, and therefore I am stating it exactly as it happened.

As she got to the end the waiter came with the drinks, and she held the document against her chest as if it were a poker hand. Keeping it there with her left, she reached for the glass with her right and took a big swallow of scotch. I took a sip of mine to be sociable.

'It's a pack of lies,' she said indignantly.

'It sure is,' I agreed. 'I have good ears, so keep your voice down. Mr Wolfe is perfectly willing to give you a break, and anyhow it would be a job to get you to sign it if it told the truth. We are quite aware that the studio door was locked and you opened it with your key. Also that – no, listen to me a minute – also that you purposely picked up the gun and put it on the bust because you thought Mrs Mion had killed him and left the gun there so it would look like suicide, and you wanted to mess it up for her. You couldn't –'

'Where were you?' she demanded scornfully. 'Hiding behind the couch?'

'Nuts. If you didn't have a key why did you break a date to see me because of what I said on the phone? As for the gun, you couldn't have been dumber if you'd worked at it for a year. Who would believe anyone had shot him so it would look like suicide and then been fool enough to put the gun on the bust? Too dumb to believe, honest, but you did it.

She was too busy with her brain to resent being called dumb. Her frown creased her smooth pale forehead and took the glisten from her eyes. 'Anyway,' she protested, 'what this says not only isn't true, it's impossible! They found the gun on the floor by his body, so this couldn't possibly be true!'

'Yeah.' I grinned at her. 'It must have been a shock when you read that in the paper. Since you had personally moved the gun to the bust, how come they found it on the floor? Obviously someone had moved it back. I suppose you decided that Mrs Mion had done that too, and it must have been hard to keep your mouth shut, but you had to. Now it's different. Mr Wolfe knows who put the gun back on the floor and he can prove it. What's more, he knows Mion was murdered and he can prove that too. All that stops him is the detail of explaining how the gun got from the floor to the bust.' I got out my fountain pen. 'Put your name to that, and I'll witness it, and we're all set.'

'You mean sign this thing?' She was contemptuous. 'I'm not *that* dumb.'

I caught the waiter's eye and signaled for refills, and then, to keep her company, emptied my glass.

I met her gaze, matching her frown. 'Lookit, Blue Eyes,' I told her reasonably. 'I'm not sticking needles under your nails. I'm not saying we can prove you entered the studio – whether with your key or because the door wasn't locked doesn't matter – and moved the gun. We know you did, since no one else could have and you were there at the right time, but I admit we can't prove it. However, I'm offering you a wonderful bargain.'

I pointed the pen at her. 'Just listen. All we want this statement for is to keep it in reserve, in case the person who put the gun back on the floor is fool enough to blab it, which is very unlikely. He would only be –'

'You say he?' she demanded.

'Make it he or she. As Mr Wolfe says, the language could use another pronoun. He would only be making trouble for himself. If he doesn't spill it, and he won't, your statement won't be used at all, but we've got to have it in the safe in case he does. Another thing, if we have this statement we won't feel obliged to pass it along to the cops about your having had a key to the studio door. We wouldn't be interested in keys. Still another, you'll be saving your father a big chunk of dough. If you sign this statement we can clear up the matter of Mion's death, and if we do that I guarantee Mrs Mion will be in no frame of mind to push any claim against your father. She will be too busy with a certain matter.'

I proffered the pen. 'Go ahead and sign it.'

She shook her head, but not with much energy because her brain was working again. Fully appreciating the fact that her thinking was not on the tournament level, I was patient. They the refills came and there was a recess, since she couldn't be expected to think and drink all at once. But finally she fought her way through to the point I had aimed at.

'So you know,' she declared with satisfaction.

'We know enough,' I said darkly.

'You know she killed him. You know she put the gun back on the floor. I knew that too, I knew she must have. And now you can prove it? If I sign this you can prove it?'

Of course I could have covered it with doubletalk, but I thought, What the hell. 'We certainly can,' I assured her. 'With this statement we're ready to go. It's the missing link. Here's the pen.'

She lifted her glass, drained it, put it down, and damned if she didn't shake her head again, this time with energy. 'No,' she said flatly, 'I won't.' She extended a hand with the document in it. 'I admit it's all true, and when you get her on trial if she says she put the gun back on the floor I'll come and swear to it that I put it on the bust, but I won't sign anything because once I signed something about an accident and my father made me promise that I would never sign anything again without showing it to him first. I could take it and show it to him and then sign it, and you could come for it tonight or tomorrow,' She frowned. 'Except that he knows I had a key, but I could explain that.'

But she no longer had the document. I had reached and taken it. You are welcome to think I should have changed holds on her and gone on fighting, but you weren't there seeing and hearing her, and I was. I gave up. I got out my pocket notebook, tore out a page, and began writing on it.

'I could use another drink,' she stated.

'In a minute,' I mumbled, and went on writing, as follows:

To Nero Wolfe:

I hereby declare that Archie Goodwin has tried his best to persuade me to sign the statement you wrote, and explained its purpose to me, and I have told him why I must refuse to sign it.

'There,' I said, handing it to her. 'That won't be signing something; it's just stating that you refuse to sign something. The reason I've got to have it, Mr Wolfe knows how beautiful girls appeal to me, especially sophisticated girls like you, and if I take that thing back to him unsigned he'll think I didn't even try. He might even fire me. Just write your name there at the bottom.'

She read it over again and took the pen. She smiled at me, glistening. 'You're not kidding me any,' she said, not unfriendly. 'I know when I appeal to a man. You think I'm cold and calculating.'

'Yeah?' I made it a little bitter, but not too bitter. 'Anyhow it's not the point whether you appeal to me, but what Mr Wolfe will think. It'll help a lot to have that. Much obliged.' I took the paper from her and blew on her signature to dry it.

'I know when I appeal to a man,' she stated.

There wasn't another thing there I wanted, but I had practically promised to buy her another drink, so I did so.

It was after six when I got back to West Thirty-fifth Street, so Wolfe had finished in the plant rooms and was down in the office. I marched in and put the unsigned statement on his desk in front of him.

He grunted. 'Well?'

I sat down and told him exactly how it had gone, up to the point where she had offered to take the document home and show it to her father.

'I'm sorry,' I said, 'but some of her outstanding qualities didn't show much in that crowd the other evening. I give this not as an excuse buy merely a fact. Her mental operations could easily be carried on inside a hollowed-out pea. Knowing what you think of unsupported statements, and wanting to convince you of the truth of that one. I got evidence to back it up. Here's a paper she *did* sign.'

I handed him the page I had torn from my notebook. He took a look at it and then cocked an eye at me.

'She signed this?'

'Yes, sir. In my presence.

'Indeed. Good. Satisfactory.'

I acknowledged the tribute with a careless nod. It does not hurt my feelings when he says, 'Satisfactory', like that.

'A bold, easy hand,' he said. 'She used your pen?'

'Yes, sir.'

'May I have it, please?'

I arose and handed it to him, together with a couple of sheets of typewriter paper, and stood and watched with interested approval as he wrote 'Clara James' over and over again, comparing each attempt with the sample I had secured. Meanwhile, at intervals, he spoke.

'It's highly unlikely that anyone will ever see it – except our clients. ... That's better. ... There's time to phone all of them before dinner – first Mrs Mion and Mr Weppler – then the others. ... Tell them my opinion is ready on Mrs Mion's claim against Mr James. ... If they can come at nine this evening – If that's impossible tomorrow morning at eleven will do. ... Then get Mr Cramer. ... Tell him it might be well to bring one of his men along. ...'

He flattened the typed statement on his desk blotter, forged Clara James' name at the bottom, and compared it with the true signature which I had provided.

'Faulty, to an expert,' he muttered, 'but no expert will ever see it. For our clients, even if they know her writing, it will do nicely.

VIII

It took a solid hour on the phone to get it fixed for that evening, but I finally managed it. I never did catch up with Gifford James, but his daughter agreed to find him and deliver him, and made good on it. The others I tracked down myself.

The only ones that gave me an argument were the clients, especially Peggy Mion. She balked hard at sitting in a meeting for the ostensible purpose of collecting from Gifford James, and I had to appeal to Wolfe. Fred and Peggy were invited to come ahead of the others for a private briefing and then decide whether to stay or not. She bought that.

They got there in time to help out with the after-dinner coffee. Peggy had presumably brushed her teeth and had a nap and a bath, and manifestly she had changed her clothes, but even so she did not sparkle. She was wary, weary, removed, and skeptical. She didn't say in so many words that she wished she had never gone near Nero Wolfe, but she might as well have. I had a notion that Fred Weppler felt the same way about it but was being gallant and loyal. It was Peggy who had insisted on coming to Wolfe, and Fred didn't want her to feel that he thought she had made things worse instead of better.

They didn't perk up even when Wolfe showed them the statement with Clara James' name signed to it. They read it together, with her in the red leather chair and him perched on the arm.

They looked up together, at Wolfe.

'So what?' Fred demanded.

143

'My dear sir.' Wolfe pushed his cup and saucer back. 'My dear madam. Why did you come to me? Because the fact that the gun was not on the floor when you two entered the studio convinced you that Mion had not killed himself but had been murdered. If the circumstances had permitted you to believe that he had killed himself, you would be married by now and never have needed me. Very well. That is now precisely what the circumstances are. What more do you want? You wanted your minds cleared. I have cleared them.'

Fred twisted his lips, tight.

'I don't believe it,' Peggy said glumly.

'You don't believe this statement?' Wolfe reached for the document and put it in his desk drawer, which struck me as a wise precaution, since it was getting close to nine o'clock. 'Do you think Miss James would sign a thing like that if it weren't true? Why would –'

'I don't mean that,' Peggy said. 'I mean I don't believe my husband killed himself, no matter where the gun was. I knew him too well. He would never have killed himself – *never*.' She twisted her head to look up at her fellow client. 'Would he, Fred?'

'It's hard to believe,' Fred admitted grudgingly.

'I see.' Wolfe was caustic. 'Then the job you hired me for was not as you described it. At least, you must concede that I have satisfied you about the gun; you can't wiggle out of that. So that job's done, but now you want more. You want a murder disclosed, which means, of necessity, a murderer caught. You want –'

'I only mean,' Peggy insisted forlornly, 'that I don't believe he killed himself, and nothing would make me believe it. I see now what I really –'

The doorbell sounded, and I went to answer it.

IX

So the clients stayed for the party.

There were ten guests altogether: the six who had been there Monday evening, the two clients, Inspector Cramer, and my old friend and enemy, Sergeant Purley Stebbins. What made it unusual was that the dumbest one of the lot, Clara James, was the only one who had a notion of what was up, unless she had told her father, which I doubted. She had the advantage of the lead I had given her at the Churchill bar. Adele Bosley, Dr Lloyd, Rupert Grove, Judge Arnold, and Gifford James had had no reason to suppose there was anything on the agenda but the damage claim against James, until they got there and were made acquainted with Inspector Cramer and Sergeant Stebbins. God only knew what they thought then; one glance at their faces was enough to show *they* didn't know. As for Cramer and Stebbins, they had had enough experience of Nero Wolfe to be aware that almost certainly fur was going to fly, but whose and how and when? And as for Fred and Peggy, even after the arrival of the law, they probably thought that Wolfe was going to get Mion's suicide pegged down by producing Clara's statement and disclosing what Fred had told us about moving the gun from the bust to the floor, which accounted for the desperate and cornered look on their faces. But now they were stuck.

Wolfe focused on the inspector, who was seated in the rear over by the big globe, with Purley nearby. 'If you don't mind, Mr Cramer, first I'll clear up a little matter that is outside your interest.'

Cramer nodded and shifted the cigar in his mouth to a new angle. He was keeping his watchful eyes on the move.

Wolfe changed his focus. 'I'm sure you'll all be glad to hear this. Not that I formed my opinion so as to please you: I considered only the merits of the case. Without prejudice to her legal position, I feel that morally Mrs Mion has no claim on Mr James. As I said she would, she accepts my judgment. She makes no claim and will ask no payment for damages. You verify that before these witnesses, Mrs Mion?'

'Certainly.' Peggy was going to add something, but stopped it on the way out.

'This is wonderful!' Adele Bosley was out of her chair. 'May I use a phone?'

'Later,' Wolfe snapped at her. 'Sit down, please.'

'It seems to me,' Judge Arnold observed, 'that this could have been told us on the phone. I had to cancel an important engagement.' Lawyers are never satisfied.

'Quite true,' Wolfe agreed mildly, 'if that were all. But there's the matter of Mion's death. When I –'

'What has that got to do with it?'

'I'm about to tell you. Surely it isn't extraneous, since his death resulted, though indirectly, from the assault by Mr James. But my interest goes beyond that. Mrs Mion hired me not only to decide about the claim of her husband's estate against Mr James – that is now closed – but also to investigate her husband's death. She was convinced he had not killed himself. She could not believe it was in his character to commit suicide. I have investigated and I am prepared to report to her.'

145

'You don't need us here for that,' Rupert the Fat said in a high squeak.

'I need one of you. I need the murderer.'

'You still don't need *us*,' Arnold said harshly.

'Hang it,' Wolfe snapped, 'then go! All but one of you. Go!'

Nobody made a move.

Wolfe gave them five seconds. 'Then I'll go on,' he said dryly. 'As I say, I'm prepared to report, but the investigation is not concluded. One vital detail will require official sanction, and that's why Inspector Cramer is present. It will also need Mrs Mion's concurrence; and I think it well to consult Dr Lloyd too, since he signed the death certificate.' His eyes went to Peggy. 'First you, madam. Will you give your consent to the exhumation of your husband's body?'

She gawked at him. 'What for?'

'To get evidence that he was murdered, and by whom. It is a reasonable expectation.'

She stopped gawking. 'Yes. I don't care.' She thought he was just talking to hear himself.

Wolfe's eyes went left. 'You have no objection, Dr Lloyd?' Lloyd was nonplussed. 'I have no idea,' he said slowly and distinctly, 'what you're getting at, but in any case I have no voice in the matter. I merely issued the certificate.'

'Then you won't oppose it. Mr Cramer. The basis for the request for official sanction will appear in a moment, but you should know that what will be required is an examination and report by Dr Abraham Rentner of Mount Sinai Hospital.'

'You don't get an exhumation just because you're curious,' Cramer growled.

'I know it. I'm more than curious.' Wolfe's eyes travelled. 'You all know, I suppose, that one of the chief reasons, probably the main one, for the police decision that Mion had committed suicide was the manner of his death. Of course other details had to fit – as for instance the presence of the gun there beside the body – and they did. But the determining factor was the assumption that a man cannot be murdered by sticking the barrel of a revolver in his mouth and pulling the trigger unless he is first made unconscious; and there was no evidence that Mion had been either struck or drugged, and besides, when the bullet left his head it went to the ceiling. However, though that assumption is ordinarily sound, surely this case was an exception. It came to my mind

at once, when Mrs Mion first consulted me. For there was present –
But I'll show you with a simple demonstration. Archie. Get a gun.'

I opened my third drawer and got one out.

'Is it loaded?'

I flipped it open to check. 'No, sir.'

Wolfe returned to the audience. 'You, I think, Mr James. As an
opera singer you should be able to follow stage directions. Stand up,
please. This is a serious matter, so do it right. You are a patient with a
sore throat, and Mr Goodwin is your doctor. He will ask you to open
your mouth so he can look at your throat. You are to do exactly what
you would naturally do under those circumstances. Will you do that?'

'But it's obvious.'

James, standing, was looking grim. 'I don't need to.'

'Nevertheless, please indulge me. There's a certain detail. Will you
do it as naturally as possible?'

'Yes.'

'Good. Will the rest of you all watch Mr James' face? Closely. Go
ahead, Archie.'

With the gun in my pocket I moved in front of James and told him
to open wide. He did so. For a moment his eyes came to mine as I
peered into his throat, and then slanted upward. Not in a hurry, I took
the gun from my pocket and poked it into his mouth until it touched the
roof. He jerked back and dropped into his chair.

'Did you see the gun?' Wolfe demanded.

'No. My eyes were up.'

'Just so,' Wolfe looked at the others. 'You saw his eyes go up? They
always do. Try it yourselves sometime. I tried it in my bedroom
Sunday evening. So it is by no means impossible to kill a man that way,
it isn't even difficult, if you're a doctor and he has something wrong
with his throat. You agree, Dr Lloyd?'

Lloyd had not joined the general movement to watch James' face
during the demonstration. He hadn't stirred a muscle. Now his jaw was
twitching a little, but that was all.

He did his best to smile. 'To show that a thing could happen,' he said
in a pretty good voice, 'isn't the same thing as proving it did happen.'

'Indeed it isn't,' Wolfe conceded. 'Though we do have some facts.
You have no effective alibi. Mion would have admitted you to his
studio at any time without question. You could have managed easily to
get the gun from the base of Caruso's bust, and slipped it into your
pocket without being seen. For you, as for no one else, he would upon

147

request have stood with his mouth wide open, inviting his doom. He was killed shortly after you had been compelled to make an appointment for Dr Rentner to examine him. We do have those facts, don't we?'

'They prove nothing,' Lloyd insisted. His voice was not quite as good. He came out of his chair to his feet. It did not look as if the movement had any purpose; apparently he simply couldn't stay put in his chair, and the muscles had acted on their own. And it had been a mistake because, standing upright, he began to tremble.

'They'll help,' Wolfe told him, 'if we can get one more – and I suspect we can, or what are you quivering about? What was it, Doctor? Some unfortunate blunder? Had you botched the operation and ruined his voice forever? I suppose that was it, since the threat to your reputation and career was grave enough to make you resort to murder. Anyhow we'll soon know, when Dr Rentner makes his examination and reports. I don't expect you to furnish –'

'It wasn't a blunder!' Lloyd squawked. 'It could have happened to anyone –'

Whereupon he did blunder. I think what made him lose his head completely was hearing his own voice and realizing it was a hysterical squawk and he couldn't help it. He made a dash for the door. I knocked Judge Arnold down in my rush across the room, which was unnecessary, for by the time I arrived Purley Stebbins had Lloyd by the collar, and Cramer was there too. Hearing a commotion behind me, I tuned around. Clara James had made a dive for Peggy Mion, screeching something I didn't catch, but her father and Adele Bosley had stopped her and were getting her under control. Judge Arnold and Rupert the Fat were excitedly telling Wolfe how wonderful he was. Peggy was apparently weeping, from the way her shoulders were shaking, but I couldn't see her face because it was buried on Fred's shoulder, and his arms had her tight.

Nobody wanted me or needed me, so I went to the kitchen for a glass of milk.

MURDER AT THE OPERA

by *VINCENT STARRETT*

Place: Chicago
Time: 1934
Performance: *The Robber Kitten*

Two circumstances marked the première of the new opera as notable, even in anticipation. First, and perhaps foremost, it was by all accounts a sensational musical event; something that was going to be talked about in the press and from the pulpit. Second, in spite of her recent scandalous divorce from Palestrina, Edna Colchis was going to sing – and Palestrina was going to direct her.

The murder of Mrs Emmanuel B. Letts during the sulphurous first act was, of course, unpredictable.

From her seat in the 'diamond circle' – specifically, the Hassard box (Mondays and Fridays) – Sally Cardiff watched the surge and flow of opulent Chicago, with the little smile of one for whom such spectacles were providentially ordained. When, occasionally, she replied to the remarks of young Arnold Castle, at her side, she did so pleasantly but without removing her eyes from the scene of colorful congestion.

Young Mr Castle was cynical. 'Fifty per cent of them are here to see what happens between those two,' he observed. 'This Colchis now,' he continued irritably, 'what do they expect her to do? Blow up in the middle of the performance?'

His cigar lighter, which he clicked exasperatingly as he talked, was a magnificent affair. It was of gold, by Lemaire, and contained everything but running hot and cold water.

'If she felt that way,' said Miss Cardiff, 'she would not appear at all. But nothing will go wrong. They are both artists – and egotists.'

'As for the opera,' persisted Castle, 'I suspect it has been greatly overrated. They say there isn't a *tune* in the whole show. Just discord!'

She laughed lightly. 'Why do you come?' Then she blushed: 'Never mind!' her smiling gaze swung to the nearer boxes and her voice fell. 'Mrs Letts is wearing her fabulous necklace tonight. You see, it isn't a myth, after all.'

'It's vulgar,' said young Mr Castle. 'She's a lighthouse. Besides, it's dangerous. In times like these she should keep her jewels in a vault. I wouldn't feel safe with that thing in a church. Who's the fat bounder behind her?'

Miss Cardiff said '*Sh!*' The fat bounder had turned his head in their direction. Mrs Hassard answered the question. 'That's Higginson,' she said briefly.

'Get out!' cried Castle, enlightened. Everybody knew who Higginson was. He was Mrs Letts' secret service department, an ex-prize-fighter employed by Mrs Letts as private detective and, if occasion should arise, slugger. The job was a sinecure, for the police also kept a friendly eye on the exits and entrances of the wealthy Mrs Letts. It was easier to prevent an attempt upon her middle-aged person than to imagine what might happen to the heads of the department if any such attempt were made.

'He looks uncomfortable,' added young Mr Castle.

Hassard grinned satirically. 'He doesn't like dressing up. He'd be more at home at the back of the house, talking to the fireman.'

'Do you think so?' murmured Miss Cardiff. 'I was thinking that he rather liked his part.'

'He's too fat,' observed the critical Castle. 'Out of training. Soft living and locking up nights agrees with him. A child could stop him. I think I might even take him on myself,' he added appraisingly.

Miss Cardiff again said '*Sh!*' and continued immediately: 'Please don't! I never shall forget the time you tried to thrash a taxi driver.'

'I won't touch him tonight,' grinned Castle. 'I suppose he's here to keep an eye on the necklace. Anyway, there are plenty of dicks in the house – eh, Hassard?'

Hassard thought it likely there were a number of detectives

scattered through the house – all as uncomfortable in evening dress as Higginson.

Sally Cardiff continued to be fascinated by the audience. From time to time she put her glasses to her eyes, the better to observe some specimen of interest. She saw everything. Everything pleased her. The human values represented were, she knew, in large part spurious; but the circumstance had no power to spoil her appreciation of the cosmic whole. Life was like that. And life was exhilarating – quietly exhilarating.

Mrs Letts, meanwhile, sat calmly in her chair, nodding occasionally to an arriving acquaintance, but for the most part placid and phlegmatic. She had once been beautiful, and she was still an attractive woman. She had oodles of money – more money than any of the peacocks around her – but she was not a snob. She was simply elderly and a bit tired. She had greeted the Hassards and their party as they came in, and then had forgotten about them. After a time she appeared to nod, and was not shaken from her lethargy until a rapturous burst of applause noted the coming of the famous maestro.

Palestrina paused in his impressive march and bowed profoundly. The applause redoubled. He raise his baton, and it subsided almost abruptly.

'He's got the hair, all right,' commented young Mr Castle.

'*Sh!*' said Miss Cardiff, for the third time.

The baton descended and there stole through the house the opening notes of the overture to 'The Robber Kitten' – a small, wailing cry from the violins, quickly abetted by the bull fiddles. The audience shivered deliciously. The cry mounted eerily on little cat feet until it was a strident shriek; then it dropped to the first whispering wail. The crescendo was repeated. It was heard a third time. Then all the violins and fiddles went crazy together and filled the auditorium with harsh, discordant sound. This continued for some time. Somewhere in the background of it all a wild, high melody persisted – a tortured, uncomfortable strain – and the brasses joined the uproar, at intervals, with savage gusts of laughter.

The critics, in retrospect, decided that the whole had been 'a succession of unpleasant sense impressions telling a brutal story with dramatic emphasis.'

Whatever the critics may have thought, the house was stunned; then thunders of applause swept the auditorium. Palestrina turned and bowed in several directions. ...

151

But the questing eyes of Sally Cardiff, at that moment, caught a familiar face in the glow of an orchestra light; and she put up her glasses for a better view. *Interesting!* The man playing one of the first violins was almost the double of Palestrina, the conductor. They might even have changed places without suspicion – as far as personal appearance went.

Again the baton was upraised, and again the kittens' wail crept through the place, to end abruptly with the shriek of the adult felines. And as the wild cry failed and dropped the figure of a man stole from the wings, costumed to represent an enormous cat. He was in full evening dress below the jaw, but a furred headpiece set with pointed ears created the impression of feline masculinity; his tremendous mustachios stood out like bristling antennae. Orlando Diaz, the famous tenor. As *Grimalkin*, the Robber Kitten.

He began to sing.

Nobody, of course, paid the slightest attention to Mrs Emmanuel B. Letts. Yet it might have been observed that at the beginning of the performance she had leaned forward in her chair – to use her glases – and that a little later she had leaned back again. In point of fact, she did this several times. Her interest in cats, however, was notorious. She was interested in a cat hospital.

The performance went on. More cat-eared, whiskered singers stole on and off the stage. The row was terrific. Colchis appeared and sang divinely – if the word may be applied to the singing of an almost diabolic rôle – and no mishap occurred to mar the flagrant felicity of the situation.

At the conclusion of the first act the applause was boisterous. Colchis popped in and out of the wings like an animated jack-in-the-box, receiving flowers, while Diaz was even more modest than usual. He was, indeed, the last to appear, to take his bow, and he contrived to lend to the simple act a suggestion of protest. In every gesture he seemed to say that the triumph belonged to Colchis.

'Smart man,' commented Sally Cardiff, on whom no nuance of behaviour was lost. 'He minimizes the Colchis triumph by appearing to abet it.'

But at last the ovations were at an end, and the audience dispersed to the lobbies and lounges to smoke and wrangle over the performance. Many sat on in their seats, among them Mrs Emmanuel B. Letts, to whom – after a respectful moment – Higginson bent forward and addressed a superficial word. What he said, it developed later, was merely: 'Well, modom, what did you think of it?'

But Mrs Letts was already quite dead. She was never to know how the story ended. Rather, she was to furnish – for days to come – a news sensation more fascinating than any the city had known in years.

'Murder!' shrieked the newsboys in the snowy streets, even before the first performance of 'The Robber Kitten' was at an end. And then they shrieked: 'Murder-wurder! All about the turrible-urrible murder-wurder in the opery-wopery!' Or words to that effect. Emerging from the great casino into the worst blizzard the city had experienced since '69, the jackdaws and peacocks of the social set were assaulted by the ferocious clamor of the gamins.

Only a few had the faintest inkling of what had occurred almost under their noses.

And Mrs Emmanuel B. Letts sat on in her gilded box, her fabulous necklace still gleaming on her mottled throat, while silent men stood by and waited the emptying of the great barn that had become her tomb.

II

Robbery, it seemed apparent, could not have been the motive. There was the famous necklace to prove that. Unless the murderer had somehow failed at the last moment. Was it possible that he had – with consummate cleverness – committed his crime, then been forced to escape without his plunder?

The idea occurred to Dallas, chief of the Detective Bureau, but he put it out of his mind for the time. It seemed unlikely. Jealousy, thought Dallas – or hatred – would be a more likely motive. These wealthy society women! He knew them. They purred and cooed and 'deared' one another, but each loathed the ground on which the other walked. For that a woman had turned the trick, Dallas had no doubt at all. It looked, he said, like a woman's job. Academically, a detective has no right to a strong opinion until he has a fact or two upon which to base it; but in actuality all detectives are prejudiced from the beginning.

Only two opera parties had been asked to remain – those occupying the boxes immediately adjoining that of Mrs Letts. It was obviously impracticable to hold the entire audience. But the theatre staff was on hand in a phalanx – all the ushers, and the box office bandits, and the hat check robbers, and the numerous management. Not to mention a terrified young man and young woman from the audience, who were regarded by Dallas with the deepest possible suspicion. The two had occupied main floor seats on stolen tickets, which they averred they had purchased from a scalper.

Around the scene of the crime a magnificent activity was apparent. Detectives from the Bureau and from the Coroner's office dashed in and out of the lethal box. Reporters jostled and quarreled around the door. Flashlights exploded, and the acrid powder smoke drifted out across the vacant auditorium like an aftermath of battle. In the mezzanine lobby beyond the tier of boxes, the presumptive witnesses huddled on long sofas or paced nervously in the deep pile of the carpet.

Dallas and the coroner sat perilously on the extreme outward ledge of the box, facing the corpse, with Higginson at one side. The background was occupied by two burly detectives from the Bureau.

'Well, Higginson,' the detective chief began abruptly, 'it looks as if the first explanation ought to come from you.'

There could be little doubt of it, since presumably the man had sat behind the murdered woman throughout the whole first act. There was, however, this in his favor: he had himself reported the demise at the conclusion of that first installment. Thereafter, for two long and ghastly further installments, with Dallas as his shadowy companion, he had continued to sit behind the stiffening body. Somebody had to sit there, to keep Mrs Letts from toppling from her chair.

This had been Dallas's idea. It had occurred to him that nothing was to be gained by stopping the performance and dismissing the audience. And removal of the body would only have created a sensation that he had no wish to father. There was always the possibility, too, that the murderess – if unsuspicious – might return to the scene of her crime. She would hardly dare to leave the building, argued Dallas, thus inviting an individual attention. It was the detective's whim to ascertain which of the friends of Mrs Emmanuel B. Letts – female – would first attempt to greet her, after the performance. He held a high opinion of the nerve and subtlety of women.

As it happened, nobody made the attempt.

Higginson, although subdued, was faintly peevish. He knew Dallas very well indeed. 'Honest to God, chief,' he answered, speaking his own tongue for the first time in weeks, 'I told you all I know about it.'

'Tell me again,' said Dallas. 'I want Marlowe and Duffield to hear the whole story. And the coroner,' he added.

Messrs. Marlowe and Duffield, of the Bureau, bent their united gaze on the unhappy man.

Higginson's wild eye avoided contact with the body in the gilded chair. The incredible scene was now lighted by a blaze of electricity, in which the fabulous necklace glinted and sparkled like a proscenium arch.

'I got a telephone call, boys,' said Higginson, in a low voice. 'That's the way it was. During the first act. An usher came to the box. He just put his hand in and touched my arm. I was sitting back a bit – just over there. I slipped outside, and he said I was wanted on the telephone. It was a message for Mrs Letts, he said.'

'Did you tell her you were leaving the box?' asked Duffield swiftly.

'No, I didn't, Duffy.' Higginson also knew Messrs. Marlowe and Duffield. 'There didn't seem to be any use. It was probably some nuisance, I figured, and I could take care of it as well as her. If I'd told her, she'd just have sent *me*, anyway.'

Duffield nodded.

'So I just slipped out and went to the 'phone myself. It was downstairs in the lobby – the public telephone nearest the east door. Oh, I know what you're all thinking! I ought to have known better. Who would call her on that telephone, eh? Who would know the number? I know! Good God, do you suppose I'd have gone if I'd known what was going to happen?'

'What happened at the telephone, Hig?' The question came from Marlowe. There was a certain sympathy in his voice that Higginson was quick to sense and appreciate.

'Not a damn' thing, Joe! Just a voice I didn't know, saying, "Is that you, Higginson?" And I said, "Yes – who's this?" And he said, "Hold the wire a minute. There's an important message coming for Mrs Letts."'

'And you held the wire,' finished Duffield dryly. '"Meanwhile, this bird – or somebody else – was beating it around to the box you'd left and knifing Mrs Letts!'

Higginson nodded slowly. 'Yes,' he agreed. 'I guess that's what happened, Duffy.'

'It was a man on the telephone, though. You're sure of that?' The detective's voice was strident. Outside, the witnesses pricked up their ears.

'Oh, it was a man on the *telephone*, all right,' cut in Dallas, with a faint sneer. 'But it wasn't necessarily a man that did this job.'

'Why so, chief?' There was disagreement in Duffield's query.

'Motive,' answered the chief laconically. His voice sank. 'You can't imagine a *man* caring enough, one way or another, to kill this old woman, can you?'

'One way or another about what?' asked Duffield.

'Anything,' said Dallas vaguely. He added: 'If it was a man, Duff, it'd be a case of robbery – and the necklace would be gone. Look at it!'

'*Mmmm*,' admitted the other. 'It's a whooperdoo, all right.'

'It's a lallapaloosa,' said Dallas.

'Ever any attempts on her before, Hig?' asked Marlowe.

'Not in my time.'

'Is that her glove?' The detective indicated a long and crumpled white object on the floor of the box.

'It's hers,' answered Higginson gloomily.

The left hand and arm of the murdered Mrs Letts were bare to the shoulder. The right hand and arm were gloved to a point above the elbow. They all studied the impassive woman for a moment, while Mrs Letts' eyes continued to stare blankly across the empty pit. She seemed to be accepting, with her usual placidity, this new experience of death and dissolution.

Her opera glasses lay on the floor a little distance from the body. Duffield picked them up. 'Looks as if somebody had stepped on these,' he observed. 'This scratch is pretty fresh.'

Higginson shrugged. 'Afraid *I* did that, Duffy,' he confessed. 'Last week. She lent 'em to me – at 'The Love of Three Oranges.' I dropped 'em and kicked 'em around a bit.'

'At the *what?*' demanded Duffield, incredulously.

'"The Love of Three Oranges,"' said Higginson. 'It's another opera.'

'My God!' said Duffield.

'Forget that,' snapped Dallas, impatiently. 'It's obvious what happened. Hig got his call – I *suppose* he did – and left the box. While he was gone, the dame who did the job slid inside, crawled up behind the victim, and pushed a knife into her back. A very neat job, too! Not a sound, apparently – although there might have been a little squeal, with perfect safety. I understand there was noise enough on the stage to cover almost anything. There was during the last two acts, anyway, while I was here. Then she slipped back to her own box and waited

156

for the show to go on. All we've got to do,' he concluded sardonically, 'is find the woman.'

The coroner was thoughtful. 'It took nerve,' he remarked, at last. 'You think one of these dames ... outside ...?'

'Sure, it took nerve,' said Dallas. 'No, I don't think one of these we've got did it – not necessarily. But they were nearest to this compartment. Maybe one of them saw something – or heard something. Anyway, if there was any society row on, they'll be sure to have heard of it. We've got to start somewhere. Let's have 'em in and get it over with.'

'All right,' said the coroner. 'When did Higginson discover Mrs Letts was dead?'

'At the end of the first act. He didn't notice anything wrong when he came back. It was dark in the box. He was tired of waiting at the telephone, and he sort of sneaked in and took his seat quietly. That right, Higginson?'

'That's about it,' agreed Higginson.

'When he did discover it, he called *me*,' concluded Dallas, 'and I called you. And here we are,' he added cheerfully.

'How about the usher that called Higginson away?'

'Left with Higginson and didn't come back. Knows nothing about it – he *says*.'

'Call them in,' said the coroner.

There entered first, as it happened, Miss Sally Cardiff. The summoner – Detective-Sergeant Duffield – for obscure reasons of his own (reasons having to do with her eyes and hair), had singled her out as the first victim of the inquisition.

She stopped short inside the curtains. Her eyes were very wide. They were even eager.

'Then it's true!' said Sally Cardiff.

Slightly taken aback, Dallas answered. 'What's true?' he asked.

'That Mrs Letts has been murdered!'

'Where did you hear that?' asked Dallas.

'I can *see* it – now! But I knew it before. It could only be that. Why else should the place be running over with policemen and reporters? What else could all the whispering mean? Why detain the box-holders nearest to Mrs Letts and send the rest of the audience away? And, by the way, I think *that* was a mistake, Mr Detective.'

Her eyes sparkled with animation. 'Why,' she said, 'I knew there was something up when I saw Higginson bolt out of the box. And when *you* returned ...!'

'The deuce you did,' said the chief of detectives. He recovered a bit from his astonishment. 'When would that be, Miss Cardiff? I mean, when you saw Higginson bolt out of the box.'

'At the end of the first act. I saw him lean over and say something to Mrs Letts. Perhaps I didn't actually *see* it – but I sensed his movement – you know? And a minute later I saw him get up and leave. I supposed Mrs Letts had been taken ill.'

'Do you know Higginson?'

'I do not. But I have seen him before – with Mrs Letts.'

'It is Mrs Letts that you know?'

'Only casually – to speak to – in such places as this. She nodded to us all when she came in, but there was no conversation.'

'Not in the same set, perhaps?' inquired the detective, with pensive malice.

But there was no sting in the question for Sally Cardiff. 'Exactly,' she smiled. Then the words burst from her quickly: 'Who killed her?'

Dallas laughed shortly and silently.

'That's what we are trying to find out. You appear to be a young woman with ideas. Have you any that might help us to answer your own question?'

Miss Cardiff was suddenly apologetic. 'I'm sorry,' she murmured. 'I just can't help being curious. I'm a – a nuisance that way! I haven't a suspicion in the world.'

But her eyes still glanced avidly in all directions – seeing everything, appraising everything. She was burning to ask a dozen questions, and a little ashamed of her curiosity.

After all, what was it to her? She was probably under suspicion, herself! Oddly, she felt no sense of crawling flesh in the presence of the murdered woman. Only a desire to look – to question – even to touch. To go down on her hands and knees and hunt upon the floor for clues. Good heavens! Was *this* the result of all her philosophy and reading? To make of her an amateur detective – stirred to a morbid *Who-lust* by the smell of blood?

For an instant she felt a little silly. Dallas was watching her.

'So you think it was a mistake for me to send away the audience?' he continued. 'Just why, Miss Cardiff, if you don't mind?'

She hesitated. 'I hardly know,' she answered. 'It was an impulsive remark – perhaps intuitive. I know, of course, that nobody from our own box went near this place; but I suppose I *can't* answer for the persons in the box beyond. I think your action struck me as being rather the obvious thing, Mr ...'

'My name is Dallas,' said Dallas, politely.

'Mr Dallas. So obvious, in fact, as in all likelihood to be wrong. You see? That is, the man who did this would hardly – unless, of course, he were very clever indeed, and realized that the obvious thing might be overlooked ...'

She was speaking, ultimately, to herself, and frowning very prettily over it, it occurred to Duffield.

Dallas studied her with profound interest. 'Why do you say the *man?*' he asked suddenly.

'But wasn't it?' she cried. She stooped swiftly to the floor of the box. 'Mrs Letts's glove! See how it has been torn back from the elbow. No woman ever removed a glove that way. Why, it's almost inside out. And he's snapped a button off. Did you find the button, Mr Dallas?'

Dallas laughed harshly. 'We hadn't quite got around to that glove yet, Miss Cardiff,' he answered, and swung sharply on his underlings. 'Find that button, quick!'

Miss Cardiff studied the distance between the chair occupied by the corpse and the low railing of the box. 'It might have jumped over the rail,' she observed, 'if the glove was removed in haste. And probably it was.'

'Hustle downstairs and see if that button's under the balcony, Marlowe,' snapped the chief of detectives. 'You, too, Duffield!' Then he cleared his throat with some violence. 'You are a remarkable young woman, Miss Cardiff,' he continued mildly. 'What else does the glove tell you?'

He waited almost respectfully for her reply.

'You see,' she answered, holding out the glove for his inspection, 'in a long glove of this sort there is a gusset, or opening, in the centre of the palm; it extends to a point some inches upward on the wrist. This is buttoned at the top by three buttons, and it's easier to open the buttons and work the hand out through the opening than it is to take off the glove. That's the way Mrs Letts would have done it, herself, if – for instance – she just wanted to cool her fingers.'

'I see,' said Dallas. 'And a man wouldn't do it that way?'

'He might, I suppose; but it's unlikely. His first thought would be to turn the glove back at the top and rip it downward.'

159

'And a woman *wouldn't*? I see!'

Miss Cardiff turned the glove back into its proper shape. 'Now here,' she continued calmly, 'is a point that is perhaps in favor of *your* theory. Notice how the fingertips are stained. They at ...'

But Dallas fairly snatched the glove from her hand.

'It's blood!' he crowed. 'By George, Miss Cardiff, it's blood!'

By his gleeful shout he tacitly accepted her, for the moment, as his fellow worker in the vineyard of detection – a tremendous compliment.

Miss Cardiff retrieved the glove and sniffed it. 'No,' she said, 'it's rouge. I thought it was; that's why I said what I did.'

For an instant Dallas was petrified. Then, 'Of course!' he bellowed. 'Of course, it's rouge!' He smiled. 'Then it *was* a woman, after all.'

'It *may* have been,' admitted Miss Cardiff, and then they both looked accusingly, for a moment at the dead lips of Mrs Emmanuel B. Letts. It was plainly to be seen that no rouge had been upon those lips for a long time. Certainly no scarlet rouge.

The chief of detectives thrust his head over the railing and called down to his searchers below.

'Just got it, chief,' floated upward the voice of Duffield. 'By golly, she was right! It popped over like a blooming poker chip.'

'Come up here again,' said Dallas jovially, 'and take some lessons from a detective that knows her business.... By George, Miss Cardiff,' he continued with enthusiasm, 'you are a howling wonder! There's one thing, though, that you won't discover for a time – and neither will I.'

Miss Cardiff looked anxious. 'What is that?' she asked.

'*Why* the murderess found it necessary to remove that glove. It's certain that Mrs Letts didn't take it off, herself; so the other woman must have. You've made that clear, at least.'

Miss Cardiff's brow cleared.

'Oh,' she said, 'I thought you knew why the glove had been removed. Surely the impression of the ring is quite plain on the poor woman's third finger. And from the little bulge in the corresponding finger of the glove, the stone must have been a heavy one. Obviously, a valuable ring has been stolen.'

Dalas sat stunned. For a long moment he stared his complete amazement. When he spoke it was in a husky whisper.

'A ring,' he echoed. 'A valuable ring?' Then his eyes swung to the gleaming, glittering toy on the dead woman's throat. His bewilderment at last found other words. 'She took a ring – and left that necklace?'

'Of course,' smiled Sally Cardiff cheerily. 'The necklace is an imitation.'

III

Could a woman have committed the crime? Sally Cardiff doubted it. Dallas, of course, was simply prejudiced. Intuition was a funny thing. It whispered to Dallas – a man – that a woman had done this deed. To Sally Cardiff – a woman – it whispered that a man had done it. Perhaps she, also, was prejudiced.

The blow, of course, delivered from behind – and by a person stretched along the floor, and therefore *upward* – had been, no doubt, a vigorous one. But there were powerful women in the world. Some of them, doubtless, had been in the audience that night. And perhaps the murderer had *not* stretched himself on the floor to deliver his blow. Mrs Letts had sat well back in the box – it was dark – he could have been in the shadow of the curtains. It was all really much simpler than it appeared. But the glove button *was* an evidence of masculinity, Dallas to the contrary notwithstanding.

And yet – what of the rouge on the fingertips?

Women, at times, shook hands with one another. And not heartily, as men did. They purred softly and touched fingertips! It was possible that Mrs Letts had greeted some creature before entering the box – and that the creature, an instant before, had dabbed at her lips.

If only the weapon could be found! Mrs Letts had been wearing an evening dress of silver metal cloth. It had been cut high, since her back was none too lovely. The knife had penetrated the cloth to reach the flesh. Miss Cardiff hummed softly to herself. There were possibilities in the situation. But the knife was with the murderer – or the murderess. Have it your own way, Mr Dallas! Probably it had been cleaned, anyway, and restored to its original innocence.

'And yet ...' murmured Miss Cardiff, puckering her forehead.

It was quite late. Indeed, it was quite early. It was, in point of fact, 3 A.M. Mrs Letts had been dead about six hours, roughly speaking. Maybe five-and-a-half. Let Dallas figure it. What difference did it make? But it *did* make a difference – didn't it? It was a legitimate supposition that the murderer – who was not a fool – had selected his time. Roughly. He couldn't be sure of Higginson, of course. Higginson *might* have left the telephone without waiting for the 'important message for Mrs Letts'; in which case. ... Anyway, the murderer had worked rapidly.

He had telephoned from somewhere *inside* the opera house. Even Dallas must be sure of that. However, there were a number of telephones in the building; they were scattered about the several lobbies and lounges, in convenient corners. For that matter, there were telephones in the *office*! At the ticket window! In every room occupied by a member of the management!

It was a shocking thought.

'*Tut!*' said Miss Cardiff.

A minute later it was less shocking. Even a member of the official staff would not have been fool enough to telephone through the switchboard. He would have gone to a public telephone. His call would then be received by an *outside* operator and would re-enter the opera house by way of another public telephone. The number of the second public telephone would be known, of course, to the murderer. Very simple. Very clever.

Miss Cardiff drew her robe more comfortably about her shoulders. The room was cooling off. It seemed that weeks had passed since her interview with Dallas. She had been at home for more than an hour. On the way home there had been much conversation. The others had been able to tell Dallas nothing at all. Young Mr Castle had been all for arresting Higginson at once. The Hassards had seen nothing – heard nothing – but the opera. Had the occupants of the other box? They were all closer to Mrs Letts than the Hassard group. Closer socially. They knew more about her.

But what was there to know?

There was Emmanuel B. Letts, of course. He was still living – somewhere in the East. The divorce had occurred at least ten years before the première of 'The Robber Kitten'. It had been quiet enough: whatever scandal attached – and there was nothing sensational that one remembered – had attached to the banker Letts. As far as the murder was concerned, he seemed a bit out of the picture.

Miss Cardiff reviewed the episodes of the opera. Mrs Letts had died during the first act. At what point? Was the uproar, at the moment, particularly furious? The overture, after all, had been the noisiest part of the performance; and Mrs Letts was placidly alive when the overture had concluded. She recalled a trifling incident to prove it. The overture had ended, the applause of the audience had subsided, and the lines of the opera had begun. Mrs Letts had put up her glasses and leaned forward in her chair. After a time she had leaned back again. That was all. But it proved conclusively that Mrs Letts was not murdered during the overture.

But did it prove ...?'

'Oh dear!' murmured Sally Cardiff.

Was it conceivable that Mrs Letts had been murdered in that instant of leaning forward and leaning back again? The moment would have been admirably propitious for a murderer intent on avoiding the chairback. And the racket, at the time, surely had been sufficient. Diaz was singing an aria describing his exploits as the Robber Kitten, and doing a good job of it. The house was intent on the stage. Immediately thereafter there had been a duet between Diaz and Colchis, which could hardly have been described as a lullaby. It was a bit screechy. The orchestra, in the instrumental intervals, had been consistently boisterous. A tiny little scream in Mrs Lett's box might well have gone unnoted.

Miss Cardiff continued to recall the incidents of the evening. Something had struck her as odd. What was it?

After a moment it occurred to her. The man in the orchestra pit who had looked like Palestrina!

She bit her lips on the fantastic thought that flashed through her mind. Mrs Letts was a noted patron of the opera. She knew everybody. Without her guarantee it was doubtful if the opera could survive. Undoubtedly she knew Palestrina.

But did musicians use rouge?

Absurd!

Did conductors? Did Palestrina?

What wild and ridiculous nonsense! Palestrina, in point of sober fact, was actively conducting his orchestra at the moment Mrs Letts lay back in her chair and died. Wasn't he? Of course, he was. A houseful of people could testify to that. He had been right there from the beginning.

Very well! But for the sake of the argument – what if Palestrina had *not* been there, behind the conductor's stand, all the time? And *any* time! Was the likeness between himself and the violin-player in the orchestra so great that one could pass as the other? Was it possible that a violin-player could, without the genius of Palestrina, conduct an orchestra with Palestrina's genius?

Would it have been possible for a violin-player to escape from the orchestra pit – at the conclusion of the overture, say – and go about another business?

'Oh dear!' murmured Miss Cardiff again. She sat up straight in her chair. 'I'm getting quite, quite mad. But I do wish I had looked for that man in the orchestra again. *Did* he go away? And if he did, *did* he come back?'

Then another thought occurred to her, more paralyzing than the first.

IV

The newspapers, in the morning, called attention to the statement of the coroner's physician with reference to the violence of the blow given Mrs Letts by her assailant. It had been, it appeared, very powerful. The flesh about the wound was bruised and discolored. The inference was that only a man could have delivered such a stroke. The newspapers were, in point of fact, inspired to this utterance by Dallas, himself, who was anxious that his private theory concerning a woman should remain in obscurity. No use warning one's suspects in advance of the big pinch. His woman obsession was one he was loath to give up, although Sally Cardiff had shaken it.

Duffield, meanwhile, had turned up a sensation. It completely revolutionized Dallas's notions when he heard about it. The word came to him over the telephone, and the chief of detectives banged his fist on the desk and swore with savage triumph.

'Good work, Duff,' he said. 'Wait there till I join you. I'm coming right away.'

Duffield, a bit of a genius himself, had been visited by an inspiration ... A pilot had crashed the night before – a commercial pilot – while eastbound for New York, and now lay cursing in a small hospital in northern Indiana. The newspaper account had been brief. Duffield had read it in an early edition. The pilot, it appeared, was concerned about the fate of his passenger; but as there had been no passenger found in the wreckage, the Indiana authorities had assumed the man to be delirious.

Duffield, without orders, had hurried to the Indiana hospital – by fast plane – and was at the pilot's bedside when he telephoned his superior. Dallas joined him at top speed, by early train. Top speed was what the company called it; but in actuality the middle west was all but snow-bound.

'Listen, chief,' said the subordinate, when he had taken his superior aside, 'he said it again, right after I telephoned you!'

'The deuce he did!' said Dallas.

'Yep. There was a doctor with us, and he heard it too. He thought the fellow was trying to say "Let's go!" which is a common phrase, it seems, among flyers. I didn't try to tell him anything different.'

Dallas grinned happily. He inhaled the aseptic odours of the hospital corridor with appreciation. 'It looks good to me, Duff,' he said.

'It's the goods,' said Duffield. 'What the pilot was saying was '*Letts*,' as sure as you're a foot high. His passenger was Emmanuel B. Letts – and Emmanuel B. Letts is missing! They must have left Chicago some time last night. They got caught in the blizzard, tried to go over it – or around it – or something – and finally they crashed.'

'Is this fellow going to die?'

'No – he's going to pull through.'

'I suppose,' said Dallas reflectively, 'it couldn't have been that ...'

'Not a chance,' interrupted Duffield. 'I thought of that. I thought maybe this fellow had done the job, himself, and was making a sneak. But why? He ain't a gunman or a gangster. He's a professional pilot. It only makes it harder, that way, chief! There's no sense looking for a hard answer. This fellow couldn't have had anything against Mrs Letts. He couldn't have done the job – the way it was done. The other way it's easy. A woman's husband ...'

'All right,' said Dallas. 'It just occurred to me. Well, we've got to find Letts. Where was the crash?'

'About five miles from here – out in the country.'

'Who found the pilot?'

'A farmer. He lives near where it happened. He telephoned the police here, when he heard the crash, and they went out and got him. Got the pilot.'

'No suspicions, of course,' said Dallas, 'so they wouldn't look around. I'll bet they've trampled the snow like a flock of elephants.'

Duffield shrugged. 'Well,' he said, 'the snow's been falling pretty steady ever since. There wouldn't have been any footprints, anyway.'

'He couldn't go far,' mused Dallas. Then he brightened and spoke more cheerfully. 'Maybe he was hurt! He'd almost *have* to be. Maybe the farmer's got him. Anyway, he's hiding somewhere.'

'They ain't always hurt,' said Duffield, morosely. 'First thing he'd think of 'd be a train. He'd have to get that *here*.'

'Would he?' questioned Dallas. 'Well, that's something. You've looked up the morning trains, I suppose?'

'The storm has shot schedules all to hell,' said Duffield. 'The train you came on should have left Chicago last night. There's plenty of time as far as trains are concerned.'

'This fellow have anything in his pockets.?'

'Nothing we want.'

'*Hmph*,' grumbled Dallas. 'Well, you're a good dick, Duffy! Let's get going.'

They assured themselves that there was no chance of the pilot's miraculous recovery and disappearance during their absence, then plunged into the snow-clad streets. Their first visit was to the railroad station. No stranger had been inquiring for trains east, however, and they pushed on to police headquarters, where their advent created a sensation. Dallas was a very famous detective.

'I'll go with you, myself,' said the chief of police, with flattering emphasis. 'My driver knows every road in the county.'

'He'll need a snow plow,' observed Duffield grimly. 'I wish criminals would stop operating in the winter.'

The drive to the scene of the accident was cold and difficult; but at last they stood beside the twisted framework of the plane – a gaunt and melancholy spectacle with its insulation of gleaming snow. A glance was sufficient to tell the experienced Chicagoan detectives that a hunt for clues would be useless. They stood in snow to their knees and looked gloomily at the tragic tangle of wood and metal. They kicked their aching feet against the dead motors, and swore thoughtfully.

'Any roadhouses near here?' asked Dallas, at length. 'Hotels? Any place he could have gone?'

'There's Braxton's,' said the police chief. 'It's five miles the other way.'

'Letts wouldn't necessarily know his directions,' said Dallas. 'All right. Let's go to Braxton's.'

They drove toilsomely to Braxton's – a two-story shack whose creaking signboard, festooned with snow-bunting, announced its *raison d'être* in a single laconic word: *Tourists*. The slattern in charge was unimpressed by their descent. No guests had come to her the night before, nor during the morning hours either. She brightened when they ordered coffee, which they drank standing.

Then again the snow-piled highway took them. They were heading back, now, toward the town. On all sides stretched desolate miles of glistening white. Trees were hung with it. Fences dropped with its weight.

Not far from the wrecked plane the land fell away into a hollow, from out of which now rose a lazy question-mark of smoke.

'What's that?' asked Dallas.

'Neilson's,' answered the police chief briefly. 'The fellow that found the pilot,' he explained. 'He don't know anything about it.'

'Oh?' said Dallas. 'Let's have a look at him, anyway. There seems to be a bit of a path there.'

They swung inward and upward for a piece; then their wheels spun uselessly in unbroken drifts of snow and ice. Duffield climbed out of the car.

'Get back to the road, if you can,' he said. 'I'll go up to the house.'

He plunged forward on foot, wading in snow to his waist, and at length breasted the hillock. Behind him the stalled car fumed and chugged, endeavoring to back.

Duffield's eyes fell first on the low dwelling of the farmer Neilson, all but snow-bound in the hollow. Then he saw something else. From an upper window a man was watching him, who, after an instant, began frantically to wave his arms. He seemed to be summoning Duffied to the house. Neilson, no doubt – but what the devil did the fellow want? Had he seen the car?

He strode onward with large steps and at length burst a path to the farmhouse door. The man at the window had disappeared. In the doorway, suddenly, were two men. The second man was obviouly Neilson; he could be no one else. But the first man was a man of substance and position if ever Duffield had seen one. He was tall and powerful, running a bit to flesh, and his garments were expensive and of the latest cut. Obviously, too, they had been exposed to the elements.

The big man was excited. 'I heard your car from the window,' he said, 'and I thought I had a glimpse of it. Are you going up to town?'

There was no doubt in Duffield's mind. He had never seen Emmanuel B. Letts or his portrait; but he knew this was Emmanuel B. Letts.

'Why, yes,' he drawled. 'Wanta come along?'

'You bet,' said the stranger. 'I had a breakdown, last night, and had to put in for repairs. I'll tell you about it as we go along.'

'Reckon I heard about that,' smiled Duffield. 'Your pilot's in the hospital, ain't he?'

'Pilot?' echoed the other. 'No, no – I heard about that, myself. Poor chap! No, I was driving. Wait till I get my traps.' He hurried away upstairs, leaving Neilson staring at Duffield with deep suspicion.

'You don't belong in these parts,' said the farmer, after a moment. 'What was it you was wanting, when you came along?'

'Your house guest,' answered Duffield promptly. He swung his heavy overcoat aside, then swung back the jacket underneath. Before the menace of his little badge the farmer fell away. 'Not a word out of you,' continued the detective. In a swift whisper he asked: 'What did he give you?'

Neilson's eyes fell, then lifted. 'A hundred dollars,' he said defiantly.

'Keep it,' said Duffield. 'What'd he tell you?'

'He was with the pilot that was wrecked; but he didn't want it known. It was a secret trip, he said, and would hurt business if it was spread around.'

'Keep your mouth shut till you're told to open it,' said Duffield, 'and I'll keep still about the hundred.'

Letts was lumbering down the crooked stairs, clutching his satchel. He was now attired in a significant leather jacket.

'I'll be glad to get away,' said the big man happily. 'Not but what your hospitality has been fine, Mr Neilson; but I've got things to do, after all.' He turned on Duffield with belated suspicion. 'You live around here, I suppose? Just breaking a path to town, eh?'

'Right you are,' said Duffield jovially. 'And glad to have you with me, Mr ...?' He hesitated before the name.

'I'll make it worth your while,' nodded Letts. 'My name is Rogers. Maybe you can tell me about the trains out of town. I'm a stranger in the neighborhood, myself.'

They fought their way through the drifts, stepping where possible in the holes made by Duffield in his advance upon the house. As they crested the rise, the detective noted that his companions had worked the car back into the road. Two of them – Dallas and the local chief – were performing a slow dance in the snow, pausing occasionally to kick their aching feet against the framework of the car. The chauffeur sat stolidly behind his wheel.

'Friends of mine,' said Duffield, in answer to the other's inquiring glance. 'All going up to town, the same as we are.'

They finished their plunge to the roadway and stopped beside the car. Dallas and the police chief were trying not to stare.

'In you go, boys,' cried Duffield. 'This gentleman is going along as far as the railway station.'

The police chief climbed in beside his chauffeur. Dallas slipped into the rear seat and made room for the newcomer beside him. The last to enter the car was Duffield. The car started with a jerk.

'This is Mr Rogers, chief,' said Duffield, chattily. 'He wants to catch the first train east.'

Dallas smiled blandly on their sudden prisoner. He had looked at a portrait of Emmanuel B. Letts before leaving Chicago. He softly rubbed his knuckles.

'I sympathize with Mr Rogers,' he murmured; and laid his heavy hand on the other's shoulder.

V

Young Mr Castle was annoyed. He had no objections to playing chauffeur to Sally Cardiff – it was his ambition to land a permanent job in that and other servile capacities – but her detectival activities set his back up. The excitement of Mrs Letts's murder had gone to her head, apparently. He was forced to admit, however, that Miss Cardiff was not unduly excited. She was eager, but calm enough, all things considered. She was even dispassionate. Her theories of the murder were fantastic, they were the utmost nonsense; but she argued them plausibly. Somewhere, he felt certain, there was a flaw in her reasoning; but he was never able – while she was talking – to put his finger on it.

'And the publicity of it,' he had stormed at her. 'Suppose you were right! Can't you just see the newspapers? My dear girl, there would be nothing left for you to do but open a private inquiry agency.'

'My curiosity is impersonal,' she explained. 'It's just – just curiosity! I really don't care two straws whether the murderer gets justice or doesn't. It's the chase – you know? My wits against his – and both of us against the police. I don't think I'm morbid, Arnold.

169

As for Dallas – can't you see him taking all the credit? Why, I'll *hand* it to him. I'll toss it to him as I would to a – a fish!'

'Good old sea lion,' grinned Castle.

That had been their latest discussion of the subject. It all flickered, cinema-like, through his mind as he sat behind the wheel of his gray roadster and looked up at the gloomy windows of the big warehouse beside which, at the moment, he was parked. Sally Cardiff was inside.

In time she emerged. On the instant all his dissatisfaction fell away. Her face was beaming. Her step was brisk and triumphant. With what decision her tall heels clicked on the stone flags! And what a glorious small person, in all aspects, was this same Sally Cardiff!

'Don't get out,' she said, climbing in beside him. She sank back with a long sigh of relief. 'It's over,' she said.

'You've failed?' he asked quickly – hopefully.

'I've won!'

He drove the roadster furiously through a narrow crack between two taxicabs, beat a changing traffic light by an eyelash, and turned a corner in haste.

'Where to?' he asked, after a time.

'I'm wondering,' said Miss Cardiff. 'To the Detective Bureau, I suppose. Not that I fancy myself, now, in the rôle of tale-teller; but there's a chance that I'll be able to keep Dallas from making a fool of himself.'

'You're quite sure you're not making – *er* – committing an error, yourself?'

'Oh, quite!'

He sighed. 'What did you find in the warehouse?' There had been a package under her arm when she emerged. Now it lay across her knee. He eyed it with suspicion.

But she did not lift the parcel. Instead, she opened her small purse, with infinite care, and extracted a tiny envelope.

'Slow down,' she ordered, 'and look inside.'

He almost expected to see a human eyeball staring at him.

What he saw was exactly nothing. Or did she mean that thread of dust that had settled in a corner of the envelope? As he looked, she shifted the container in her hands; and the thread of dust turned over on its side and glinted.

He looked quickly away. 'What is it?'

'Mrs Letts, you will recall, wore a metal cloth evening dress. It was cut high. The knife passed through it. This is a shred of the material.'

170

'Get out!' he scoffed. But he was astounded.

'Actually. It can't be anything else. It adhered to the point of the knife.'

Castle was stunned. 'Oh, come off it, Sally!' he cried at last. 'It couldn't!'

'It did. Ordinarily, it wouldn't. I mean, it wouldn't adhere to an ordinary knife. This kinfe was not ordinary. It was rather a blunt knife, with a damaged tip. You remember what the coroner's physician said about the wound? An unusually violent blow was required. That was why. The blade didn't have a point.'

He was still incredulous. 'And you found it – still clinging to the knife?'

'Oh, no! It was on the jacket of the other man. Almost under the arm. I'm glad it was a rough jacket. The knife, of course, was cleaned – but this little shred – just a twisted thread or two – remained in the broken tip. It was dislodged by the murderer's second thrust – *later* – and remained among the hairs of the jacket.'

'Well, I'll be hanged!'

'Somebody will be,' smiled Miss Cardiff. 'No – they don't hang them, any more, do they?'

'And the knife proves this, too?'

'Yes – the point is damaged, as I explained. I've got it here, with the jacket.'

'How on earth did you get away with them?'

'I simply dared them to stop me.'

'Great Scott!' said young Mr Castle, feebly inadequate. After a moment he asked: 'Won't they tell?'

'I don't know. I warned them not to – but I suppose they know, by now, what I was really after. I don't care much. The rest of it is up to Dallas. After all, I'm not a policeman.'

Castle smiled a mirthless smile. 'No?' he interrogated; and answered himself with grave irony: 'No – I suppose not!'

'Nevertheless, I suppose we must get to Dallas with our evidence.'

'I suppose we must,' agreed Mr Castle.

They were incongruous figures on the steps of the Detective Bureau – that sinister gray building with its dingy corridors.

A staring desk sergeant directed them to Dallas's office. In the outer chamber a hard but smirking secretary stopped them. Dallas, it appeared, was in conference.

'My God,' said Castle, 'do they have them here, too?'

Miss Cardiff smiled attractively. 'If you could just slip my name in to him,' she whispered, 'I think he might consent to see us. In fact, I'm sure of it.' She proffered her visiting card.

The secretary smirked and frowned and smirked again. 'I ain't saying I haven't heard of you, Miss Cardiff,' he observed. 'Well, just wait a minute, and maybe –'

He disappeared through a swinging door, into a room across which they saw another door. They heard the second door close behind him.

They waited exactly two minutes.

Then Dallas came hurriedly into the anteroom. He was very courteous.

'I'm glad to see you, Miss Cardiff,' he said, ignoring Castle. 'But I *am* busy – there's no use denying it. If it's important ...?' He smiled a hard, ingratiating smile.

'It *is* rather important, I think,' answered Miss Cardiff. 'I've come to tell you who killed Mrs Letts.'

The chief of detectives stared, speechless. After a moment, 'Oh!' he murmured. After another moment he grinned. 'To tell you the truth, Miss Cardiff, we've got the fellow, ourselves. Brought him up from Indiana, last night. I was questioning him when you arrived. You were certainly right about his being a man.'

'He was running away, then?' cried Sally Cardiff.

'Just as fast as he could go,' agreed Dallas.

'And he has confessed?'

'He *will* confess, before I get through with him,' said Dallas grimly. 'At the moment, between ourselves, he's holding out.'

'What does he say? Of course, he hasn't a leg to stand on!'

'I agree with you, but he hasn't been able to see that – yet. Look here, have you got proof?'

'Positively.'

'Good enough! It isn't customary to discuss these matters, but with *you* I will.' Dallas was at once flattering and unctuous. He needed proof – it was all he did need.

'He admits he attended the opera – privately – but swears he knows nothing of the murder. Gave a very good imitation of a man being shocked, when we told him. Says his presence in Chicago was entirely due to business matters – very important! So important that he came here from the East secretly. Something to do with a bank merger which, if it got out, would upset business to beat he- to beat the band. Affect the stock market, and so one. Very plausible. He had his story all ready, obviously. So secret that, after the opera – and incidentally after the murder – he took a fast plane to get back to New York. Unfortunately, he crashed in Indiana. We were on the job – we got him.'

Miss Cardiff had listened to this explanation with growing wonder. 'Who under the sun are you talking about?' she asked, at length.

'Emmanuel B. Letts,' said Dallas. 'Former husband of Mrs Emmanuel B. Letts, deceased. Who are *you* talking about?'

'Oh, my goodness!' cried Sally Cardiff. 'You've got the wrong man!'

For an instant they stared at each other in silence. It was Dallas who spoke first. 'Oh, I think not,' he said. But his eyes were worried.

'But you *have*,' she insisted. 'I *know* it!'

The smirking secretary put his head in at the door for an instant. He made signs to Dallas.

'Get out of here!' roared Dallas in a fury. Then with an effort he controlled himself. 'You were saying, Miss Cardiff?'

'I think,' said Sally Cardiff, 'I'd better tell you my story from the beginning, Mr Dallas. I'm sure you must have forgotten the most important clue of all – the rouge on Mrs Letts's glove.

'That rouge!' said Dallas scornfully. 'It had nothing to do with it.'

'It had everything to do with it. Does Mr Letts use rouge?'

'Of course not. At least, I'm certain he doesn't.'

'So am I. If you'd said he did, I'd have been bothered. Listen, Mr Dallas. Mrs Letts wasn't killed by anybody in the audience. She was killed by someone on the stage.'

Into the harassed eyes of the detective chieftain crept a look of relieved understanding. He understood it all now. This attractive girl had simply gone cuckoo. She had been thinking too hard about the murder. It often happened that way.

He smiled tolerantly. 'I hardly think that can be the case, Miss Cardiff,' he said. 'After all, the people on the stage had their own business to attend to. They were singing – and dancing – and carrying on – and Mrs Letts, you will remember, was killed during the first act.'

'You think I'm crazy?' Sally Cardiff laughed delightedly. 'I give you my word, Mr Dallas, if you arrest Mr Letts for this crime, you will have a very nasty time on your hands – afterwards!'

The worried look again crept into Dallas's eyes.

173

'Well, well,' he cried jovially, 'let's hear your story, Miss Cardiff. I'm sure it will be an interesting one – and very clever.'

'I'll tell you,' she answered, 'for the sake of Mr Letts. Once more, I say, Mrs Letts was killed by somebody on the stage.'

For the second time she opened her tiny purse and extracted her envelope. She laid it in his hand. Then she fumbled with her parcel. There emerged a shaggy jacket of theatrical aspect and a gaudy dagger somewhat battered at the tip – but all the more formidable by reason of the damage. A toy that had become an ugly weapon.

'The envelope,' continued Sally Cardiff crisply, 'contains a few threads of Mrs Letts's dress. These other things came out of a theatrical warehouse, this afternoon – the warehouse where "The Robber Kitten" is in storage till its next performance. This is the knife that murdered Mrs Letts. The threads clung to this battered tip, you see, and later were transferred to the jacket of an actor who was murdered in the play. Not really murdered, you understand. In the opera! It took nerve to pretend to murder a man on stage after *really* murdering a woman in the audience!'

She paused impressively; but Dallas had no words to utter.

'There is a rehearsal on at the opera house, right now, Mr Dallas. It will last until five o'clock. Our man will be there. Will you come with me?' For a long minute Dallas met the challenge of her eyes. Then he wilted.

'And Letts?' he questioned.

'Why not bring him along?'

There was another silence. Then Dallas spoke with epoch-marking decision.

'I'll do it,' he said. 'Wait till I get my hat.'

VI

The orchestra was hard at work and, miraculously, playing something tuneful. But there was little time for listening, and after a few moments of unconscious lagging Castle hastened after his companions. No questions were asked of them. Here and there in the darkened house were other groups, standing or sitting; officials, critics, members of the company not engaged on the stage.

They crowded through a small door, concealed by curtains, climbed a flight of steps, and suddenly found themselves backstage. Only Letts and Dallas – and on different errands – had been in such a place before. A number of performers were standing around; but small attention was paid to the newcomers. The light behind the scenes was gratifyingly dim.

'Now, Mr Dallas, we must work quickly – before we are suspected. I almost wish you had worn a disguise.'

'Good Lord!' gulped Dallas. 'I never wore one in my life.'

'We've simply got to find the telephone he used,' said Sally Cardiff. 'The one he *must* have used. Remember, it was a public telephone. He would never have operated through the switchboard. Now where would the dressing rooms be, Mr Letts?'

The mountainous Letts indicated.

'I see. Very well, then – he would go first to his dressing room, remove his mustache and his furry ears, pick up his dagger, then return to this section. Without his costume – it was only a headdress, after all – he would appear to be just a man in evening garments. The house was in darkness – the play was going on. Everybody was intent on the story. His makeup would not be noted. If he left by the door by which we entered, he would be out among the audience in a jiffy – just a quiet man walking up the aisle.'

'There are no telephones in the auditorium proper, Miss Cardiff,' said Emmanuel B. Letts positively. 'They're all in the lobbies and lounges.'

'Yes – and so he did *not* go out into the audience. The nearest exit light is over there.' She walked swiftly to the door she had indicated and opened it. 'Exactly! this is an entrance to the mezzanine lobby – an exit, if you like.' She put her head outside and cocked it at an angle of interrogation. 'And at the far end of this corridor there's a telephone booth! Quite perfect, you see. He knew beforehand exactly what he would do. He knew the number of the other telephone he was to call. From the first booth he called the second booth; and when a boy answered, he asked that Higginson be summoned from Mrs Letts's box. Higginson came – and was asked to hold the wire. Then the other man quietly stood his receiver on the shelf and hurried to the front.'

She stepped into the corridor, and the others followed.

'Why did nobody see him?' asked Castle suddenly. 'The lobbies and lounges are studded with pages and ushers.'

For a moment Sally Cardiff was stunned. It was a question she had never asked herself. Was it possible, after all, that there had been more than one person in the plot? *Had* somebody seen the murderer and kept silence?

'For that matter,' said Dallas, a shrewd eye suddenly on Emmanuel B. Letts, 'why did nobody but the boy who summoned him see Higgingson go to the telephone and return? We questioned the whole staff about that.'

But Emmanuel B. Letts knew the answer. 'I think I can answer both questions, Miss Cardiff,' he said gallantly. 'The opera was being presented for the first time. The ushers, once their charges were safely seated, slipped off to their own points of vantage – wherever they may be – and watched the opera. They always do it, unless it is something familiar and boring to them. Most of them, in fact, are students of music – that's why they have these jobs.'

'Why, yes,' smiled Sally Cardiff, 'I think that must have been it. At any rate,' she continued, briskly, 'he met nobody – nobody, at any rate, who later connected him with the crime. He knew Mrs Letts's box, and slipped in quickly. Then I think he dropped softly to his knees. Mrs Letts's back was to him. She must have been very close to his hand.'

Dallas nodded. 'It's a good thing his knees didn't crack when he knelt!'

But Sally Cardiff answered him in all seriousness. 'He knelt,' she said, 'at a moment when the orchestra was playing its loudest, or when the orchestra and chorus were in full swing together. Obviously he had no immediate business, himself, on the stage. Everything was planned with the utmost care.'

'And the rouge?' asked Dallas.

'He had it on his face. It was part of his makeup. Some of it he rubbed off no doubt, before leaving his dressing room. But it worried him. He knew it would be noticed if *he* was noticed. I think as he hurried along the corridors, before reaching the lounge and entering the box, his nervousness kept him dabbing at his cheeks – possibly he thought that way to conceal his features. The rouge would adhere to his fingertips, and then – after the murder – when he tried to remove the glove – you see?'

Dallas nodded unwillingly. 'The rouge was on the fingertips of the glove,' he reminded her. 'It was once your opinion –'

'No, yours – *yours* always! I said it *might* have been a woman *or* a man; but I always believed the murderer to have been a man. First he attempted, as I pointed out, to tear the glove off by turning it inside out – a wholly masculine idea. It wouldn't work that way – so, he tugged at the fingers.'

'Why did he want the ring?'

'I don't know – but I think, now, that robbery was not his motive. I doubt that he knew the necklace wasn't genuine. To him it would seem real enough. It was only when I saw it at close quarters that I realized it was false.'

'Why did he kill her?'

'I don't know, Mr Dallas – I only know he did.'

'What was she to him?' persisted the chief of detectives.

'I can only guess.'

Emanuel B. Letts was registering embarrassment. He coughed deprecatingly. 'One hears gossip,' he said. Then he stopped and tried again. 'I don't pretend that this has hit me very hard, Dallas. There's been nothing between Mrs Letts and myself for a long time. Still, I'm shocked; and I'd like to see justice done. As I say, one hears gossip – whether or not one wishes to. People persist in believing that I must still be interested in her actions.' He shrugged and his face twisted.

'Well, she met him in Italy, when she was there. She helped him, as she had helped others. I suppose, ultimately, she thought she had fallen in love with him. She was not –' he hesitated – 'wholly admirable. I'm sorry to say that. For him, of course, it was – to be brutal – just duck soup! An elderly woman with tons of money; and all she asked in return was a little – shall we say? – attention.'

Sally Cardiff looked at him with horror and compassion. And over and above and backgrounding his unhappy disillusionment rose now from the theatre the triumphant strains of a great love chorus.

'Then that,' said Sally Cardiff, in a low voice, 'explains a great deal, Mr Letts. When she discovered that –'

'Exactly.'

'Exactly what?' demanded Dallas, annoyed.

'He was the co-respondent in the Colchis-Palestrina divorce,' said Sally Cardiff. 'Obviously, he was through with *her* – with Mrs Letts. She had helped him to rise, and then when he no longer needed her –'

Dallas digested this information.

'That would give *her* a reason for hating *him*,' he agreed. 'If *she* had killed *him*, I could understand it. But –'

Miss Cardiff nodded. 'It's still puzzling,' she admitted.

'It's crazy,' said Dallas.

'Unless she were going to break him, in some way,' contributed young Mr Castle, with sudden inspiration.

Miss Cardiff looked startled, as so did Dallas. Emmanuel B. Letts, wiser in the ways of the world even than the policemen, only nodded his head.

A glorious tenor voice was now ringing through the auditorium – soaring on wings of song to the utmost peaks of infinity. When its last note had died away there came from the stage and from the interior of the house a burst of spontaneous applause that reached the group that stood and plotted in the lobby.

Then voices were heard – closer at hand.

'They're coming,' gasped Sally Cardiff, in sudden panic. 'Mr Dallas – shall you – shall I –?'

For the first time she was nervous. But it was not fear – if anything it was stage fright.

'Leave it to Dallas,' counselled young Mr Castle; and he attempted to draw her away. But she slipped from his grasp and stepped quickly through the lobby door into the wings.

A tall young man, obviously Italian, was striding toward the dressing rooms. His face was still flushed with pleasure at the recognition of his peers. He paused and looked with benevolent curiosity at the group that suddenly confronted him – prepared, if it was their wish, to be amiable for a moment or two. Perhaps an autograph ... Perhaps ...?

'Mr Diaz,' said Sally Cardiff casually, 'there is only one thing that still bothers me. Well, two! But first of all – what was your *reason* for murdering Mrs Letts?'

Orlando Diaz did not collapse. For an instant, though, he wavered, and Dallas stepped forward. Then a long sigh passed the tenor's lips and he drew himself upright. He bowed profoundly to the small person who stood before him.

'It was because, dear lady, she had threatened to end my operatic career – and because I knew that she would do it.'

'And the ring?' she continued. 'The ring you took from her finger?'

'It was my own, dear lady – one that I had given her. It was foolish to take it. It would have been foolish to leave it. Either way, it would have pointed to me. As it has done.'

She nodded her understanding, and, turning, took the arm of Arnold Castle. Even as they moved to leave they saw Dallas step forward.

But at the door she stopped him. 'I can't go yet,' she said. 'I simply can't, Arnold. Run back, like an angel, and find Palestrina. I've simply *got* to know. Ask him if he has a brother in the orchestra.'

Mr Castle ran back. After a time he returned.

'He *has*,' he reported. 'A *twin* brother.'

'I was sure it must be something like that.'

After a long silence, during which the car sped nowhere in particular, his secret admiration burst its seals. 'Sally,' he said, 'you're simply *great*! There aren't any words in the dictionary to touch you. *Do* you mind if – like good old Watson – I ask one final question?'

'Of course not, silly!'

'What under the canopy was the first thing that led you to suspect Diaz? Someone on the stage, rather than someone in the audience!'

'It was that belated curtain call. You remember it? They clapped and clapped and clapped – and still he didn't come. At last he *did* come. It was most unlike him – unlike *any* opera star. I wondered where he had been, and what he had been doing. And after a while I knew something had kept him. He just got back in time – and I think it was a very narrow squeak for Diaz.'

'It was,' agreed Arnold Castle, with conviction. 'All the good it did him in the end! Do you know, Sally, I think I'm a little afraid of you! It's rather alarming to contemplate – *er* – having a detective in the family – *er* –'

Miss Cardiff blushed a little.

'Don't be silly,' she said. 'There'll be times when I'll be grateful for a good old Watson.'

MELODY IN DEATH
by *BAYNARD KENDRICK*

Place: The 'Knickerbocker' Opera, New York City

Time: 1942

Performance: *Cesare*, by Rudolpho D'Auria

Gina D'Auria, youngest star of the Knickerbocker Opera Company, repeated the last few bars of the aria from *Cesare*, flooding the confines of the small rehearsal-room with an overplus of sound. She held the top note with a distinct physical effort and, breathing skillfully in spite of her weariness, allowed her strong young voice to flutter gently down. It still was not right. She knew it as soon as the last note died. A glance at the face of Paul Metcalfe, the taciturn assistant conductor, seated at the piano, confirmed her knowledge.

Instead of asking her with his unvarying politeness to try it again, as she feared and expected, Metcalfe looked at his wrist watch and closed the lid of the upright with a tiny bang. 'It's half past eleven,' he announced. 'That's enough for tonight.' He rolled up the score, tucked it under his arm, and vanished abruptly into the corridor, leaving Gina alone.

With the door left open and her own singing stopped, she could hear from another rehearsal-room the clear, powerful voice of the famous tenor, Michl Soulé. Gina listened for a moment, and then walked slowly to her dressing-room four doors down the corridor.

She sank down on the skirted chair in front of her dressing-table and stared with annoyance into the triple mirror. There were lines of fatigue marring the oval purity of her face, and, unless she was careful, portending crow's-feet at the corners of her deep, intelligent black eyes. She added more by wrinkling her forehead, high and smooth beneath the classical set of her hair. She had worked like a fool, much too hard, but she wanted to be at her best when the Knickerbocker produced *Cesare*. Gina crossed her arms on the table and lowered her head to rest against them, closing her eyes to keep back unshed tears.

Her grandfather, Rodolfo D'Auria, was dead. The old musician had been ailing for several years, but he had managed to finish his opera, *Cesare*, before the end came. Gina could picture his frown if the granddaughter he had trained from childhood should sing his aria badly. Her grandfather had stood for perfection. She could give him no less, since he had given her everything.

The sound of hammering drifted in from the stage and beat against Gina's door. Michl Soulé's singing stopped abruptly at the noisy intrusion.

The telephone rang. She raised her head, stared at the phone with hostility, suppressing an impulse to push it from the table. Then she uncradled it and said, 'Hello.'

It was Jacqueline Marlowe, laughing through her words: 'I'm phoning from a pay booth in a cigar store, darling. I'm just a block or two away and I'll be right up. I'm taking you out for rarebits at Reuben's.'

'Jackie, I'm too tired.'

'You'll always be too tired, darling, if you never play. Dane's joining us, and he'll be terribly disappointed if you don't come. Besides that, Arthur Considine's with me.'

Gina sighed inwardly. Dane Marlowe and his attractive wife were more than old friends to Gina. They were powerful and important factors in any young prima donna's career. Dane's company had made and installed the mechanical stage equipment – orchestra lifts and counter-weight systems – in Knickerbocker Opera House as well as in nearly every large theater in the country.

It was not good policy at any time to disappoint Jackie and Dane, but her weariness overcame business caution and even the lure of a midnight snack with Arthur Considine didn't tempt her. She made another try: 'Jackie, I simply can't.'

'I'll be right up, Gina. I have something important to tell you. You can wait five minutes anyhow and tell me how tired you are when I arrive.'

Mrs Marlowe disconnected. Gina sighed and slowly replaced the telephone.

Jacqueline Marlowe never got tired, but then it was easy to stay rested and refreshed when your husband was as wealthy as Dane Marlowe and you were further mattressed by five million dollars of your own. Gina realized she was being catty, but there were times when Jacqueline's silk-sheathed slenderness in its nutshell of mink touched her with irritation by its very unvarying perfection. Gina knew that Jacqueline's gold-blond hair would be upswept into her neat coiffure without a waving tendril, and that the mink would fall in harmonious lines even though Jacqueline had packed herself into a booth to use the telephone.

It was more trouble to compete with Jacqueline's energy that to give way to it. Gina might be dead on her feet, but she would finish up at Reuben's eating rarebit. She looked at herself in the mirror and decided that the print she was wearing must do. Jacqueline was always on time.

Gina paused with a lipstick halfway to her full red lips, her black eyes widened. The noises of the crew busy on the stage had ceased, leaving the building unnaturally quiet. Audible now in the frame of silence was the sound of somebody humming.

The melody was quaint and haunting. It reached down into Gina's heart with reminiscent fingers, holding her motionless at the table with her hand half raised. In it was the tragic history of a nation and something of slumbrous nights and velvet stars, with Italian mothers crooning a million babies to rest. In it was a slice of Gina's childhood.

The humming grew closer and footsteps approached her dressing-room door. Mixed with the footsteps was something else – the scratching of nails on the concrete floor and the gentle pad of four soft paws. They came nearer.

Gina left her chair, crossed the room, and flung wide the door. The corridor was dim and she drew back startled and a little embarrassed.

A man was outside. He wore a loose English ulster of pepper-and-salt and was carrying gloves and a gray felt hat in his right hand. In the dim light of the corridor he loomed inordinately tall. He stopped both walking and humming as Gina opened the door. His left hand was clutching a U-shaped brace harnessed to the most beautiful German shepherd dog Gina had ever seen.

The dog turned its head, gazed at Gina, and yawned deliberately, exhibiting boredom by its curling tongue. The man stood rigid, as he seemed to gaze down the length of the deserted hall.

Gina said, 'I'm sorry if I startled you. Were you just humming a song?'

The man's head turned slowly. Light from the dressing-room lit up furrows in his strong, mobile face and brought a strange, reflecting glint into perfect eyes. The eyes made Gina uncomfortable, for they seemed to stare straight through her, fixing their gaze on the opposite wall.

'I'll plead guilty to humming, but it's not exactly a song.' He smiled, and his whole face came alive, creasing itself into tiny hills and valleys with a marvelous play of expression which reached from his square-cleft chin to his crisp dark hair. His eyes stayed blank, still holding her. It took her several seconds to reach the conclusion that the man was totally blind.

Surprise at his ease and self-assurance immediately blanketed her first, quick surge of pity and momentarily drove from her mind the reason why she had stopped him. It was difficult enough for a person with eyes to negotiate the backstage tiers of the Knickerbocker Opera House. The hall itself was cluttered with lockers, trunks, and scattered props left over from many operas. An archway thirty feet to the left of Gina's dressing-room led to a vast stage, where the traps in the floor and the jumble of scenery and ropes made walking dangerous even for a sure-footed stagehand.

He brought the melody to her mind again, speaking reflectively: 'I've been listening to Michl Soulé rehearse the tenor part of *Cesare*. The melody I was humming is part of the tenor aria. I'm an old friend of Michl's and privileged, I guess, on account of my blindness. Not many outsiders get to hear rehearsals.'

'No,' said Gina, 'they don't.' She touched his arm with her fingers. 'I'm Gina D'Auria. My grandfather composed *Cesare*. I'm waiting for a friend here in my dressing-room. I you have a few minutes I wish you'd come in and sit down.'

'That's kind of you,' he said without hesitation. 'I'd love to.'

She guided him in from the hall, the German shepherd keeping close to his side until they reached a chair.

'I'm Captain Duncan Maclain, and this is Schnucke,' he told her as they settled down.

'I'd guessed that already,' said Gina. 'Michl and Jacqueline Marlowe have both mentioned you.'

'Oh, so you know Jackie, too. Of course. I'd forgotten that she is practically godmother to the opera.'

183

'As a matter of fact,' said Gina, 'I'm expecting her here right now. She phoned from a couple of blocks away that she'd be right over.'

The Captain took out a heavy silver case and offered her a cigarette.

Gina said, 'That's another of life's pleasure forbidden by my singing. But smoke if you want to. It doesn't bother me at all.'

She watched him as he flashed his lighter and applied the flame with neat precision. Then, picking up a silver tray, she placed it on the table beside him.

Maclain smoked thoughtfully, inhaling with enjoyment, letting the smoke trickle out slowly from mouth and nostrils. 'I'm curious,' he said frankly, depositing some ashes accurately in the tray.

'About me?'

'About the melody I was humming. Your grandfather wrote the opera and you're singing in it. How is it you didn't know it was part of the score?'

'Because it happens to be in the tenor part, and I'm a soprano. I probably won't hear the whole opera until the first rehearsal with the orchestra, and I haven't had a chance to look over the score in its entirety. All the principal parts are rehearsed separately, as Michl has probably told you.'

The Captain nodded and rumpled his crisp dark hair. 'My blindness has endowed me with an insatiable lust for asking questions. Jackie's probably told you that. If I become presumptuous, you can always throw me out. But there was something more than idle curiosity in your voice when you asked me about that song.'

She was silent for a moment, toying with a gold-backed mirror. 'When I was six or seven, my grandfather composed it for my brother and me. Our parents died when we were babies and we lived with our grandfather in Naples. We had a governess who was very strict and who thought that sweets were bad for children. Grandfather used to hide candy and cookies in the piano. When we'd come in from playing he'd casually give us the signal by humming or singing that little song.'

She paused and put the mirror down. Maclain snuffed out his cigarette in the tray. As though it were a signal, a burst of song came from the stage, flooding the opera house with a good-night accolade from Michl Soulé.

Gina said, 'My brother died when he was ten. Later I translated the Italian words of the song into English. It makes a little rhyme. Would you care to hear it?'

The Captain nodded.

She sang very softly.

> '*The laughter of happy children*
> *Is the memory of a dream.*
> *The little prince and princess*
> *May not be what they seem.*'

The Captain touched his braille watch.

'I hadn't heard it for years,' Gina said. 'Not until I heard you humming it. To think that he put it in his opera for me and I didn't know until now.'

Her dark eyes closed and her thoughts went back to Naples – the smell of the harbour and fishing boats and the ragged sails – a villa on the white, dusty road, and children playing in the sun.

When she opened her eyes again she saw that the Captain was listening. His finely chiselled head was tilted at the slightest of angles. His strong, fastidious hands were crossed in his lap, the nervous fingers in repose. Only one well-shod foot was moving as he gently stroked the back of the dog beside him with a polished toe.

The leather-bound clock on Gina's dressing-table showed five minutes to midnight. She said, 'It's almost time for the night stage crew to come in. Jackie must have got sidetracked some place.'

'Does she know where your dressing-room is?' The Captain asked the question as though his own smooth voice might disturb his concentration.

'She's been in here a dozen times.'

'Theaters fascinate me,' said Duncan Maclain. 'Theaters and all types of auditoriums. They're the only buildings I know of constructed to enhance the qualities of sound.'

He stood up abruptly. 'I have to identify my friends by voices and footsteps, Miss D'Auria. I live in a world of sound. If Jackie got sidetracked, it was somewhere here in the opera house. I'm certain I heard her footsteps on the stage many minutes ago. She was crossing with someone else just as Michl started to sing. If you'll take my arm we might go out and look around.'

Gina said, 'She was probably with Arthur Considine. He drove her down.'

They went to the door together. Schnucke pressed close to her master's left side, then dropped back and hesitantly settled herself on the floor again as he gave a command to lie down.

Gina opened the door and guided the Captain through, her hand nestled lightly in his arm.

Maclain walked with confident stride beside her, his lithe, well-knit body standing straight and strong.

She turned him right, through the arch at the end of the hall, and stopped in the wings, pressing closer to him. A single dim worklight burned straight ahead, lost in the vastness of a sixty-foot stage that was nearly a city block long. Far overhead two other lights shone dimly, helping not at all. Darkness swept on up above them to touch the gridiron, where, during a performance, high-perched workmen looked down on the singing puppets eighty feet below.

Gina forced herself to speak: 'I don't see any sign of anyone. If those were Jackie's footsteps you heard, she must have gone.' Her voice sounded flat and dead, smothered with silence.

Far above her, a man laughed. The laughter was leaden, too, striking incongruously into the darkened silence, chunks of mirthless sound tumbling over the trailing of the scene painters' fly sixty feet overhead and plummeting swiftly down.

'The night crew's coming in,' said Duncan Maclain. 'Suppose we cross the stage and see if the doorman's seen anything of Mrs Marlowe.'

'She couldn't have been here.'

'Come along.' He was moving forward, assuming the role of leader himself, dragging her into nothingness.

'I think we'd better wait until the night crew comes in and puts on some lights,' said Gina. 'I can't see very well, and I'm afraid the stage would be hard to cross even with your skill in the world of sound.'

He chuckled, and the sound reassured her.

'What are you laughing about?' she asked him.

'People with eyes,' he said. 'The blind have an edge on them. We never have to worry when the lights are out or even when they're turned down.'

They were close to the edge of the proscenium arch, where Gina had so often made an entrance to take a bow before the great gold curtain. To their left was a cubicle in a dented niche about the size of a large clothes closet, set in the edge of the proscenuim arch. There, during each performance, a stagehand stood to raise and lower the great gold curtain.

Gina said, 'If a dog can lead you, I can, too.'

Two steps onward, the Captain stopped abruptly, as though some giant magnet had glued his feet to the ground. The arm that Gina was holding straightened, barring her way. She peered through the dimness, searching his face, and found it tight and knotted with a worried frown.

'What's the matter?' Her mouth was dry.

'Mind where you step,' he told her, and suddenly bent to touch one finger to the floor beside his shoe. Straightening, he held out his hand with a finger extended.

Gina moistened her lips and leaned closer. In the feeble light of the night bulb, the tip of his finger looked brown.

'I feel faint,' she told him weakly.

He said quite softly, 'Go back to the dressing-room and sit down.'

For the moment, she could not move. His arms extended before him, he found the door to the cubicle and disappeared inside. Then, hypnotized, Gina followed, groped for a hanging light, found the chain, and pulled it. The Captain was standing by a big, red sign, his hand on an empty leather sheath which was fastened to the wall. Close to the sign and the empty sheath, a taut, heavy rope extended from floor to ceiling.

Gina's lips moved numbly, mumbling the words on the sign:

IN CASE OF FIRE USE THE KNIFE
TO CUT THIS ROPE TO DROP THE ASBESTOS
CURTAIN
The knife must not be removed from here
under penalty of the law.

Gina moved one foot, and found that the sole of her shoe was sticky.

The Captain said, 'I warned you to go to your dressing-room.'

Again she found she could not move. Her eyes were held to Jacqueline's slender body stretched out straight in an angle of the wall. The fur of the dark mink coat was matted where the knife hilt stuck up sharply in her back, casting a single shadow against the upswept golden hair.

'Look!' Gina breathed, and pointed, forgetting he was blind.

'I don't need to look,' she heard him say. The words were tiny, irresistible hammers beating at her through an enveloping dizziness. Gradually they shut out everything and sent her mercifully slumping to the floor. . . .

Gina coughed against the sharp, choking fumes of smelling salts and turned her head. The smelling salts followed persistently, scratching at her throat and searing her nostrils. Her eyelids fluttered, and the naked lights of her dressing-table hurt her with their brightness. She shut them out quickly, trying to find blackness again. Firm, gentle fingers closed on her wrist, and a voice muttered something in soothing French to the effect that she was going to be all right.

A hand rested on her forehead. She raised her lids and stared up mistily into the gentle, sympathetic eyes of a seal. No, it wasn't a seal – it was a man in a sleek fur coat, his round, comical face furrowed with worry.

'She's chilled perhaps, *non?*' The man in the fur coat spoke English that was touched with the accent of many languages fluently mastered. There was only one man in the Knickerbocker who lived in a world where the atmosphere remained at a constant point of freezing. That was Michl Soulé.

Gina reached up and closed her fingers around the hand on her forehead and clung to it tightly. The mistiness of her eyes decreased and revealed two other faces floating above the satin couch on which she was lying.

One was Ed Trapper, her manager, his silvery white hair brushed tightly back and slicked as tightly down, his businesslike pale blue eyes under the heavy white brows touched for once with a glint that might have been softness.

The other face thrilled her and warmed her inside. It was a face that depicted joy and sorrow and understanding, with a hint of fiery passion in the delicate set of the lips – things that its owner could wring from a grand piano with a touch of his tapering fingers. The face belonged to Jacqueline Marlowe's latest protégé, twenty-five-year-old Arthur Considine. He grinned at Gina reassuringly, and the grin was as helpful as a draught of golden wine.

'Come, come; snap out of it, Gina baby.' Ed Trapper's smooth voice struck against her with fatherly slaps. 'You're old enough not to be pulling faints. You're apt to cook your voice for the opening. That would be fine.'

'The voice, the voice.' Michl shrugged, raising two waves of shimmering fur, then touched his throat above the coat collar with a finger and emitted one clear liquid note. 'Always it is the *voice!* Never what is in here.' He slapped his heavily padded heart. 'It is freezing in this room. Does anyone care for *me?*'

From the other side of the dressing-room Captain Maclain said, 'If it's eighty in this place, Michl, it's a hundred and nine.'

Gina forced herself to sit up. For the moment she had completely forgotten the Captain and Schnucke. His back was toward her. He had shed his overcoat and was standing in front of her dressing table. His sentient fingers flitted from object to object with the delicacy of a gardener testing new buds on a vine.

'Are you looking for something, Captain Maclain?'

Arthur Considine's voice sounded strained and hard.

'The police will be here any minute now.' Maclain sat down on the bench with his back to the make-up table. 'They're naturally inquisitive, but Inspector Davis is a very close friend of mine. The more I know about the room I'm in, the more I can save him time.'

The telephone rang. Ed Trapper started forward, but the Captain reached around without turning his head and lifted the phone from its cradle.

Gina sat quite stiffly on the edge of the couch and tried to read something from the Captain's immobile face. It was strange that a face which could portray so many emotions by a lift of the eyebrows or a twitch of the mouth could remain so impassively blank, staring unseeingly back at her over the phone.

'I'm sorry to tell you that your wife's met with a serious accident.' The Captain's lips were moving.

Dane! She'd forgotten about Dane.

'Yes, it's serious. You'd better come right down.'

The door opened quietly and a man stepped in, closing the door behind him. He backed up against it and traveled the room with his quick-moving eyes. At the sight of Gina he took off his hat. His close-clipped mustache was sandy and touched with gray. He was not much more than five feet ten, but the clever drape of his well-cut coat and his slim, hard-muscled erectness made him look tall.

Maclain said, 'Inspector Davis, unless I'm mistaken. Good Lord, Larry, it took you long enough to answer my call.'

The inspector removed his gloves, packed them together, and put them in his overcoat pocket. 'Have I got B.O. or something, Maclain?'

The Captain smiled and shook his head. 'It's your footsteps, Larry. I've told you a hundred times. They're unmistakable. I heard you when you came up to the door five minutes ago. You've been standing out there in the hall.'

189

The inspector's eyes were on Soulé. 'Are you going or coming?' he demanded, his eyebrows drawn together.

'I am freezing, monsieur,' said Soulé, and hunched himself into a ball.

'What's your name?'

Michl unwound, rose, and faced him. 'I resent that question, monsieur,' he announced with furry dignity. 'It proves one of us very ignorant. I have supported a so-called press agent and his entire family for some ten years. Either I am very ignorant for having supported him, or you are very ignorant for not knowing that my name is Michl Soulé and I sing. In answer to your first question, which I also consider insulting, I am going.'

'Where?' asked Davis.

'To my dressing-room, where it is warm enough to avoid encroaching pneumonia. It's across the stage to the right, at the end of the hall. You can find me there if you need anything.' He brushed the inspector firmly aside and ambled out.

'Well, I'll be damned,' said Davis. He leaned out into the hall and yelled, 'Be careful you don't trip, Caruso. You'll never get up if you fall.'

Inside again, he took out a clean white handkerchief and wiped his forehead. 'How many singers are there in this place?' he inquired of Maclain.

'Well, there are three or four hundred people involved in every production,' the Captain told him. 'They're not necessarily all singers.'

'They will be with me on the case,' said Davis. 'And I'm the guy that'll have to interview them all.'

Davis, having disposed of Michl, found a toothpick in his pocket and began prodding his clean, white teeth, while he leaned inertly against the wall.

Arthur found a straight-backed chair and perched rigidly on the edge. Ed Trapper looked around and, finding no other place to sit, settled himself on the couch beside Gina.

Trapper, who never could wait long for anything, began to fidget, and finally bellowed. 'Great God, man! Why are we wasting time?'

Davis said, 'I thought if I waited long enough somebody'd tell me who made that telephone call.'

Everyone looked at the Captain.

'Dane Marlowe,' said Duncan Maclain.

'Her husband?'

The Captain nodded.

'Where from?' Davis planted his feet more firmly and slid a couple of inches lower against the wall.

'From Reuben's.'

'Who was he calling?'

Gina said, 'Jackie and I were to meet him, and I guess he wondered –' She was surprised to find that her voice sounded calm.

'That's right,' Arthur put in eagerly. 'I drove her down from her house to pick up Gina. We were –'

'Let's take one thing at a time,' Davis interrupted. 'We won't get any place if I try to listen to you all. Now, let's see. Captain, you answered the call?'

Again Maclain nodded.

Arthur slid back farther on the chair, tugging at his lower lip.

'Are you sure he was at Reuben's?'

Maclain said, 'They have an operator there. If you have any doubts about it you can easily check the call. He should be here any minute now. He said he'd come right down.'

Someone rapped on the door. Davis stepped outside, closed the door behind him, and was back again in a minute.

'Let's begin at the beginning.' The inspector took out a notebook and resumed his task of holding up the wall.

He was staring at Maclain, and Gina was a couple of seconds late in answering when he asked, 'You're Gina D'Auria, the opera singer?'

Ed said, 'Yes, and she had nothing to do with this at all.'

The inspector studied Trapper's white hair, appraised the cut of his pin-stripe suit, and settled on his twenty-five-dollar shoes.

'I'm Edward Trapper, her manager. She's scheduled to open here in a few nights in her grandfather's opera, *Cesare*. Miss D'Auria spent a lifetime training –'

'You've got me all wrong, Mr Trapper.' The inspector raised a restraining hand. 'I'm on the staff of Police Headquarters, not a newspaper. There's a woman outside with a knife in her back.'

Gina said, 'Please, Ed. I'm quite all right,' and put her hand on Trapper's arm.

'Thank you, Miss D'Auria.' Davis's stern face softened. 'Now, suppose you tell me just why Mrs Marlowe was meeting you here and just what happened.'

Gina told him quietly, keeping her hand on Trapper's arm.

The door opened and Dane Marlowe, white as marble, stepped in.

He was as tall as Maclain, and as straight and well-knit. A short, black mustache swept up over his wide, straight mouth, giving him a slight Mephistophelian air. Wide, deep-set eyes glittered under slightly curved black eyebrows.

Gina, who had seen him in many moods, was shocked into silence. He closed the door very softly behind him and stood swaying a trifle, as though the wound might have been in his own straight back.

The Captain said quietly, 'Hello, Dane.'

The sound of his words appeared to stiffen Marlowe. In a single breath he blurted out, 'I'm glad you're here, Maclain. How about taking this over for me. Have you got any whisky, Gina?'

Arthur stood up and said, 'Here, Mr Marlowe, take this chair.'

Gina went back of the screen in the corner and poured him some whisky from a half-filled bottle. When she returned to where Dane Marlowe was sitting, he took the whisky without a word, tossed it down, and gazed at the inspector with a maniacal stare.

'Are you the police?' His voice was cutting.

'Yes,' said Davis, and gave his name.

Marlowe said, 'Well, if you're in charge, what the hell's the idea of letting her lie out there?'

The inspector said, 'I'm sorry.'

Dane suddenly broke. He set down the glass and pressed his fingers hard to his eyes. His shoulders trembled. Speaking from between his hands he said, 'Hell! I know there are things to be done. But I didn't know how bad it was, and the sight of her got me. Her eyes that were always so full of fun – staring up at me with that frightened stare.'

He removed his hands and raised his head toward Arthur: 'You drove her down here, Considine. Where were you when Jackie was murdered? This might not have happened if you had been there.'

Gina whispered, 'Oh, Dane.'

The Captain spoke as smoothly as rolling marbles: 'If you let the inspector handle this, Dane, you'll save a lot of heartaches and headaches. I'm sure you will find him impartial and very fair. Larry tolerates my butting-in because I really try not to interfere.'

The inspector said softly, 'I'm certain Mr Considine can tell us why he wasn't there.'

Arthur walked to the side of the dressing table and steadied himself with one hand. The Captain lit a cigarette, fitted it into his holder, and held it between two fingers. Schnucke glanced up as he flashed his lighter, then settled her head on her paws again, looking up from under at the smoke rising into the air.

'Mrs Marlowe helped finance my musical education – a loan, no more.'

He was struggling to find the right words and Gina wanted desperately to help him. Everything in life was a struggle for anyone as sensitive as Arthur, or for any musician. No matter how he put it, financial help from a woman as beautiful as Jackie was going to sound bad to the practical police.

Davis had it already. 'Your musical education?'

'I'm a pianist.'

'He's an artist, Larry,' said Duncan Maclain. 'He takes the steel strings out of a piano and puts in heart-strings. Now, suppose for once you skip riding someone and let him tell his story in his own sweet way.'

'I was introduced to Mrs Marlowe at a concert given by the conservatory where I was studying,' Arthur began. 'She took an interest in me –'

Dane picked up the glass beside him, looked at it, and found it was empty. 'Enough interest,' he remarked, quite low, 'that up until tonight I always thought you called her Jacqueline.'

Colour rushed into Arthur's face, and his hand pressed more tightly on the table. Gina felt her own cheeks grow hot in a wordless protest.

The inspector dug his toothpick out from his pocket again and broke it in two. The snap sounded loud. He examined the pieces as though he had never seen them before, and finally restored them to his pocket.

Maclain took a placid puff of his cigarette and raise his eyebrows enough to attract attention. 'I called her Jackie,' he remarked, speaking to no one. 'Gina called her Jackie. Nearly everyone connected with the opera who knew her called her Jackie. It makes the use of her full name Jacqueline sound quite formal to me.' He swung his sightless eyes toward Dane. 'Shock is apt to warp our perspective, Dane. Don't you think that's true?'

'If you'd seen her eyes,' said Marlowe, 'you'd be crazy, too.' He left his chair and vanished back of the screen, and returned with his glass half filled with liquor.

Trapper slicked his smooth white hair still slicker and said kindly, 'Go on, Arthur; spill it. Let's get this finished. Skip the background and start with this evening. I was in the publicity-room looking at clippings and waiting for Michl when this thing happened. What did you do?'

193

'Gina was to join us for dinner at Larue. She had to rehearse and couldn't come.' He was speaking with mechanical stiffness. 'We had dinner together and Jacqueline asked me to come to the house on Fifth Avenue. She was arranging a concert tour for me and wanted me to play several of the numbers.'

Dane swallowed half of his whisky noisily. Arthur stopped with resentment, his face growing darker.

The Captain took two more puffs and snuffed out his cigarette. Gina felt that some mental clairvoyance had drawn him a picture of every resentful line on Arthur's face and the antagonistic set of Arthur's body.

He confirmed her intuitive guess by saying, 'There's nothing more difficult than being meticulously accurate under stress, Mr Considine. You have all my sympathy and everyone else's. A murderer not only kills one victim. He invariably reaches out a number of horrible tentacles that strive to crush others.

'Minor facts have become important. You went to Mrs Marlowe's home and played the piano. The inspector is interested in everything that happened from the time you got there until the time you left – messages, phone calls, visitors, guests, and plans. I'm merely trying to make helpful suggestions. What, exactly, did you and Mrs Marlowe do?'

Arthur visibly relaxed under the Captain's soothing, and some of Gina's own uncomfortable tenseness left her.

'I was driving Jacqueline's town car. She didn't like to drive herself. We drove uptown from Larue. The maid let us in, and Jacqueline asked if Mr Marlowe was home. The maid said no, but that he had telephoned and left word he'd call later.'

The inspector moved his head a quarter of an inch toward Dane, who said, 'That's true.'

'We went into the music-room and Jacqueline showed me the original score of *Cesare*, which Gina had lent her. I played part of it for her.'

'The tenor aria, by any chance?' asked Duncan Maclain.

Davis tugged his mustache and said, 'The night's still young. Let's send for the freezing tenor and get him to sing it. Then we might put in a call for a music critic and get him to give him an interview.'

'This part, Arthur?' the Captain asked unperturbed, and hummed the little song which had introduced him to Gina.

'No,' said Arthur, puzzled. 'I don't believe I played that.'

194

'Thank you, Arthur,' the Captain said calmly. 'Go ahead.'

'Jacqueline telephoned here three times during the evening. We got no answer.'

'I was in the rehearsal-room,' said Gina.

The back of her mind was filled with a tiny, tinkling carrousel repeating over and over again the words of her grandfather's little song. Was it playing also in the Captain's quick brain? Why had he wanted to know if Arthur had played that song?

'Jacqueline had a caller, a man, about half past ten.' Arthur looked at Dane and paused, as though expecting a question that might help him go on.

The Captain supplied it: 'Did you get his name?'

'The maid who announced him said he refused to give it.'

'She was always having mysterious callers – musicians and singers needing money,' said Dane.

'Let's hear about this one, Arthur,' suggested Maclain.

'I don't know anything about him except that he was a bent old Italian with a lot of matted silver hair. He said he wanted to speak with Jacqueline in private. So I stepped out into the hall and smoked a cigarette.'

The Captain asked, 'You're sure he was Italian?'

'He spoke it,' said Arthur.

'Do you?'

'Quite fluently. I stayed in the hall about fifteen minutes, looking at a magazine that was on the table. He did most of the talking, speaking very low, but I didn't hear anything. When the maid showed him out, I went back in again.'

'And that was all?' asked Maclain.

'There was something I forgot,' said Arthur. 'When he came in the room he spotted the score of *Cesare* which was standing on the piano. he went over to it, Gina, and repeated your grandfather's name.'

'You say he was bent. Could he have been a hunchback?' asked Duncan Maclain.

'Perhaps. Or very old,' said Arthur.

The tiny carrousel stopped its whirling in Gina's brain. 'He was my grandfather's friend.' She spoke aloud, her hand clenched tight. With an effort she disengaged her aching fingers and pointed toward the dressing table, flanked by two heavy, framed bronze plaques. Everyone turned except Duncan Maclain.

'He was the best-known sculptor in Naples,' said Gina. 'His name

195

is Pietro Nucci. When I was a child, he cast those plaques of my brother and me. Grandfather had them fixed to the gateposts of his villa outside of Naples. It was a whim of his to have them there. They were smuggled out of Italy just before the war by Jacqueline at Grandfather's request. When she got back from her trip, she gave them to me.'

The Captain got up and felt the two plaques, tracing their outlines and touching each of the faces with reverent dignity. He turned and said, 'They are signed by Nucci.'

Davis crossed the room and looked, his eyes held close to the metal. 'There are times,' he said, 'when I wish I had fingers that could see.'

The Captain said, 'Gina, I'd like to look over the room where you rehearsed tonight. I wonder if you'd take five minutes and act as guide?'

Davis asked, 'What are you up to now?'

The Captain smiled. 'This is a matter of music, Larry. You'd better leave it to Gina and me.'

She took his arm and led him outside, her thoughts still whirling dizzily. Once again he left Schnucke gazing inquiringly. As the door closed on the others, the Captain stopped.

'The rehearsal-room's down this way,' said Gina.

'We'll rehearse right here,' said Duncan Maclain, and bent quite close. 'The blind get funny hunches, probably because they can't see. It's better that I frighten you than to have you found like Jackie.' He paused, then quoted softly, '"The little prince and princess may not be what they seem." Until we find out what they really are, you'd better stick close to me.' ...

It was after two when the Captain's limousine slid to a stop in front of Gina's apartment house on East Eighty-second Street. The quiet neighborhood was dim, and frozen into desertion by the penetrating cold.

Cappo, the Captain's giant Negro chauffeur, left his seat behind the wheel and held open the door.

Maclain said, 'I wish you'd change your mind, Gina, and be my guest until this blows over. My partner's wife, Mrs Savage, has been my secretary for years, and looks after my penthouse for me, too. He's away and we have plenty of room.'

Gina set her chin. 'I can think of no one in the world who would want to harm me, Captain Maclain. I'm certainly not going to start jumping at shadows and inconveniencing you.'

196

'You weren't able to think of anyone who would want to harm Jackie,' said Maclain.

She reached out and took his hand. 'You've been wonderful tonight to me – and to Arthur. I don't think either of us could have stood that inquisition if it hadn't been for you.'

Maclain said, 'I like your singing. And your bravery, too.' He handed her a card. 'This is my private telephone. Call me if you need anything. Sometime in the morning I'll probably call you.'

'You're not angry with me, are you?'

'Years ago,' the Captain told her, 'I learned that life held two futilities. Trying to change the mind of an artist is one. The second – still more hopeless – is arguing with a stubborn girl.'

Cappo aided her across the icy sidewalk and up the steps, and waited while she traversed the darkened vestibule and stepped into the dimly lit hall. Gina thanked him and stood still, her fingers tight about her handbag, until he left and the limousine rolled away.

Once it was gone she found that the familiar old apartment house had unaccountably changed. The long, tiled hall made a narrow path between duplicate marble stairways at front and rear. On each side of the path two blank, impersonal doors faced each other with mute antagonism.

She was beginning to learn what the Captain meant when he spoke of horrible tentacles. One of them had already wrapped around her at the very first moment she found herself alone, squeezing her into a frightful depression. She shook it free with an actual physical effort and forced herself to climb the stairs to the second floor. Under the tap of her heels, the marble and metal rang resoundingly. She clicked down the hallway, found the key in her alligator bag, and opened the first right-hand door.

A scalding bath would relax her, make her feel better, she thought as she crossed to the table to light the lamp.

Out of the darkness a gentle old voice said, 'Gina, *carissima,* no!'

She was startled to a point where she couldn't move.

'Gina, *carissima,* I've frightened you. It's Pietro – Pietro Nucci.' The Italian words were tender, solicitous, and worried.

She drew the window curtains closely and lit the lamp. The circle of its radiance reached out and stroked the ebony sheen of her piano, high-lighted the gray silk cushions of the English divan, polished the highboy in the corner, and softened the marble of the antique fireplace.

It took her an instant to find the old man, hunched in a chair and half

197

cloaked by the shadows beyond the piano. The sight of him sent pity surging through Gina.

His hawklike face was sunken and wrinkled beneath the silvery hair, but his penetrating eyes still held a twinkle. He wore a thin black overcoat, now rusty and shapeless, with the collar turned high. From the inadequate sleeves, his hands jutted out and clung like delicate claws to the arms of the chair.

'Pietro, darling.' She ran and knelt beside him, and suddenly put her arms about his bony shoulders and kissed him with affection. 'You frightened me nearly silly, sitting here in the dark like this.'

Questions poured out with nervous quickness as she spoke her familiar Italian: 'How did you get in? How did you find out where I live? Why didn't you telephone, or come to the opera house?'

She gave him no time to answer, but got to her feet, quickly disposed of her hat and fur coat, and settled herself on the floor at his feet.

He reached out and touched her hair with a bony hand.

'Do not be shocked by my appearance, child,' he said 'I am an old man and I have been ill. Things have not been easy for us since the war. I have only been in your country a few days. I had your address and Signora Marlowe's. I called you by phone from Grand Central Station, but you were not here. So it was the Signora I first went to see. Then I came here. Your cleaning woman let me in when I convinced her that I was old and harmless, a friend of your grandfather's. I was waiting in the dark for you because the light is very painful to my eyes since I have been sick.'

'Poor darling,' she said softly.

'I bring you a message from Rodolfo who is dead, child. I am very tired, *carissima*.'

Gina left him, poured a glass of wine, and brought it back to his chair. He sipped it slowly, and his old eyes brightened as she settled herself at his feet again.

'I bring a strange story of plaques, child – the ones I cast many years ago of you and your brother. It is very short. Years ago Rodolfo saw that some day the Fascists would strip him of everything. He took those plaques from the gateposts of his villa and brought them to me with much money. I recast them in solid platinimum, which I covered with bronze. He took them back to the gateposts and replaced them there.

'When he was in prison, he got word to Signora Marlowe, who secured the plaques and brought them to you. He could trust the guard, who was friendly, to carry the message asking her to bring you family keepsakes, but to tell their value he didn't dare. He didn't even dare put the information in a letter. I doubt that you would have received the letter anyway.'

'Platinum,' Gina whispered. 'The little prince and princess – Grandfather was very clever, Pietro. He finished his opera and in it he put a little song that he used to sing to my brother and me when we were children. The song was to tell us that he had hidden something which we would like very much – usually sweets and cookies, which our governess forbade. He must have figured that some day I might hear *Cesare* or sing in it and that I would recognize the little song.'

Gina sighed. 'It just so happens that the words fit, too. It was a hint for me if I was smart enough – a hint that might tell me the truth if your attempt to reach me should fail. Still, I probably would never have learned without your coming, if it hadn't been for the insight in a blind man's brain.'

The wrinkled face clouded in anxiety. 'The plaques. Do you still have them?'

'Yes.' She kissed him, and his deep-set eyes were misty.

'My mission is finished, child,' he said. 'It's time I go.'

Gina's attention was divided between his words and a footfall, no more than a scrape of leather against tile, in the hall outside her door.

At the sound, the old man changed. He came to his feet with surprising speed, and his thin right hand flashed up his sleeve, to appear with a shining stiletto.

Gina spoke with infinite patience: 'If nobody followed you here, Pietro, the sound we heard in the hall just now was made by a policeman. He's been sent here to guard me from danger, I'm sure. Put your stiletto away now.'

'I'm sure I wasn't followed here.' He took his hand from her arm, and the cloth of his coat swished softly. 'You spoke of the police and danger, *carissima*. Have I brought you danger?'

She waited impotently, searching for an answer. Already she was wise enough in the ways of the New York police to realize that after Pietro's visit to Jackie they must want him for questioning in connection with the murder, if nothing else, and would have broadcast a statewide alarm.

Well, let them find him without her help! She believed him and was positive everything he had told her was true. He loved her and trusted her. She certainly was not going to turn him over without giving him a chance. There would be questioning, internment, and perhaps deportation. He would never understand. Loss of faith in Rodolfo D'Auria's granddaughter would leave him an old, old man with nothing to cling to, and destroy the burning spark that had kept him alive.

'Danger?' Determined to say nothing of Jackie, she contrived to make her voice sound light, despite her concern. 'I exaggerated, darling, as singers do. I have some jewels, and an attempt was made to break into my dressing-room. My manager, seeing a chance for publicity perhaps, has arranged for a policeman to guard me.'

Gina listened but heard nothing. 'I think,' she said, 'that in view of what you have told me tonight, Pietro, it would be best if you left here without being seen, even by the police.'

He silently agreed.

Gina went on. 'There's a stairway at the back. I will go out first, see that this second-floor hall is clear, and you come out and prepare to go down the rear stairs halfway. I'll walk down the front stairs, making a noise with my heels. Under cover of the noise I make, you go quickly to the stairway in the rear, go down halfway, and wait in the turn. I'll go out the front door, and the policeman will be sure to follow me. Give me time; then you come out, and you're free.'

His arms went about her, and for one brief instant he held her close and kissed her.

Gina turned on the light, put on her hat and coat, and turned out the light again. Opening the door, she stepped out unconcernedly. The badly lit corridor was vacant.

She walked to the stairway at the front and noisily started down, alert for any signs of life in the lower hallway. She tried to hear Pietro, but the second-floor hall was as silent as the one below.

She paused for breath at the landing. Her caution began to seem silly. The footsteps she and Pietro had heard might have been any late homecomer slightly the worse for wear. Racked by strain, for a time she had forgotten that others lived in the building. She put a hand on the banister and went on down.

The downstairs hall was empty. She gave it a glance, tried the front door, and found it hard to open. After some tugging, it came quite easily, wrapping her up in a sheet of freezing wind.

Behind her an unoiled door hinge creaked. That would be the policeman. She knew she should leave without looking, but she had to turn around.

The door of the first apartment on the left had blown open. The dim hall light was enough to show her a man in a camel's-hair coat. He was lying still, with his legs out straight, and his face was quite white. A clouded bruise marred his forehead. The shoes on the man were brown.

The cold knob she was holding slipped from her fingers. The front door closed, with a sigh from the big, brass door-check up at its top. She ran down the hall, screaming, 'Pietro, Pietro, Pietro!' and tore up the stairs to the landing.

Not until she had gathered his frail old body up into her arms did she notice the slim stiletto over his heart. The shaft was nearly hidden in the folds of the rusty coat. Blood dripped down and matted her furs, as Jackie's furs had been matted.

'Pietro,' she whispered.

He looked at her once, and died without a sound. ...

Sunlight streamed in through the diamond-paned doors of the Captain's penthouse terrace and made designs on the office floor. Gina shifted uncomfortably on the red leather divan and tried for the twentieth time to find a restful position.

Maclain reached into a drawer, took out a box, and dumped the pieces of a jigsaw puzzle onto the desk-top before him. His fingers made journeys through the pieces of cut-up wood, tracing outlines, selecting, and swiftly rejecting. Two pieces fitted together, and then a third – a legerdemain too swift for Gina to follow.

Michl pulled at his chair to move it closer, and sank back in quick frustration.

Davis relaxed his sombre face. 'I've been here a hundred times at least, and I still can't remember that the chairs are made fast to the floor.'

'I'd banged into those chairs a hundred times at least,' said the Captain, 'before I found there was one sure way to keep my guests from putting them in my path from the desk to the door.'

He raised his head and turned, as though he might read the expressions of those about him. 'Because of my blindness, my office has certain peculiar features. Everything that is said in here is picked up by a detecto-dictograph set in the wall, and recorded on a dictaphone in the adjoining room.'

Michl said. 'I'll have to watch my singing around here, then. I'm under contract for my records.'

Ed Trapper put his pencil away and asked, 'What's all that for?'

'My personal use only,' said Maclain, 'but I felt that, in fairness, all of you should know it before any of us says anything more. You've been most considerate, all of you, in answering my request for a conference, since I'm acting for Dane.'

The Captain's fingers resumed their task. 'Gina was here before the rest of you,' he announced, his blind eyes holding the room. 'A lot of things may be made much clearer if you hear what she said to me.'

Ten pieces of the puzzle were together on his desk, a splotch of colour against the polished top, forming an irregular design.

He turned in his chair, selected a record from the rack beneath the dictaphone, and slipped it on the machine. The cylinder began to whirl, the reproducer went down, the Captain flicked a switch, and voices came from the radio-phonograph across the room startlingly loud and clear.

Gina sat transfixed, hearing herself as she answered the Captain's questions and poured out her story of Pietro's nocturnal visit. The voices ceased, and she found she had wadded her handkerchief into a tight, hard ball.

The Captain removed the cylinder and replaced it in its felt-lined case amid a silence deep as the sea.

Ed Trapper broke it: 'So those plaques are platinum. Ingenious, what?' He whistled softly. 'No wonder there were a couple of murders. Well, at least you have them safe, Gina baby. I know a man who'll get you top prices and have them reproduced in bronze. Until then, you'd better turn them over to me.'

The Captain swung back to his puzzle. 'Mr Trapper has a knack of getting at the heart of things. It's a pity that two rather violent killings can't be dismissed with such nice simplicity.'

Davis said, 'At least, we know what the murderer was after,' found another toothpick, and gnawed moodily. 'He evidently spotted Callahan, whom I sent to guard Miss D'Auria, and lay in wait for him in the vestibule. Callahan came up the steps and our friend conked him, dragged him inside and into that vacant apartment. Then he must have heard Miss D'Auria coming down the front stairs and he started up the back stairs. But he ran smack into the old Italian. The old man probably got frightened and pulled his stiletto. Only, our friend was stronger.'

The Captain picked up a piece of the jigsaw puzzle and held it extended before him. 'Barring the facet that Gina hasn't the plaques, Davis, that she didn't take them home last night, and that they've disappeared from her dressing-room at the Knickerbocker Opera House, it's a simple as one-two-three.'

Trapper started to his feet, his white eyebrows bristling. 'But they were gone right after you left, Gina. We went out onto the stage with Davis, and when I looked back into your dressing-room they were gone.'

The Captain asked, 'Who's "we"?'

Davis told him, 'Mr Marlowe, Trapper, and Considine.'

The Captain slowly moistened his underlip. 'And that left no one in the dressing-room.'

'No one,' said Davis, 'but there was a man on the door.'

'The man you left on the door followed us onto the stage,' said Arthur Considine.

Ed Trapper turned to Gina: 'Good Lord! Is that right? You didn't take them home?'

'I'm quite positive she didn't,' said Duncan Maclain. 'Two plaques that size would make quite a tidy package, Mr Trapper, and heavy, too. Gina was carrying nothing but her handbag when she got into my car. I drove her directly home.'

Dane Marlowe snapped out, 'Whoever took those plaques certainly must have known their value.'

'In the words of Jerry Colonna, it's silly, isn't it?' The Captain fitted another piece into his puzzle. 'The murderer finds out a ten-year-old secret known only to Pietro Nucci and Gina's grandfather. This impetuous fellow kills Mrs Marlowe before she can pass the news on to Gina –'

'Damn' silly,' said Davis. 'Whereupon, he steals the plaques right from under our nose, and after he's stolen them he hides them away so that he can go make another attempt to steal them from Miss D'Auria's home.'

'Maybe you have it, at that, Davis.' The Captain swept the pieces of his jigsaw puzzle into a box and put it in the drawer. Under Gina's eyes he seemed to lose his radiating quality of human warmth and stiffen like a figure turned to stone.

'Have what?' asked Davis.

'The reason why the killer went to Gina's.' The Captain was talking to the ceiling. 'You know and I know that the outstanding trait of any brilliant crook is that he can't let well enough alone.'

'Then you think this killer's brilliant?' the inspector demanded.

The Captain thoughtfully chewed one finger. 'It's the sort of thing

I might do myself,' said Duncan Maclain. 'If I killed a woman to get a valuable pair of plaques, and then succeeded in stealing them, I might very well stage a second attempt – *attempt* I said, Larry – particularly if I thought that my theft was undiscovered.'

'It wasn't undiscovered,' Davis protested.

'Oh, yes, it was,' the Captain persisted. 'You've admitted, yourself, that you and everyone in the opera house thought that Gina had taken the plaques safely home.'

'Okay, brilliant brain.' Davis stuck out a finger with theatrical emphasis. 'Let's be frank, open, and gay, like girls dancing around a maypole. You cloud up your dictaphone disks with so many blind deductions that I'd rather hear the radio play *Night and Day*. Just for once, suppose I ask and you answer.'

'Those elks' teeth on your watch chain jingle when you wave your finger at me, Larry.' The Captain leaned back, grinned, and became more human. 'Your impetuous method of handling things will probably confuse me no end, but I'll do my best. Take it away.'

Davis sank back resignedly, staring at his offending hand. 'The killer knew about the value of the plaques. At least, that's what you say. How?'

'From Nucci.' The Captain locked his hands behind his head.

'Then why didn't he make an attempt to steal them before last night?'

'Because he didn't know about them before last night, Larry. Does that sound okay?'

'It has its points. Go on.'

Gina was suddenly conscious of Arthur flushing uncomfortably. He was being gazed at by Ed Trapper, Dane Marlowe, and Michl Soulé.

The inspector was shaking his head. 'It doesn't make sense, Maclain, and you know it. Why should old Minestrone keep his mouth shut for ten long years and then start bleating his brains out yesterday?'

'He didn't consider telling his secret to Mrs Marlowe bleating his brains out.' The Captain's voice was a monotone. 'Servants are much like detecto-dictographs, Larry. Sometimes you don't even see them, yet they unerringly record every word you have to say.'

'I have a houseman and a maid,' said Dane, 'and neither of them speaks Italian.'

Arthur Considine left his chair as though pulled by strings. 'It's easy to see what you're driving at.' His color had faded away. 'I'm sticking to my story. I drove Jacqueline downtown and waited outside in her car until I got worried and went in. Nobody saw me enter, because even the stage-doorkeeper had run inside to the stage. I sat in the hall while Nucci talked with Jacqueline and heard nothing that was said. You know I couldn't have taken the plaques.'

'Not unless you were very quick and hid them some place near the dressing-room.' The inspector's words were speculative only.

'You know there's no possible way I could have killed her.' Arthur's voice slipped into a slightly higher key.

'Not unless you left the car right after she did and ran around to the front of the opera house and got in somehow and out again through the auditorium.'

Gina realized her fingers were hurting badly. Looking down, she saw they were clenched to whiteness. There was a door in the front of the opera house, and how many of the cast used it to escape the eye of the vigilant stage-doorkeeper, she didn't know. She did know that she and Ed and Dane and Michl all had keys and that she had given one to Arthur Considine herself. She did know the stage-doorkeeper had said that Jacqueline Marlowe had entered the opera house alone.

Shaking inside, she watched Arthur standing stiff and still, his mouth half open. There was something worse – something that threatened to tear her composure into shattered ribbons. He had a key to her apartment, a key she had lent him so that he might practice on her piano every day.

Maclain began to speak – words that seared like cold dry ice in the midst of her quandary: 'Mr Marlowe informed the inspector that his wife had willed you twenty-five thousand dollars, Mr Considine. Did she tell you about it during the evening? It seems that her will was altered only yesterday.'

'Yes.' Arthur's mouth closed, fishlike, on the single word.

'Did you think it so unimportant that you haven't even mentioned it?'

'Yes.' Two bright spots popped out of Arthur's cheeks.

In the corner someone chuckled, and it sent a ripple up Gina's spine.

'You might call me doubly guilty, monsieur. I learned this morning that she willed me fifty thousand. She must have liked me, *non?* Even though we were married for two long years and most unhappy,' said Michl Soulé.

More talk and more questions. Were murders all talk and questions? Voices rolled on interminably about Gina, divorcing Pietro and Jackie from any resemblance to figures who had ever lived and breathed,

205

spoken to her, been sorrowful and gay. She became involved in a network of complicated thoughts which held her steadfastly twisting her handkerchief into more shapeless form. Finally she found herself seated at a lunch table with Arthur and Duncan Maclain, wholly unconscious that the others had gone away.

Cappo, a black-faced giant in a starched white coat, served them crabs *en coquille*, which she ate but could not taste, salad, dessert, and coffee. Arthur sat woodenly, resenting the luncheon invitation, which he felt to be a command, pushing untasted dishes away.

The Captain talked, making light of his blindness, explaining how life in darkness could be fun, how books became more vivid, music more alive and poignant, people more interesting when you heard only voices and pictured their owners as actors in a play. He told why he had become a private investigator after losing his sight in the first World War; of his endless drive to prove to his own satisfaction that blindness had not robbed him of life – that Duncan Maclain was as good as, or better than, any man who could see.

Eating skillfully and finding his food without apparent effort, he chatted of his dogs: Schnucke, trained by the Seeing Eye, gentle as a lace-capped old lady; and Dreist, a second German shepherd which they had not seen, trained for police work – no pet, Dreist, but a powerful weapon which attacked without warning at any hint of danger to his master, fast and dangerous as a loaded sho-sho gun.

Gina forced herself to listen, interspersing comments of reticent politeness. What was he thinking beneath his endless chatter? Was his smile sympathetic or full of amusement at human transparency?

He shifted with the coffee, stabbing out as adroitly as a conversational boxer who has feinted, parried, and at last found an opening to strike through a tight defense.

'You could have killed Jacqueline Marlowe if you had had a key to that door in front of the opera house, Arthur' – footwork with words, a straight, flat punch giving no time for Arthur to resume his guard.

'I have a key,' said Arthur.

Gina spilled coffee in her saucer. 'I gave it to him. I'm entitled to have friends visit me in my dressing-room if I want them to. There are lots of others who have keys. You don't keep beating them down, Captain, questioning them again and again.'

The rebuke in her voice brought a sober smile to his mobile face. 'Sometimes I am most harsh with the people I like the best. I have to be if I hope to outsmart Davis. He's one of the most intelligent men I know. He's already learned about the key. The fact that both of you failed to tell him is sure to annoy him. His methods of questioning may be far worse than mine. I presume you're innocent, Arthur?' His eyebrows arched in inquiry.

'I've never harmed anyone in my life. I don't intend to –'

The Captain lifted one hand in a gesture. 'Innocent but touchy, Arthur. The police have a job to do. If I can make you mad enough before Davis gets to you, I may be able to save you a lot of pain.'

Gina reached across the table and touched Arthur's hand. 'Please trust Captain Maclain.'

'They think I killed her. They think I murdered the woman who helped me – killed her for money and to steal the plaques that belong to you, Gina.'

'They certainly do,' said Duncan Maclain. 'Maybe you and I had better take a trip up to the music-room of the Marlowe house and start all over again.' ...

Gina caught a sky-top cab downtown. Winter sun poured through the transparent roof. Under the heady combination of brilliance and snapping cold, she huddled back in the corner, listening in desultory fashion to the talkative driver. The years of rigorous musical discipline overcame her distraction and brought her back firmly to the problems of *Cesare*. There was much rehearsing still to be done. She hummed a few bars of her part, and temporarily murder was far away.

Gina started across the stage, her light footsteps echoing in a hollow resonance which intermingled with the other noises. The heart of the Knickerbocker was under the stage, and the floor was laid on a hollow gridiron of supports checkerboarded with trap doors of different sizes and functions. The resonance was dispelled during a performance by laying down stacks of coloured canvas cloths arranged in the reverse order of the acts, so they might be peeled off one by one as the scenes were changed.

The effect of walking on such a gigantic drum brought back Duncan Maclain's remark of the night before while she was waiting for Jackie: 'I'm certain I heard her foot-steps on the stage many minutes ago. She was crossing with someone else just as Michl started to sing.'

With someone else – Gina stopped and stared, horrified , at the door to the little cubicle straight ahead, filled with the first real glimmer of what might be working in the mind of Duncan Maclain. If the murderer had used the key to the door at the front of the house and gone down through the Auditorium to hide in the cubicle, Jackie would have crossed the stage alone.

Someone touched her arm, and she started violently.

A voice said, 'Don't take it so hard, Gina. It's done and we can't help it.'

She turned to face Dane. He looked tired and wilted, and had lost the spruce appearance and some of the cockiness he had displayed during the morning while interviewing Maclain. The expensive blue suit was dusty and marred by a grease spot on one knee.

Gina said, 'You startled me.'

'Obviously.' He forced a grin which looked ghastly under his waxed mustache. 'As I said, you're wrecking yourself. Not that I can blame you entirely, for everything since last night has been startling me.'

'I can't forget it, Dane.'

'Neither can I, but yet, much as I hate the expression, Gina, I have to remind you that the show must go on. It's your business and mine. Look!' He pointed to the right. 'They're setting Act Three of your grandfather's opera. That's the old tower by the water, where the mist rolls in from the sea and hides the dying Caesar as the curtain comes down. I've been supervising the mechanical equipment – a new set of steampipes to bring the mist in from the sea.'

He was talking about steampipes and the handle beneath the stage which turned them on, but Gina's mind was far from steampipes as he held her arm and walked her along. It was on footsteps crossing the stage the night before and Jackie pushed suddenly into the cubicle by someone who must have known the knife was there, not to be removed under penalty of the law.

They passed the darkened doorway.

Dane said, 'God, I'm tired. I hope all your whisky isn't gone.'

Across the stage the powerful voice of Michl Soulé was raised in a burst of song.

She was glad to find Ed in her dressing-room, and for once found herself welcoming his businesslike censure:

'Metcalfe's been playing Chopsticks on that piano in the rehearsal-room for an hour, Gina baby.' Ed's belligerent eyebrows bristled at Marlowe as though Dane were personally to blame for her lateness.

Dane vanished back of the screen in search of stimulant, and Ed turned his fatherly tirade toward his charge.

'Even if they kill the whole ballet you're still under contract,' he began inpatiently. 'You're not reading lines in a melodrama, Gina baby. You're supposed to be singing an aria. Metcalfe says that so far you've been lousy.'

'I'm sorry, Ed. I know I'm late.' Gina hung up her furs in the closet.

'Of course,' said Trapper, 'I can always get you a job if they revive *The Merry Widow* again, or perhaps *The Prince of Pilsen*. If you don't like rehearsing you can always sing a song.' He started a restless pacing.

Dane appeared from behind the screen, swallowed half a tumbler of whisky neat, and said to Trapper, 'For the love of God, sit down.' He disposed of the tumbler and went out, leaving Ed with a farewell frown.

Gina said weakly, 'Ed, I can't rehearse until I've rested half an hour.'

He stopped pacing, stared at her hard, and was instantly solicitous, his brusqueness gone. 'Lie down, Gina baby. You're better than any of them without any rehearsal. I'll be back in a minute. I'll explain to that Metcalfe clown.'

She stretched out on the silken couch and closed her eyes.

A few minutes later Ed came back and sat down. 'He'll wait. What's the matter, Gina – Arthur?'

'Partly.' She opened her eyes. 'He's so helpless, Ed.'

'Yeah. What else? Did Marlowe upset you?'

'Oh, this morning, and crossing the stage just now.'

'What about this morning? You're not letting that blind man get you down?'

'It's Michl, Ed.' Her hands lay laxly beside her.

His keen blue eyes changed colour. 'Michl? What the hell has Michl –?'

'He never said anything last night about being married to Jackie. He was joking after–'.

'He's like that, Gina baby. He probably thought everybody knew it. Pagliacci – he laughs, and hurts inside.'

'Whoever stole the plaques knew about their value, Ed.'

'What's that got to do with Michl?' He leaned forward, his hands tight on his knees. 'You don't think Nucci went to Michl?'

'There was a way Michl might have guessed those plaques were valuable,' said Gina. She told him about Maclain and her grandfather's song.

Ed said, 'I've managed him nearly fifteen years, Gina. You've got him all wrong. You're trying to cover Arthur.'

'There's the fifty thousand dollars, Ed.'

'You've got him all wrong. What the hell does he need with fifty thousand dollars and your plaques? He's the king of song.'

'There's more, Ed.'

'What?'

'A trust fund of two hundred thousand dollars. Jackie set it aside for him after their divorce and kept it a secret.'

'Her attorneys would know it, and Dane's.'

'No.' Gina shook her head. 'She didn't want Dane to know it, so she didn't tell her lawyers because they'd be sure to tell him. He was jealous.'

Trapper got up. 'Look, Gina baby; I don't blame you for breaking your neck to cover Considine. I think you love him. But if there's any such trust fund set aside for Michl I'd know about it, just as I know everything about you and your financial affairs.'

'But she told me. She was always fond of Michl, even though they split up. She felt that he was just an overgrown kid and temperamental, Ed, and that she was the one to blame. He spends money like water –'

'While he earns it like wine,' said Ed.

'I know,' Gina agreed, 'but Jackie wanted him to have a backlog. She told me she'd set aside two hundred thousand dollars in bearer bonds for Michl before she married Dane.'

'Where?' asked Ed.

'She didn't say, but she did say that if Michl learned about it he would run through it in no time.' Gina was plaintive. 'Singers do occasionally end up penniless, Ed, even the best of them. I've heard you say so yourself. You keep telling me that it's part of the game.'

Trapper shook his head. 'You're all wrong, Gina. You just said Michl knew nothing of this fund. Then why in the devil would he want to kill her without knowing he had something to gain?'

'He may have found out.'

'I still claim that I'd have known about such a fund,' Ed maintained seriously.

'But she told me,' Gina persisted.

'All right,' said Ed. 'She told you, but think about Dane.'

'What about Dane?'

'You're trying to point out, Gina, that Michl gets two hundred and fifty thousand dollars by Jackie's death. Dane gets five million. You've said yourself Dane was jealous. I'll tell you something else – he and Jackie had quarreled – at least, she was leaving for Europe within the next couple days, to be gone for months, maybe longer.'

'She never mentioned that to me,' Gina protested without much ardor.

'Well, it's true,' Ed continued. 'Suppose he was spying on Jackie and Considine last night. He could have overheard Nucci's conversation. He'd know about the plaques and their value. Maybe he pinched them himself to make it look like Arthur. Those plaques would be a fortune to anyone as broke as Considine. Also, he'd be the first one to hear that Jackie had left twenty-five thousand to her pet piano player.'

'Ed, you can't –' His calm, unimpassioned words were engulfing her, dragging her down.

'There's more,' he said. 'All of us here thought you'd taken the plaques home. Dane could have made a fake attempt to steal them if he knew that Considine had a key to your apartment. He could have run into Nucci in the hall and had to kill him because the old man pulled his stiletto. Think about Dane, Gina baby, and you'll see that you've got Michl wrong.'

'Ed!' She sat up quickly. 'What are you going to do?'

'I'm going to the police,' said Trapper. He picked up his hat and coat and was gone ...

Her attempt to relax had only made her more tired. She gave it up after fifteen minutes and walked down the hall to the rehearsal-room, to find that Metcalfe was not there. She sat down to wait, strumming idly on the piano.

Gina waited in the rehearsal-room a little longer than ten minutes, then went in search of Metcalfe. If she didn't find the assistant conductor soon she'd lose an entire day.

When she left the rehearsal-room she stood in the wings for a moment, close to the spot where she and Maclain had stopped the night before. There were only two men on the stage now, busy with some piece of construction. As she watched, a backdrop went up slowly into the flies, raised like a window sash by heavy counterweights which worked over pulleys in the gridiron eighty feet above.

The assistant conductor had a small office off the third fly floor. Gina started across the stage to take the elevator up on the other side.

She had covered a third of the distance when an unseen voice from one of the flies above called, 'Joe!' One of the two men working on the stage looked upward just as Gina circled a small chest of carpenter's tools which stood in her path.

It was then that panic froze her, and the world stood still at the sight of the guy named Joe. His face had turned into a wild, white mask surrounding two crazy eyes. His wide-open mouth emitted no sound. Running toward Gina, he suddenly flung his heavy body straight through the air, crashed into her middle, and knocked her ten feet backward in a stunning, breath-taking blow.

Within a foot of the carpenter's tool chest a sandbag crashed with the force of a canvas bomb, raising great splinters from the heavy wooden stage. Men appeared from nowhere, yelling futile curses into the flies above.

The stagehand picked up Gina, who clung to him weakly.

'I'm sorry I had to tackle you, lady,' he said contritely, 'but there wasn't much time, for when one of them sandbags starts falling it don't fall slow.' ...

Melody in death! It had started back in childhood and, crawling like an invisible virus, had worked its way along. Since the night before, it had sprouted like the deadly amanita, attaching itself with a fungus growth to her grandfather's little song, and now the opera house Gina loved so well had become a place of danger.

Gina was afraid. She was frightened of Dane Marlowe and Michl Soulé and Trapper and Arthur Considine. She was panic-stricken.

Life had been reduced to one stark fundamental – inertia. She dared not leave the only two men who spelled safety: the tireless, toothpick-chewing inspector, pacing back and forth before the door, and the blind man, who had both of his dogs with him now.

Another stagehand came and went, leaving more answers to Davis's impersonal questions. The ballet rehearsal-room was large. The inspector walked to the farther end, noisily dragging back a kitchen chair to near the door. Gina felt her own keyed-up body relax when he finally sat down. He took out a thin, expensive cigar, bit off the end, and lit it. When it was going nicely, Michl coughed.

'Monsieur, again I beg of you. My throat is unable to stand it. Twice before I have asked you, and you have been so kind as to put them out.'

'So you sit there and let me light a third one!' the inspector remarked with poison. 'Well, this time you can choke to death.' He blew a lungful toward the scowling tenor, who fanned it away protestingly. 'It might have been an accident, that sandbag falling down.'

'Yes,' said Dane. 'I remember a similar case in a Shriners' temple seventeen years ago. It turned out that some boys had sneaked up into the flies and were fooling with the rope. Personally, I think a deliberate attempt was made on Gina. With the stage so cluttered, you have to cross near the footlights from wing to wing. That sandbag was right in line. Anyone waiting up in the flies and watching –'

The Captain twisted a music rack with his restless fingers and asked courteously, 'Where did you go this afternoon, Arthur?'

'I thought you and Arthur went up to Dane's.' Gina moved her hand so quickly to her throat that Dreist's muzzled head snapped up, and the Captain ordered, 'Down.' The dog relapsed.

'I changed my mind,' said Duncan Maclain. 'I left Arthur shortly after three o'clock and made a trip downtown.'

'And you, Mr Considine?' asked Davis.

'I went to a music store and then to Gina's apartment on Eighty-second Street, where I practiced. A couple of hours ago I called her up for dinner. She told me what had happened here and that I'd better come down.'

'The process of elimination is a fascinating thing.' The Captain resumed his torture of the music rack.

Davis stiffened up in his kitchen chair. 'What are you going to eliminate now?'

'Dead wood,' said Maclain.

'Is that why you brought that murderous dog?'

The Captain gave a pontifical smile. 'Dreist? He's not murderous, Larry. He's just efficient. He dives into the centre of things, looking neither to right nor left. He'll scale a twelve-foot fence if it's in his path, or go through fire and water to get at a killer who's brandishing a gun.'

The inspector chuckled grimly. 'I remember once not so long ago when he took a gun away from a G-man. Even at *my* job I occasionally have a little fun.'

'Tenacity of purpose,' said Duncan Maclain. 'He still goes straight at the object in view and ignores the smoke screens.'

'I shall ignore one myself, monsieur,' said Michl, and pulled his chair to another part of the room.

The inspector's gray eyes followed. 'What smoke screens?'

The Captain gave the music stand an added twist.

'The platinum plaques, for one. No matter how much smoke gets in my eyes, Larry, I still can't see. That leaves me only thinking and listening.'

'Listening to what?' The inspector dropped ashes on the floor.

'Questions and answers,' said Maclain. 'Questions and answers buried deep in a smoke screen of platinum plaques. They've gone round and round like this music stand.'

'And my head,' said Ed Trapper. 'For the love of God, quit twisting that thing! It's getting to be quite a bore.'

Dane asked, 'What do you mean by saying those plaques were a smoke screen? I thought they were stolen. At least, we all know they're gone.'

'Gone for a purpose,' said Duncan Maclain. He placed his hands flat on his knees, and the music rack ceased to twirl. 'I'll take things in order. We'll dispose of the plaques and of the people, and then of the attempt that was made today to take the life of a girl.'

'If it was an attempt, monsieur le capitaine.'

'Which I am certain it was, Monsieur Soulé. We will start with a simple premise. Nucci had told Mrs Marlowe that Gina's two plaques were made of platinum. So far as we know, she died without revealing that fact to anyone. I had a hint of the value of the plaques from a line in your aria, Michl – "The little prince and princess may not be what they seem."'

'My aria! But what –?'

'I told the Captain about it last night,' said Gina. 'It was a song my grandfather wrote for me and my brother when we were children. He used to hum it to fool our nurse and tell us that he had hidden candy in the piano.'

'The devil with the plaques. Let's get down to the people involved. What about them?' The question came tight as a snare drum from Arthur Considine.

'The plaques will lead to the people, Arthur.' Maclain leaned down and unmuzzled his dog and twirled the leather mask around his finger. 'The plaques weren't stolen. At my suggestion, Davis took them from Gina's dressing-room last night and sent them down to headquarters for safekeeping.'

'That was a peach of a crazy idea.' Dane moved his chair closer to Gina's. 'That lunk of a cop' – he pointed at Davis – 'told everyone there that Gina had taken them home. She might have been murdered, as Nucci was.'

The inspector's clipped mustache set fiercely in warning. 'There are two people living who can call me a lunk. One's Larry Davis and the other's my wife. This happens to be one of the times, Mr Marlowe, when I'll make an exception. The Captain told me to guard Miss D'Auria and watch her apartment. We're shorthanded since the war. I put one man on a four-man job, and he was half asleep on his feet. If any thing happened to Nucci the fault was entirely mine.'

'It seems to me the blame rests on the killer,' said Duncan Maclain. 'Blaming ourselves for what has happened is merely a waste of time. . . .

We'll go back to our simple premise: Mrs Marlowe drove from her home down here with Arthur Considine. She told him nothing of Nucci's conversation while he was waiting in the hall. I am coming now to the three people concerned with known motives for killing Jackie: Dane Marlowe, her husband; Michl Soulé, her ex-husband; and her protégé, Arthur Considine.'

Dane Marlowe said, 'Now, wait a minute.'

'We've waited too long,' said Duncan Maclain. 'Four persons only were told by Davis that Gina had taken those plaques to her home. None of the four knew their value, and I had only guessed it through a song and chanced it might bear on Jackie's death.'

'Did you count me in?' asked Trapper. He got up and stood behind Gina's chair, resting his hand on her shoulder.

'You,' said Maclain, 'and Michl and Dane and Arthur Considine.'

'You now come into the swim, monsieur,' said Michl Soulé. 'You will find that the water's fine.'

'Maybe she's got me down for a hundred thousand in her will,' said Ed. 'That's all I need to find.'

'No,' said Maclain. He crossed his long legs and capped his knee with Dreist's muzzle. 'I talked to her attorney this afternoon. That's why I left Arthur and went downtown. Her only bequests of importance, outside of Dane's, were those to Michl and Arthur.'

'She never mentioned mine to me,' said Arthur Considine.

'No,' said Maclain. 'Nor Michl's to him. There's where we come down to the interesting process of elimination. I'm about to eliminate hours instead of people. By accepting Arthur's story as true, I'll show you she never had time.'

'For what, mon ami?' asked Michl.

'To speak of her bequest to you. And of something else that Gina told me when I arrived here late this afternoon – the fact that Jackie was going overseas within the next few days.'

Dane said, 'But I knew she was trying.'

The Captain closed his sightless eyes. 'Gina knew she was going. Ed Trapper told her this afternoon. You slipped there, Ed. The only person that Jackie could have told that to was the man who killed her.'

'You're crazy,' said Ed.

'Follow me closely,' said Duncan Maclain, 'and I'll prove that she never had time. You realized it yourself after you'd talked to Gina – that's why you dropped that sandbag, loosening the rope up in the fly. She mustn't be allowed to tell anyone where she heard of Jackie's departure. It would leave you far too much to explain. It was rather neat, your telling the assistant conductor that Gina wasn't going to rehearse. It made it almost certain that she'd cross the stage to see if he was in his office.'

Gina started to speak, but sat quite still. There was danger in the ballet-room. Ed's hand lay light on her shoulder, but the other was down at his side, and a cold, hard circle of metal death was pressing into her spine.

'Jackie went to her lawyer's at five,' said Maclain. 'She decided to alter her will, leaving fifty thousand to Michl and twenty-five thousand to Arthur. She also asked if her lawyer knew an auditor who could do some confidential work for her today. I've guessed that it had to do with a secret trust fund which Gina mentioned to me – a fund that Jackie had set aside in bonds for Michl Soulé. Two hundred thousand, wasn't it, Gina?'

She nodded like an automaton.

Ed said, 'Rot!'

Davis said, 'Let the Captain talk.'

'Two hundred thousand!' The little tenor shook his head. 'Nom d'un nom! Was it worth two hundred thousand to her to be rid of Michl Soulé?'

Maclain went on, 'I think those bonds were left with Trapper, as Michl's manager. I think they're gone. I think if Jackie had stayed alive that's what her auditors would have found out today.'

'You'll have to prove it,' said Trapper.

'No,' said the Captain, and shook his head. His face looked worn and gray. 'She left her lawyer's at six o'clock and had dinner with Arthur Considine. She saw no one else between six o'clock and the time she crossed the stage with the man who killed her. I heard her cross with someone – so, obviously, her killer did not come in the opera house front door. Your story is, Ed, that you were waiting in the publicity-room by the opera house entrance when Jackie was killed – waiting for Michl Soulé. A couple of people saw you there, it's true, including Jacqueline Marlowe as she entered alone.'

The Captain straightened suddenly and his voice grew stern: 'I might take a shot at constructing your conversation. She told you first what Nucci had said about Gina's plaques. But then she told you the thing that made you kill her – the fact that she was leaving for overseas. She was telling you that as you crossed the stage. And of Michl's trust fund that was going to be audited today.'

'And what about Nucci?' said Davis, his hand in his right coat pocket.

'Mr Trapper overplayed his cards, like most good killers,' said Duncan Maclain. 'Arthur could have overheard Nucci's story. He had a key to Gina's apartment, and whoever made the attempt to steal the plaques must have known their value. So Ed made the attempt himself to make it look like Considine. Only, he didn't knew that Gina hadn't taken the plaques home. And he didn't know Nucci was there. I'll give him the benefit of the doubt and say that Nucci attacked him and Ed had to kill him.'

'If your man Callahan hadn't been so dumb, we'd have had Ed last night and he wouldn't have slipped by telling Gina of Jackie's departure. Michl couldn't have known about it. He was singing in his dressing-room and she hadn't seen him. Arthur's story I believe, for we know she came into the opera house alone. Dane was at Reuben's, so she must have told Ed at the time she was killed. It could have happened no other way.'

Ed said, 'Stand up, Gina baby,' and the metal disk pressed hard. 'I have a gun in Gina's back,' he told them all. 'It's hidden where your dog can't see it, Captain. You're very clever, but a lot like me. You talk too much. It's better now if you let me walk out quietly. I've killed twice already since midnight last night, and I'll kill again if I have to, to get away.'

'Ed, you can't get away with it.'

'I'm trying.'

'You're mad.'

'Quite mad, Gina baby. Keep marching.' The gun in his pocket pressed strong in her back. 'We're going downstairs and out the street door.'

'There are police there, Ed.'

'Keep marching. Quickly, across the bridge! You're a good actress, Gina. If we meet anyone, start acting. If it isn't good you'll have sung your last song.'

The dark, tortuous passage had closed now. Nine-foot walls of sheet iron hid them from workers on the stage eighty feet below. The footsteps rang. The ballet bridge was narrow and very long.

The house electrician stopped them at the other end. 'That was a narrow squeak you had, Miss D'Auria, when that sandbag dropped. I don't understand it. Something must have gone wrong.'

The gun in Ed's pocket was pressing close.

'Well, anyhow, it missed me.' She hoped her voice was casual.

The electrician wanted to talk more.

Ed said, 'We haven't had any dinner. We have to be pushing along.'

Instruments tuning in another big rehearsal-room. 'Keep marching, Gina. You're doing fine.' His voice was low. 'Maybe you'll live to sing another song.'

Two stage hands on the closed-in stairs. 'Hello, Miss D'Auria. Evening, Mr Trapper.'

Fly floor number four, and a quick look down at pygmies moving about on the stage below.

'They'll stop us, Ed.'

'Not while I have you with me.' The gun barrel nudged her. 'Keep moving, Gina baby.'

Fly floor three, and a painter. 'That sandbag –'

'Yeah,' said Ed. 'It nearly hit her. We haven't had dinner. We have to keep pushing along.'

'The policeman on the door will stop us, Ed.'

'We're going out the front of the house. Keep walking.'

Fly floor two. A glance at the stage, much nearer now, and a silent prayer that he hadn't seen a sandbag that was dropping swiftly from up above on the other side. Standing on the sandbag and clinging tight to the stong hemp rope in a perilous ride to the stage below was Arthur Considine.

Dane would have thought of that – Dane, whose blue-print mind was a record of every piece of equipment in the theater. Gina pictured the bank of sandbags hanging close to the fourth floor tier. Even with Dane to handle the rope and play it out with some semblance of safety, it took a man of iron nerve to ride the sandbag down. In one swift instant she had learned a lot about the sensitive Arthur Considine.

She forced herself to turn and look at Ed. His eyes, thank heaven, were on the stairs, his bush eyebrows set at attention, his forehead creased with a frown. Gina moved swiftly ahead into the shelter of the stairwall, and the stage was hidden from view.

Ed's voice was low in her ear, his breath warm on her neck. 'When we reach the bottom of this flight, Gina baby, keep right on going down.'

'Under the stage?'

'You got it.' The gun edged her on. 'We'll cross underneath to the other side and come up there near your dressing-room, then out through the house. Keep right along the right-hand aisle until we find an exit.'

They were on the stage level, starting down the narrow stairs which led below, when Arthur jumped from behind with a shout of 'Run, Gina, run!'

There was no place to run except straight ahead into that gloomy mass of platforms and pulleys and threatening machines.

Ed's gun fired twice. Arthur sat down on the narrow steps and slowly slumped forward, his talented hands dangling limp and still.

The bullets might well have struck Gina, for her heart seemed to die.

Ed's tone had changed: 'Keep going, Gina. That Considine always was a fool. He's only made me kill again.'

'They'll close in, Ed. You're trapped here. They'll use gas or something.'

'Not with you here, Gina baby.'

Footsteps were pounding overhead and voices were shouting: 'We've got you surrounded, Trapper. There are men at each of the stairs with machine guns. Send Gina out first and give her your gun and you'll have a chance to stay alive.'

Gina said weakly, 'Ed, you'd better.'

'When we go up, we go together.'

They passed a short flight of railless steps, dark, and roofed by a sliding trap in the stage above. She had reached a state where her head was light and terror had made her buoyant.

The voices above were louder. For a moment the gun was gone from her back and Ed was twisting a heavy valve in the steampipe. Above their heads the voices were raised, and then grew silent as though in awe.

'Ed, what have you done?'

He was back close to her again, painfully gripping her arm. 'I've started the closing scene of *Cesare*,' he told her. 'I've opened the steam, and in five more minutes the stage will be thick as a London street with fog rolling in from the ocean to surround the dying Caesar.'

He pulled her fast to the railless stairs beneath the sliding trap and held her there while the seconds ticked. The gun pressed into her back again. They ascended a little. Reaching above him, Trapper tugged until a white line showed at the stairhead.

'You'd better help,' he warned her. 'Dead or alive, you're going up this way.'

Gina set her teeth and helped him pull. The trap slid open a yard or more. She looked up into a swirling mist – thick and white and dimming the light of an opera day.

'Stick close,' said Trapper, 'and don't try tricks.'

They made an entrance near centre stage, coming up through the floor. Steam swirled about them everywhere, billowing out from the fog pipe hidden in the wings.

The gun pressed close, as both knees buckled beneath her. She flung an arm about Ed's neck, closed her eyes, and let her weight go dead.

For a second he held her, muttering curses, then dropped her roughly, and stepped across her motionless body.

Ed's footsteps sounded loud in her ear pressed close to the floor – the only sounds in the silent house. He had gone ten paces when out of the fog she heard the voice of the Captain say, 'Damn you, Trapper, you're walking alone. I've lived in a fog for twenty years, and now I'm coming to get you. I shoot by sound and not by sight. If you've killed that girl on top of the others, I'm going to make you pay.'

Ed fired twice through the opera fog, and then, quite close, a big gun banged three shots so quick that they sounded like one.

Some one fell, and she raised her head. A blue automatic loose in his hand, Maclain was standing not two feet away. Driest left his side with the speed of a boxer's fist and dived through the fog. Another body dropped the stage.

'Hell, Maclain!' came the angry voice of Davis. 'If after ten years you don't know how well you shoot, you ought to be shot, yourself. Your man's quite dead. Now call of this idiot Dreist, for he's taken my gun away.'

Gina got to her feet and found she was staggering. A furry brown bear waddled out of the fog.

'It is cold, petite, by the sea, *non*? And the voice, it is gone.' Michl's comical head popped up from the thick fur collar to emit a rusty note. He held out both arms, and Gina crept into their grateful warmth.

'The so brave Monsieur Considine is still quite alive, petite, and will play again his very bad music. A bullet in his arm and thigh.' His pudgy hand patted her shoulder, and she began to weep comfortably on the fur of Michl Soulé.

When she raised her head, Maclain was gone. 'Where's the Captain, Michl?'

'Who knows?' he said. 'I have known him long, and sometimes he's here and sometimes – *non*. He hates to kill and he loves life much, as you and I love music.'

'I wonder if I could love life so well,' said Gina, 'if I knew that my life had neither night nor day.'

'I doubt it,' said Michl softly. 'My friend, monsieur le capitaine, is very strong.'

THE PTOMAINE CANARY

by HELEN TRAUBEL

Place: New York, The Metropolitan Opera
Time: 1949
Performance: *Die Walküre*, by Richard Wagner

On stage of the Metropolitan Opera House, Brunhilde Wagner, the celebrated dramatic soprano, was a stately figure commanding the rapt attention of an audience that literally bulged the walls of that ancient structure.

From the orchestra pit the music of *Die Walküre* rose in wild and savage splendour as Otto Furst's baton quivered in the air. Tonight's performance was one that would be long remembered and that would find the critics tossing their hats into the air. Even the musicians and the supers backstage were enthralled. Never before had they heard Madame Wagner sing so magnificently. From that golden throat poured notes of such voluptuous beauty as to make the senses reel.

High in the galleries, voice students felt like tearing up their voice teachers.

And yet no one, not one single person in that vast auditorium, so much as supected that a great frustration burned like an unholy fire in the breast of the famous prima donna.

It was a frustration of long standing, and one to be carefully considered in the light of subsequent events.

At her side, the bearded Wotan briefed her with orders for the day.

Brunhilde cut loose with her battle cry, 'ho, yo, to ho'. The orchestral accompaniment swelled with the turbulence of a storm-tossed sea, and she galloped off to the fray.

Two people were waiting for her in the wings. Her husband, Bill Wagner, and her friend, Lily Furst, the conductor's ex-wife.

'You were wonderful, darling,' breathed Lily.

Others closed in for congratulations, but Bill shooed them off. 'You have a few minutes for your next cue,' he said. 'You need some relaxation. Here –' and he thrust a book into her hands.

Brunhilde lowered herself into a chair. At once her interest was captured by the title of the book, *Embalmer's Holiday*. The jacket design showed a female sitting on a gravestone combing her hair.

Avidly Brunhilde turned to page one, hoping that this book would be as good as the last which she had finished just before tonight's performance. For Brunhilde belonged to that vast army of fans who find escape and intellectual exercise in the reading of mysteries. Her yearly expenditures were said to keep a number of authors in a state of economic solvency.

As the opera proceeded, Madame Wagner became immersed in blood, mayhem, and detection, oblivious to her surroundings until the director called, 'Ready, Mme Wagner, your cue.'

From the stage, Fricka's summons shook the rafters.

Handing the book back to her husband, Brunhilde opened her mouth, got wired for sound, turned up the volume, and strode back onto the stage.

She took her cue from the music, trying to avoid the conductor's eyes. They were not on good terms. Otto Furst, a tall, not unhandsome man, with baleful eyes and a disordered crop of hair, had many female admirers. Only a few days ago, a wealthy old widow in White Plains had died, willing him her fortune.

And then, while she sang, something else swam into the line of Brunhilde's vision.

Faces in the front row – familiar faces – she had seen them before. But where? And then she remembered. They were faces she had seen on the backs of many books.

Brunhilde blinked, unable to believe her own eyes. It couldn't be possible. It must be some trick of lighting, or wishful thinking, or something conjured by her imagination.

And yet – there they sat, smiling up at her, a galaxy of her favourite authors.

Agatha Christie, John Dickson Carr, Rex Stout, Erle Stanley

Gardner, Q. Patrick, Raymond Chandler, Ellery Queen, and many others she instantly identified. People who had entertained her and chilled and thrilled her, made her laugh, and kept her awake through many a night.

Her gaze veered into the wings.

Bill Wagner stood there, smiling.

Then she knew. It was true. This was no figment of her imagination. They were all there, out front. She and Bill had often discussed inviting these virtuosos of gore and extinction to hear her sing and later to meet her personally. She was a fan of theirs and she wanted them to be fans of hers.

Her pleasure was communicated to her voice, and it soared now with new glory.

The curtain fell on a thunderous ovation. There were eleven curtain calls. Ushers poured down the aisles carrying flowers and baskets filled with the latest mystery novels presented by her admirers. But Brunhilde was scarcely aware of the plaudits. The ovation found her impervious and abstracted. Her acknowledgments to the audience were purely mechanical.

Something else occupied her mind.

Tonight was the night when certain long prepared plans were about to be realized.

I

In the wings, Lily Furst kissed her impulsively. 'You were never better, darling. Listen to that applause.'

Brunhilde, overflowing with emotion, spared her a brief smile and grasped her husband's hand.

'Bill, you angel,' she said breathlessly. 'You did it. You actually invited all those wonderful authors.'

'Sure, Bruny, it was what you wanted, wasn't it?'

'Oh, yes! When will I meet them?'

'They're coming up to the apartment for cocktails and a bite.'

'Can I come too?' asked Lily.

'I don't know, Lily.' Bill was dubious. 'That's up to you. Otto will be there.'

'Otto!' Both women made distasteful faces.

'Did you have to invite him?' Lily wanted to know.

Bill shrugged. 'Well, Lily, there's no reason why you can't be civilized about it.'

'But after all, Bill. The divorce trial was last week. I only got my decree yesterday.' Lily relented and sighed. 'I guess I can tolerate him for another evening.'

Brunhilde's protest was more vehement. 'You shouldn't have invited him, Bill. You know we don't like each other. You know how we fought and disagreed all during rehearsals.'

'That's precisely why I did invite him, Bruny. This constant wrangling has got to stop. It's perfectly senseless. We can't have friction between a singer and her conductor. Now be a good girl and try to make up.'

Brunhilde sulked. 'I don't like the man. He's arrogant and sarcastic.'

'Okay. Don't like him. But try to be friendly with him. For the sake of your art.'

Brunhilde smiled. After all, this was no time to remain bitter. The smile became a chuckle, and the chuckle grew into a laugh. It was a magnificent thing, that laugh, contagious and convulsing, thrilling everyone within earshot into paroxysms of merriment.

'All right,' she conceded, when she finally caught her breath, 'let, him come. No one can spoil this evening for me. Where are our authors?'

'They're meeting us at the apartment.'

Two hours and ten pounds of sauerbraten later, Brunhilde Wagner and her famous guests sat back to relax. The authors were assembled around the table, all talking shop. In the corner, a small canary in a large cage kept exhibiting musical talents. Its whistling was incessant. At the singer's feet, unimpressed, sat a French poodle, wearing a necklace of pearls and diamonds. The conversation was animated and Bill and Lily did the honours at the bar.

The conversation, mostly, however, was dominated by Brunhilde. She had strong opinions and no intention of buttoning them up. The opportunity to express herself about their characters to the authors who had created them was a rare one. She leaned forward, earnestly addressing Mr Rex Stout.

'One of my great favourites,' she said, 'is Archie Goodwin. He's breezy and bright, and he has such a wonderful way with the ladies. But that fat boss of his' – she made a helpless gesture. 'How can I keep my diet when he describes such wonderful food? And when I surrender and try to buy those ingredients and spices he talks about, no one has them. I wish Nero Wolfe would invite me for dinner some time.'

Mr Rex Stout sat and beamed.

Brunhilde looked at John Dickson Carr. There was that in her manner which you may see in the face of a Mohammedan who turns east at the muezzin call, worshipful reverence.

'I have read every one of your locked room mysteries, Mr Carr, and never, not once, have I solved the puzzle before Henry Merrivale or Dr Fell. I confess, sometimes I tear out the last chapter to keep me from peeking.'

John Dickson Carr stood up and bowed.

She went on. There was no need to wind her up. Tonight Brunhilde's turntable was running on an electric motor with an inexhaustible supply of power. Her eyes, going clockwise around the table, glowed with pleasure.

'If there were only more lawyers like Perry Mason,' she said, 'why, I almost think I'd enjoy being sued. I would rather hear him defend a client in court than sing before all the crowned heads of Europe.'

Erle Stanley Gardner sat basking in her delight.

In the corner the little canary kept showing off, whistling encores of its own composition.

Brunhilde continued the circuit.

'Philip Marlowe,' she said, sounding awed. 'There is a man! What punishment he absorbs. What coolness – what wit – what imagination. What self-control with the ladies. What a sardonic sense of humour! Mr Chandler, I am overwhelmed. But' – she waggled an admonitory finger – 'you mustn't make your public wait so long between books.'

Mr Raymond Chandler sucked on his pipe and nodded.

Her next target was a woman. Brunhilde spoke in a voice that carried firm conviction.

'Understand, dear, I like my stories occasionally leavened with romance, because I am myself a romantic. But why must your heroines go stumbling into dark attics and cellars just because they hear suspicious sounds? That's very silly, especially after six or seven murders have already been committed.'

The author addressed managed a polite smile. Then her face reddened, for Brunhilde was quoting a passage from her last book.

'Had I but known on that fateful night as we sat around the campfire on Angler's Island what ghastly horrors were in store for all of us, especially Casper, and how it would end with Lucy's lovely throat ...'

226

She stopped and left the rest of it hanging unspoken.

'Know what I mean?'

'Can you do better, Madame Wagner?'

'Yes,' said Brunhilde. 'As a matter of fact I already have.'

She was instantly the bull's eye for a barrage of inquiry.

'You mean you wrote a mystery?' demanded Ellery Queen, the detective novelist and editor, sniffing out material for his magazine.

'Yes,' Brunhilde was placid.

'What's it about?' asked Dashiell Hammett.

She shook her head. 'I'm not telling.'

'How many murders?'

'Twelve.'

'All done the same way?'

'Nope. All done differently.'

The assembled authors were now suffering from an acute attack of curiosity. Twelve different murder methods. It seemed impossible. Hanging, drowning, shooting, poisoning, strangling, stabbing, bashing – what else was there?

But Brunhilde was adamant. She refused to tell. Some day, perhaps, they would see her story in print.

'Can you tell us the title?'

She just smiled.

'Please.' Agatha Christie was pleading.

'All right,' said Brunhilde. 'It's called: *Murder At The Met.*'

'Admirable,' said John Dickson Carr.

'Excellent,' said Van Wyck Mason.

That seemed to be the consensus of opinion.

Then Agatha Christie pointed at the bird cage and said, 'That is the singingest canary I ever heard. What do you feed her?'

'Italian coloraturas.'

Everyone joined into her roar of laughter. As usual, there were some moments before she had her breath back.

'And not only does the canary sing,' she said, 'but her repertoire contains a very unusual trick.'

'Oh no,' groaned Otto Furst, making a sour mouth. 'Not again.'

'Oh yes.' Brunhilde was firm. 'I want them to see how clever Galli is.'

'Galli?' Erle Stanley Gardner looked puzzled.

'That's the canary's name. Galli-Curci. She doesn't have quite the same range, but she loves singing every bit as much as her namesake.'

227

'What is the trick?' asked Ellery Queen.

'You shall see.' Brunhilde arose, went to a highboy, pulled open a drawer, and found a small box of birdseed. Then she went over to the cage, slid the door back, and held out a finger. The canary fluttered her wings and made a perfect three point landing. This was admired by everyone except Otto Furst and the French poodle.

With her free hand, Brunhilde extracted a seed and offered it to Galli-Curci. Taking the seed in its beak, the canary flew straight to John Dickson Carr and put it between his lips.

'Go ahead,' urged Brunhilde, 'swallow it. Galli-Curci is very sensitive and she'll feel hurt if you don't.'

It was a small seed, and easy to swallow; and since Mr Carr, a very gallant gentleman, had no desire to injure the little creature's sensibilities, he forced the seed down. The others, observing him closely, saw that his face registered no expression to indicate an unpalatable taste.

Thus encouraged, each accepted one of Galli's seeds.

The single major objection was filed by Otto Furst, who nevertheless fell into line, looking sour as ever. Galli placed a seed on his protruding lower lip. The instant he got it down, he shot up out of his chair and repaired quickly in the direction of some plumbing facilities, presumably to upset the laws of gravity.

II

At the conclusion of her performance, Brunhilde returned the canary to its cage and closed the door, fencing it in.

By now the beverage supply had become depleted, and the guests were showing signs of wear. But a mass exodus was not what Brunhilde had in mind. She preferred to convoy each guest separately.

First to be so escorted was Mr Rex Stout.

'Did you notice the French poodle?' Brunhilde asked him.

He had.

'Wasn't that a cute necklace?'

It was.

'Her name is Zita. She belongs to a friend of ours who is away on vacation. We're taking care of her for him. He has a simply spectacular apartment on the next floor. I want you to see it.'

He followed her up a flight of stairs. Brunhilde had the key ready. When she opened the door, a wave of shimmering heat engulfed them.

The singer nudged Mr Stout over the threshhold. All the windows were closed, the radiators turned on, and several electric heaters going full blast. The temperature was high enough to wilt a tropical cactus. Its effect upon the eminent author was instantaneous. He closed his eyes and spiraled very slowly to the floor. For a moment Brunhilde inspected the horizontal figure, completely unconcerned.

Then came the detonation. Her laugh echoed and rolled around the room, the same laugh that had convulsed radio audiences from coast to coast. The seizure finally subsided, leaving her weak but happy. She sighed, went out, closed the door, and returned to her own apartment.

This identical performance was mounted and staged with only slight variations for each of the novelists. Ellery Queen, Agatha Christie, Q. Patrick, Raymond Chandler, John Dickson Carr, all of them wound up, three deep, dead to the world.

Alone at last with her husband, Brunhilde stretched and relaxed. It had been a wonderful evening, she said. Nothing in her manner hinted at what had taken place in the apartment above.

'What a night,' Bill said. 'I'm tired, really bushed.'

'Nevertheless, I think you ought to walk Zita before retiring.'

Acting as a valet for a French poodle is a job few men relish. But since it was therapeutically unavoidable, Bill reached for his hat with resignation, got a leash on Zita, and descended to the street.

Like most dogs, Zita had considerable difficulty reaching a decision. It was while he stood patiently on the pavement that Bill Wagner heard the scream and instinctively recognized its source.

Back in the apartment, many floors above him, Brunhilde, about to enter the bathroom was greeted by a sight that congealed the blood in her veins and impaled her to the floor, pop-eyed with fright.

Mr Otto Furst, the famous conductor, lay crumpled on the white tiles, quite unmistakeably dead. About that, there was no doubt. It had not been an easy death, and his face was twisted like a cruller.

The sight paralyzed every muscle except those which control articulation. How many decibels went into Brunhilde's scream no one will ever know. The mechanical instruments that measure sound were not at the moment available. Backed by some twenty years spent in developing her lungs, larynx, and diaphragm, and strengthened by countless Walkürie war cries, it was a most awe-inspiring sound. Honest burghers as far away as Hoboken awakened in a cold sweat. The sudden and violent agitation of the seismograph at Fordham

University threw two undergraduate scientists into a dither of excitement. For the first time in operatic history, a dramatic soprano hit an F above high C, turning a coloratura on Staten Island green with envy. Telephone calls began pouring into police headquarters.

Zita stopped what she was doing and then suddenly went skidding along the sidewalk as Bill plunged for the building entrance, taking off like Citation breaking the barrier at Belmont.

Despite his shattered nerves, the elevator boy managed to get his car to the proper floor.

Bill found Brunhilde at the entrance to the bathroom, her eyes rigidly fixed on the corpse, her face devoid of colour.

'My God!' Bill's voice was a hoarse whisper. 'What happened?'

'I – I don't know.' Brunhilde swallowed with considerable difficulty. 'I just found him here like this. Is he dead?'

'Of course he's dead, look at him.'

'Wel, don't just stand there. Give him an aspirin or something.'

They stared at each other blankly. Bill shook his head, still dazed. His ears were still ringing. Suddenly his spine grew rigid and his face grew stiff with shock.

Brunhilde was alarmed. 'What is it, Bill?'

'The others, those writer chaps.' His voice was curiously strained. 'Where are they?'

'They went home. Why?'

His fingers gripped her shoulders. 'Don't you see? It was that birdseed. He came in here right after he swallowed it.'

Brunhilde blanched. Her fingers clutched frantically at his sleeve. 'Oh no, Bill. It – it couldn't be –'

'I hope not,' he muttered fervently, thinking of newspaper headlines:

WHOLESALE SLAUGHTER
BY METROPOLITAN OPERA STAR.

Brunhilde grasped the back of a chair for support, steadied her lips between her teeth, and wailed, 'What are we going to do?'

'We haven't any choice. We have to call the police.

'Police!' It was a breathless gasp.

'Of course.'

There was a mute appeal in her eyes. 'Couldn't we – well, just sort of get rid of him?'

'Nonsense. He wouldn't fit down the incinerator anyway. Besides, he'd be missed. Otto's a famous man.'

'He'll be twice as famous tomorrow,' Brunhilde murmured irreverently and irrelevantly. A sudden thought brought her hand up to her mouth and she spoke between her fingers. 'Bill, they'll suspect me. We've been having such terrible fights.'

'I know.' His face was grim. 'But you didn't kill him, so we have nothing to worry about.' His voice lacked conviction. 'Come away from here, darling. He's not a very pretty sight.'

'He didn't look any better to me when he was alive.'

'That's not the point.' He led her toward the bedroom, heading for the telephone on the night table.

Detective Lieutenant Sam Quentin of Homicide was a tall, purposeful man with penetrating blue eyes, a resolute mouth, and a challenging jaw, somewhat like the prow of a battleship. His manner, however, was mild, and his voice surprisingly soft.

His first step upon arrival, accompanied by a battery of city employees, was to view the corpse at close quarters. He sniffed and straightened and made his first deduction.

'Smells like bitter almonds,' he said. 'Must be cyanide.'

After that he put his henchmen to work, dusting with fingerprint powder, exploding flashbulbs, making chalk marks and chemical analyses of the various edibles and liquids still remaining.

While all this was taking place, he got the facts of the party from Bill Wagner. His eyes went up, appealing to the heavens.

'Mystery writers, yet. So many of them. Guys who spend their lives cooking up murder brews nobody could solve but a genius.' He called to a plainclothesman. 'Rollo, take these names.'

When the roll of guests had been called and inscribed in the detective's notebook, he was told to work on the phone and get them all back to the apartment at once.

Lieutenant Quentin went over to inspect the canary. Galli-Curci sang to him. He turned away finally, looking frustrated.

'Furst ate the same food as the others?' he asked.

'That's right,' Bill said.

'He drank the same liquor and ate seed out of the same box?'

'Yes, sir.'

'He was a close friend of yours?'

'Of my husband's,' Brunhilde said. 'I didn't like him.'

'You didn't?' His eyebrows were up.

231

'Not a bit.'

'Why?'

She shrugged. 'Artistic temperament.'

He chased the scent but was unable to pin her down, pausing when one of the lab men came over.

'No trace of cyanide, Lieutenant.'

'You checked everything, the glasses, the liquor, the food plates, the birdseed?'

'Yes, sir.'

'Okay. Call the medical examiner and tell him I want an autopsy tonight. If they're open –'

He stopped as Detective Rollo came back in a high state of excitement, gesturing wildly.

'Listen, Lieutenant –' Rollo was overcome.

'Go ahead, spill it.'

'Those authors, none of them, not a single one ever got home.'

'Huh?'

'That's right, sir. They're missing.'

The Lieutenant catapulted to his feet. 'Holy smoke! Maybe they all dropped dead on the street. Call headquarters. Call the Commissioner. Call the Sanitation Department.' He slumped back into his chair.

Bill Wagner stood motionless, his mouth open. Brunhilde gave him a sickly smile. She was about to speak when there was a sudden commotion and Lily Furst came sailing into the apartment.

'I was told to come right over, darling. What happened? Who are all these men?'

Bill cleared his throat and gave it to her straight. 'Otto died.'

'Yes, that's –' Suddenly she looked stunned. 'What did you say?'

'Otto is dead. He was poisoned. Lieutenant, this is Mrs Furst.'

Quentin discarded the amenities. 'How come you left here and went home without your husband, Mrs Furst?'

'The ex-Mrs Furst,' she informed him. 'We were divorced last week.'

'Oh!' He seemed disappointed at the evaporation of a possible motive. 'On what grounds?'

'The usual. Infidelity.'

'Ah, then he must have had a lady friend.'

'He did, at least twenty of them. Hero worship, I suppose.'

'Lieutenant,' broke in Detective Rollo's agitated voice. He had just come through the door with a uniformed building attendant in tow.

'Get a load of this, Lieutenant. Here's the elevator operator. Brother, we really got a case here that –'

'All right, all right.'

Rollo gulped. 'He says he never took any of those authors down, and he never saw any of them leave the building.'

This extraordinary intelligence caught the Lieutenant totally unprepared. His chin hung on his tie-knot. He shook his head like a boxer who has just had one bounce off his ear.

'Ridiculous,' he exploded. 'A gang of famous men can't vanish, just go up in thin air.' He looked at the operator. 'Were you on duty all evening?'

'Ever since ten o'clock, sir.'

'Could they have left while you were in the car between floors?'

'No, sir. I keep the front door locked at night and open it only to let people in or out.'

'Hold it,' Bill Wagner growled. 'Somebody's lying. I saw those people leave this apartment with my own eyes, and I saw my wife take them to the door.'

Quentin looked at Brunhilde. 'That's true, Mme Wagner?'

Brunhilde was not happy. She was, she knew, in a very delicate spot. The thing was getting out of hand. There was no telling where it might end. She exhumed a frail smile and decided to explain this segment of the mystery.

'Yes,' she said. 'I accompanied them to the door. But not to the elevator. I took them upstairs to an empty apartment.'

'What?' They were all gaping at her.

She nodded morosely. 'They're up there now, all of them. Unconscious.'

'Unconscious?'

'Yes. Come, I'll show you.'

It was a bewildered and apprehensive safari that trooped after her. Bill was holding tightly onto her arm. When her fingers fumbled with the key, he took it and opened the door. The sight of the authors, spread out on the Persian rug, peacefully snoring left them slack-jawed with astonishment.

'The heat did it,' Brunhilde explained. 'The heat and a drug I soaked the birdseed in. But it wasn't cyanide and I didn't kill Otto Furst.' As she spoke, she seemed withdrawn and thoughtful.

Bill was incredulous. 'Buy why, darling, why did you do it?'

233

'That's what I want to know,' snapped Lieutenant Quentin. 'What in sanity's name was your motive?'

Brunhilde did not answer him. The word 'motive' struck a chord, and it kept clacking through her mind like a square wheel on a hump-backed railroad track; motive, motive, motive. So great was her preoccupation that she failed to hear Quentin's barked order to get the heat turned off and the windows open. The blast of cool air found her impervious.

Motive. There was the crux. Who had a motive for killing Otto Furst? The gears in her brain slowly meshed. Ideas from the numberless mystery stories she had read, long buried in her subconscious, came seething to the surface. There were various motives, she remembered, for murder – love, jealously, fear, gain – that was it, the greatest of these was the last.

Who stood to gain by Otto's death?

Something nudged her memory. Excitement quickened her blood. Suddenly she had it. She knew. It came to her in a flash of logic. Slowly her eyes went around the room, and she lifted a finger and pointed it.

'You!' she breathed. 'You killed Otto!'

The silence was oppressive. All eyes centred on Lily Furst.

Lily laughed shortly, off-key. 'That's not very funny, darling.'

'It's not meant to be. You killed him. You know you did. It has to be you. You were serving the drinks and it was you who gave Otto a cyanide highball.'

Lily, drawing herself up straight, looked at Lieutenant. 'She's crazy. Absolutely unhinged. She must be. Look what she did to these authors. Why would I kill Otto? All I wanted from him was a divorce and he gave it to me.'

'He gave you a settlement, too,' Brunhilde said. 'But it wasn't enough, was it?'

'How would killing him get her any more?' Quentin demanded. 'After all, they were divorced.'

'Oh no, not quite. If you remember, the case was held last week and she got her decree only yesterday. But it was an interlocutory decree. It takes ninety days to become final, so officially she was still his wife. I remember the law. As Otto's wife, she stands to inherit a lot of money. I guess you didn't know about that old woman in White Plains who left him a fortune several days ago. It happened after she started her divorce suit. Poor Lily, she just couldn't stand losing so much money.'

Lily Furst stood cold and pale, her nostrils wide. Her voice went up a full octave, shrill with denial. 'Nonsense. Sheer, utter nonsense.'

'Is it?' Brunhilde said. 'You killed him with cyanide. You thought this would be a perfect chance to get rid of him, with so many others around.' And then she applied the *coup de grâce*. 'I bet they find some of the poison left when they search your apartment.'

It hit home. The significance struck Lily all at once, and the blood fell out of her face, turning her deathly white. Her knees trembled and she swayed backward. Bill Wagner caught her before she spilled to the floor.

'Oh, let her down,' Brunhilde said.

The air in the room, cooling rapidly, brought life back to the authors. There was a faint muttering and stirring.

Lieutenant Sam Quentin embraced them with a wide gesture. 'Okay,' he said. 'That covers the murder. But how about these birds? Explain this clambake.'

Brunhilde, twisting her fingers with embarrassment, looked sheepishly at the floor.

'Go ahead,' Bill urged her gently. 'We'll try to understand.'

She took a deep breath and plunged. 'You remember that mystery I wrote: *Murder At The Met*? Well, I wrote one before that I couldn't sell, *The Post Mortem Of Mortimer Post*. It meant so much to me to have a story published and I was afraid to take a chance with this new one. So I thought, well, if I kept all the best authors drugged for a time, there would be a terrible shortage, and then the publishers would have to buy my story.'

'My God!' muttered Bill.

The Lieutenant put his head between his fingers and squeezed. 'Women!' he groaned from his abdomen, as if that explained everything.

Suddenly Brunhilde brightened. 'I don't care,' she said. 'What happened tonight will make a wonderful plot. I'm going to write it and they won't have any choice, they'll just have to print it.'

235

THE SPY WHO WENT TO THE OPERA

by EDWARD D. HOCH

Place: London, Covent Garden
Time: 1982
Performance: *La Gioconda*, by Amilcare Ponchielli

Rand was on one of his periodic visits to London when his old chief Hastings took the two tickets from his desk and passed them over. 'Do you and Leila ever go to the opera?' he asked.

'I doubt if I've been to one in fifteen years,' Rand admitted, 'though we've watched one or two television performances.'

'Well, here are two good seats for *La Gioconda* at Covent Garden on Friday evening. I'm sure Leila will enjoy it.'

Rand hesitated. He'd never known Hastings to be so generous without expecting something in return. Still, he'd helped the man out of a difficult situation last summer and perhaps this was merely Hastings' way of repaying him. 'No strings?' he asked with a slight smile.

'Of course not!' Hastings shuffled some papers on his desk. 'Honestly, Rand, your old department isn't the same since you retired. All these bright young men solving ciphers with their computers! I doubt if there's one of them ever heard of a Vigenere or a Pigpen.'

'I'm sure they get the job done,' Rand remarked.

'Ever think about coming back to us?'

'No, no! Leila and I are quite happy as we are.'

'There's so much you could do, even on a part-time basis. Just talking to people, for instance.' He paused, averting Rand's gaze, and added, 'Like Sergio Guendella.'

'Who's Sergio Guendella?'

'I see you really don't keep up with opera! He's singing the role of Barnaba in *La Gioconda*.'

'I see.' Rand dropped the tickets back on the desk.

'Oh, really now, Rand! I'm not asking you to do anything except talk to the man. Go backstage after the performance and tell him how much you enjoyed it.'

'How will they allow me backstage?'

'He'll be expecting you. He'll leave word that you and Leila are to be admitted to his dressing room.'

'And what do I say to him?' Rand asked, still not retrieving the tickets from the desk. He wondered what Hastings was really up to.

Hastings leaned back in his chair, trying to appear at ease, as if the little favour he was asking was the most natural thing in the world. 'Well, you see the entire company's leaving for Warsaw soon. We'd like Sergio to contact a friend of ours there, if he's able.'

'Since when do you use opera singers as couriers, Hastings?'

'Oh, it's nothing like that. But naturally he'll be entertained by the Polish arts world during his stay. He'll have natural social contact with some dissident factions.'

'How would I approach him on this?'

'I don't have to tell you, Rand. Chat with him casually. Make the suggestion obliquely. You know the drill.'

'Backstage, after the performance? Won't there be scores of people dropping in?'

'You'll find a way. I have confidence in your abilities.' Rand thought he said it with just a twinkle in his eyes. He sighed and picked up the tickets, wondering what Leila would think of all this.

Leila didn't think very much of it. 'But Jeffery, you *know* that's the night of my lecture at the university!' she said when the words were barely out of his mouth. She taught a course in archaeology at Reading, and occasionally gave evening lectures on special occasions.

'I forgot,' Rand said. 'I'll phone Hastings right now and tell him to get someone else. He must have a dozen bright young chaps in the department who'd love a night at the opera.'

But he found it was not so easy getting off Hastings' hook. 'Oh, come now, Rand, couldn't you go alone?'

'I'd really stand out then, wouldn't I? A lone male going backstage to see Guendella after the show? Who knows? Maybe the Russians are watching the cast too. They'd spot me in a moment without a wife in tow.'

'Oh, very well,' Hastings said cheerfully. 'I suppose we can supply you with a wife for the night. That should be easy enough.'

Rand had no immediate answer.

It developed that the woman's name was Vesper O'Shea, and as Leila remarked upon hearing it, 'Her name alone is enough to make me jealous!'

Nevertheless, Rand went off to London on the Friday afternoon train, having arranged to meet Vesper O'Shea for a bite to eat before the theatre. They dined at an inexpensive restaurant on the Strand.

Vesper proved to be an attractive young woman in her late twenties who worked as a code clerk in Rand's old Department of Concealed Communications. 'I understand we're to be married for the night,' she said with a jolly smile, extending her hand in greeting.

'Only till after the opera, unfortunately,' Rand replied, steering her to a table in the crowded restaurant. After they'd ordered a drink, he asked, 'Are you enjoying Double-C?'

'Oh, certainly! I only wish I'd been there when you were in charge, though. They still talk of you as sort of a grand old man.' She grinned at him. 'Frankly, I'd expected someone with white hair and a cane.'

'Thanks.' He sipped his drink. 'How did you happen to get chosen for tonight?'

'Hastings knows I like opera. He thought I could fill you in on the libretto.'

'He told you about seeing Sergio Guendella afterwards?'

'Yes.'

'What do you think?'

She shrugged. 'I think it's ironic. Sergio plays a spy in the opera, you know. A man called Barnaba.'

'In *La Gioconda*?'

She nodded. 'He's a terrible villain in it – a spy for the Inquisition in seventeenth century Venice, who plots to destroy a nobleman in love with the title character, so Barnaba can have her for himself. In the end Gioconda kills herself rather than submit to him.'

'Sounds like a lot of laughs.'

'Well, one goes to an opera for the music, not the plot. Actually, *La Gioconda* is rarely performed in London, though it's had many successful productions in New York. Some of the greatest stars of opera have performed in it – people like Enrico Caruso, Ezio Pinza, Gladys Swarthout, Richard Tucker, Maria Callas and Eileen Farrell.'

'Did you memorize all that for my benefit?'

She shrugged. 'I just have a good memory for facts. It comes in handy in this business.' He wondered if she meant spying or the opera.

They dined pleasantly and then set off on foot for Covent Garden. When they'd taken their seats on the left side of the orchestra, near the front, Vesper had more facts for him. 'The music in *La Gioconda* is by Ponchielli, of course.'

'Of course.'

'He was Puccini's teacher and very famous in Italy, although *La Gioconda* is the only one of his operas to bring him universal renown. The libretto is by Tobia Gorrio, whose real name was Arrigo Boito. It was based upon a play by Victor Hugo, and was first performed at La Scala in Milan on April 8, 1876.'

'You even have the date memorized?'

'Well,' she confessed, 'I just saw it in the program.'

The opera was in four acts, and as the curtain rose for the first of them Rand could see he was in for a long evening. The scene was the courtyard of a palace in Venice, where a festival was under way. As the townspeople sang, a tall, burly man with a guitar stood off to one side, observing them. 'That's Guendella in the role of Barnaba,' Vesper O'Shea whispered. 'He's disguised as one of the merrymakers in order to spy on them.'

When the courtyard emptied of singers, Barnaba took centre stage as Guendella's powerful baritone voice filled the theatre. He strummed his guitar as he sang, and though Rand could understand very little Italian, he found himself marvelling at the man's voice. 'He's overheard something that tells him where a fugitive from the Inquisition is hiding,' Vesper explained. 'And he sings of his desire to snare his greatest prize – the street singer La Gioconda.'

As he finished, Gioconda herself entered with her blind mother. The part was sung by Amanda Faye, a young British soprano who'd been getting much press attention because of her role opposite the great Guendella. Gradually Rand found himself falling under the spell of the opera, and he settled back to enjoy it.

By the third act, as the evening wore on, he'd grown a bit restless again. But scene two brought the familiar *Dance of the Hours*, with a spectacularly staged masked ball, and his enthusiasm was rekindled.

Finally, when the curtain descended following the death of Gioconda and Barnaba's last lament, Rand was on his feet applauding with everyone else.

'I think we've made an opera fan of you,' Vesper announced happily.

'Not quite, but I do appreciate good music. Guendella's voice is superb.' He helped her squeeze through the crush of the crowd. 'We'd better get backstage.'

They were indeed expected, and a young stagehand led them to the star's dressing room. He was alone with Amanda Faye, the lovely Gioconda, as they entered. 'Your guests are here, Sergio,' she said with a smile. 'I'll leave you with them and get out of my costume.' She hurried out the door.

The baritone rose to greet them. 'I could not introduce you,' he said by way of apology. 'The names –'

'I'm Jeffery Rand and this is my wife Vesper. I wanted to tell you how much we enjoyed your performance.'

'Ah, thank you! This is the first time I have done *Gioconda* in London, and the response has been overwhelming.'

'I'm sure it will be just as overwhelming in Warsaw.'

'Ah! You are a man who comes directly to the point! My manager said it was a matter in the national interest, and though I am not a British citizen I have always felt very close to your country. But you could have come to my hotel!'

'It was felt this would seem more casual,' Rand explained. 'A great many people go backstage after a performance.'

Guendella gestured towards his face. 'Please – may I remove my makeup as we talk?'

'Certainly.'

The baritone smiled at Vesper. 'You have a charming young wife, Mr Rand. It is good to have a young wife. It keeps one young in spirit. Here, Mrs Rand, allow me to offer you the best of my meagre chairs.' He scooped up a pile of sheet music and Vesper seated herself with thanks.

Rand remained standing as he spoke. 'Your journey to Warsaw could be quite important to us, sir. You will be there for two weeks, and we understand you are to be honoured by several groups of Polish intellectuals including some dissidents.'

'That is correct.' He was watching Rand in the mirror as he wiped the makeup from his face. 'But what do you want me to do? Will I be a spy for you?'

240

'No, no – nothing like that. But every country has its dissidents. We have them in England, Lord knows! We want you to speak with them, especially with certain names on a list I'll be giving you, and perhaps ask them a few questions. These are mainly people we've been unable to reach by any other means. It is not exactly a free society over there, you know. Talk to them, ask them questions, and bring us back any information you can about their situation. We especially want to know about the chances of a revolt in the aftermath of the recent unrest. And we want to know what sort of an independent leader the intellectuals would support.'

Sergio Guendella nodded. 'You want the name of someone acceptable to the West who could –'

They were interrupted by a sudden knock at the door. It opened at once and a youngish bearded man in a dressing-gown entered. Rand recognized him as Franc Bougois, the French tenor who'd sung the part of the nobleman Enzo in the evening's performance. 'Pardon, Sergio – I did not know you had visitors.'

'What is it, Franc?'

A package was left for you at the stage door. I was passing by and said I'd bring it to you.'

'Thank you, Franc.' Guendella took it and set it down on his dressing table without a second glance. 'A box of candy, no doubt,' he told Rand. 'An Italian interviewer once printed a story about my love of candy. Now fans send it to me everywhere.'

Franc Bougois retreated, closing the door after him. 'He's a very good tenor,' Vespor commented.

'One of the best,' Guendella agreed. 'But back to the business at hand. You want me to seek out and question Polish dissidents, to bring you a report of what I learn – correct?'

'Correct,' Rand said, 'though you put it a bit more bluntly than I did.'

'You understand that I cannot formally agree to work for you – for British Intelligence, if I may use that phrase. But I will do what you wish. Where is this list of names?'

'Here in my pocket. Naturally we'll be happy to reimburse you for any expenses you incur, and to reward you with a small token of our appreciation.'

Sergio Guendella held up a hand. 'Do not speak of money. I am not in your employ.'

'Of course not.'

241

Rand handed him an envelope containing the list of names. 'We leave for Warsaw on the weekend,' Guendalla said.

'The questions are in here too. Good luck on your trip, and my thanks for a wonderful evening.'

The baritone smiled. '*La Gioconda* is always a popular work. I suppose someone in your line can admire its violence and melodrama.'

'I have no line of work,' Rand said simply. 'I'm retired.'

He left the dressing room with Vesper, and after a quick drink at a nearby pub they parted. Rand caught the late train back to Reading, assuming incorrectly that his opera assignment was at an end.

When he woke up the following morning the bedroom was bathed with sunlight and Leila was shaking him. 'Jeffery, it's Hastings on the telephone from London. He says it's important.'

He lifted his head from the pillow. 'What time is it?'

'Quarter past eight. Time you were up anyway.'

He put on his slippers and robe and went to the phone. Hastings' voice was brisk and grim. 'Rand, how did it go last night?'

'Fine. I thought Vesper would report to you.'

'She's not in yet and there's a problem.'

Rand sighed. There was always a problem. 'What is it?'

'The Russian embassy sent a radio message to Moscow at 1:27 this morning, using their special diplomatic code – the one reserved for urgent dispatches. You want to hear it?'

'Not particularly. I'm retired, remember?' Still, the fact that Double-C could read the Russian diplomatic texts with such ease certainly interested him. Those young chaps with their computers weren't half bad.

'Listen anyway,' Hastings said. 'It reads: *Guendella contacted by British agent on eve of Warsaw trip. Please instruct what action to take.* The signature is a code name: *Dean Lugel.*'

'Has there been a reply?'

'Unfortunately we're not quite as skillful at reading the Moscow-to-London messages. Something about the Moscow computer being more sophisticated at generating one-time ciphers. We'll get it in time, but it might take a day or two. I'm worried that Guendella might be in danger.'

'Put a guard on him,' Rand suggested, wishing he was back in bed.

'It looks as if we'll have to scrub the whole Warsaw mission now. There seems to be a spy in the opera company.'

'Perhaps.'

'What other explanation could there be?'

Rand didn't answer. Instead he asked, 'Have you ever intercepted previous messages from this Dean Lugel?'

'Not that we can find. But he's probably using a changeable code name.'

'Or no code name at all, since the entire message was already encoded. I'd suggest you check the university directories to see if there really is a Dean Lugel. And the ecclesiastical directories as well.'

'Good idea. We'll get on it.' He hesitated. 'But Rand –'

'What is it?'

'I wish you'd come in on this. We think that a warning should be passed to Sergio Guendella. After all, we owe the chap that much.'

'All right,' Rand decided. 'I'll be in as soon as possible.'

'I'll look for you.'

'One other thing –'

'What's that, Rand?'

'Did Vesper know the nature of the mission before last night?'

'Just in general terms, not specifically. Why do you ask?'

'No reason. Just curious.'

After he hung up, Rand got out the program for the opera and went over the names of the large cast. There was no Lugel among them, but then he hadn't expected to find one.

When he arrived in London, Rand telephoned the hotel where Sergio Guendella was staying and asked to be put through to his room. When the baritone's familiar voice answered, rand told him, 'This is your friend from backstage last night.'

'Oh, yes! How are you?'

'Fine, but there's been a change of plans. The word seems to have got out.'

'But how could that be?' Guendella asked, genuinely concerned.

'We're wondering the same thing. I called to warn you to be on your guard. We don't know what will happen.'

'Who could –?'

'Did you talk to any of the other cast members about it? Amanda Faye or that Frenchman Bougois, for example?'

'Certainly not!'

'There must have been someone, after I left the theatre.'

'The leak may have come from your end, my friend.'

'Did you talk to anyone at all last night?'

'No one but my manager.'

'What did you tell him?'

'He knew someone was coming. Your people contacted him first, remember. I said you'd stopped in after the performance and we had a nice chat. I gave him no details.'

'What's your manager's name?'

'Hyram Wendel. His office is here in London.'

Rand jotted down the address and then, with a final warning to Guendella, hung up. Twenty minutes later he alighted from a taxi just off Fleet Street and made his way up to a second-floor office in an older but well-tended building.

Hyram Wendel was a man in his sixties with an unlit cigar in his mouth. He sounded more American than British as he greeted Rand. 'What can I do for you, mister? You want to book Sergio, the world's greatest baritone? Why else come to me on a Saturday?'

'I believe you were contacted regarding his forthcoming journey to Warsaw,' Rand began.

'Well, the opera's producers handled all that.'

'No, I mean someone here in London asked you if Sergio might be willing to do a little private business while he was there.'

'Oh, you're with those guys! Look, I'll tell you, mister – I don't want to know anything about it. I asked Sergio and he said sure, and I passed the word along. That's his own business. I don't commission on it.'

'Who did you tell about it?'

'No one, I swear! Not even my wife! I know when it's smart to shut up.'

He seemed sincere enough, but that proved little. Rand chatted a bit and then asked, 'What about the others in the cast? Do you handle any of them?'

'Amanda. I manage Amanda Faye. She and Sergio are close friends, you know what I mean? He wanted her for Gioconda.'

'Had she ever sung the role before?'

'Once, a few years back. You know, opera singers have a wide repertoire. Sometimes the same company will stage two or three different operas on successive nights.'

'Do you know anything about Amanda's politics? Does she campaign for leftist causes?'

'No, nothing like that. She sticks to her singing.'

'Well, thank you, Mr Wendel. You've been a great help.'

244

'I hope Sergio isn't in any kind of trouble.'
'I hope so too.'

When Rand reached his old office overlooking the Thames, he found that Hastings had been called away for a meeting with the Prime Minister. Instead, Vesper O'Shea was awaiting him in the outer office.

'Hastings left a message for you,' she reported. 'They've been unable to locate any Dean Lugel in church or education records and he even checked the staff at the Russian embassy. None of them has a name even close to Lugel.'

Rand nodded. 'It's a code name, of course. I suspected as much from the beginning. It probably changes every day or week, along with the cipher itself. Someone found out that we'd contacted Sergio and had the embassy pass the word to Moscow.'

'Someone in the opera company?'

'Probably, but not necessarily.' He told her about his meeting with Sergio's manager. 'I'd suggest we get over to Covent Garden. There's a matinée performance today.'

When they were still a few blocks away in Vesper's little Fiat, Rand heard the sirens. By the time they'd parked a block away, the area around the opera house was filled with police cars, fire engines and ambulances. 'What is it?' Rand asked a constable, as Vesper flashed her Whitehall identification.

'Looks like a bomb, sir. Backstage.'

He allowed them to pass the police line and Rand led the way over fire hoses to the stage door. The dressing room area was a mass of confusion, and they were stopped twice more before they managed to reach Sergio Guendella.

He sat dazed in his dressing room while ambulance attendants finished bandaging his hands and armds. 'Only powder burns,' one of them told Rand, taking him for a police official. 'He was lucky.'

'A bomb?'

A detective nodded. 'But the main charge misfired. We only had a little flare-up when he opened the package.'

Vesper tugged at Rand's sleeve, pointing to the scorched wrappings on the floor. 'That looks like the package he received last night.'

Rand crouched down in front of the dazed baritone and spoke softly to him. 'This is Jeffery Rand. Do you recognize me?'

'Of course I recognize you! The bomb didn't hurt my head!'

The detective looked nervous and tried to intervene. 'Are you with the official police, sir?'

Vesper cut quickly in front of him, showing her card. 'This is a security matter.'

'You'd better come with us in the ambulance, sir,' the attendant was saying to Sergio. 'We just want to take x-rays and check you over.'

Suddenly Amanda Faye was in the room, pushing through the crowd to his side. 'Sergio! What happened? They said there was a bomb!' She glared at Rand and Vesper. 'Can't you move back and give him air?'

The baritone was struggling to stand up. 'The matinee goes on in an hour. We must –'

'Forget the matinee! Sit down and tell me what happened.'

'The box,' he muttered, obeying her order. 'The candy box that arrived last night. I unwrapped it and opened it to have a bite, and it flared up!'

'It's a wonder you weren't killed!' She glanced around. 'Where is this box?'

'The bomb squad removed it,' someone explained.

Rand bent to pick up the torn wrappings, but other than Sergio's name and the address of the theatre there were no markings. 'Taking candy from a stranger wouldn't seem like a very good idea under any circumstances,' he observed. 'Mightn't it have been poisoned or drugged?'

'I am very careful,' Sergio replied. 'Usually there is a fan letter inside, but this time I found nothing.'

Rand spotted the tenor, Franc Bougois, in the dressing room doorway. The crowd was thinning out as the firemen rolled up their hoses and prepared to depart. 'You brought that box to him last night after the performance. We were here at the time,' Rand said.

Bougois bristled at the veiled accusation. 'It was left at the stage door. I know nothing of any bomb! Do you think I would harm the man? Without him singing Barnaba, the whole production would shut down and we would all be out of work!'

Someone from the management arrived to announce that they were cancelling the afternoon performance. Sergio Guendella prepared to go to the hospital, though he insisted he was all right and would be back for the evening show. He would not allow them to carry him out on a stretcher and insisted upon walking to the ambulance. 'I still have my pride,' he told Amanda, giving her a kiss on the cheek.

Rand walked by his side to the stage door. 'Forget our conversation of last night,' he advised. 'I'm sorry we got you into all this.'

'My friend, it is not your fault. One attracts enemies at times.'

'In the company? A jealous tenor, perhaps?'

Sergio smiled. 'You are very perceptive. But bombing would not be his manner.'

'He brought you the package. Could anyone else have tampered with it in your dressing room?'

'No. The wrappings were undamaged, and I had locked it in my drawer overnight.'

'Did you ever hear the name Lugel before?'

He thought about it. 'I do not believe so.'

'He may be a dean of some sort. Or Dean may be his name.'

'No. But one meets so many people –'

'This way, sir,' the ambulance attendant beckoned, and he stepped into the waiting vehicle as a cheer went up from a crowd of onlookers. Sergio acknowledged the greeting with a wave of his hand as the ambulance sped off.

'We were too late,' Vesper observed at Rand's side.

'I've been a great deal later than this on occasion. At least he's not dead or badly injured.'

'Hastings said this Lugel sent a message to Moscow. Do you think a reply came back to kill Sergio?'

'I don't know, but I think we should pay a return visit to the opera tonight, just to make sure the next attempt isn't successful.'

Somewhat to Rand's surprise, Hastings decided to accompany them to the evening performance of *La Gioconda*. 'But won't that blow our cover?' Rand argued. 'A great many people know you by sight.'

'Not so many as you'd think. Government regulations prevent the press from publishing my name or photograph in connection with my intelligence work. If they know me, chances are they know you as well.'

Hastings made a call and there were three tickets awaiting them at the Covent Garden box office. As they settled into their seats an announcement was made that Sergio Guendella would be playing the role of Barnaba with bandaged hands as the result of an injury earlier in the day. Rand opened his programme and settled back for the overture, a sweeping refrain based upon a theme from one of the first act songs.

He glanced down at the title page of the programme.

And suddenly he knew. It was as clear as that.

He sat through the four acts of the opera with growing impatience, anxiousd to get backstage. Finally, when Gioconda had once again plunged the dagger into her chest and Barnaba had sung his lament, Rand rose with the others for a standing ovation at the curtain call. Then he told Hastings, 'Come on. We have to get backstage.'

They hurried down the side aisle with Vesper trailing along. 'What's the rush?' she asked.

'I know who put the bomb in Sergio's candy box, and who sent the message to Moscow.'

'This Dean Lugel fellow?' Hastings asked.

'Yes, Dean Lugel.'

Then they were inside the dressing room and Rand had introduced Hastings. 'Did you enjoy the performance?' Sergio asked him.

'Very much. Until that bomb I was hoping you could demonstrate for us that you were as good a spy off stage as on.'

'I think he's already demonstrated that,' Rand said quietly. 'How long have you been working for the Russians, Sergio?'

The blood drained from his face as he sat staring up at Rand. 'I do not know what you mean.'

'What I mean is that British intelligence tried to recruit you for exactly the same sort of mission you were already performing for the Russians. I imagine you've been contacting dissidents and leftist groups in western Europe and reporting back to Moscow on ones that seemed ripe for further contact. You were quite willing to work for us, and I imagine you were just as willing to work for the other side when they approached you.'

'You cannot know this!' the baritone protested. Then, turning to Hastings and Vesper he said, 'Do not believe a word of it! I was almost killed by their bomb!'

'The candy box supposedly containing the bomb was delivered to you last night,' Rand observed, 'hours before the spy's message requesting instructions went off to Moscow. You told me yourself that the wrappings hadn't been tampered with, and the box was locked up overnight. So there could have been no bomb in that box when it was delivered – unless we're to believe in the coincidence of some fan with a grudge against you choosing this moment to strike. But such a person would have been far more likely to poison the candy than to rig up a bomb inside the box.'

'Why would I risk killing myself with a bomb?' Sergio demanded. 'The whole thing is foolishness!'

'There was no risk. You very carefully rigged it so you'd get powder burns on the hands and nothing more. The rest was acting. You *are* an actor, after all. As for your reason, when I phoned to tell you that the word was out, you saw that you had to protect your own position. You feared we might begin to suspect you'd sent that message to Moscow yourself, so you faked the bombing.'

Hastings was still frowning. 'You mean Sergio is the mysterious Dean Lugel?'

'Of course. We should have known it at once. The opera in which he's performing is about a spy, and the libretto for that opera was by Tobia Gorrio, whose real name was Arrigo Boito. Vesper told me that last night, and I saw it again when I looked at the title page of *La Gioconda's* programme this evening. The author hid his identity with a simple anagram. Isn't it likely that a spy playing the lead in *La Gioconda* might choose to do the same thing? *Dean Lugel* is merely an anagram for *Guendella*.'

The fight had gone out of Sergio with those last words, but Rand persisted. 'He got the Russian embassy to send his message telling Moscow he'd been approached by us, and asking for instructions. Then he faked the bomb attempt to stop us suspecting him.'

'What sort of spy would use an anagram that simple to conceal his identity?' Vesper asked.

'A not very good one,' Rand admitted. 'Though keep in mind that the entire message was transmitted in diplomatic code. It probably seemed safe enough to him at the time.'

Hastings turned to Sergio Guendella. 'How can we let you go back to them? You'll tell them we broke their code.'

'Look,' Sergio pleaded, holding out his hands. 'I only want to sing! I agreed to work for the Russians because I thought it would bring peace. That is why I sent the message, to warn them you wished to stir up the Polish dissidents. Maybe I was wrong. Maybe we should talk more. I will do whatever you ask.'

Rand decided his work was finished. Any further deals were for Hastings and Vesper to work out. As he slipped out of the stage door and headed for Paddington Station, he was glad to be retired.

Acknowledgements:

'Albert Herring': used by permission of Mr James Nines as agent for authors.

Agatha Christie: used by permission of Dodd, Mead Inc. and Aitken & Stone Ltd. From *The Listerdale Mystery* © 1934, and *The Golden Ball and Other Stories* © 1971 by Agatha Christie and Christie Copyrights Trust.

O. Henry: Public Domain.

James Yaffe: used by permission of the author.

A.E.W. Mason: © 1917 by Charles Scribner's.

Hector Berlioz: translation of Jacques Barzun kindly used with permission of the translator.

Rext Stout: used by permission of Viking, Penguin Ltd.

Vincent Starrett: used by permission of Starrett Library and the Estate of the late Vincent Starrett.

Baynard Kendrick: used by permission of Mrs Baynard Kendrick.

Helen Traubel: used by arrangement with the Library of Congress. This edition © editor.

Edward D. Hoch: used by kind permission of the author.

Author's acknowledgements:

Jacques Barzun for his guidance and encouragement; David O'Dell for his advice and support; Elizabeth Gilpin of the Goldwyn Library/Los Angeles Public Library who did much of the spadework in tracking down the elusive Traubel story; Edward D. Hoch for his encouragement and suggestions; Kathy for her support and encouragement; Marvin Lachman whose piece 'Murder at the Opera' in the July 1980 *Opera News* provided a springboard for this collection; Harold Q. Masur for providing some interesting background into the Ptomaine Canary and the subsequent *Metropolitan Opera Murders*; Doris Parr for her advice and research; Otto Penzler who helped steer me to some material very early in the project; Douglas Sutherland of Occidental College who helped me secure the Kendrick story; Valerie Vanaman for her great assistance and comments.